LADY ANNE
and the
MENACING MYSTIC

Books by Victoria Hamilton

A Gentlewoman's Guide to Murder

Lady Anne Addison Mysteries

Lady Anne and the Howl in the Dark
Revenge of the Barbary Ghost
Curse of the Gypsy
Lady Anne and the Menacing Mystic

Vintage Kitchen Mysteries

A Deadly Grind
Bowled Over
Freezer I'll Shoot
No Mallets Intended
White Colander Crime
Leave It to Cleaver
No Grater Danger
Breaking the Mould
Cast Iron Alibi

Merry Muffin Mysteries

Bran New Death
Muffin But Murder
Death of an English Muffin
Much Ado About Muffin
Muffin to Fear
Muffin But Trouble

LADY ANNE
and the
MENACING MYSTIC

VICTORIA HAMILTON

Lady Anne and the Menacing Mystic
Victoria Hamilton
Beyond the Page Books
are published by
Beyond the Page Publishing
www.beyondthepagepub.com

ISBN: 978-1-958384-79-4

LADY ANNE
and the
MENACING MYSTIC

Chapter One

The drone of conversation in the overwarm sitting room of her grandmother's Bath townhome was making Lady Anne Addison drowsy. Standing still for a fitting was tedious labor to someone accustomed to movement. Feminine voices blended into a sweet, soft hum, a few words distinct in the back-and-forth exchange between her mother and her mother's good friend, who sat near the fire visiting.

"Baron Kattenby . . . most eligible fellow . . . said to be wife hunting . . . Bath, the perfect place to find a lady . . ."

Anne yawned. Wife hunting; what sport! The hounds baying, bounding along the green space by the Avon, chasing women in panniered gowns who tripped and galloped in awkward flight . . .

"Did you hear . . . ? Mr. Cleveland Courtland! Poor fellow! Recently wed to that widow, the former Mrs. Breckenridge. Died an agonizing death, I heard . . . so very sad . . ."

Death, *another* favorite topic in Bath, served up in gossip as a delicious piquant condiment, Anne reflected, blinking, wiping sleep from her eyes. A titillating shock was sudden death, good to pique the appetite for more. However . . . she had seen enough of it in the past months, and would be quite happy not to see it again. She swayed on her feet, then shook the drowsiness away and forced herself to sharpen her hearing. She again heard a few words and names . . . *"Mr. Tyler says . . ."* and *"Lady Sharples informed me . . ."* and *"Mr. Doyne announced . . ."* Tedious tittle-tattle.

"Ow!" Anne shrieked and Irusan, her cat, leaped from his slumber on a cushion near the fireplace. He growled and looked around, ears back, his thick fur standing on end and his tail lashing back and forth.

"What is *wrong* with you, Anne?" her mother, Lady Barbara, Countess of Harecross, cried out, irritated by her outburst. She had turned away from her tea table, where she sat gossiping with her longtime friend Mrs. Clary Basenstoke.

Anne looked down at the seamstress, who gazed up at her with a frantic and frightened look, pins bristling from her mouth like comb tines. The pin was still sticking in Anne's flesh at the waist from where her new *robe à l'anglaise* was being fitted. She took a deep breath and said, "I stepped on my own toe, that's all. Go back to your gossip."

Mrs. Basenstoke hid a smile and engaged Anne's mother in some fascinating topic that drew her attention. They chatted on about a certain Mr. Josiah Doyne, widower, who had come to Bath to take the health-giving waters and, at the same time, find a wife to keep his house. A Baron Kattenby likewise; an exceptional catch for a woman. They enumerated a list of young—but not too young—ladies who they thought suitable. Matchmaking was ever a fitting pastime for elegant ladies.

"I heard yesterday afternoon that the baron is already snapped up," Mrs. Basenstoke said with an unmistakable note of chagrin in her tone.

"Oh, that's too bad, Clary," Lady Harecross said.

"Never mind, I knew it was coming," Mrs. Basenstoke said, and the pair went back to low-toned gossip.

"Thank you, milady, for saying naught about the pin prick," the seamstress murmured after using the last of her mouthful of pins. She cast a fleeting glance toward the tea table. "I shouldn't like her ladyship to think me careless."

"You have worked for my mother before and no doubt have found her a difficult and tedious client," Anne said sympathetically.

"Oh, no, not at all, milady. Lady Barbara is kind. She always makes sure I have tea before I go."

Anne watched the seamstress frown and squint as she worked. "Truffle, may we have the draperies open?" she said to the butler, who had entered to make sure that the gossiping ladies' teapot was replenished. "Mrs. McKellar is having a difficult time with the lighting in this room. Mama keeps it so gloomy always." They were doing the fitting in the first-floor sitting room at Lady Harecross's insistence; she wanted to approve all of Anne's fabric and color choices, though at twenty-five Anne knew what she liked and would do what she wanted. Her allowance money was her own, and she needed no maternal approval. The butler summoned a maid to open the drapes, letting in a stream of misty Bath autumnal sunshine from the large windows overlooking the Paragon. The new gown was exquisite, and Darkefell would approve of the way the neckline flattered her figure. Darkefell. Anthony. What in *heaven's* name should she call her husband-to-be when speaking to others? In their private moments she called him Tony, but she could not speak so of him to others. She fidgeted. Just *thinking* of him made her feverish. Mrs. McKellar smiled at her image in the cheval mirror.

"You're getting rosy, milady, with thinking? P'raps of your gentleman?" she whispered. "Some like your mother or grand-mother will no doubt frighten you wi' fears of the wedding night, but don't let it worry you. A woman's duty can be pleasant, if the gentleman is gallant enough."

Anne hid a smile as she said, "I'm quite comfortable on that topic, Mrs. McKellar." She would not say it to anyone, but in a deeply unorthodox wooing she and Tony had anticipated the wedding vows while she stayed at Darkefell's estate over the summer. It was one of the few enticements to marriage for a woman, in her mind. Other than that—the delight she took in her and Darkefell's indubitable physical compatibility—it had been a struggle to reconcile her sense of independence with the expected role of a woman as a wife and mother. She would be reduced, after marriage, she sometimes felt, to fulfilling her biological destiny as dam to the next marquess.

It was a conflict in her soul that she wished she could reconcile. It wasn't Tony who made her feel uncertain; he was the one thing about their marriage she was sure of. After a few initial incidents when he was more masterful than she was comfortable with, he had never made her feel that she would be anything but his equal in a loving partnership. It was everything else around her: her upbringing, her church, her friends, her mother. *Especially* her mother, who badgered her constantly to set a date, to confirm to the world her engagement to the eligible, eminent and elusive Marquess of Darkefell. *Make the announcement before he has second thoughts,* her mother had warned her, even after Anne said that Tony was a man of his word, whether that word was given in a public forum or had been just between the two of them.

From the time she was a child her mother had been planning for her marriage and she did not understand Anne's qualms. For Lady Harecross it was natural; when a woman wed, she ceased to be. She became, legally, a part of her husband. He was responsible for her, and if she strayed he would have the right to bring her to heel. They would never see eye to eye on this subject.

"We can fit the next garment, milady," Mrs. McKellar said. The two moved behind a screen, and the seamstress helped her remove the elaborate robe. "What is he like, this man of yours? Is he handsome?"

Anne smiled and put up her arms as the woman lifted the heavy skirt over her head. "He is *very* handsome," she said. "Dark hair, dark eyes, broad shoulders."

"What about his legs? I do love a man with sturdy calves," the seamstress said with a sigh. "One who fills out a pair of stockings."

"His calves are perfection."

The seamstress helped her into another of Anne's gowns from three years ago that she was making over for her. "We can stay here for the moment, milady, while I pin the adjustments. Looks like you've lost a wee bit of weight."

"Long walks in Yorkshire, Cornwall and Kent are responsible," Anne said. *As well as other enjoyable activities,* she thought, remembering their passionate lovemaking.

However . . . lovemaking outside of marriage had deep risks. If she fell pregnant, or if a servant whispered about what they did, her reputation would be shattered, and a lady's reputation was something to be guarded strenuously. She and Tony had reluctantly made the mutual decision that there would be no more of that sort of behavior, but being near Tony and not able to be with him was dismal for both of them. So she had returned to her family home in Kent to spend time with her father and brother, and then traveled on to Bath to prepare for marriage.

"Milady, could you turn for me please?"

"What? Oh, yes, pardon me. I was wool gathering." Anne turned, then looked down at the seamstress's face in the shadowed protection of the dressing screen. Had she been too free with her acknowledgment of her engagement? "Mrs. McKellar, I must ask that you say nothing about any possible nuptials. We have not announced yet, and I wish to be free of the fuss and bother until it is impossible to avoid."

"I understand, milady. What shall I say if asked directly about your situation?"

"Tell anyone who asks that they are rude to inquire into a lady's private affairs." The seamstress gaped, aghast. Of *course* the poor woman could not say that to her curious customers. More gently Anne said, "Tell them this: as far as you know I am visiting my family and taking the time to have a few gowns made. Let them think what they will, so long as they don't bother me."

"What are you saying over there, Anne?" her mother asked, breaking off her conversation. "What are you two whispering about behind that screen? I will not have you whispering and keeping secrets in my home, Anne."

Silence.

"*Anne!* Did you hear me?" Lady Harecross was querulous.

"I *heard* you," Anne retorted. "How could I not, since you shouted it?" She swept out from behind the screen and glared at the countess. "Because our conversation was not carried out at a yell does not mean we were whispering. Besides, Mother, you cannot forbid my behavior. This is, after all, *not* your home, except in the nominal way that you currently live here. It is Grandmama's."

The seamstress had followed her out to stand in the better light by the window. Eyes wide, her hands trembling, she knelt and continued her work to pin the skirt, taking it in at the waist. Anne sighed. She and her mother were constantly at odds, but she would *not* be bullied.

The tension between them would not be eased until Anne agreed to announce her engagement. Lady Harecross and Anne's grandmother, the Dowager Viscountess Everingham, were almost frantic with irritation with Anne. She suspected they wanted it announced so neither could renege. Of the two interested parties, both her mother and grandmother thought Anne more likely to disappoint them than the marquess. They also longed for the ability to hold over every other matchmaking mama's heads the family's great good fortune: a *marquess*, with many tens of thousands a year and estates and business dealings in every county. It was success beyond what had ever been thought possible for such a contrary, independent, plainspoken and plain-appearing woman as Lady Anne Addison, even given that she was the daughter of an earl. The announcement would cause such a stir as was seldom seen in sedate Bath.

But Anne would not be forced into an announcement. Tony was

still north in Yorkshire dealing with family matters, and she would not face alone the storm that would surely accompany their wedding announcement. Until that moment she was a free woman, at liberty to speak, dance and walk with whomever she pleased, and no one the wiser.

The gown was pinned and altered, ready for sewing. She turned from regarding the changes in the mirror. "This will do nicely, Mrs. McKellar. You have a fine hand with stitchery. I'll have Mary speak with you about the finishing touches." She spotted the butler, who had again entered to make sure nothing was amiss." Truffle, will you bring tea for Mrs. McKellar and myself?" He appeared scandalized and hesitated, but Anne's mother had not noticed, back in a comfortable coze with her friend, so he must order tea for a working person, the seamstress, against his deepest prejudices.

Mrs. McKellar colored, her freckles standing out even against the red of her cheeks. "Oh, milady, you oughtn't have bothered. I always take my tea in the kitchen."

"Nonsense. I would like to speak with you in particular about my nightclothes, and some other items I wish made, and I won't sit and have tea while you work. Are you free for an hour more?"

"I am, milady."

"Truffle, before you go," she said to the butler, who had hesitated, ". . . move that small table over to the window, and make sure there are cakes with the tea. And currant buns, with butter. And a pot of jam. I'm famished and I'm sure Mrs. McKellar could use some sustenance." Anne smiled, turning back to the seamstress. "Perhaps you can smuggle some out for your children. Grandmama employs one of the best pastry chefs in Bath."

Irusan twined about their feet until Anne put some buttered crumbs on a saucer at her feet and he gobbled them up, then set about cleaning himself. Over tea the two women discussed many more wardrobe additions, and a trip to purchase the necessary fripperies: fans, stockings, gloves and other odds and ends. Then Mrs. McKellar began to carefully pack away the instruments of her trade, along with the pattern books and fabric samples. She was meticulous and neat. With no chatter between her and the seamstress, Anne would hear the subject of Anne's mother and their family friend's conversation.

"I find it most intriguing that Mother Macree is situated in rooms in Margaret's Buildings," Lady Harecross said of the townhome block named for a Lady Margaret when they were built a few years before. "They have swiftly become unfashionable, though situated so close to the Crescent. My cousin Miss Louisa Broomhall has rooms there. So *many* are saying the mystic must be telling fortunes to make money, but she insists it is all to help. I say, if it was for money, surely she would house herself somewhere more fashionable than over a shop?"

"I'm sure I don't know, Barbara. A clever woman would reason that she must appear humble to quell any rumor that she is grasping."

"You are a cynic, Clary. I never suspected it."

"Roger claims I am the opposite, too gullible, he says," Mrs. Basenstoke said, speaking of her son. "I am an easy target for anyone with a sad story, he says."

"Of whom does Roger speak?"

"I think you know," Mrs. Basenstoke said on an exaggerated sigh.

"Your nephew Alfred," Lady Harecross said with a knowing tone.

"Who is this Mother Macree?" Anne whispered to the seamstress.

Eyes sparkling, Mrs. McKellar folded a swatch of fabric, patted it into a square, and whispered, "A prophetess, milady! Some call her the Mystic of Bath. She can foretell *exactly* what is to happen in the future, and has predicted with astonishing accuracy an assortment of happenings."

"What kind of happenings?"

"Oh . . . marriages, births, scandals; all manner natural and personal. There are many in Bath who will do nothing—agree to be engaged, plan a party, buy property, or even a gown or hat—without they consult her."

"I think I may have heard of her. Has she become fashionable?"

"Yes, milady, ever so! There is not a person of standing in Bath who has not been to her."

"My grandmother can tolerate so few fashionable affairs nowadays, but she does like to get out. She told me she had visited a prophetess who had, she said, predicted I would become engaged to a man of elevated status." Since that had already occurred, it was not so much a prediction as a good guess, or perhaps a simple acknowledgment of what Anne's mother and grandmother had been hoping for ever since Tony visited them early in the summer, trying to discover where Anne was.

As Mrs. McKellar made a few final notes, Anne listened in on the other conversation.

Mrs. Basenstoke said, "He is not pleased that Alfred is staying with us."

"Roger is not pleased? But they are cousins," Lady Barbara exclaimed. "What objection has he to your nephew?"

"I don't know." The other woman paused, her forehead wrinkled, then continued, "Roger will not say. It's troubling. Alfred is a most abstemious young man, here to take the waters after a bout of illness. He's so sweet and helpful, more so than Roger."

"He's an endearing boy," Lady Harecross acknowledged. "And beautiful, like a Grecian marble bust, with a tumble of dark curling hair over his brow."

"Since his parents are both gone I feel a motherly interest in him," Clary said. "We *must* find him a bride, perhaps one with money."

"Alfred Lonsdale is a vicar, Clary. He cannot aim too high with poor health, a limited income and middling prospects for the future. He will not be able to wed until he has a living, surely. But perhaps a merchant's daughter with a hundred a year who will trade her dowry for an introduction to society could be a good match. Alfred's birth is good, after all, and can stand any inspection."

"Perhaps you're right. I shouldn't worry about his ability to find someone. He appears a most *able* matchmaker. After all, he *did* introduce me to Mr. Smythe," she said, with a youthful blush mantling her cheeks.

"Your new beau! A gentlemanly fellow, so I understand, and said to be tremendously wealthy from woolen mills in the north. I didn't know *Alfred* had introduced you."

Anne watched her mother's friend, a woman of average height, face lightly lined with wrinkles, but still with a fine figure. Mrs. Clary Basenstoke had been a widow for many years. How nice that she had a new love interest!

The lady self-consciously fanned herself and smiled. "Alfred has become quite fashionable and has a wide acquaintance, even though he has been here in Bath only a couple of months. He met Mr. Smythe through a friend, I understand, and so introduced him to me at the Assembly Rooms."

"You do appear quite . . . elevated, Clary. I have not seen you so happy for many a year," Lady Harecross stated with satisfaction.

"I should be *perfectly* happy, if only Roger had not taken against poor Alfred. It does disturb my household."

Anne firmed her lips in a grimace to keep from uttering a biting remark; she had known Mrs. Basenstoke's son, Roger, for years and had never liked him. He was presumptuous and conceited, she thought, with the outward aspect of a gentleman and the soul of a scapegrace. If Roger disapproved of this vicar, Mrs. Basenstoke's nephew, Mr. Alfred Lonsdale, then Anne approved of the gentleman on principle.

"His great friend Mr. Bertram Birkenhead has offered Alfred a room, should he need it, but I do not wish—"

"Oh, I know the Birkenheads!" Anne exclaimed, setting down her refreshed bowl of tea and looking over to the two older women. "I have known Alethea Birkenhead for ten years or more."

"Is that so?" Mrs. Basenstoke said, smiling over at Anne.

"We went to school together. Her husband, Bertram—Bertie to most of us—has become my good friend too, since they wed."

"You should not use a gentleman's given name, no matter how friendly," her mother stated. "It's vulgar and common. Bertie is a name for a rag-and-bone man, not a gentleman."

Anne ignored her and continued to Mrs. Basenstoke, "Whenever I come to Bath we reanimate our friendship. In fact, I shall be going to visit them in an hour. We are to walk today, and are engaged to the ball at the Assembly Rooms tonight."

"They seem a delightful couple, devoted to each other," Mrs. Basenstoke said.

"They are the very pair who inspire me to hope that happiness can be found within marriage."

Her mother sniffed and harrumphed. Her own marriage to the earl, Anne's father, was broken in profound ways. The problems with Jamey, Anne's brother, who had a condition that made him wildly difficult to deal with, had forced a wedge between the husband and wife. Anne's mother had been devastated by Jamey's troublesome behavior and had wished to send him away to be looked after elsewhere.

In one sense her father had acquiesced, but the place he chose for Jamey to live was a house on their estate so he could visit with his only son. Jamey had a private house and a couple whose job was to look after him and keep him happy. He mostly *was* happy with his greenhouse, his gardens and his inventions. His proximity, though, to Harecross Hall had been unbearable for Lady Harecross, a continual reminder of her failure to give the earl an heir who could act with competence.

Lady Harecross, unable to bear the strain, had moved to Bath to stay with her mother. She had never returned to her home and Anne, in her own stubborn turn, had been angry at her mother for years. Standing with her father regarding Jamey's living arrangement had broken the thin, tenuous bond they had once had as mother and daughter. She was now trying to mend their fractured relationship for the sake of her family, but she would never apologize for what she had done in the past, nor would she regret what she said.

"There's no need for comments like that, Anne!" her mother said.

"Barbara, she didn't mean anything by it," Mrs. Basenstoke said.

"I meant exactly what I said," Anne replied. "The Birkenheads are my ideal of happiness in marriage."

Mrs. McKellar, clearly uncomfortable with the palpable tension in the room, stood and said hastily, "Thank you, milady, for the tea. I will be gone now, for I must not disappoint my next lady."

"Please do take some cakes home for your children," Anne said with a smile.

The seamstress ducked her head in thanks and wrapped some delicacies in a scrap of fabric. "Milady, if you can have your maid box these two gowns and send them to my home, I will make the alterations and the final stitching on the *robe a l'anglaise*, and begin on the *robe à la polonaise* and other items. Please send me a note when you wish to shop for the accoutrements."

She hurried from the room, and her mother, looking Anne over disapprovingly, said, "I hope you are going to visit Darkefell's brother and sister-in-law while you are here? And you'll wear something appropriate?"

Anne took in a deep breath. "Mother, Lydia is not only Darkefell's sister-in-law but my particular friend. For heaven's sake, I was engaged to her brother, Reggie! Of *course* I will be visiting them, but I must respect her delicate condition. I have sent round my card and expect to hear back any time now; I'll be guided by how she is feeling. I'm going tomorrow afternoon to visit Lolly." Lolly was Miss Louisa Broomhall. "Will you have any message for her?" Anne said pointedly. "Perhaps an invitation to tea?"

"Not right now, Anne. I'm far too busy for Lolly's giddiness."

Anne stared at her mother, who was in her leisure, wearing her favorite sack gown, unpowdered and unwigged. Lady Harecross did nothing most days but visit friends, gossip and shop. Today she was "not at home" except to her dearest friend. "I will be taking a box of cook's treats to her, at least," she said. "Considering Lolly's continued penury and your refusal to help in any material way, I will do whatever is in my power to aid her. And I'll give her your love. Such as it is."

"Do not be smart with me, Anne," Lady Harecross said, her voice frozen with fury as Mrs. Basenstoke remained diplomatically silent.

Anne picked up Irusan, and as she departed the room muttered, "I have an engagement, if you'll excuse me."

Chapter Two

The Birkenheads arrived to pick her up in their handsome open landau; they were to stroll the park, or some other green space.

Mrs. Alethea Birkenhead, clad in a striking gold polonaise gown and plumed hat, waved a hand toward a gentleman and lady sitting opposite her. "Anne, my dearest friend! We have brought company with us. This is Mrs. Bella Venables, a cousin of Bertie's," she said, touching her husband's shoulder. He, garbed in a rust-figured frock coat and gold breeches, smiled benignly and bowed his head. "Bella, may I introduce you to our dear friend Lady Anne Addison?"

The two ladies bowed their heads, Anne noticing how well-looking and genteel Mrs. Venables was, clad in a magenta striped day gown, her flattering hairstyle — not as elaborate as many felt necessary — topped by a beribboned calash. She was a woman of middle years, closer to forty than thirty, Anne judged. Her face was lightly lined, as if she had suffered in her life, but her eyes were lovely, deep-set, dark and liquid, a look Anne admired greatly.

"And I hope you don't mind; this is our good friend Mr. Alfred Lonsdale. Mr. Lonsdale, may I introduce you to Lady Anne Addison?"

Anne, handed up into the carriage by a footman, eyed the soberly dressed young gentleman, who had stood, removed his hat and bowed during the introduction. He took his seat as she sat down beside him. "Mr. Lonsdale, you are Mrs. Clary Basenstoke's nephew, are you not?"

"I am, my lady," he said as he donned his hat. "Do you know my aunt?"

"I do; she is the dear friend of my mother, Lady Barbara Harecross."

"Ah . . . I have heard my aunt speak of your mother and your grandmother, Lady Everingham?"

"You are correct. Mrs. Basenstoke is a frequent visitor to our home. I enjoyed meeting her this morning and reacquainting myself with her. I arrived in Bath two days ago."

Formalities out of the way, the footman hopped up beside the driver, who maneuvered the landau around a corner on the Paragon. Carriages were not usually employed in Bath, where the streets were narrow and the distances close, but with so many it was a necessity, Anne supposed. They chatted, a cheerful group, though Mr. Lonsdale appeared a somber young gentleman, not much given to light conversation and gossip. He had been asked to make up the numbers, Alethea said, as three ladies and one gentleman was one too many ladies. Anne smiled at her friend's flighty chatter. Alethea, a friend of hers from her brief time in school, had moments of such gaiety, and then long periods of introspection. Their friendship had not been without drama, but through all the turmoil and tumult they were steadfast and true. She had attended their wedding six years ago and considered them both good friends.

Mr. Bertram Birkenhead—extremely wealthy from family investments in the fur trade with the Hudson's Bay Company in the colonies—was at least ten years older than Alethea, his dark hair threaded with silver, his mien calm and reflective. His wise levelheadedness countered her occasional giddiness, and his wife's mercurial flightiness made him smile, lightening his mood and making life zestful, he had once said. Together they were a striking couple, both tall, both elegant, her fine-boned beauty—sharp chin, wide mouth, high cheekbones—a contrast to his sober solidity. They were as close as any husband and wife Anne had ever witnessed.

They trundled no further than the Crescent, that long beautiful curved row of Bath stone townhomes and the park opposite, before stopping and dismissing their carriage for the moment. Mrs. Venables was on Bertram's other arm, so each lady had a gentleman's support.

October in Bath was a rosy month of moderate temperatures, misty sunlight, and muted colors. The trees were changing from green to golden, rust, and scarlet, and scattering leaves beneath them, a showy carpet of color. The park opposite the Crescent was a wide swath of green, with a view of trees below, beyond the ha-ha. Anne strolled, supported by the arm of Mr. Lonsdale, who was as beautiful as his aunt had said, with black hair and dark eyes. He had high cheekbones and hollow cheeks, with a suggestion of delicateness in his mien. Dark circles under his eyes hinted of suffering and perhaps sleepless nights. She was curious about him, a pleasant sensation in Bath, where nothing seemed to change much.

"Are you certain you don't wish for a more amusing walk, my

lady?" the young gentleman said anxiously, tucking her arm in his own. "I believe they promised you a park."

"This is park enough for me. I am perfectly content, I assure you, especially with my friends' choice of a companion for me." She turned to catch a glimpse of his face, not so simple a matter with her bonnet shading her eyes. "How coincidental that I heard your name and am now meeting you!" There was no reply from the young gentleman, so she continued. "As I said, I am acquainted with your aunt, Mrs. Clary Basenstoke, and your cousin, Mr. Roger Basenstoke." Anne didn't add that on her last two visits to Bath her mother, desperate for Anne to wed, had tried to matchmake her with the gentleman simply because he was eligible and wealthy. She had spent many hours with him at the card table and the Assembly Rooms, and found him gloomy, cynical, sarcastic and unappealing. "How happy you must be, with a cousin to spend time with! He has lived here most of his life, I believe, so he has been able to introduce you to all of his friends."

Faint rosy color mantled his cheeks, the only color on him for he was, indeed, pallid. He ducked his head in an affirmative nod. "I am grateful to my aunt for giving me a home for the time being."

That was evasive and ambiguous, to say the least. Anne was becoming more curious about his relationship with his disagreeable cousin. "Do you and your cousin, Mr. Basenstoke, spend much time together?"

Alethea, ahead on the arm of her husband, looked over her shoulder. "Don't speak to me of Roger Basenstoke," she cried. "He is a fiend whom I cannot like."

"Alethea, you should not criticize," her husband protested mildly. "You put poor Alfred out of countenance."

"Pish tush," she said dismissively. "Alfred can no more bear Roger than I can, but he's too polite to say it."

"Many in society find Mr. Basenstoke perfectly amiable," Mrs. Venables protested.

"You're too kind, as always, Bella," Alethea said, a sharpness in her tone that Anne caught. Was there friction there, between the two ladies?

"My cousin has his detractors," Mr. Lonsdale said in a soft voice, "but I cannot criticize him while his mother is so kind to me."

"I credit your delicacy, sir," Anne said. "I did not mean to cause a stir. Alethea, you are too warm when your sentiments are engaged."

"I will ever be fierce regarding my friends, I hope," she said, smiling back at Anne. She was one of the few who knew of the attempt to match her with Mr. Basenstoke, and of Anne's dislike of the gentleman. "Let us walk more swiftly. I wish to enjoy autumn before winter closes its hoary, crabbed fingers over the land."

They strolled along the edge of the ha-ha, overlooking the lawn and path below. "Mr. Lonsdale bemoaned the dullness of this walk and asked if I preferred the park, and I promise I am not unamused, but why *are* we walking this mundane area?" Anne asked, twisting to look back at Alethea, whom she and Mr. Lonsdale had passed in their stroll. The Birkenheads were standing, arm in arm, gazing at the long crescent of Bath townhomes, as Mrs. Venables stood apart, smoothing the ribbons of her calash and vacantly staring back at the white stone crescent of beautiful townhomes.

"I'll confess an ulterior motive to today's jaunt. Bertie is thinking of leasing or purchasing one of the Crescent houses," Alethea said, airily waving her hand at the row of elegant townhomes. "What think you?"

"It would be a costly purchase," Anne said cautiously. "Better to lease, surely. Even then, the Crescent would be a large expense."

"Bertie can afford it, can't you, darling?" Alethea said gaily, clutching her husband's arm. "He's a financial genius, which the world would know if he wasn't so modest."

"Alethea, please, no boasting," her husband said disapprovingly. Money was not a topic for conversation, or not in polite circles, anyway. "I am considering either here or the Circus, but am undecided," he said. "I'd like to find something easier for poor Quinny, something bigger that has a suite of rooms on the ground floor suitable for his health, you see. The stairs are becoming increasingly difficult for the dear boy." He spoke of his younger brother, Quin, who'd lived with them since their parents' deaths. Quin was frail, with a wasting illness that no amount of Bath waters, internal or external, seemed to aid, though he dutifully hobbled to the baths and quaffed the mineral water.

Anne and Lonsdale joined the couple and stared at the Crescent.

"I am for the Crescent; look at these expansive views! So *open*, a real vista, almost like being in the country." Alethea turned and gestured to the landscape, past the ha-ha and down the sward of green grass to a walkway and row of varicolored trees. "But Bertie prefers the Circus," she said with an affectionate look at her handsome husband. "You shall break the tie, Anne."

"No, no," said her husband with a rare smile. "I insist on Alfred breaking the tie. That way I can be sure of winning." He cast a careless look Lonsdale's way and raised his brows. "I have your vote, don't I, dear boy?"

"You know you do, Bertie," he said. "I stand with you in whatever you wish."

"Why not let Quin be the tie breaker?" Anne said. "He's the one who will be living there." She wondered, at the same time, why they did not appeal to Mrs. Venables, who also lived with them.

Alethea laughed out loud. "Always-sensible Anne. I do love you, my friend, and I'm so happy to have you back in Bath."

"Let us walk on. The carriage is to meet us at the Circus, where we can view the homes there," Bertie said. "In either case we shall have to wait until next spring, as there is nothing available until then."

They strolled down Brock Street toward the Circus, but along the way paused, at Anne's request, as they came to the lane that held Margaret's Buildings. Anne examined the narrow lane with interest, for her dear cousin and occasional chaperon, Miss Lolly Broomhall, lived in rooms above a tobacconist along the busy, if slender, thoroughfare. And as a matter of interest, so did the fascinating mystic about whom everyone in Bath seemed to be gossiping.

"Alethea, I have heard a tale that many in Bath are currently enamored of a mystic, a woman with the sobriquet of Mother Macree, who has rooms along here somewhere," Anne said. "Even my mother and grandmother have been to her. What say you? I know how much you enjoy the absurd; are you a devotee?"

Alethea didn't have a chance to respond, for Mrs. Venables stopped and stared back at Anne. "My lady, please do not make light of that woman and her powers!"

"Oh, come, Bella!" Alethea said, staring at her husband's cousin. "You and I went to her together. We listened and then came away laughing. Since then we have chuckled many a time over Mother Macree and her laden pronouncements."

Primly, the woman said, "*You* laughed. I merely smiled to see you so easily entertained."

"Not true!" Alethea cried, staring at the other woman with disbelief. "You laughed as heartily as I, surely?"

Mr. Lonsdale, who had dropped Lady Anne's arm, was silent, his expression blank of emotion, while Bertram watched, head tilted, as his wife protested.

"It is not right to laugh at her," Mrs. Venables insisted. "Not when I have reason to thank her for her enlightenment."

"And how is that, Mrs. Venables?" Anne asked.

With an arch look, Alethea said, "Do you not know the gossip? Our dear Bella has caught herself a beau; a most *eligible* gentleman indeed, though far from a beau idéal, one must say."

"Don't be cruel, dearest," Bertram said with a troubled frown.

"Not cruel, merely precise," Alethea protested. "Bella, truly, I mean no disrespect, but he is so much *older* than you! Why, he is fifty or sixty if he is a day. And you . . . you are in the full bloom of beauty."

Mrs. Venables blushed, adding softness to her expression. She was beautiful, indeed, though Anne felt there was a reserve to her, a lack of openness that she could not like. It was unfair of her to judge, though, given she had met the woman a mere half hour before.

"I count myself fortunate," Mrs. Venables said gently.

"And yet to the mystic you credit that good fortune, as you name it? I had thought it was your own beauty and wit that won the day, not some fortune-teller with bad breath."

"Who is the gentleman, then?" Anne asked to distract from Alethea's impolite, acerbic comments.

Mrs. Venables's cheeks still held that tint of palest rose, like a full-blown but fair flower. "Lord Kattenby. He is a baron, by no means a handsome man," she said to Anne, then turned to her cousin-in-law, "but he is good, and kind, and when you have had as little as I have had in life, you will learn, Alethea, to value the plain and good over the handsome and scandalous."

Alethea had the grace to look ashamed. "I am chastened and apologize, Bella, truly. Lord Kattenby is, as you say, reputedly a good man."

"And he will give me the quiet life I desire."

"And *you* will be the perfect wife to him," Alethea said. "Why,

Anne, she positively shames me, how she goes from kitchen to stillroom, darns Bertie's stockings, oversees the laundry and manages our household like the perfect little huswife!"

Anne smiled and commented, "You were not here last time I was in Bath, Mrs. Venables, last winter. When did you arrive?"

"It is an amazing story, is it not, Bella?" Alethea cried. "She was in Italy—"

"Spain," Mrs. Venables corrected with a faint smile.

"—when her poor husband caught some plaguey fever—"

"A waterborne fever known in the tropics, which occasionally breaks out in Spain, carried there by travelers."

"—and died, leaving her stranded with little to go on."

"Mr. Venables died three years ago," she said.

"We had always been correspondents," Bertie said. "After her husband died, we wrote to each other often at first, and I urged her to come back. We were childhood friends, as well as cousins; she was always kind to me. I would never allow my cousin to suffer in penury."

"I was not penurious then, Bertie, and truly . . . you have been *too* kind." Mrs. Venables had colored more deeply, giving her for that moment the elusive beauty of youth.

"But she would not come, and then I did not hear from her for two years, during which time I'm afraid she suffered terribly," he said, his expression sober and remonstrative. "When I finally convinced her to return to England and come to us, she was a changed woman."

"Illness and poverty do change a woman," she said, touching a gold and amber cross she wore around her neck. "I am so grateful for my family."

"That was the cross Mr. Venables gave to you on your wedding day, is it not?" Bertie asked, his tone gentle.

"It is," she said, her lips trembling. "I never take it off. It reminds me of all our years together in Spain and abroad. He was a provisioner for the army. We had many good years, until illness robbed me of such a good man."

"Though you have found another good man?"

"Baron Kattenby is the sort of gentleman who makes an ideal widow's husband," she said. "Good, kind, undemanding, attentive."

"What did you do in the years when Bertie did not hear from you?" Anne asked, curious about people, as always. "How did you live?"

"I sold what I had to sell," she said, her eyes tearing. "Including much that was dear to me . . . much that my beloved husband had given me. Except this cross, of course, which will be around my neck until the day I die. I was ill with the same fever that had killed my husband for much of the time, fortunate to have with me a woman who nursed me through it. Poor Betty . . . she was such a kind woman, but she, too, died of the fever, leaving me alone." She caught back a sob. "Please, I don't like to speak of that time. I was too ashamed to write to dear Cousin Bertie, too afraid of sounding wretched."

"It is a pity that poverty and illness bring with them shame," Anne said gently.

"It's over now, and I am on the way to being happy, so I do *not* wish to dwell on the past."

Anne offered her an apologetic smile. She was clearly a private woman, and to have her past dredged up like that to a stranger . . . it was hideous. Alethea looked a little ashamed, while Bertie turned his face away in compassion for her suffering.

A young man approached and bowed, misty sunlight piercing the clouds and shining on his golden hair and glinting in his sky blue eyes. "Mr. Thomas Graeme at your service, ladies. Lonsdale, how do you do this fine day?"

Mr. Lonsdale appeared taken aback to be accosted on the street. He glanced at the ladies, then doffed his hat, bowed and said, "I am well, Mr. Graeme."

There was a discomfited silence for a moment. The young gentleman's behavior was forward. "Lonsdale, will you not introduce your friend?" Alethea finally asked, censure in her tone as she continued, saying, "Since he has already been so bold as to address us?"

Anne was interested to note Mr. Lonsdale's confusion; his friend's behavior had put him out of countenance. But he acceded to her wishes and said, "Certainly. Lady Anne Addison, Mr. and Mrs. Birkenhead, Mrs. Venables, may I introduce Mr. Thomas Graeme? Mr. Graeme, may I introduce you to Lady Anne, Mr. and Mrs. Birkenhead and Mrs. Venables?"

"Good day to you all," the young man said, sweeping off his

cockade-adorned hat and bowing elegantly, one shapely leg fitted perfectly in buff cloth thrust forward.

"And how do you two know each other, Mr. Lonsdale?" Anne asked, curious. Graeme appeared young, a fresh-faced fair-haired fellow with an elegant cravat and jacket that was slightly too large for his frame.

"Our club," Graeme answered, as Lonsdale said, "Eton."

"Come now, which is it?" Bertram asked, his gaze slewing between the two men. His brow was furrowed, and a look of suspicion marred his normally elegant insouciance.

"Both," Graeme said. "I replied with the current association and dear Alfred replied with the older connection."

Lies, Anne thought, and wondered why. Such a simple thing, to tell how they knew one another, and perhaps so revealing; her suspicious nature asserted itself in the face of falsehood. Graeme whispered something to Alfred and he nodded, then the other man bowed and walked away.

"I, er, must speak to Graeme about something of import," Lonsdale said. "If you can all do without me for a moment, I will rejoin you at the Circus?"

"No, Lonsdale, that is *too* bad of you," Alethea said sharply. "We invited you so there would be no lady without an escort."

"Alethea, enough," Bertram said. His wife glanced at him, her brow furrowed, but he was frowning at Graeme, who had walked away and awaited Lonsdale.

"My friend, I am fully capable of walking alone," Anne said to her. "I have proved it many a time. Why, just the other day I took a dozen or more steps before tottering like a rotten apple tree and toppling over." Her jest alleviated the tension and they walked on, but Anne did notice Bertram casting one long assessing glance over his shoulder as he watched the two younger gentlemen walking away together, deep in conversation.

Anne, close to Bertram for a moment, murmured, "Do I sense disapproval of young Lonsdale's choice of companion?"

His lips twitched. "I have heard the young man's name before as a newcomer to Bath. Graeme is . . . light in his morals."

"What does that mean?"

Bertram merely shook his head. "I do not gossip, as you know.

Let us say he's not quite the thing, and I do not like to see Alfred led astray by such as Mr. Thomas Graeme."

"Is Lonsdale so easily imposed upon as to be led astray?" Bertram did not answer. "Where is Mr. Graeme's family from?"

"No one knows."

And that, Anne thought, gave the lie to the Graeme-Lonsdale tale of meeting, and was, perhaps, the crux of Bertie's disapproval. Family history was the all-important indicator of weight and substance in their world. To be untethered, to be a nobody, made social dealings more difficult. Still, she had not thought Bertie a prig, though, to be fair, she had her own reservations emanating from the lie of the two young gentlemen's acquaintanceship. But that could equally apply to Lonsdale, who she had also just met. She was prejudiced in his favor, she realized, because his aunt, Mrs. Basenstoke, was such a dear friend. That was hardly fair to Mr. Graeme. As bad as it seemed, who could blame the young man, if he was indeed untethered in this world, for trying to form connections with others, even if it was at the risk of appearing impolite?

They strolled to the Circus and regarded the townhomes there, the pallid sunshine struggling to make itself seen through the canopy of trees that had yet to shed their leaves. And yet no decision was forthcoming. Alethea preferred the Crescent, with its views, and Bertram thought the Circus, closer to the Assembly Rooms, was the more convenient. Quin, his foremost concern, would be able to walk so far, he hoped, and sit in the Octagon Room, or even the ballroom, as others danced.

"We can engage a sedan chair for Quin so simply from the Crescent." Alethea watched her husband, then shook her head impatiently. "Dearest, please be reasonable. You expect too much from Quinny, truly, you do. Think on it. You say the Circus will be more convenient than the Crescent, but unless you plan to walk him through one of the townhomes, out their yard and directly to Alfred Street and the Upper Assembly Rooms, he must still walk all the way to either Bennett or Gay Street and around." Exasperated, she added, "That is far too distant for dear Quinny." She sighed. "He fears your reliance on his recovery, Bertie, he truly does."

Birkenhead looked pensive and crestfallen, staring down at the cobbles and muttering his muted, unintelligible response. His brother was dearer to him than anyone in the world, Anne knew, and valued him the more for it. Her feelings for Jamey were such that though their cases were far different, she was sympathetic to Bertie's yearning for his brother to recover. Anne knew Quin was frail, but he had a fierce inner strength far beyond his physical lack.

But Alethea was right; Quin was not likely ever to increase in strength. To expect it was unfair. "I don't wish to interject myself into a family discussion, but practicality dictates that you must choose the situation that is best for you both, not disregarding Quin, but recognizing his limitations. If you are close to the Assembly Rooms and he knows you purchased on the Circus for his benefit, might he not feel compelled to try what he may not be able to achieve? You know Quin best, of course, but might he not feel guilty that he cannot take advantage of your generosity to walk all the way? On the Crescent, at least, he can walk on the green for a few minutes, and if weary, your footman can help him back to your home."

He nodded. "But the Circus, too, has a lovely green space opposite."

"But not the open view, dearest," Alethea said, with a glance of appreciation to Anne.

She shook her head. Now, having spoken, Anne feared her powers of persuasion. She did not wish to be the deciding vote after all. "What do you think, Mrs. Venables?" she asked.

"Oh, I have no say in the decision," she replied. "Nor should I. After the baron and I wed, I will, of course, be removing to his home on Camden Crescent."

So the relationship had come far enough that she was expecting a proposal, or had, perhaps, already received one! "Camden Crescent! My grandmother's home is on the Paragon, close by. Will you attend St. Swithin?"

"Yes, indeed! Shall we see you there Sunday?"

And with such chat of church and congregation, the matter of the lease or purchase of a townhome passed and they strolled the Circus until they came in sight of the landau, where Lonsdale awaited them.

Chapter Three

The afternoon was not yet gone, and Anne had a task she had been wishing to perform since she arrived in Bath two days before. She marshaled her forces and set out with her maid, Mary, Mary's son Wee Robbie, and her cat, Irusan. As Mary carried a basket on her arm laden with treats from the Everingham cook—the woman loved to display her arts and baked far too many sweets for a household of women—tea and various other sundries, Anne utilized her grandmother's creaky carriage to manage the slight distance to Margaret's Buildings. The driver let them down along Brock Street. Anne tugged at her bodice and settled her cat in her arms. He grumbled and flexed his claws, catching them on Anne's shawl, then withdrawing them with an impatient growl.

"This is it, Mary; this is where Lolly lives now," she said. She eyed the row of townhomes down the narrow lane as they strolled it. The buildings were relatively new, but already the owners were renting space to shops along the ground level, with rooms and apartments on the first and second floors.

The afternoon had turned dusky, with a dusty light from the sun that was obscured by the angling shadows of the buildings. "She has moved rooms since I was last here. It's the door beyond the tobacconist, she wrote," Anne said, hefting Irusan—a not inconsiderable weight, halfway between one stone and two—on her hip like a baby. "Look at all these townhomes that have become shops and rented rooms! I see a day when *all* are shops and rooms to let above, not homes."

"Aye, milady. Robbie, *Robbie!* Dinna run aboot so; it's ill-mannered," Mary said, distracted by her son's excitement as he dashed along the cobbled lane.

Anne had feared the stultified atmosphere of Bath would dull the boy, but she realized she had not reckoned with the difference in life experience between a lady of her age and means and a boy of the serving class. Between making friends with other tigers and scullery lads along the Paragon, escaping his lessons—his mother had been too busy with Anne's Bath wardrobe to attend to his reading and arithmetic—and stuffing his face with the Bath buns Anne's grandmother had the cook purchase from Sally Lunn's, he was rarely still.

"Let him go, Mary. He can't get into trouble along here, I don't think," she said as they strolled, and she examined the shops along the street level. "Let him run about and release his fidgets."

"He *will* visit with Miss Broomhall, or I'll know the reason why," she said sternly. "She was verra kind to him in Cornwall, and he willna advance in life by disremembering kindness."

With one sharp word from his mother, he was swiftly brought to heel. Anne located the correct building, with a stained white painted door beside a tobacconist's shop. "Oh, dear," Anne said, staring at the coal smoke–dirtied door. "This does not bode well for the cleanliness of the establishment." As she stood and allowed Mary to employ the door knocker, Anne observed a well-dressed young lady, her face veiled, departing from a house a few doors down, as an anxious-looking couple arrived, cast glances both ways, and hustled in. Her nerves tingled. Could that establishment be the infamous Mystic of Bath's residence? Something told her it was, though she was no seer.

A woman in a soiled apron answered the door. As the ladies and Robbie entered the dim entry that smelled of boiled beef, fish and cabbage, she indicated, with a laconic and put-upon sigh, that Miss Broomhall's rooms were up two floors at the top.

"Will you bring up tea, madam, while I visit my cousin?" Anne said to her, eyeing her stained apron with disapproval.

The woman glanced at Mary, Wee Robbie in his pint-sized livery, and then sized Anne up and straightened. "Aye, miss, I'll—"

"Her ladyship, Lady Anne Addison, daughter of the Earl of Harecross," Mary snapped.

The woman nodded and curtseyed. "I'll bring it up in a jiffy."

"See that you do, madam," Mary replied tartly.

When the woman had hustled away, closing her door behind her, and they began to ascend, Anne said, "I think you stand stiff on my account more than I do, Mary."

"That's my job, milady. I'll no' have you disrespected by aught."

At the top of the stairs they found a door standing open and heard a pretty humming sound from within, and then a burst of song, a bit of the saucy ballad "My Thing Is My Own" sung in lilting sweet tones, followed by a brief refrain on a piano. Mary rapped on the door, the sound silenced, and Lolly sang out, "Come in!" When she saw it was Anne, her face was wreathed in a joyful smile. "Dearest Anne!" she exclaimed, coming forward with open arms for a hug. "How nice of you to come visit me."

"My darling Lolly, how good to see you!" Anne exclaimed, her voice muffled. Released at last from an enthusiastic, suffocating embrace—something she suffered only from dear Lolly, who was plump and soft as a cushion—as Irusan grumbled and wriggled to be let down, Anne glanced around and saw, against one wall, a table with a clavichord upon it. "I'm so happy you received my gift! I hoped it was not amiss and that you could find space for it, but you should *never* stop singing. You always were a delight."

"It was most welcome," Lolly said, bustling over to it and stroking with fondness the small tabletop keyed instrument. "Such a *clever* gift, dearest Anne; you see I have found space for it after all. So thoughtful."

Mary was then welcomed, but Lolly's most effusive salutation was offered to Wee Robbie, for the two had become fast friends in Cornwall. Once she had coddled Wee Robbie, she sent him off outside with an admonition to buy at the bakery three doors down a sack of boiled sweets to share with the street urchins and sweepers. She chucked Irusan under his furry chin and held him on her lap for as long as his dignity would stand as they chatted about Anne's arrival in Bath, the Marquess of Darkefell's whereabouts, Lady Barbara's infamy in not visiting Lolly, and Anne's grandmother's steadfast ignoring of Lolly. Both facts seemed to irritate Anne more than Lolly, the object of the slights. The fate of a poor relation was merely reality to her, while Anne knew how much Lolly's life could be improved if Lady Everingham and Lady Harecross would do their duty by a kinswoman.

The housekeeper/landlady, with her dirty apron gone and her slatternly hair tidied, delivered a tray laden with tea up the steep staircase, and served the ladies. Anne offered the treats she had brought with her and insisted the landlady take some for her own tea. The woman's manner greatly improved, and she curtseyed before descending.

After catching up on family news and local gossip, Anne asked,

"Lolly, I've heard much, since I arrived, about this woman, the Mystic of Bath. She has rooms a few doors down from you, is that correct?"

Lolly's eyes widened and her lined face had a girlish look of glee. She settled her ribbons and flounces about her and said, "Mother Macree as she is known? A *fascinating* character. Oh, the bustle there has been around her of late! All sorts of people, high- and lowborn come to see her. She is quite accurate. *Amazingly* so!"

"Have you been to see her yourself?"

"Indeed I have, before she became so popular. It is difficult to get an appointment now."

Anne frowned. "Why so?"

"There is the matter of money."

"I see. She demands payment now?"

"Oh, my dear, she *must*! Don't you see? If she did not, she would be simply overrun, so popular is she!"

"What do you know of what she has predicted that came true?"

Her eyes widened with delight and her voice lowered to a mysterious whisper. "Why, she foretold this instrument coming to me!" Lolly said, indicating the clavichord.

Startled, Anne asked, "What did she say?"

"It was the most extraordinary thing," Lolly said. "I took her a pot of the ointment I use for my joints—"

"Are they still bothering you, Miss Broomhall?" Mary interjected.

"I'll never *not* suffer. So my mother did, and her mother before her. It is in the family, you know."

"About the mystic?" Anne prompted.

"Oh, yes, where was I?"

"You took her a pot of ointment."

"Of course and then . . . oh, *yes*! She told me she had a message from beyond. *Quite* startling! My heart began to palpitate . . . it thudded, you know. I felt faint for a moment, but it was my stays; they were too tight, you see. Too many Bath buns, I'm afraid. I rather indulge in Sally Lunn cakes. You must try them! I know you spend so little time in Bath, my dearest cousin, but you must—"

"Lolly, please, can we get back to the message from the mystic?"

"Oh, yes, where were we?"

Anne held her breath for a moment, as Mary bit her lip to keep from laughing out loud. Letting the breath out slowly, Anne said, "You took her some ointment and she had a message for you from beyond."

"Oh, yes! Of course." She leaned toward them and whispered, "She said I would come into some good fortune soon. She would not say what form the fortune would come in, as she did not wish to spoil a surprise, but it would come, and soon."

"And?"

"And three weeks later the clavichord was delivered! Is that not *quite* amazing?"

"I'm . . . speechless."

"Aye, and she smiled when I told her of it. Said of course it was what she meant, but it was worth it to keep the secret, for it was such a delightful surprise to me."

"What else have you heard?"

Lolly told them a long tale of the many times the woman had been correct. Children who had become ill, but then recovered, women who had discovered they were with child, money paid back that was thought to be lost, all manner of domestic mysteries. If her whole reputation had been based on such matters, Anne would have thought nothing of it. But she supposed Lolly would not hear of the other matters, the secrets told of the great and mighty of Bath and beyond. But her grandmother's assertion that the woman had foretold Anne's own as-yet secret engagement to the Marquess of Darkefell interested her. How could she know such a thing without she had an ear tuned to the universe?

"Could you make an appointment to attend Mother Macree? I'll confess, I'm intrigued. I know you said she is difficult to see now—"

"It will be no trouble now for *you*. And she knows of you, of course."

"Oh?"

"Of whom else would I speak? My fondness for you will find an ear with everyone."

So, that was one possible source for the mystic's information, but still, even Lolly did not know she and Darkefell were definitely engaged to be wed. "Will you make an appointment for two days hence? Saturday . . . perhaps two in the afternoon?"

Lolly clapped joyously. "I'll be pleased to do so! I so hope for good news for you." Her smile died. "But alas, good news is not all she imparts, of course."

"What has she foreseen that was unfortunate?"

"She has foreseen tragedy. In the summer she was devastated and I asked what was wrong. She said she knew a gentleman was going to die, but she did not know what to do, whether to tell him or his loved ones so they could prepare, or to leave it alone and let God have his way."

Anne paused and thought; there were so many possibilities, but one was simplest, and therefore most likely. "A dilemma to be sure, but Lolly . . . in a city such as Bath, which attracts more than its share of the sickly, the infirm and the elderly who come to take the water, surely—not to be too blunt—but surely death is a common occurrence."

"You don't understand, Anne, dearest; this gentleman was sickly, true, but his recent marriage had inspired a hope in him that he would recover fully. He was happy."

Anne's brow wrinkled and her mouth opened, but then closed again. What could she say? How Lolly made the leap from a sickly man to a man who was happy and therefore recovering, she didn't know how to discuss. It was nonsensical, but it was not the worst failure of logic she had ever seen.

Mary murmured a warning of the time, and Anne rose. "We must go; our carriage will be waiting. Tonight we are engaged to go to the Assembly Rooms, though I wish t'were otherwise. I am going to see my friend Lydia and her husband tomorrow, but if you will engage us to Mother Macree the next day, I will be content."

"I will happily do so. Oh, what fun we will have, dearest Anne! And what mysteries we may discover! I'm so pleased you are here."

Chapter Four

The Upper Assembly Rooms of Bath were lovely, rather new—constructed fifteen years ago, unlike the Lower Assembly Rooms, which were many decades older—and built in a U shape, two long rectangular rooms (one the ballroom and the other the tearoom) joined by an octagonal room at the far end, with a newer purpose-built card room (added nine years ago) beyond that. Mr. Tyson, the master of ceremonies, had been informed of Anne's arrival in Bath—it was a courtesy he admired greatly, and Anne's mother was assiduous in such duties—and so her name was added to the book and they had been formally invited to the fancy dress ball.

Lady Barbara was elegant in blue silk, with ostrich plumes nodding from her turban and a hand-painted fan languidly utilized as she sat among other similar ladies in the ballroom. Mothers and chaperones of eligible misses were sharp-eyed and on the hunt, competing with the widows and ladies with a few more years for the trophy of an eligible bachelor or widower. The Bath Season had begun and there were matches to be made.

Anne would, as always, be viewed as *highly* eligible—she united both a titled family and an independent fortune in one tolerable female—and her presence in Bath could be a considerable enticement. But as tedious as it would be to evade wife-seeking gentlemen, she was not ready to announce her betrothal, and that was that.

To her first Assembly Rooms ball of the Season she wore a gown of green figured silk, with gold embroidery and gold lace ruffles at the bodice and elbows, green kid gloves to the elbow and gold satin dancing pumps. She looked well enough, her mother said, though it was last year's gown. The new dresses could not be made fast enough to soothe Lady Harecross's anxiety for her daughter to appear *au courant.*

Standing along the edge of the row of chairs, looking about for her friends as the noise of conversation increased with each new arrival as the orchestra tuned up, Anne felt a familiar tingle of anticipation. She might not enjoy husband hunting, but she did like to dance. Perhaps she would be blessed with a partner who would not shame her.

"Lady Anne, what a pleasure to see you here!"

She turned to see Miss Susanna Hadley, an acquaintance of some years, and both curtseyed. "Miss Hadley, lovely to see you. What brings you to Bath this Season? In your last letter you gave no hint at such a move." Her friend, a slim, nearsighted and plain-visaged young woman, was usually content to remain in Canterbury, but the death two years ago of her mother may have affected her decisions. Perhaps she had decided it was time for her own establishment. She was of an age with Anne, so in her mid-twenties.

"I came to stay with my aunt, Lady Rebecca Sharples," she said. "My father has decided to remarry, and . . . and . . ." She bit her lip and shook her head.

Anne watched her with sympathy. While she could understand Susanna's father's desire for remarriage, his daughter had been exceptionally close to her mother. This could not be easy. Susanna was of a retiring personality; she much preferred the garden to the salon, and the library to the ballroom. "You will be a welcome addition to my Bath acquaintanceship." A woman approached, and Anne felt the tug of recognition.

"Lady Anne Addison, may I introduce you to my aunt, Lady Rebecca Sharples," Susanna said about the woman, an elegant lady of middle years. Her hair was thoroughly powdered, dressed high and elaborate, with a jaunty peacock feather nodding with every move.

As both women curtseyed, Lady Sharples examined Anne through her lorgnette and said, her voice loud, sharp and carrying, "I believe I know your mother and grandmother. Your mother is the Countess of Harecross, who will not return to her home village and prefers to board with her mother."

Anne glanced back to her mother, who was gossiping behind her fan with a close friend. Put out of countenance by the other woman's bluntness, she remained silent, simply smiling and nodding. Susanna colored faintly and looked down at the toe of her slipper, peeping out from under her dark gray gown. Fortunately at that moment the Birkenheads claimed Anne's attention. Quin was in the Octagon Room, Alethea said, and craved a visit from her.

"Excuse me," she said to the other two women with a brief curtsey. "Susanna, I look forward to reanimating our acquaintance.

I'll leave you my card in the next few days, though I am engaged for at least the next three. My friend Lydia Bestwick is in Bath and I simply *must* visit her."

"Bestwick . . . Lord John is the Marquess of Darkefell's younger brother, is he not?" Lady Sharples said, her head tilted to one side as she eyed Anne.

"If you'll excuse me," Anne said without replying. She escaped, following Alethea, who had nodded to Lady Sharples, with whom she was acquainted. As they walked, they chatted about friends, absent and present. "Is Mrs. Venables not in attendance?"

"She has her iron in another fire; she's in attendance at a musical soiree hosted by friends of Baron Kattenby."

"Ah, her prospective husband!"

"Indeed. She is expecting a proposal any day now."

The Octagon Room was large, with four deliciously blazing fireplaces, where the older and infirm could wait until the card room or the tearoom was open. It was the perfect place to view everyone who was entering, exiting, going to the card room, or headed in to tea. Quin sat by one of the fireplaces, warmly wrapped against the chill of an October evening, his profile sharp etched, lit by the fireglow. Anne paused in the doorway and examined him. Quin's head was fine-boned, his skull perfectly delineated, clothed only in thin, pale skin. She had been acquainted with the Birkenhead brothers since Alethea and Bertram first became engaged seven years before, and Quin had always been frail, but it was clear that time had not been his friend. His shoulders were stooped, his frame was thin, his hands knotted and gnarled. He wore spectacles sometimes, when he could bear them. His hair, though an attempt had been made to style it, was thin, but he could not abide a wig because it irritated his scalp. No cause had ever been diagnosed, and some doctors had told Bertie that it was a nervous refusal to eat that caused the young man's troubles. Whatever the source, his suffering was sincere. Anne pitied him with all her heart.

"Quin, my darling boy," she said to him, though he was a few years older than her. "It is good to see you." She bent over and embraced him before taking a low stool near his knees.

"Lady Anne," he said, his eyes lighting up with joy. "I have been feverish waiting to see you. I so envied Alethea and Bertie today when they came home, rosy-cheeked, from their walk with you."

Bertram, looking down fondly at his brother, touched his shoulder. "We'll leave you two to catch up, shall we? Come, Alethea, let these two flirt in peace."

With the hubbub about them, Anne found once more the joy of Quin's conversation. Those who deigned to visit the invalid found in his company ample pleasure. Denied other outlets, he read and studied as much as he was able, and could talk on any subject with good sense and knowledge. Also, he was kind and good-natured, bearing his ailments with stoicism. After speaking a few moments, she looked into his gentle gray eyes. "Quin, I would value your opinion on a matter of interest to me. I'm sure you've heard of this Mother Macree, the supposed Mystic of Bath. What think you of her and her claims?"

"So you have heard of her already!" he cried. He grinned, mischief lighting his eyes until they sparkled in the firelight. "Have you seen her?"

"No, but I am going day after tomorrow with my cousin, who knows her."

"How I *long* to go!"

"Go with me!" she said, then felt her stomach lurch. Had she committed a faux pas? "If . . . if you'd like, that is," she said, giving him an opportunity to slip out of any commitment if it was too much for him. "Would you like it?"

"I should enjoy it above all things." He didn't seem to notice her hesitation. "I have been reading of Dr. John Dee, Queen Elizabeth's astrologer. Fascinating! That a woman of immense ability would place so much faith in a man of such a nonsensical—I suppose I must call astrology a science, for so it was and still is viewed by some people—but Good Queen Bess's reliance on his science is beyond belief. I shouldn't scoff; he was also a scholar of some note and an accomplished mathematician who helped calculate voyages of exploration."

She eyed him with a smile. "You are a never-ending source of wonder, how you accumulate all your knowledge."

"It's not magic," he said drily, "but reading." He turned reflective and said, "Back to John Dee . . . those were different times, I suppose. But now about this so-called mystic . . . it's alarming that people still will place their lives in the hands of quacks, even in this enlightened time of true science."

"If you are game we shall visit her together, then, day after tomorrow."

"Leave it to me to arrange my transport, dear Anne," he said, taking her hand in his, cold despite the roaring fire. "I go every other day to the Cross Baths with my doctor for a plunge and a soak, but other than that I rarely emerge. Tell me what time, and I shall be there."

"Two in the afternoon, then. You have her direction?"

"Every child in Bath knows how to find Mother Macree," he said with a smile.

She stood. "I must get back to my mother. She is inclined to complain of neglect if I leave for too long, and also, I am promised for the first dance. Shall I sit out the fourth dance with you and we can take tea in the tearoom?"

His smile faltered. "I doubt I will stay so long. I'll listen to the first music, but probably go home after."

She laid a gentle kiss on his forehead as several ladies looked on aghast at such an open display of preference. There would be rumors circulating about them swiftly, but as carefully as she guarded her reputation in general, in this case she did not care. "Good evening, then, my dear Quin. I shall see you Saturday."

She took a deep breath and started back toward the ballroom. Susanna, tears filling her large gray eyes, stumbled into the Octagon Room as Anne was approaching the door. "My dear friend, what's wrong?" Anne asked, steadying the other woman with one hand.

She shook her head, the tears spraying like raindrops, catching the light as they scattered, dotting the dull silk of her gown. "It is nothing, really . . . nothing important, anyway. I just arrived a week ago and I'm so *dreadfully* weary of it all already; the tittle-tattle, the fakery, the lies, the flirtation, the gossip. Dear Lady Sharples *means* to be kind, I know, by introducing me everywhere as her spinster niece with a considerable dowry, but it's simply too much. She puts me so out of countenance I don't know where to look. I don't know what to *do* anymore."

Regarding her closely, Anne saw her friend was close to the edge of her ability to withstand the crowd. Susanna would not allow

Anne to accompany her to the ladies' withdrawing room, insisting she must go back to the ballroom soon, or Lady Sharples would seek her out.

"Nonsense. *I* will return to the ballroom, make sure she is entertained and give you time to collect yourself," Anne said. A sudden inspiration came to her, and she led Susanna to a vacated seat by Quin and introduced the two, knowing the gentle fellow's conversation was the best tonic for a woman weary of the usual gallantry. "I shall tell Lady Sharples your whereabouts, and that you are chatting and flirting with a very *eligible* young man," she whispered to her friend with a smile. She walked away, but stopped in the doorway and looked back. Already the two had their heads together as they spoke softly in the hubbub of the increasing crowd.

She did as she said she would, informing Lady Sharples that Susanna was accompanied by an eligible gentleman of wealth and good family, perfectly chaperoned by the crowd in the Octagon Room. The ballroom was filling quickly. The music for the first dance started and she was claimed by her partner, a gentleman she knew from her last Season in Bath, two years before. He was still unwed, as he said with some heavy emphasis, and so was she. Perhaps fate —

Not fate, she firmly told him. She wanted to follow it with the undeniable fact that he set his sights too high. He was a baronet, but every woman he had courted — and she was among them — had been an earl's daughter or higher. A brewer's daughter of modest attractions was more his limit. If he had brilliance and good looks he may have aimed higher, but he was vacuous, dull, pedantic and pompous. Was she vain for thinking herself out of his reach? It wasn't just her birth and wealth, it was her mind and heart and spirit. She was beyond him, though perhaps that fact was not as obvious to society as she would have liked to think.

Inevitably, she compared him to Darkefell; the contrasts were laughable. As she avoided his tedious and heavy-handed flirtation, waiting impatiently for the moment when their dance would be done and she could move on to her next partner, she acknowledged the truth. What kept her from announcing her engagement was one inevitable fact: she feared the hubbub it would create. There would be astonishment, but she knew society very well, perhaps too well.

Why would a man of such wealth and property and title stoop to choose the plain Lady Anne Addison? The answer, gossips would say, was her sizable dowry, of *course*. Even though he had money of his own, even though he was a marquess, with land and an abundance of houses scattered over England like dewdrops on a rose, still . . . it *had* to be money. What else would make her tolerable?

Perhaps she was not so vain as she feared.

Finally their dance was done, and she was claimed by her next partner, a gentle man who simply enjoyed the dance. His concentration and the intricate but well-known figures of the dance left her free to enjoy, and enjoy it she did, the lilting music, constant rhythmic movement and the smiles and laughter of friends . . . she was finally enjoying herself.

However, by her fourth partner her recurring asthma left her breathless and feeling faint. She was weary of chatter and gossip anyway, and was happy she had promised no one beyond that. She retreated, with her mother and their companion, Lord Westmacott, an elderly beau who was attached to Lady Harecross at most public events, to the tearoom. Her discomfort passed as she watched the crowd, how people flicked glances at each other, then bent their heads to gossip, how many petty cuts were made, the flirtations that were taking place unnoticed. There was a buzzing undercurrent in Bath that she had forgotten in the time she had been away from it.

Her dance partner after tea was Bertie Birkenhead. As Mr. Tyson called the cotillion, Alethea was claimed, to her obvious misery, by Mr. Roger Basenstoke. The cotillion was a lengthy dance, to complete Alethea's wretchedness. As Anne and Bertie joined in, held hands and circled, she mentioned his wife's dislike of the man.

"I think it is his disdain for poor Lonsdale that makes her dislike him so," Bertie said as he crossed his hand behind her back to grasp hers, and led her in the circle. "She is a ferocious supporter of Lonsdale's, and you know her tender heart," he murmured below the music. "His manner is not appealing to her, but Roger is not a bad soul. We went to Oxford at the same time."

"How long have you known Mr. Lonsdale?"

His handsome face turned away as they parted in the dance and he took his wife's hand. She watched him smile encouragingly at

Alethea and squeeze her hand. A trembling smile quivered on her lips. When Anne and Bertie came back together he answered her question.

"We met Lonsdale some time ago, I cannot be precise. A few months; not more. We are acquainted, of course, with Mrs. Basenstoke and her son, and met him through them, I suppose. Bath society is small, out of Season. We Bathonians must stand together in summer, in the desultory heat, to have any entertainment at all."

They parted once again, and she smiled and nodded to Mr. Basenstoke, noting his grim countenance and proper gait. He danced well, if stiffly, but with little feeling or flair. As the ladies met together in the center of their dance, she sent Alethea a sympathetic look and her friend smiled.

It was one dance. She'd survive.

After, Anne accompanied the Birkenheads when they headed to the Octagon Room to collect Quin, who had, after all, stayed through the sixth dance. She was amazed to see Miss Susanna Hadley there still—it would cause endless chatter and gossip, that they had spent a couple of hours together—and more amazed to see the fond look she gave Quin as they parted. Her sadness and tears of earlier were gone, and when she returned to the ballroom it was with a pretty smile on her face.

• • •

At long last the evening was done. Anne was silent in their carriage as she and her mother departed. Lady Barbara was weary, but once she did start talking it was to complain endlessly about everything, from the tea (weak!) to the band (raucous!) to friends (absent!). She criticized a friend's inappropriate gown and an enemy's expensive jewelry. That continued as they entered the townhouse and mounted the stairs to part ways.

At the top, Lady Harecross turned to her daughter in the muted candlelight, her expression cross and disgruntled, her pouchy face lined with weariness. "Anne, I was pleased to see so many gentlemen eager to court you, but it is beyond my comprehension, when I know your opinions of Bath society, why you would not stop them all by announcing your engagement."

"Goodnight, madam," Anne said to her mother and parted on the landing as a footman followed to douse the candles.

Irusan was awaiting her on the bed, and Anne leaned over and petted him, then sat at her dressing table. Mary, quiet and efficient, took pins from her hair, undid the coiled style, and began the complicated task of preparing her hair for nighttime, tying a scarf around it to keep it tidy. As Anne removed her gloves and jewelry, she told Mary all that had occurred and all she had witnessed.

Once done she turned and regarded her maid. "Mary, when Darkefell joins us here in a week, we shall announce our engagement."

"Aboot time, milady, begging your pardon. What made the final decision for you?"

"Believe it or not, my mother has something to do with it. As much as she annoys me, I love her and Grandmother, and I know I am tormenting her to no end by delaying it. I promised her I would do it soon, and there will be no reason to delay any longer once he is here. I love him. He loves me, though I can't think why, the torment I've put him through."

"Milady, having come to know him, I think he would be bored witless by anyone with less spirit and intelligence. He's a man who'd rather be challenged than wearied wi' dullness. You're never dull."

She smiled. "You're too kind, Mary."

"By the by, a note came by hand this evening." She handed it to her mistress.

Anne unfolded it and read the tidy script. "How nice! Mr. Boatin has arrived in Bath after visiting Father to see how the new secretary is working out," she said of Darkefell's African secretary. "He's to find a house for Tony to rent here in Bath."

"Why does Lord Darkefell not stay with Lord and Lady Bestwick, then?" Anne gave Mary a look, and the maid bit her lip. "Of course; what was I thinking? Lady Lydia, the puir dear, would drive him daft, even more so now in her condition. And how does he find your father's new secretary? Does Mr. Boatin say?"

Anne smiled as she read the muted words and saw through to the profound happiness underneath. How very "Osei" the letter was. "He sees what I witnessed with my own eyes. You saw it too, when we were staying with Father. The young woman has surpassed all expectations. Her knowledge of Greek and Italian has pleased my father greatly. Honestly, that young lady is a joy to behold, how she manages Father's business affairs as well as his correspondence and research. And how she manages *him!*" Recent changes had been made at the estate, including employing Mr. Destry's son as an assistant to the elderly Harecross land steward. The estate was on its way to becoming much better run with so much able support. She could rest easy when she married that her father would have all the help he needed.

She sighed. "I hope the young lady finds the neighborhood amenable. She has caused a sensation. We went into the village together on occasion, as you know, and there she is followed by all the children who have never seen an African before. Thank goodness she is as good-tempered as she is intelligent."

"That'll wear off, milady."

"I hope you're right." She folded Osei's letter and handed it to Mary. "Could you put it on my desk for me? I'll send a note to him tomorrow. I wish to have him write Tony for me, so I know exactly when to expect him."

And so to bed. She curled up with Irusan, who purred and lulled himself to sleep. But her eyes were open for hours as she thought of what life with Tony would be like.

Chapter Five

Lord and Lady John Bestwick had taken a modest house on Milsom Street, midway along the row of Bath stone townhomes and —increasingly—shops. Anne had engaged to visit Lydia in the evening, when she thought her friend might be most at her ease. The maid led Anne up to a first-floor sitting room decorated in waist-high white paneling, above which the walls were hung in blue wallpaper. The furnishings were blue silk, with rounded lines. Lydia, well wrapped against any imaginary puff of air, sat on a sofa by a fire, a pretty ornamented screen keeping the heat from her face. Anne crossed the room and leaned down to embrace her friend awkwardly over her growing stomach.

"Dearest Anne," the younger woman said, her eyes gleaming with emotion. "I've been *longing* to see you, but you have been here in Bath for *days* and have not visited."

"You know my mother would not allow me to have any rest the first few days without I must have in a seamstress and order a whole new wardrobe."

"But you've been visiting others. I hear you were walking with the Birkenheads, and attended the Upper Assembly Rooms for the ball last evening. John was in the card room and saw you, but you were again engaged with the Birkenheads and dancing *every* dance." Lydia was pouting, one tear trailing own her pale cheek.

If her friend and the sister of her late fiancé was in good health Anne would not have put up with being reprimanded for abandonment, but the young woman was heavy with child and clearly uncomfortable. Anne sat beside her. "I'm here now, my dear," she said, putting one hand over her friend's. "Please, let us not quarrel."

"I don't wish to quarrel, Anne. But I'm so lonely."

"Oh, my dearest friend, I'm sorry, I should have visited earlier. I promise you I will make amends. Where is John?"

After they exchanged news, drank tea, and discussed John, who was out playing whist with his cronies, Lydia seemed calmer. But something was troubling her.

"Are you certain everything is all right, my dear?" she asked Lydia.

"As well as can be expected, I suppose. Dr. Haggarty says I am in the bloom of health." She sniffed. But when Anne pressed her, Lydia merely shook her head, brooded and touched her distended belly.

"Have you seen friends in Bath since you have been here?" Anne finally asked.

"A few. When we first arrived I was not so enormous and it was not so bad, but no one *truly* wishes to see a woman heavy with child. It is a *most* unsavory sight, I swear. Vulgar. As bad as a goiter or other protuberance. 'Tis like I have something catching, for all the young ladies avoid me."

Anne bit her lip to keep from smiling. But childbirth was no smiling matter, a sobering thought. Too many women brought to bed with a baby never again saw light of day. Was this the sole source of Lydia's uneasy demeanor, her prenatal state? It was difficult to imagine how to speak about it with her, as Anne would offer no facile reassurances.

Instead she tried to soothe her with stories and gossip. She relayed her new acquaintance with Mrs. Bella Venables, the Birkenheads' cousin, and how Mr. Quin Birkenhead had looked, and how he and Miss Susanna Hadley made friends. Over tea they spoke of the Season so far. Already there were scandals and gossip. Anne also spoke of her father and his work—Lydia almost dozed off during that part of the conversation—then returned to livelier news. Thinking to entertain her, Anne said, "I visited Lolly yesterday. She is in rooms in Margaret's Buildings, you know, close to the Upper Assembly Rooms a few doors down from the latest Bath fashion, Mother Macree. I'm sure you've heard of the woman?"

"John has forbad me from speaking of her," Lydia said with a sulky pout. "I so wish to see her, but he says it is foolishness and will make the baby come early."

"How would it make the baby come early?"

"He thinks I will fuss myself about it. He fears I am fretful."

Lydia *was* fidgety and abstracted at times. "I don't think merely visiting a mystic would make the baby come early. Perhaps he will change his mind."

Darkly she said, "He's become so stiff lately. He won't allow me to secure a hunchback!"

"A hunchback? Lydia, whatever are you talking about?"

The young woman shook her head. "Never mind. Don't you go being harsh with me, Anne, for if you do, I won't be able to stand it. John is a perfect bear lately. I can't say *anything* without him jumping at me."

Anne frowned. "That doesn't sound like him." Lord John was indulgent to a fault with his wife. Perhaps Lydia was exaggerating, a bad habit with her. And yet she was troubled about something more than her pregnancy, Anne would swear it. "I should go," she said, vowing to herself to talk to John as soon as she could, to get his opinion as to Lydia's health. "I told my grandmother I'd look in on her tonight. She fancies herself ill when it is boredom that brings her to bed, I fear."

There was a sound in the hallway and John entered, bringing with him the odor of tobacco and port.

"How are you, John?" Anne asked, rising. "I was about to leave."

"I pray you stay, my lady. We have much to discuss."

"Another half hour, perhaps."

He brought with him a more lively spirit. Lydia made an effort to be her usual self with him there. They talked of all they had done so far in Bath, and he spoke of his most recent letter from his eldest brother. "He is dealing with our mother right now," John said with a sigh. "She's being impossible, as usual."

Anne was silent on that topic, though she longed to retort that she was only being impossible if one defined that as doing what *she* wanted, rather than what the men around her wished. John would not understand her meaning if she said it, so it was useless to try. Anne had spent two long days traveling north in a carriage with the dowager marchioness a few months before and now had a deeper understanding of the woman. Lady Sophie was prey to melancholy but would not discuss her dark imaginings with her sons. It was an unspoken pain she withstood, preferring to suffer in silence than try to explain herself. "Osei sent me a note yesterday; he is in Bath and looking for a townhouse for Tony," Anne said, to change the subject.

"I don't know why my brother can't stay with us," John groused. "We have room. Waste of money."

His own money, Anne thought. And as his money was also paying for the Bestwicks' Milsom residence it was not John's place to criticize. But he would be her brother-in-law; they *must* get along. She promised to come back for an evening of cards with Lydia and John, and said she would bring a fourth, if they liked. She had a couple of friends who would happily fill another chair at the card table. "You have met Miss Susanna Hadley, have you not, John?"

"I know *of* her. She is another spinster, is she not?" he said, his tone careless.

"She is unwed," Anne admitted. "Her father is remarrying, and I'm not sure she is happy about it."

"So you think she's finally serious about husband hunting?" Lydia said with a malicious gleam in her eyes. "Bath may not be the place for her. There are many more ladies than bachelors and widowers. One such as she—plain, you know, and shy—should go to Tunbridge Wells, or Lyme Regis."

"She's not pretty enough to tempt the fellows of Bath, I don't think," John said, gazing with satisfaction at Lydia, who, with chestnut curls, pale skin, a bow mouth, pink cheeks, and beautiful blue eyes, like a Yorkshire sky in summer, was the portrait of beauty.

Anne was silent and rose again, readying to go. She would not indulge cruel gossip. Susanna was a friend, as was Lydia; to defend one at the expense of the other would only result in hurt feelings. "I must go."

"I'll walk you out, my lady," John said, polite as always.

As they descended to await her grandmother's carriage, he paced the foyer. He finally turned and examined her with an unusually serious expression. "My lady, may I ask . . . did you notice anything different about Lydia?"

She was touched; he *had* noticed and was clearly worried. "She appears nervous, but that's not unusual for her state," Anne commented cautiously.

"I understand that. However, she was anxious but comfortable until one day about two weeks ago. I went out that morning and she was in good humor; when I returned that evening I found her in tears and frightened. She would not tell me what she fears."

"Did she have any visitors that day? Someone who may have frightened her with tales of the difficulties of childbirth?" There were women who gloried in frightening expectant mothers, to the point that nothing but a frantic outbreak of tears would suffice.

"I questioned the housekeeper and maid thoroughly, you may be sure, and there was no one."

"And she didn't go out that day?"

"Not at all."

"Were there any other calls? Not visitors but a seamstress, or milliner, who may have carried worries or unpleasant gossip to poor Lydia?"

"No one."

Anne pondered. "Did she receive a letter from anyone, then? Could she have received bad news?"

"If she did, she would share it. You know Lydia; she's not the type to suffer silently."

Anne smiled despite the seriousness of their conversation. John had married in haste and now was learning that Lydia, though sweet-natured most of the time, would never suffer alone. If she had a fear or tremor she magnified it, talked it over incessantly, and asked for advice from every person she knew, advice she would be as likely to ignore as take. But this time was different. She had not asked anything of Anne, nor apparently of John. The fact that she had not shared whatever was bothering her was more troubling than the most exaggerated frights expressed eloquently and often. Whatever it was, it must be bad for her to hide it from her husband and friend.

"I will not pretend, John, this concerns me. Let me think it over. Bring her to St. Swithin Sunday morning; we have the Everingham family box . . . my maternal family side, of course. My cousin, Viscount Everingham, is seldom here—he's a scholar, and is studying in the Holy Land right now—but is happy for us to invite friends. It will do Lydia well to get out of the house. I'll try to discover what could be bothering her."

He looked relieved to have shared his concern. Her carriage arrived and he accompanied her to the street outside and handed her up into the vehicle. "Thank you, Lady Anne," he said. "I cannot say enough how you marrying Tony relieves me. Of all the young ladies in the world, you suit him—and our family—best."

Anne smiled and touched his hand. "Thank you, John. Take care of Lydia. I'll see you Sunday morning."

Chapter Six

The next morning Osei visited Anne at her grandmother's townhome.

"Osei, how good of you to come!" Anne cried, advancing across the ground-floor reception room to where he stood by the bay window, overlooking the Paragon.

He turned and bowed. "My lady, how wonderful to see you!"

Anne stared at his dark face and eyes, behind the glint of his spectacles. Rarely had she met someone with whom she had shared such an instant sympathy. He was intellectual and learned, but also gentle and with great feeling. Even deeper was his connection to her father, who valued Osei's curious mind and vivid intelligence. Perhaps that was the attraction; he was very much like her father, but united with their similar traits was Osei's ability to tactfully manage the world around him. He was scholarly but engaged; wise but with his feet firmly planted on the earth. "I'm happy to see you," she said with profound feeling, taking his proffered hand and squeezing it. "Will you sit and take tea? I can have the maid bring some within minutes."

"I think I have shocked your household quite enough for one day. In London I deserve no more than a passing glance, but I am finding Bath a new experience."

"It's a little more parochial, I'll admit. If I can help smooth your way, let me know."

With a faint smile he replied, "I find all I need to do is mention the Marquess of Darkefell's name. That opens all the doors necessary."

"And have you found him a townhome to rent?"

"I came to see you for that reason. You know this city better than I; I have three areas in mind, with a few leaseholds available in each location. Perhaps you can help me decide? You know the marquess; he will not care which I choose, but it is my business to make him comfortable for the time he is here." He held out a neatly scribed list.

"Let us sit."

He bowed and sat in one of the dainty chairs, his dark blue coat and dove gray breeches a sober note in an overtly feminine room.

She examined the list. He was considering the Crescent, the Circus and a townhome on the Paragon. Her heart thudded in her chest at the thought of Tony being so temptingly close. She swallowed and breathed. "I'm surprised, given the Season, that you have found such a wealth of homes to lease. My friends Mr. and Mrs. Birkenhead have been looking, but Bertie confessed that if he was to take one, it would not be available until next spring."

He shifted and looked uncomfortable. "And therein lies a problem; the moment I mention my employer's name, *every* place is available. For the marquess, existing leases would be broken to accommodate him."

"O-ho, the mighty marquess will unhome others, will he?"

Osei shook his head, shamefaced. "I'll admit, my lady, I am at a loss. The estate agent for several of these will not tell me which are actually to let and which have leases he would break for his lordship. I don't think Lord Darkefell would want to evict others for his comfort. You know him; as long as he has a place to lay his head he'll be happy. What should I do?"

"Mr. Boatin, I think this is the first time I have ever seen you at a loss and I'm sorry to tell you that it pleases me." She smiled to show it was a jest. "Leave this with me. As I said, I have friends who have been looking for a place to move to, and they know what is coming up for lease apart from these addresses. Perhaps Gay Street, or Monmouth. I'll see them later today."

He looked relieved. "Thank you, my lady. May I visit again tomorrow morning?"

"Join us at church, St. Swithin, up the Paragon from Grand-mother's home. We attend service at eleven."

"Will that be appropriate, my lady?"

"I don't see why not."

• • •

Anne, accompanied by Mary, walked the short distance to Margaret's Buildings and her cousin's rooms. Lolly awaited them outside. They strolled down the street and were met by Quin, who emerged carefully from a sedan chair conveyed by two stout carriers. Mary agreed to await them in the foyer on the ground floor, while Lolly, who made fast and immediate friends with Quin, climbed the stairs, huffing and puffing. Quin slowly followed suit and Anne ascended last.

Quin was pale and trembling from the effort, and Lolly not much better, so both took a moment to catch their breath at the top of the stairs while Anne looked around her with great curiosity. They were in an anteroom of sorts, with a bench set along one papered wall and two chairs on another, both now occupied by Anne's companions. Portraits by painters of little ability and less imagination adorned the walls, a group of angry strangers forced to share a room, staring at each other in disdain. The room was lit by sconces every few feet, the candles giving a soft glow to the room and the cheery-patterned — though stained — wallcoverings. They could have been in any home anywhere, for this certainly did not seem the entry into a mystic's abode.

"What think you, Quin?" she asked, glancing over at her friend, who had regained what little color he possessed.

"I think Bertie would be alarmed if he saw me here," he joked. "My brother would think me mad, and perhaps I am. But this is the most fun I've had for a while, I must say. Alethea tells Bertie that he keeps me too bundled up."

"And yet she's the one who is worried that Bertie is expecting too much from you."

"My sister-in-law is a dear soul. She wishes to keep Bertie from thinking that I'll someday magically recover if we find the right physician, or right home, or right circumstance, when she and I both know that I will never recover. There will be good days and bad days, and someday a final day."

Anne remained silent. What was there to say to someone who acknowledged so openly his mortality?

"Is there no treatment, young sir?" Lolly asked.

"Bertie is convinced that exercise is the cure. He wants me to go nowhere that I do not walk, but Alethea would rather I get out and about even if a footman or sedan chairmen must carry me." Distressed, he shook his head. "No amount of Bath mineral water is going to cure me, but Bertie still hopes."

Lolly put her hand over his where it rested on the chair arm and smiled. "My dear boy, I don't know you well, but I can see already that your purpose on earth is to teach patience. Perhaps your brother will learn in time."

"I rather doubt it. His impatience is with nature, and I observe that once the habit is set, it lasts a lifetime. It is not just my infirmity with which he quarrels, but with the weakness of others' ideologies, their reliance on signs and portents, and any form of faith in an otherworldly being."

"He does not believe in God, then?" Lolly gasped, hand to her heart.

"Do not judge him harshly, dear lady; Bertie is kindness itself. His belief is in the goodness of people. It is when humanity falls short that he becomes incensed and impatient. Cruelty of any kind wounds him. It is unfortunate, but humanity often falls short of his hopes and expectations."

"You must pray for him," Lolly said, her voice faint.

"I wouldn't dare, dear lady. He would consider that an impertinence," Quin said lightly, and with a smile. "I'll leave that between my brother and God."

They chatted for a few minutes longer, as Anne grew increasingly impatient. Finally a young girl, dressed in a neat maid's outfit with a snowy apron over top, came out of the interior chamber and curtseyed, not meeting their gaze. "An' it please you, ladies and gent, come inside to meet Mother Macree."

Anne took Quin's arm and helped him rise. With an effort that etched lines in his brow and tightened his lips, he straightened and together they followed Lolly into the next room. Lolly, having been there before, knew the protocol and led them through that sitting room to the next, quite a distance to a dimmer chamber at the back. Even in midday, the windows were draped in fusty fabric, darkening the room.

A woman sat huddled by a lace-draped table with three other chairs around it. Anne, Quin and Lolly sat. Mother Macree looked up and surveyed her visitors. Anne wasn't sure what she expected, but she was let down. The mystic was an average elderly woman gowned in some dark fabric that swallowed the remaining light nearby. She wore a lace-trimmed tucker around her neck, tucked into her bodice, and a lace-trimmed white cap over wiry gray and white hair. She was heavy but not quite corpulent. Her face was unremarkable: a doughy ball with pale eyes set deep in red-rimmed flesh, she seemed almost sleepy. One eye closed more than the other, and one side of her large blue-veined mouth drooped.

"Good morning, Mrs. Macree," Lolly said gently. "Thank you for seeing my friends, Lady Anne Addison and Mr. Quin Birkenhead. They have many questions."

The woman fastened her gaze on Quin. She eyed him with an unemotional gaze. "What's wrong with ye?" she said bluntly, her voice raspy.

Quin, startled, stuttered as he spoke. "I-I don't quite know. D-doctors have been unable to diagnose it so far. It is some disturbance of the digestion system, they say." It was clear to anyone with eyes that Quin suffered some disorder, from his hunched back to his odd way of sitting, leaning to one side.

"And you," the woman said, slewing her gaze to Anne as she spoke abruptly. "What are *you* here for?"

"I have heard of you, of course, and one seeks amusement in Bath. You are said to be amusing."

Lolly gave her a startled sideways look. "She jests, of course, Mother Macree. She is interested in her future, as are we all, and your abilities have attracted her."

"If she meant that, why didn't she say it?" the woman said, her words faintly slurred.

"I do not jest, Lolly," Anne said. "I'm completely serious, Mother Macree. I am here for amusement."

The woman ignored her and focused on Quin, who was watching with fascination. "I see much within ye, young gentleman. It's misty. You doubt yer mending, but there is much that can help yer heart. Will ye be wanting me to read you, then?"

"*Read* me?"

"Read yer future?"

He hesitated.

"Are ye afraid of the future, then? Sore troubled by yer health, as I said."

Too easy, Anne thought again. *Anyone* looking at Quin would say that.

"But yer brother worries more than ye."

The audible gasp, Anne realized, emanated from her. How did the woman know Quin had a brother?

"You're right about that," Quin said. "Bertie has always worried about me."

"But 'is wife . . . ye like her *very* well, don't ye? Like the sister you never had." She paused, staring at Quin with her oddly intense glare. "The sister you never 'ad. . . aye, I see 'er! The sister you *would* 'ave 'ad, if she'd *lived*."

Anne stared, then looked over at Quin. He blinked, rapidly, and nodded. A tear welled in his eye. "Cordelia would be twenty-five this year," he said, his words catching on a sob. "She was a delightful child, and I loved her."

"I didn't know you had a sister," Anne whispered, staring at him.

"She died when she was three. I took it hard, but Bertie . . . he acted as if she had never lived. It made it doubly hard for me." He paused and wiped a tear from his eye. "We've never spoken of her since."

"I'm so sorry," Anne whispered. Despite her best intentions, she was impressed, and returned her gaze to the seer. This was unexpected and disturbing. She shifted in her chair, uneasy, not knowing quite what to think.

Mother Macree said, in a hushed, slurred tone, "But *ye* have never forgotten 'er. She knows this, and loves ye for it. She grew up in 'eaven, you know; aye, they do," she said, as Quin appeared startled. "Folks think they stay children forever, but 'eaven lets 'em grow up. She forgives yer brother. Though 'e seems hard of heart it's just that 'e don't believe in heaven, and don't think 'e'll meet her again."

"It's true," he murmured, his voice choked. "I've always thought it." Quin was breathing hard and staring at the mystic. He was so thin Anne could practically see his heart pounding in his chest under his coat. A vein throbbed at his temple.

Lolly laid her hand on Quin's arm. Anne took a deep, steadying breath and looked back to the mystic through narrowed eyes, determined to be rational. How did the woman know all this? She could not have researched Quin beforehand, for Anne hadn't told Lolly who she was bringing. It must be a trick, a cunning stratagem, else she must begin to believe in seers and the spirit world.

Mother Macree swiveled her beady gaze to Anne. "*You*, lady . . .

ye have always fancied yerself a woman of reason, but yer heart is befuddled. Ye fear yer future. I see a man . . .a *dark* man—"

Lolly gasped. "Lord Darkefell!" she blurted out. "Anne, it's Lord Darkefell! She sees him."

Anne sighed in exasperation. She had been determined to remain stoic and composed if the seer made any correct guesses concerning her and her life, the better to judge her performance, but Lolly's outburst made that impossible. She should have known that reserve was impractical with her irrepressible cousin present.

"Lord Darkefell? I have heard the name," Quin said.

"It's her beau, the Marquess of Darkefell," Lolly gasped, breathless, hands clasped together. "Such a handsome man he is. So *commanding*, as Mother Macree said. Fancy that, her seeing Lord Darkefell and describing him so clearly!"

The mystic swayed in her seat and closed her eyes, moaning and rocking. "Ah, yes! I see it all now. He has asked you to *marry* 'im."

"Lady Anne, how exciting!" Quin said. "You didn't tell us you were engaged."

"She isn't telling anyone," Lolly blurted out. "She didn't tell me, though I had my suspicions. But how amazing that Mother Macree knew it before any of us!"

"Stop; *enough!*" Anne said. Annoyed and baffled, she stared at the mystic for a long minute, but the woman looked for all the world as if she was sleeping, her chin sunk on her chest, soft snufflings emanating from her lips. Anne turned to her friend. "Quin, please don't tell anyone what you've heard here today. I never intended . . . that is, I have made no announcement."

"But you'll soon have to, won't ye?" the woman said with a malicious cackle, lifting her chin and staring at Anne with her odd squint-eyed gaze. "For 'e won't be toyed with. One so plain as you . . . yer a lucky woman, and you'd best grab onto 'im wiv both hands or 'e'll move on, won't 'e?" Her tone bordered on spiteful, her gaze malevolent. "He'll find a lass more easy."

"Nonsense," Lolly said. "He's a gentleman, and if he has asked, he is bound."

"But she 'asn't announced and it is the lady's choice, yes?" She cackled with laughter that ended in a raspy cough, a spray of spittle jetting across the table. The little maid rushed forth with a handkerchief. The seer grabbed the handkerchief then slapped the girl away with a vigorous backhand. The child retreated. "Don't toy with a man like that or 'e'll find a prettier maiden to bless 'is bed." She chortled and ended coughing again.

"We must leave," Anne said, her whole body quivering. She had not thought her secrets would be divulged in such a rude way.

"Wait! I 'ave a message for the young gentleman," the woman said. She wiped her mouth and laid the handkerchief down, then eyed Quin. "I 'ave a message, but not for you; fer someone you care for, someone *close* to you. Or . . ." She squinted and moaned, rocking in her chair. "Mayhap someone close to someone ye love. There's danger all about 'im. Trouble, there is, an' secrets that'll cause danger, aye, and turmoil too; guard against 'em, and *give freely* to those who can help."

"What does *that* mean?" Anne demanded of the mystic. She looked over at Quin and was alarmed to see that he was frightened. He'd gone white even to his lips. "Quin! Are you—"

"We must go," he said, stumbling to his feet. "I'm not feeling at all well."

On the street he unsteadily declined Anne's company home. Mary trotted off to the end of the street to summon a sedan chair. Quin, pale and trembling, was transported away, refusing all help. Anne hoped that when she next saw her dear friend—she was engaged to the Birkenheads that evening of music—she would find him well again.

Shaken, she and Mary returned with Lolly to her rooms and accompanied her upstairs. "What am I to think of all that?" Anne said, pacing to the clavichord. "I'm no believer. But the woman appeared to know things she could only know if she saw into one's soul." She took in a deep and trembling breath. "It has upset me, I will admit it."

"I told you, Anne; she is truly remarkable. She has the sight. 'Tis a God-given talent!" Lolly said, watching Anne pace.

Mary was silent. She was a skeptic—almost as much so as Anne— but it appeared that what the women said of Mother Macree's ability troubled her.

"I should go. We'll see you at church tomorrow morning, dear Lolly," Anne said.

"See that you mind Mother Macree's warning, Anne dearest. Don't toy with a man like Darkefell. He'll not wait for you forever."

It was a brilliant autumn day, warmer than usual and with misty sunlight bathing the streets in a golden glow. Despite the beauty of the day, though, Anne was distracted and perturbed. As they walked the short distance to her grandmother's home, she told Mary everything that occurred. It had left her with a variety of warring emotions: fear, trepidation, worry, and most of all anger. Anger for herself; she would *not* be told what to do, and the contrarian in her urged her to wait, now, to tell Tony she'd announce their engagement, as silly as that was. But she was worried more for Quin; something had frightened him badly when the mystic issued her dire warning, and Anne wished she knew what it was.

Chapter Seven

Dressed and with her hair perfectly coiffed, Anne descended from her room ready to attend the Birkenheads' musical evening. She greeted Lord Westmacott, who awaited Anne's mother and grandmother in the main-floor reception room. Bewigged and dressed, as always, in a perfectly tailored figured satin frock coat, knee breeches, and elegantly clocked stockings, he was the vision of an elderly beau idéal, his figure still good after many decades on the town (though his figure might owe its svelte lines to stays that creaked under his frock coat when he moved too rapidly), even though there were lines in his face and pouches under his protuberant eyes.

He was attending the two ladies for an evening of cards. They were to be joined by Lolly, who had been recruited at the last minute when another guest disappointed them. Courtly and sweetly flattering, Lord Westmacott was an old favorite of Anne's, a bachelor baron of her grandmother's generation who could be relied on to accompany the ladies to the Assembly Rooms, the Pump Room, or to enjoy a simple evening of whist or backgammon.

"My dear, you look simply stunning, as always," he said, taking her hands and holding her away from him, eyeing her lush figure gowned in a purple *robe à l'anglaise*, a gold lace fichu, an amethyst-encrusted comb in her hair, with amethyst earrings dangling from her ears. "Every time I see you I marvel at your continued single state. If I were but ten years younger . . ."

Given that he was at least seventy, that was an interesting compliment to pay, Anne thought, but hid her smile. "Thank you, Lord Westmacott. I fear I have overdone my plumage for a simple evening of music at a friend's, but my maid insisted."

"Ah, I understand. I am a slave to my valet. The dear fellow will never allow me to leave the house without proper attire." He preened, touching his snowy lace cravat, with a gold crested pin nestled in the fabric. "The Birkenheads will appreciate the trouble you have taken, though, for they value the little social niceties." He then smiled and raised his eyebrows with a significant expression on his lined face. "I hear you are to be wed at last?"

"I beg your pardon?"

He held one finger to his lips and winked. "I know all about the marquess, my dear. You needn't fear I'll say a word to anyone," he murmured, leaning toward her. "But I know he is coming to Bath, and I *do* hope to meet him and look forward to seeing an announcement of an imminent event in the near future. Single no more, hey?"

Anne was summoned to the carriage and departed discomfited. As an American wit wrote in an almanac, three may keep a secret if two are dead. It did make her consider, though, the source of the mystic's seeming knowledge of her and Darkefell's secret engagement. Mayhap it was not so miraculous after all.

The Birkenheads' leased home was on Pierrepont Place, conveniently near the Old Orchard Street Theatre, perfect for the art-, music- and theater-loving couple. Her carriage passed through a stone arch and stopped in front of a nondescript door on a narrow cobbled street. Her grandmother's driver handed her down, and Anne entered the plain house. She understood why Bertie was looking for another home for his family. Though this was a good address, it was cramped and could not compare with the spacious and elegant newer buildings on the Circus and the Crescent. They enjoyed entertaining often, and their wealth had increased greatly in the last ten years, so something more suitable to their status must be found.

There was an adequate morning room and dining room on the ground floor. The more expansive drawing room lounge, with a withdrawing room beyond, was on the first floor. Therefore the bedchambers must be on the second . . . two flights of steps up for Quin, and she had seen how exhausted the one flight up to Mother Macree's had made him. But the couple had made the home comfortable, with Turkey carpets on the wood floors and tapestries warming the plain plastered walls. Elegant furnishings loaned the rooms an aura of refinement.

Others had already arrived. She greeted those she knew: Miss Susanna Hadley, who was already seated on a low stool at Quin's side; Mrs. Venables; Mr. Alfred Lonsdale; Mr. Thomas Graeme; and Lady Sharples, of course, who accompanied Susanna. Anne was introduced to those she did not yet know, including a friend of Alethea's, Mrs. Meredith Hughes, who appeared shy, clinging to her with a timid expression on her pretty freckled face.

Among the others was a Mrs. Honoria Noakes and Mr. Josiah Doyne. Ah . . . Mr. *Doyne!* She recognized the name. He was the gentleman of whom her mother spoke as looking for a wife; perhaps matchmaking efforts were too late, given how firm a hold Mrs. Noakes had of his arm, upon which she leaned. Also, there was Lord Kattenby by Mrs. Venables's side; he bowed elegantly over her hand. He was indeed older, as Anne had learned from Alethea in their walk from the Crescent to the Circus, and his face was drawn by suffering, but there was something about him that Anne liked immediately. *Well done,* she thought of Mrs. Venables. He seemed a good match, though at least twenty years the lady's senior.

Mr. Doyne and Mrs. Noakes appeared lost, almost frightened by the crowd of elegantly dressed gentlemen and ladies. They didn't appear to have any friends present. They drifted close by Mrs. Venables and Lord Kattenby, but that lady turned hastily away—either a deliberate slight or the lady overlooked them—and led her beau to the fireside to chat with Quin Birkenhead.

There was much chatter, the place full of good cheer, warmth provided by cheery log blazes and light by several candelabra and sconces. The doors between the drawing room and withdrawing room had been thrown open and both chambers were full, more so than was comfortable. There was a small sitting room beyond set aside for the ladies who needed respite. The performer that evening was Signore Fiore Valentini, a young Milanese gentleman. Accompanied by Bertie, who was accomplished on the piano, he stood at the pianoforte and sang, acquitting himself well with his rendition of a song from an Italian opera, then a couple of sentimental pieces, then English fare, including "O Cruel Cruel Case" from *The Beggar's Opera*—an odd choice, Anne thought, though it showed off his voice. Polite applause greeted him as he finished, and he bowed with an elegant flourish.

After, there were refreshments. As Susanna departed the fireside to retrieve punch for herself and her new friend, Anne took the young woman's seat and spoke to Quin. "How are you, my friend?" she murmured, examining his face anxiously. There was some color in his cheeks, but he still seemed subdued.

"My lady, please do not worry for me. I have recovered from our earlier jaunt." He said it was the unexpected words from Mother

Macree about his sister that had upset him. He still could not imagine where she got her information from. He was not, in general, a believer in such things as mystics, but that day's visit had him rethinking that position.

"Quin, what do you think her warning to you meant at the end, when she said someone you knew was in danger, and mumbled something about secrets?"

He shook his head, his lips firmed into a tight line; he would not reply, and he stared into the fire, his expression troubled.

Miss Hadley brought a glass to him at that moment, and Anne rose gracefully, to leave space for her friend. "I'll speak to you again, Quin. Miss Hadley, your servant." She curtseyed a farewell for the moment. As she turned away she spied, through the crowd, Mr. Lonsdale by the other fire, moodily staring down into it. He had seemed out of sorts all evening. Young Thomas Graeme strolled to his side and muttered something to him, and the look on Lonsdale's face was illuminating; he appeared annoyed and turned away from the other gentleman. She was about to amble over to eavesdrop — her curiosity at the exchange had been piqued — but was accosted by Lady Sharples, who greeted her.

"The tenor had a fine voice, do you think, Lady Anne?" the woman asked. "He acquitted himself well, given Mr. Birkenhead's unequal piano playing."

Anne defended Bertie's piano skills, and in such inconsequential chatter they passed a few moments, when the woman asked, "What think you of this new closeness between Susanna and Mr. Quin Birkenhead?"

"He is my ideal of a gentleman: intelligent, genteel, kind. With her warmth, kindness and sensibility I think it a good friendship."

"Hmm, as long as that's all it is, friendship. I did not wish to come here this evening. We had another much better invitation, one that would have exposed her to more eligible suitors, but Susanna proved surprisingly mulish and would not be convinced to my wishes." Lady Sharples looked most perturbed at such an event as her charge proving to have a mind of her own. "I want what is best for her. I worry that she is spending too much valuable time with someone who cannot give her all she deserves."

Anne examined her face, the hard, set lines, the dour turned-down mouth. "You see injury in such a harmless acquaintance?"

"Not active injury, but she is getting no younger and will not be happy at home with her father's choice of a wife. Therefore she *must* marry. She has an adequate dowry, but not one such as will tempt a man of substance. She should be actively pursuing gentlemen in a different sphere, but she refuses to play the part."

"What do you mean?"

"Now, see Mrs. Venables," she said, indicating with her glass of sherry that woman, who stood with Lord Kattenby, her arm tucked in his, her head bent to listen to his conversation. "He is as tedious a gentleman as any with whom I could ever wish to chat, and yet she makes it appear that he is the most fascinating man in the room. That takes some decided effort on her part, and I like her the more for it. She knows what she wants and is unafraid to pursue a husband and a good situation."

"With a man you condemn as tedious."

"Yes, and so what?" she bellowed. A nearby couple turned to glare at her, but she did not notice. "One *must* marry. Tedious is better than exciting; I know whereof I speak. Exciting men will invariably break your heart and bankrupt you. And yet I cannot make Susanna attend the Pump Room, where she will find the eligible widowers. I must force her to go with me by saying I need the waters, dreadful as is that cup of warm pus."

Anne choked back a laugh, clamping her mouth shut. From a practical standpoint she knew Lady Sharples was right. It was the sad truth for many a lady; a female must find someone suitable, attract his attention, attach him and marry. For many young ladies it was a difficult and stressful occupation destined to bring only partial happiness. And for someone shy and retiring, like Miss Hadley, it was doubly difficult and distressing.

All of that aside, though, why should Susanna not enjoy the company of a gentleman as kind as Mr. Quin Birkenhead? She was about to say as much, when the other lady again spoke.

"Now examine those two over there," Lady Sharples said, holding up a lorgnette and turning her quizzical gaze to a man and woman standing together. "Mrs. Honoria Noakes and Mr. Josiah Doyne."

"Why do I examine them?" Anne asked, not revealing what little she knew of Mr. Doyne's wife-seeking.

"I point to them as an example of a lady who knew what she wanted and found it at the Pump Room. He is a widower of uncertain health, seeking a genteel wife."

"And she is . . . ?"

"*That* is the question," Lady Sharples murmured, watching the couple, how the lady leaned on the gentleman and hung on his every word. "I can discover nothing of her except that she is *said* to be of unexceptional background and with some money. No one knows her family, no one vouches for her, and yet everywhere she is spoken of as genteel. That opinion seems to be based on her ability to hold a glass of wine without spilling it. I have tried to engage her in conversation. She knows nothing of music, or art, or polite society. She cannot even gossip."

"Heavens, how *does* she live?" Anne murmured, smothering a laugh. For Lady Sharples that was condemnation indeed; to be unable—or unwilling—to gossip was social failure. "Not everyone feels about gossip as you do, though, my lady."

"They should." Lady Sharples looked unhappy and flicked her lorgnette closed within its tortoiseshell casing, which was also its handle. "You may think me small-minded, but to be unable—not unwilling, *unable*—to gossip indicates unfamiliarity with society. I suspect she does not know enough people to gossip effectively."

That was interesting. In society one knew people, their history, their relationships. It was about connections, who had them, and who did not. "How did they meet?"

"The Pump Room, through a mutual friend."

"A mutual friend?"

"Yes, young Mr. Thomas Graeme, that fellow who seems to know everyone. I blame myself for not pouncing more quickly. Susanna would have been perfectly comfortable with Mr. Doyne."

"Pouncing? How catlike you sound, Lady Sharples, rather like my Irusan when he sees a mouse."

"Aye, a *widower* mouse, squeaking and nibbling on cheese," she said with a bark of laughter. "Mr. Doyne could have been Susanna's saving grace."

"Saving grace?"

"A husband, of course! Don't be dull, Lady Anne. I know you to be sharper than that. He would be a husband with a comfortable income and not overburdened with healthy male urges."

"Heaven forbid he should be burdened with male urges. Is he ailing?"

"No more than your mother," Lady Sharples said with a sharp glance sideways to Anne. "One does not merely seek healthful waters at the Pump Room unless one has some reason to require aid, however it can be as simple as dyspepsia, or trouble sleeping."

"True," Anne murmured.

"But he is older. *That* is the idea for Susanna, a bookish maiden like her . . . she should have a husband who will not demand more than company and someone to pour his tea."

"So what is your objection to Quin Birkenhead, then?"

"*He's* never going to marry! His brother and sister-in-law . . . those two are not going to *let* him."

Anne shook her head, unwilling to engage in a battle over something neither of them could know. "Why were Mrs. Noakes and Mr. Doyne invited tonight?" she asked. "They seem an odd couple for the Birkenheads to mingle with."

"That is one thing I cannot quiz. What do two such fashion leaders see in a dull gentleman of middle years and a not-quite-genteel lady?"

"Not quite genteel?"

"I have, as I said, spoken with them both. There is something wrong about her, and besides her inability to gossip, I can't figure out what it is . . . a restrained brassiness, a theatrical expression subdued with effort. Perhaps you can discover it, if you would so choose."

"Are you enlisting me for some nefarious purpose?"

Lady Sharples chuckled and shook her head, tucking her lorgnette in her deep bosom. "The woman is a mystery, and I don't like mysteries."

Chapter Eight

Anne drifted and spoke to others, as some gathered at the pianoforte for the talented amateurs among them to play and sing. Finally, she found herself next to Alethea, who looked splendid, gowned in gold lace and burgundy silk, her golden hair piled high and adorned with gold and ruby combs. After congratulating her on the choice of singer for their musical evening, Anne said, "Where is your friend Mrs. Hughes, who I met earlier?"

Alethea grimaced. "Her importunate husband—a *most* unpleasant man—has arrived in Bath. A note found her here; he demanded her presence at home."

"So she is not a widow? Everyone in Bath seems to be a widow or widower."

"No, sadly she is *not* a widow."

"Alethea, how naughty!" Anne cried, smothering a laugh. "One would think you had a dislike for poor Mr. Hughes."

"He's a bully and a domestic tyrant," she said, more seriously now. "You saw how gentle and unassuming she is? How beauteous, how sweet? She is an angel and he takes advantage, Anne; he truly does."

"That is unfortunate," Anne said absently, watching across the room as Lady Sharples stalked her prey, which was always whomever she did not know enough gossip about. "I was speaking with Lady Sharples. We were both wondering how you came to know Mr. Doyne or Mrs. Noakes?"

"I don't know them at all," Alethea replied. "Or . . . let me rephrase that. I know them as nodding acquaintances at the Pump Room, when we accompany Quin there."

"I see. How about Bertie? Perhaps he knows Mr. Doyne from a club or some such?"

Alethea looked over her fan at Anne and frowned. "What is this about? Why the sudden interest in Mr. Doyne?"

"No reason. You know me . . . I get curious."

"What did you mean by a *club*?"

Anne stared at her friend, whose tone was sharp and full of suspicion. "Gentlemen belong to clubs. I simply thought that would explain the invitation to Mr. Doyne and Mrs. Noakes, if Bertie knew the gentleman from a club."

Alethea nodded and her frown disappeared. "I believe it was Bertie's friend Lonsdale who invited them."

"That elucidates the mystery, then. I didn't realize Bertie and Alfred were so close that Mr. Lonsdale would feel free to invite someone to your home."

Alethea gave an elegant shrug. "I don't mind the extra people, as long as they are sociable and moderately elegant."

The lady in question was neither, according to Lady Sharples. "I was *more* surprised to see Mr. Graeme here after hearing Bertie's opinion of the fellow. He said the gentleman had light morals; coming from Bertie that is criticism indeed." Bertie didn't mind a little scandal, as long as it was in good taste. The couple had hosted, in their home, many a lady or gentleman recovering from a disgrace in their life. Their own social standing was so high they could afford to loan some to a friend in need. "He does not consider amorous adventure to be shameful, I recall, so the gentleman must be scandalous indeed to earn such censure."

"You know my husband; he can abide many scandalous attributes but will not suffer a liar or gambling table cheat. Perhaps that is Graeme's story. I cannot say. One cannot avoid people of light morals in London, and perhaps that is now extended to Bath," Alethea said with a shrill laugh. She bustled off to speak with a maid, who was lingering by a doorway looking for her mistress.

Anne watched after her a moment, then turned to find Alfred Lonsdale close by. Curious now about many things, she moved to his side. "Mr. Lonsdale, how are you this evening?"

She had caught him in a brown study and he appeared startled, but he recovered and bowed. "I'm well, my lady. How are you?"

"In perfect health, thank you. And how is your cousin Mr. Roger Basenstoke? I have seen your aunt since I arrived in Bath, but not that gentleman."

"Roger was to attend this evening but was called away. We were going to travel here together."

"What could have taken him away in the evening?"

"He owns property in Bath, and there have been problems with tenants recently. He's serious about infractions against his lease; he is an Inner Temple man, you know," he said, referring to one of the four law schools in London. "And is assiduous about enforcing the leasehold terms."

They chatted a moment, then Anne said, "I saw you speaking with Mr. Graeme earlier. He seems a pleasant young man. You've known him for a long time, I suppose?"

"It depends on how you quantify time, my lady, but not so long."

"I thought you were at Eton together?"

"Ah . . . there is my cousin now!" he said.

Mr. Roger Basenstoke had just come in and was bowing to Alethea, perhaps making his apologies for being late. He was a handsome man in a sinister way. In a world that valued fair abundant hair, or at least the wigged appearance of it, he made no concession to fashion and wore his fine black hair short and combed back off his high forehead, away from his sharp-featured face.

He caught sight of her and Lonsdale standing together and crossed the room, bowing to acquaintances along the way. Finally he stood before them and summoned a wintry smile that did not diminish the severity of his appearance. "My lady, how delightful to see you here. I was regrettably not able to secure your hand for a dance at the Assembly Rooms. I count myself fortunate to see you this evening, given my delayed attendance."

"Mr. Lonsdale says that it was business that took you away from company this evening."

"Trouble over leasing terms. I am plagued by complaining tenants who want to change wall coverings and move furnishings. It seems a leased residence is absolute perfection until the moment a tenant moves in."

Lonsdale bowed and murmured that he was being beckoned from across the room, though Anne saw no one beckoning. However, she knew the two gentlemen did not get along overwell, and assumed the younger man was making a polite escape. "Mr. Basenstoke, I am fortunate you *did* come this evening. I was asked by an acquaintance if I knew anyone who understood the rental market in Bath at the current time. I was hoping to speak with Birkenhead, but he's taken up with his guests. As my acquaintance is seeking a house to rent for a short period, I thought our mutual friend, searching the market himself, might have a good idea of what is available, but you may know better."

"I am at your service, my lady."

"You must know other property owners who lease their townhomes?"

He nodded. "How can I be of assistance?"

"I have an acquaintance who is seeking to rent, for a period of some months, an elegant townhome near the center of Bath. His secretary had visited several, but because of the eminence of his employer, as soon as he mentions the name every place is suddenly available, even when it appears to be tenanted. For his employer's convenience, it seems many landlords will break the lease terms of their tenants, despite a risk of legal action. Knowing his employer will not approve of such concessions, the secretary wishes not to evict someone, but is sorely troubled by how to know what is truly available. Do you have advice?"

"Not advice, but I will gladly help. As you say, I know many of the other owners of property in Bath. Have the fellow call on me at my office on Monday," he said, giving Anne the direction of his commercial office.

Anne bit her lip. Should she tell Basenstoke about Osei? She was caught in a dilemma; for the world she would not see Osei hurt by any bad reaction on the part of someone she had heard of in a negative light, and yet . . . the marquess's secretary was stalwart and had faced with humor and unusual grace prejudice in England against his African origin. It was not her place to "explain" him to anyone. In fact, it was presumptuous of her to think it, she decided, given what Mr. Boatin had been through with Mr. Hiram Grover recently. "I will tell him. Thank you, Mr. Basenstoke."

He nodded, but his attention was elsewhere, she could tell, and when she followed his darkening gaze it was to see Mr. Thomas Graeme and Mr. Alfred Lonsdale in a whispering conference. "Excuse me, my lady."

She nodded and watched him stalk toward his cousin, who broke away from Graeme and faced Basenstoke. The two had words, but Bertie Birkenhead intervened and guided Lonsdale toward Alethea. He swiftly returned to Mr. Graeme and the two spoke briefly; the young man whirled and stormed out the door, into the passage and staircase.

Puzzling over the acrimonious pantomime, she drifted to the

window and looked out over Pierrepont Place. It was a dark evening but lanterns were lit, illuminating the street below. The Birkenhead residence overlooked, across the narrow street, a home with ornate Ionic pilasters on either side of the door supporting decorative depictions of urns bearing pineapples. There was some movement below, on the pavement; as she stared into the gloomy shadows she noticed someone emerging from the front door of the Birkenhead home. He paused and looked up at her window. She drew back into the draperies. His face illuminated by the oil lamp sconce mounted by the door revealed his identity. It was Thomas Graeme, his expression one of baffled fury. He whirled and pulled a cloak about him, then strode away.

"What in heaven's name are you doing?" Alethea asked.

Anne emerged from the folds of the draperies and smiled. "I am hiding away, what do you think?" She passed it off with a laugh, and accompanied her friend, who led her to Mrs. Noakes and Mr. Doyne. Both seemed uncomfortable and isolated in a room where it appeared they knew few people.

"Please help me entertain these poor souls," Alethea whispered as they approached the couple. "They look like ramshackle skiffs adrift in a harbor of yachts."

After introductions and light chat, Alethea was called away once again by her maid, and Anne began the delicate probe of what acquaintance they might have in common. Mr. Doyne, a salt importer and widower, meekly acknowledged that they were unlikely to have any acquaintance in Bath in common. He was there for a few months staying with his sister and her husband while he recovered from a feverish illness he had suffered during his family's time in the West Indies. That same illness had claimed his wife and left his brood of three young children—who were staying with their mother's family in the north—motherless. His illness had left its mark on him in a feverish complexion and a yellowish cast to his protuberant pale eyes.

Anne turned to Mrs. Noakes, an attractive woman of about thirty with a frowzy wig from under which peeped ginger sprigs of hair. "Are you a native of this city, Mrs. Noakes?"

"No, I am from another place, of course," she said in a careful accent. "Most of us in Bath are not from here, is that not true?" She tittered politely, and beamed a smile that betrayed her gaps in teeth.

An answer that gave no illumination, Anne noticed. "I am Kentish, myself. My mother and grandmother reside in Bath. Do you have family here, then?" She bordered on being rudely over-inquisitive, but she was curious.

Mr. Doyne looked on, beaming with an approving smile.

"No, I am quite alone in the world, I fear," the woman said with a mournful sigh.

"Perhaps you stay with friends?"

"No, I do not."

Another answer with little information. "How did you and Mr. Doyne meet?"

"Through mutual acquaintance in the Pump Room, your lady-ship," Mr. Doyne said, bowing low.

"What acquaintance would that be?" she probed relentlessly.

"A young gentleman I have come to know in Bath," the gentle-man replied.

"And who would that be?" Mrs. Noakes was looking at her with something like fright, Anne observed, and indeed, her questions were pointed. Too pointed for courtesy, but her curiosity was roused and would not be quieted.

"A young gentleman . . . mutual acquaintance, you see . . . he is the most genteel fellow, with a sweetness of temperament I have rarely met in my years." Mr. Doyne had lost his way again and named no name.

Anne bit back a sharp question. "Perhaps he is one of *my* acquaintance. Would that be Mr. Lonsdale?" she said, risking the name.

"No, oh, no, for I only met Mr. Lonsdale when Mr. Graeme, the estimable young man I spoke of just now, introduced us."

"Mr. Thomas Graeme! How interesting. He was here but has now departed." Mrs. Noakes appeared miffed at her betrothed, and Anne wondered why. "I met the gentleman the other day. He introduced himself to me."

Mr. Doyne looked shocked at such a breach of polite manners. Even a salt importer, be he of a polite frame of mind, knew how outrageous that was. "He introduced *himself* to you?"

"Yes, in fact not just me, all of us. He approached us on the street—I was with Mr. Lonsdale, Mrs. Venables, and Mr. and Mrs. Birkenhead—and made himself known. It was disconcerting, I'll admit, though Mr. Lonsdale was a common acquaintance between us."

"It was presumptuous of Mr. Graeme to push himself forward, though. A shocking breach of manners. As Mr. Lonsdale was with ladies unknown to Mr. Graeme, he should have waited for his friend to greet him and introduce him to you all if he so decided."

"True." Anne thought of the expression on the young man's face as he left. "What do you know of him, Mr. Doyne? Is your acquaintance with Mr. Graeme of longstanding?"

"I would not say that, no; he introduced himself to me, too, in the Pump Room. Not the done thing, but not so bad to another gentleman, you know." Mrs. Noakes sagged against the gentleman and he noted it with concern. "Are you well, madam?"

"I am parched, sir, and the heat in this room . . . could you find me a place to sit so I may have a cup of punch?"

He took the hint and led her away, after excusing them to Anne. She watched them make their way through the crowd. It was not so heated in the room, certainly not enough to make a lady faint. For some reason Mrs. Noakes had not been happy about their conversation. Why? What did she have to do with Mr. Thomas Graeme? It was a puzzle, and she did not like puzzles except as an exercise for her brain.

She chatted with other acquaintances, and lingered near the pianoforte for a particularly affecting performance of "Blest Be the Tie That Binds," a newer song by John Fawcett, a vicar. It was a pretty air, and sweetly sung by a young gentleman to whom she had been introduced, though she couldn't recall his name at the moment. She then drifted on feeling out of sorts. The room was noisy, and she was weary. Quin did not need her; Susanna and he were thick as inkle weavers now, with eyes only for each other. Lady Sharples had cornered Mr. Doyne and Mrs. Noakes, new food for her voracious appetite for gossip. The lady was looking perturbed and tugging on the gentleman's arm, perhaps ready to depart, but her ladyship was not letting them go for the moment.

Anne found a spot to sit by the window, near a door that led to the staircase. As she filtered out the noise and tumult of singing, piano and chatter, she could hear two male voices in urgent, muttering anger nearby, outside the door. One was Bertie, the other was Mr. Lonsdale.

". . . *shocking* breach of trust to bring him here, Alf. How could you after . . ." He broke off, then continued, saying, "What were you thinking? You know I do not like the fellow, nor do I trust him."

It must be Graeme of whom they spoke; Anne recalled the young man's thunderous expression as he stomped away from the Pierrepont Place home.

Sullenly, Lonsdale muttered, "You had no right to order him gone."

"I had the perfect right. This is *my* home, as much as I have invited you to make us your refuge, and do not forget it."

"Can I have no friends of whom you do not approve?" Lonsdale cried.

Anne frowned. That sounded for all the world like a son's lament to his father, oddly familial.

Bertie muttered some expletive, but Anne could not understand him.

"You've made trouble for me," Lonsdale continued. "I'll suffer—"

"Suffer *how*? What hold does that fellow have on you? Is it . . . *tell* me what it is!"

"I can't!" the younger fellow wailed. "You don't understand, Bertie. I have made a terrible mistake, and now—"

There was a clatter and an outcry near the refreshments; a maid had dropped a tray and spilled some food on Mrs. Noakes, who was plaintively wailing in exaggerated horror. A footman rushed to her aid and tried to help tidy the mess, but she made it worse by weeping and flapping her hands.

Lady Sharples, who *had* been close by, edged away from the woman, who was now in near hysterics at the incident, loudly complaining that it was Mrs. Noakes's own fault, for she had jostled the maid. Alethea called out for her husband to manage the situation. Bertie and Mr. Lonsdale entered the room together, both dark red of face, both with obstinate expressions. The host soon had the problem sorted and the maid was banished, sobbing, from the room while a footman took over. Mrs. Noakes was guided to the ladies' withdrawing room; Mr. Doyne said he would make sure she got home and was comfortable with her maid.

Anne watched the tumult in abstract thought, as Lonsdale bolted from the place and clattered down the stairs. What was his and Bertie's angry confrontation about? Why was it Bertie's place to disapprove of Lonsdale's friendship with Mr. Graeme? And why *did* he disapprove?

The puzzle deepened.

Chapter Nine

Sleep eluded her for most of the night, and when she did slumber, it was to be chased by clumsy maids, angry young men, and a haunting vision of Darkefell, asking why she hadn't yet announced their engagement. She tried explaining how different it was for a woman than for a man, especially one so accustomed to having everything her own way, to give it all up and commit to a man being put over her, in charge of her life, her fortune and her body. Why was she considered something between a beloved pet and a valuable carriage? And yet even in her dreams there was no explaining it adequately in terms he could ever understand without walking in her uncomfortable shoes for a day.

Sunday morning dawned bright and warm, a golden Bath autumn day. Though she would see him at church, before breakfast Anne sent a note to Osei with Mr. Roger Basenstoke's direction and his kind offer to share information about the Bath leasing market, along with a separate note to forward on to Tony. She then sat at her dressing table as Mary did her hair for church. They talked over the night before, and Anne pondered aloud the various interesting mysteries she was wondering about. What was at the root of the tension among Bertie, Alfred Lonsdale and Thomas Graeme? Why did Bertie behave like an angry father and berate Alfred about his friendship with Graeme?

And another bothersome moment from the night before: why did a perfectly capable maid suddenly spill a tray on Mrs. Noakes as that woman was becoming nervous and fretful? There was an answer that occurred to Anne. The poor woman had looked out of her depth and unhappy the whole evening. Had she instigated an incident so she could ask Mr. Doyne to take her home? It would be easy to jostle a maid's arm and cause a spill; that was what Lady Sharples had loudly suggested.

Mary had no answers, and worked silently, letting Anne talk it out as she pinned and coiled the thick hair into a modish style. Finally, Mary gave her hair a pat and said, "I think you're ready, milady."

Anne stood; she wore one of last year's gowns, a blue satin *robe à la française*, with exquisite Brussels lace at the neck and sleeves, enough to show she could afford the luxuries, not enough to be ostentatious at church. It had been freshened with a new stomacher in white silk with blue embroidery, an old-fashioned look contrasting the gown, but one that Anne thought was pretty. Mary helped her with her gloves.

When her mistress was perfect, Mary went back to the subject of Anne's chatter. "Nouw, milady, don't ye think you're making up mysteries to avoid thinking of his lordship?"

"I've been doing nothing *but* thinking about him, in between other things, of course."

"Aye. So . . . *why* are you in such a tumult?"

"I have asked myself that question, and myself has many excuses and answers, but few that will suffice. I consult myself like an Oracle, but myself merely bids me *ask another question, for the future is clouded.* Mayhap I should consult again the Mystic of Bath."

"I'd no think you the fool if you did, milady; many an answer has been captured by such as yon mystic. P'raps it is that they delve into the innermost longings of their subject and fish out the answers from there."

"You may have something, Mary. In part that did seem to be her method, to divine what the subject most wished, and to tell them those secrets within themselves. But still . . . there is much she knows that I don't understand how she knows it."

"Aye, milady; that is how life works, is it not? With mystery abounding? After all, are not mystery and the mystic allied?"

• • •

St. Swithin Church was a short walk along the Paragon, a perfect distance on a warm autumnal morning. The air was perfumed with the nutty aroma of fallen leaves and the faintly fishy tang of the river. Anne and her mother walked, arm in arm, while Lady Everingham took a sedan chair with two perspiring carriers. Despite their burden they outpaced Anne and Lady Harecross, and the older woman was settled in the family's rented box in the upstairs gallery of the church by the time the two younger women arrived.

Built over an ancient crypt, on a site of worship to many generations of Bathonians, St. Swithin was popular. The new edifice had been constructed a few years before but had to be expanded not long after, and there was talk of continuing expansion, for it was in the increasingly fashionable section of Bath known as Walcot. After arriving they were joined by Lolly, who accompanied Lydia and John in their carriage and supported poor Lydia up the stairs. Anne appreciated John's kindness in escorting the older woman. It was more than her grandmother and mother — Lolly's cousins — had thought to do even though Lolly had obliged them the evening before by making up their card table of four.

Mrs. Clary Basenstoke was accompanied by both Mr. Lonsdale, who Anne had invited, and his cousin, Roger, who Anne had *not* invited. Lady Harecross had extended the invitation to their church to Mrs. Basenstoke's new beau, Mr. Smythe, but he was not able to join them, so perhaps Roger was a replacement.

They took their places — their box in the upper gallery was crowded because of all of their guests, invited and otherwise — then there was a stir and a wave of whispers. Anne turned. Osei had entered on the lower level and stood at the end of the nave, glancing around the church. Anne stood and caught his eye. He found his way upstairs and joined them, murmuring a greeting, his ineffable grace allowing him to ignore the stir and the whispers and the eyes of everyone on him. Lydia welcomed him with pathetic gratitude, for Osei was a familiar face, and patiently kind and courtly with her in her uncomfortable state.

Anne's mother greeted him with frosty civility. Anne's grandmother ignored him. The others politely nodded at Anne's introduction, and prepared for service. Anne introduced him to Mr. Roger Basenstoke, whom she had spoken with the night before concerning Osei, explaining that she had not expected to see Mr. Basenstoke at the church. She was gratified that after a brief moment of surprise on the gentleman's face he nodded and said he would be happy to speak with the secretary after service.

Baron Kattenby and Mrs. Bella Venables attended the service, as it was his parish church, but sat in a pew in the nave. There was whispering and much attention; that they had come together and without other accompaniment — Alethea and Bertie attended Bath Abbey, close to Pierrepont Place — revealed much about their relationship.

Anne's mother leaned in to Clary Basenstoke and shared her opinion. "It can mean aught but that the vicar will read the banns. How *awful*. Especially after he courted you so assiduously all summer, only to turn from you in the wink of an eye and the turn of a pretty ankle. It is unconscionable."

Mrs. Basenstoke kept her eyes rigidly forward and did not respond.

As the service approached the end, the vicar cleared his throat and declaimed, loudly, his resonant voice echoing in the upper reaches, "I do today publish the banns of marriage between Baron Tedrick Kattenby of Somerset, now residing in Bath, and Mrs. Bella Venables, widow, of Bath. This is the first time of asking. If any of you know cause or just impediment why these two persons should not be joined together in Holy Matrimony, ye are to declare it."

There was silence for a moment, and the vicar closed the service with the blessing and grace, "The grace of our Lord Jesus Christ, and the love of God, and the fellowship of the Holy Spirit, be with us all evermore. Amen." There was then the usual rustle of cloaks and fans and hymn books, as well as the murmur of conversation, as congregants gathered themselves to depart, their weekly duty done.

Anne and her family had descended to await a sedan chair for Lady Everingham and a carriage for John, Lydia and Lolly. Lonsdale, as a vicar himself, had paid close attention to the service. He appeared thoughtful after, standing alone and looking down at his feet, hands clasped behind his back, as his aunt and Mr. Basenstoke stood talking to Lady Harecross. Anne's grandmother wished to speak with the vicar—she was adamant that she had something she needed to see him about—and Lydia wished to remain inside and seated in a pew near the door until their carriage arrived. Lolly, out of gratitude to the young couple for bringing her in such comfort, remained at Lydia's side as a kind of attendant.

As Clary stood chatting with her son, Anne's mother took hold of Osei and talked earnestly with him. Anne overheard some of their conversation, which as far as she could tell consisted of the countess probing him about when the marquess could be expected in Bath, and him responding with vague assurances. Mr. Basenstoke stood courteously supporting his mother and awaiting the secretary's freedom from the countess's importunity.

With nothing else to occupy her time or mind, Anne decided to discover what the previous evening's disagreement between the young vicar and her friend Bertie was about. She moved quickly and quietly over to Basenstoke's cousin's side. "Mr. Lonsdale, I feel a need for some air. Would you escort me outside?"

The young man nodded solemnly, and they exited into the sunny warmth of autumn and the St. Swithin garden. The grounds were neatly maintained. Mr. Lonsdale offered her his arm; she nodded in gratitude and together they strolled. There was a wide grass lawn with a border wall, below which was the Paragon. Along the wall were hedges of yew and some pretty flowers.

"I wish I were a gardener to know what those are," she said, waving her fan at the small lilac-colored blossoms, naked of leaves. "Brave little blossoms! They look like crocuses, but crocuses are spring flowers."

"These are colchicum, my lady, often confused with autumn crocus, but a different species." He dropped her arm and knelt, tipping the flower slightly with slim gloved hands. "See, in the crocus there are three stamens, but this flower has six, therefore it is a colchicum, not an autumn crocus."

"How knowledgeable you are," she said, watching him as he straightened and dusted his hands.

"A vicar often finds joy in such simple pleasures as the garden, milady," he said, taking her arm again. Almost to himself he said, "I find God in the garden, and talk to Him."

"If He is anywhere, surely it is in the garden," Anne agreed. "What thought you of today's service?"

"Not earthshaking. As one comes to expect, I suppose, but I am in no position to critique another vicar's service."

"Whyever not?" she asked lightly.

"I fear I would suffer by comparison."

"How unfortunate."

He smiled faintly. "Do not mind my melancholy frame of mind, my lady. I think I came to service this morning looking for moral clarity, for a higher voice to show me the way."

"Show you the way?"

"Have you ever had a choice to make, a choice between what you feel is right and what is expedient?"

"I don't think so."

"What would you choose, in that case?"

"Why, I hope I would choose what is right, of course."

He shook his head and squinted into the misty light. "What if 'right' is not so easy to tell because . . . what if to do what *seems* right will almost certainly hurt someone you love, while what is expedient will protect that person, but possibly hurt more people . . . people you don't know or care for?" He glanced at her anxiously. "Do you understand, or am I making a muddle of it?"

"That *is* a dilemma," she murmured, feeling out of her depths. How could one advise someone on a moral tangle when one did not know what the issue was? And yet, she knew him so slightly it would feel forward to ask. She was beginning to think it impossible to plumb the depths of the previous night's quarrel. He had been so thoughtful and questioning. To scrutinize someone who was so clearly struggling would be an imposition, a manipulation. They strolled on and came to an ancient tree, leaning for support on the wall of the churchyard. To lighten the subject matter, Anne said, "To test your garden knowledge, what bush is this, sir?"

He smiled. "I fear you are having a joke at my expense, my lady, for I'm sure you know the answer. It is a yew, of course, ancient, by the looks of it. To impress you, though, I will tell you that our pagan ancestors are thought to have worshipped this venerable tree. It holds symbolism both of death and rebirth."

"How did that come to be?"

"Perhaps it is the yew's poisonous nature that makes it a tree of death, but how it became a tree of life in Celtic folklore I cannot say."

They walked on in silence, his gloom impenetrable. She felt it flowing from him to her by way of their linked arms. Perhaps there was a way to introduce the previous night's quarrel without being discourteous. "Pardon me for dreadful inquisitiveness, Mr. Lonsdale, but I could not help but notice a friction between you and Bertie last night, and some tension between you and your cousin, Mr. Basenstoke. Bertie is a dear friend, and I dislike seeing him disturbed. What is wrong among you gentlemen, or is it private? Am I being fearfully prying?" she asked, leaving him a way to refuse to answer.

He was pale and quiet, paused, then shook his head. "It *is* private, my lady. I will say . . . Bertie is something beyond a friend or a brother; he is a steadfast soldier of rectitude and someone I view with unrelieved admiration. I fear I have fallen into disfavor with him."

"And Mr. Basenstoke? What disagreement is there between you?"

"My aunt is a wonderful woman, as I'm sure you're aware. She has been so kind to me, and guided my education and vocation with a steady and friendly hand. Since I lost my own dear mother, she has stood in that stead. Roger was like a much older brother to me as a child. I worshipped him. He's clever, and sure of himself, neither of which attributes I possess."

Anne remained silent, hoping he would speak more, and he did.

"Somehow, somewhere along the way, Roger and I fell out. He does not approve of me."

"Why is that? You appear an abstemious, learned and good-natured gentleman."

He shook his head and stared at the yew. "I have faults; he can be cruel concerning them. My lady, another question, if I may: do you think it is right for someone with a deep moral failing to preach to others?"

He was one for asking difficult questions of a stranger, she mused. "It depends on the moral failing," she said, gazing at him with a smile. When she saw his sad, unchanging stare, she wished she had answered more thoughtfully. She was searching for a better answer when he spoke again, almost to himself, it seemed.

"It matters little. I don't suppose I will be a vicar much longer. There are some failings the church will not . . . that is . . ." He shook his head. "Pardon me, my lady, for my sadness today. I have few friends and have fallen out with those who matter most to me."

"Like Bertie?" she said softly. "I know you said it was private, but I dislike seeing him troubled. You had words."

He looked over at her in alarm.

"I overheard the argument between you in the hall last night, after Mr. Graeme left in what appeared high dudgeon. I did not mean to eavesdrop, but I was too close not to hear. It seems unfair of him to berate you over your friendship with Mr. Graeme."

His pale cheeks colored pink and he held one hand over his stomach, appearing ill. "Don't think that Bertie had no *right* to say what he said; I would not have you think ill of him. I have failed him."

"I don't think I understand, Mr. Lonsdale."

"I cannot explain; there are others involved, and private matters among them. But what think you of someone who would stand by and say nothing, knowing that someone is doing something wrong? What should a person do, someone who, with one word in the right ear, could keep people from immeasurable heartache?" He was becoming agitated, dropped her arm again and paced away, then turned back to stare into her eyes.

She tried to form an answer, but could not without knowing more. It was all so vague, so tangled. She wondered if it had to do with the moral dilemma he had, of whether to do the right or the expedient thing?

"One should do something. One should take action, speak up, be *brave*," he said, his mouth trembling as he formed the words. He wrung his hands, his gloves pinching and puckering. "But some of us were not formed for courage, and if there is a bitter personal price to be paid . . . it is unthinkable, but some put themselves ahead of others, and that is surely not how society should advance."

"Is this the same moral dilemma you questioned me concerning earlier, sir? I fear I am at a loss as to how to answer."

"I beg your pardon, my lady, I am being *most* unreasonable. I abuse your kindness. I have in my life right now several moral dilemmas, and I must untangle my thoughts before making any decision." He swayed on his feet.

"Mr. Lonsdale, are you unwell?"

"I slept but little last night. I'm so weary. If you don't mind, Lady Anne, may I return you to your family? Though you may not think so, in hearing me out you have helped immeasurably. My dilemma is clearer to me now. I have something I need to take care of, something I must do *now*, while I have screwed up my courage to the sticking place."

• • •

Anne returned to Lydia and John's comfortable townhome to spend the day with them. Her uneasiness over Lonsdale's moody depression dissipated in the homely atmosphere of the Bestwicks' company. Setting aside all her own confusion, she focused on her friend. Lydia was pale and fretting, and John was worried about her. It seemed to be more than the normal anxiety of a woman heavy with child, to Anne, but who could know what "normal anxiety" was? She sat quietly with Lydia late into the evening as John retired to his study to write letters. Try as she might, her friend would confess no concerns or worries.

"I cannot say, I'm sure, dearest Anne," the pretty young woman said in response to Anne's repeated request to explain what was troubling her. Dark circles under her eyes spoke of her lack of sleep, but she shook her head when asked why.

Turning to more practical matters, Anne said, "Then is there anything I can do to distract or comfort you?"

Lydia slyly peeped at her through her thick fringe of lashes. She leaned forward, resting one hand on her bulky stomach. "Take me to see Mother Macree tomorrow," she whispered.

"Why are we whispering?"

Tears welled in her eyes. "John is being horrible. He says he will not allow me to do such a thing, that it is foolish and not good for me. But I say it is worse for me that I can do nothing entertaining, that I am kept in like a cow in a barn, waiting for birth."

"Lydia, that's vulgar."

"It's true!" she wailed, then hushed, her gaze slewing toward her husband's study door across the entry hall. "*Please*, take me," she said, grasping Anne's hand. "I am so weary of being shut in. You went with Lolly, and she said it was ever so entertaining."

Against her better judgment, Anne agreed. "All right. We'll go tomorrow. But I'm telling John."

"No! Please don't. He doesn't understand."

Anne sat and watched her young friend. As silly as she sometimes was, Lydia was an adult woman, and if the law insisted on treating her like a child or halfwit, Anne should not, or she made a lie of her own rebellion. To ask permission of John was behaving as if she agreed with society that a woman needed a keeper. "We'll go, and I'll not tell John unless he asks." She rose and bent over, kissing her friend on her soft tearstained cheek. "I'll come get you tomorrow morning. We'll have Lolly meet us there, shall we? She is acquainted with the woman and can get us an appointment. Then after we'll go to Sally Lunn's for teacakes and indulge ourselves."

She left her friend radiant, and accepted John's suggestion that he walk her home.

On the way, a linkboy carrying a lantern before them, they talked. Lord John was not as intelligent and dynamic as his older brother, the marquess. Nor was he as charismatic and attractive as his other brother, the marquess's twin, Julius. But for Lydia, he was perfect, as he was patient and kind and content with her lack of intellect. He didn't need a woman of learning, he simply wanted a wife, and a family.

But he had come to enjoy talking to Anne, as surprising as she found that. His mother was critical and difficult, his older brothers impatient with Lydia's lack of depth and constant emotional turmoil, so John perhaps found her his best choice to confide his uncertainties over his wife's health and well-being. "I am worried about Lydia," he said, holding Anne's arm in his tightly against his side. He matched his stride with hers as they headed the short distance to the Paragon through the dark, the linkboy's lantern casting a bobbing pool of light.

The weather had changed, and a wind had hastened to a chill that buffeted them. Anne pulled her cloak around her tightly. "What do you fear?"

"She's fretting about something, but she won't say what."

So John was not oblivious, as Lydia appeared to think. If she wouldn't confide in him, nor in Anne, maybe seeing the mystic was a good idea to get her talking. "I think she is chafing at being home so much. She's in Bath, and yet not allowed to be out in society." She slid a glance over to him, his face mostly shadowed, his expression concealed. "Lydia is feeling constrained by her condition."

John pondered that. "I don't wish to imprison her, my lady, I want her to be well. Should she not already be lying in?"

"I sincerely sympathize with your concern, but perhaps we should be guided more by what Lydia *wants*, or even feels she needs, rather than traditional notions of what is correct."

"My lady, surely tradition is the best guide society has!" he exclaimed.

Anne sighed, knowing how impossible it would be to explain to the poor fellow that for women, "tradition" was too often an excuse to keep them restricted and behaving as men wished them to behave, rather than following the dictates of their own hearts and knowledge of their capabilities. Maybe that was unfair. Certainly men were also constrained by society and tradition, but at least they had outlets that allowed them much more freedom of movement and choice. "We are going out tomorrow. I'll try to find out what's wrong," she said without mentioning their destination.

"I do appreciate it, my lady." His mind relieved on that track, he moved on to other matters. "So Osei is in town and looking for a townhome for Tony. I do not understand why my brother will not stay with us."

Anne sighed inwardly. They had already canvassed this topic, but John was not one to let go of something that puzzled him. "You know your brother; he's determined to have his own way."

John cast a sly glance her way. "*Will* he have his own way and convince you to announce your engagement?"

She evaded that question with a shrug. "I introduced Mr. Boatin to an acquaintance who can help him find Darkefell a townhome to rent for a few months. Had you met Mr. Roger Basenstoke before this morning?"

"Mrs. Clary Basenstoke's son? I *have* met him before. A solid fellow, trained in law. I would have succeeded at the Inns myself, you know, if I had been allowed." It was a familiar lament. The family had a troubled relationship among them and the youngest son had always felt he suffered by comparison to his brothers.

"You could take training now, you know. Some gentlemen attend the Inns in their twenties."

"It's far too late for me," he said, shaking his head. "I'm a married man, going to be a father. Other things are more important to me now."

Or perhaps he didn't *want* the rigors of intellectual study, and it was just something to grumble about.

"I hope to manage one of our estates if Tony will but let me." He paused and glanced over at her. "Could *you* speak with him for me? There is an estate in Cornwall that I have always been fond of. It would be perfect for Lydia, closer to her family than Ivy Lodge at Darkefell. Her mother has not been well lately, or she would be here."

Anne knew of Lydia's mother's bouts of sickness, which most often coincided with anything she didn't particularly want to do, such as leave home. "I fear I have no sway with Tony on anything," she said, though she knew that was not completely true.

"You underestimate yourself," John said as they approached her grandmother's townhome. Truffle tottered out and bowed, holding the door for Anne. John bowed over her hand. "Good evening, my lady. I look forward to seeing you again soon. Please, speak with Tony for me."

Chapter Ten

Morning dawned, revealing that the inclement weather presaged by the rising wind the night before had settled in. A steady chill rain pelted down, tapping against the windows like a nosy neighbor asking to be let in. Anne sent Lolly a note about her excursion to the mystic with Lydia, and then breakfasted alone in the dining room. She would usually walk with Mary the relatively short distance from the Paragon to Margaret's Buildings, but for Lydia's sake and privacy, she decided to make them comfortable and take the Everingham closed carriage.

And so they arrived at the mystic's residence midmorning, with Lydia complaining of nerves and being unwell, an expression of her fear of what was to come. When Lydia was frightened, she said she was unwell.

"We can stop now, my dear," Anne said, hand on the carriage door handle. "We don't have to do this."

"No!" Lydia exclaimed, rather too vehemently.

Anne watched her for a moment in the dim interior of the carriage. "Lydia, if there is anything you wish to tell me—"

"Please, let us go!"

"All right."

The driver, an elderly gentleman who had worked for the Everingham family his whole life, gently aided Lydia's descent from the carriage to the street. It had stopped raining but appeared ready to start again any moment. Lolly had received Anne's message and met them at the door of the mystic's residence. Her anxious solicitousness was perfectly designed to calm Lydia, making her feel there was one person, at least, who was wholly engaged in her well-being. Anne was relieved. As much as she loved the young woman, it wore on her to constantly reassure Lydia, while Lolly never seemed to weary of the task.

They were ushered in by the little maid, climbed the stairs, and sat in the small anteroom once more, and Lydia chattered about her baby, her discomfort, John's lack of sympathy, and her fears of the process of childbirth. Finally, they were summoned and entered the seer's den, Lydia wide-eyed and quivering, with Lolly jollying her along. Mother Macree was sitting at her table as before, but the light was dimmer because of the nasty weather outside. She was huddled in her chair and said not a word as the three women were guided to seats by her little maid.

The mystic muttered and laid out some cards, then looked up sharply into Lydia's eyes. "Yer frightened, child. Worried about yer baby, yes?"

Lydia nodded, her breath catching on a sob in her throat.

With the cards laid out in front of her, the mystic then began to read them, passing one wrinkled, spotted hand over the backs, turning some up, nodding and sighing. Finally, she said, "All will be well, child, all will be well. Even now ye feel the babe stirring in yer womb and are afeared, but fear not; ye'll be delivered of a healthy child."

"Do you . . . do you know if it will be a boy or girl?"

The woman muttered and turned more cards, then shook her head. "The future is unclear. Yer husband wishes a boy, I know this, but it is unclear."

Lydia watched her carefully, appearing uncertain, and sighed, moving in her chair. She opened her mouth, then shut it again.

"What is it, Lydia? What do you wish to say?" Anne asked.

The young woman glanced at her and ducked her head, tears shimmering on her lashes. "I wonder . . . is . . ." She stopped and shook her head. "I can't," she said, her voice clogged.

The mystic turned to Anne. "Ye've returned. The young man you were with . . . he's all right, yes?"

"Yes."

"But *you* are worried and tormented by fear. Ye wait for yer man to join ye here, and yet don't know what to say when he does. You risk everything in yer doubt."

Lydia, wide-eyed, stared, her tears drying on her cheeks, leaving tight paths of stained skin. She then looked at Anne. "Why, she's right! You've been hedging and fussing about announcing your engagement. Oh, Anne, you must not toy with Darkefell. He is the very devil when crossed. When you told him no before I thought he'd go out of his mind, he was so angry!"

"Hush, Lydia," Anne said crossly. "Why must everyone poke their nose in my business?"

"You did come to a mystic," Lolly pointed out with perfect logic.

Ruffled, Anne exclaimed, "Since I don't believe she is in contact with some divine personage, and believe this is all nonsense, I would say even given my attendance here, she should keep her nose out of my business."

Lydia, frightened by Anne's forthright speech and acerbic tone, quivered and tears welled again. "You're not helping, Anne! Please, Mother Macree, don't pay any attention to her. I wish to know more."

Darkly the old woman glared at Anne. "Not with *her* in the room. Go, both of ye," she said with an impatient gesture to Lolly. "I'll speak to the girl alone."

"Out of the question," Anne said, folding her hands on her lap. "I'll *not* leave this room. Lydia, dearest, you can rely on—"

"*Please*, Anne, go! Let me speak with her in private," Lydia said crossly. "I wish to talk to her without your disapproving glares."

Anne narrowed her eyes and stared at the mystic. It went against the grain to give in, but she was doing her utmost to be supportive of Lydia in her struggle for some degree of independence. And what harm could the old woman do? "If you're not out in five minutes I'm coming back in to get you," she said, and rose, following Lolly out of the room to sit in the antechamber.

Less than five minutes later Lydia emerged from the inner room, her face glowing and with a smile on her rosy lips. Any trace of tears was gone, any suspicion or hint of trouble dissipated. The transformation seemed too good to be true. It was like another young woman stood before her. "Is everything all right?"

"Of course. Let us go and eat now."

At a cozy tearoom not far from the mystic's house in Margaret's Buildings, they partook of hot Bath buns, liberally doused in melted butter. Lydia smiled and chattered, watched other ladies, commenting on their clothes, and ate with great appetite, then expressed a desire to return home, as she was sleepy. She put her hand over Lolly's on the table. "Miss Broomhall, could I possibly impose upon you to come and stay with me for a few days?" she said with her prettiest manners. She was a charming girl when in good spirits.

"Lydia, you cannot ask Lolly to give up—"

"Anne, please, hush up!" Lolly blinked once, a rapturous

expression of delight crossing her face. "My dear girl, Lady Lydia, I would be absolutely *delighted* to stay with you for however long you need me."

"Not everyone is as hard-hearted and difficult as you," Lydia said to Anne with a sniff.

Anne sighed and restrained the urge to roll her eyes at her young friend's pettish pout. It was quite clear that Lolly was eager to help Lydia, and who was she to stand in her way? Though living with and helping Lydia, as much as she loved her friend, would be her last choice in the world.

Remembering Lolly's financial constraints, and how much easier it would be to live with the Bestwicks, with the benefit of a cook, housekeeper, maids, laundress, good food, and warm fires, Anne softened and smiled at her cousin. "Shall we retrieve some of your things, then, Lolly? I'll carry you both to Lydia and John's townhouse on Milsom."

• • •

The steady rain set in again, pouring down in sheets. Anne had an evening in and visited her grandmother in her rooms, reading to her the letters her son had sent from the Holy Land, where he was deeply involved in theological research. Lady Everingham's deepest regret was that her son had never married, nor had he an heir. His country estate in Oxfordshire was perfectly maintained by the heir presumptive, a cousin from his late uncle. But Viscount Everingham was a dutiful son and faithful correspondent. Anne took pleasure in reading to her grandmother the letters he sent, full of description of the tombs of antiquity, and his most recent travels through Persia. She had few memories of her uncle, as he had traveled for most of his adult life, but his letters revealed an intelligent, thoughtful man of deep sensibility.

Leaving her grandmother to read her Bible in peace — she felt most connected to her son when she was reading of the places he had been and the ancient sites he had seen for himself — Anne joined her mother and they sat in the sitting room, drinking tea and gossiping for a time. Finally, though, as Anne turned to a piece of embroidery she was attempting, Lady Harecross spoke what was on her mind. In her comfortable saque robe, her hair covered by a lace cap, she thumbed through a list of her friends and enemies. "Anne, I will not countenance any more nonsense. We *must* have a party when the marquess arrives in Bath, so he can become acquainted with our friends." She consulted a notebook that held the list, then looked up at her daughter with a frown. "Can you not give me a more precise idea of whom I should invite? And *when*? How can we plan anything this way when I don't even know when he is arriving?"

Anne held her tongue. She understood her mother's frustration; she was unaccustomed to having her plans determined by someone else and Anne suspected she didn't know what to think of her future son-in-law. "I'll be sure to take it up with the marquess when he arrives. I know you must have a dinner or a party, but please don't plan anything until I speak with him."

Discontented with such an answer, the countess shifted in her seat and threw down the book. "I do not know what to think, Anne. After Reginald's death," she said, naming Anne's late fiancé, "I thought we could find you another husband quite easily, once you were out of mourning, but you have thwarted my plans for any potential suitor I have presented to you. Some quite rudely, I must say. Clary doesn't show it, but she was *quite* hurt you wouldn't marry Roger."

"He never showed the slightest interest in me, Mother. I cannot respond to a proposal that never came."

Forced to admit the justice of that, Lady Harecross grumbled, "At least you caught a much better beau. How you did it I will never know, though your grandmother insists that I value you too lightly. How is that possible, I ask her? I *know* your value to a farthing. *And* you are the daughter of the Earl of Harecross, an important distinction that would always hold significance on the marriage market."

Anne restrained herself from asking how much a pound she could fetch. Better to hold her tongue than unleash the derision her mother would not understand.

"I must admit, I was deeply concerned you would reject him."

Anne was tempted to tell her mother that she *did* reject his first proposal, *and* his second, but she had no wish to be the cause of her mother's death by apoplexy. In truth, it had taken her some time to understand Tony, that as prickly and commanding as he could be, he was unlikely to become the overbearing husband she had avoided her whole life. With Darkefell she was safe. He had finally concluded, he told her, that it would take too much energy to attempt to restrict her vigor, so he would lengthen the reins and give her freedom. She had briskly replied that he made it sound like she was a horse, and he laughed aloud.

She smiled at the thought, remembering his dark eyes and sensuous lips; she longed to kiss him and indulge in the other shocking and forbidden caresses that had made their time together so revelatory. In intense lengthy conversations they had come to terms, and he confessed his beliefs had amended to the realization that women were *not* the frailer sex, as some condemned them. He was more likely to see Anne as an equal than any man she had met, though she was fortunate to be able to count her father and Osei Boatin as being equally as enlightened.

"Anne, did you hear me?"

"What? No, Mother, I did not. I was woolgathering."

Sighing heavily, Lady Harecross said, "As usual. I asked, should we invite your father?"

"Of course."

"He loathes Bath."

"But he loves *me*," she said, and bundled in a fist the sewing she was trying to attend to. "And as much as he hates Bath, he is also one of the few people Tony can talk to on equal terms. There is certainly no one else among our immediate circle who Tony will have the slightest respect for."

"But . . . but the *party*—"

"—will be *awful*. Darkefell will offend everyone with his manners—"

"Ridiculous. He has absolutely perfect manners. You forget, Anne, your grandmother and I have met him."

"Yes, but he wanted something from you," she said bluntly, unwilling to raise expectations about her husband-to-be that he would fail to fulfill. "He was attempting to find out where I had gone, and he knew that offending you would not gain him the information. He is devious where once he is committed. Otherwise,

he can be careless about offending those who find honesty and
forthright truth alarming or unpleasant, and that, Mother, includes
most of our mutual friends."

"You make him sound *most* disagreeable."

"And so he is, for many. But not for *me*." She flung the wrinkled
sewing aside with a pettish exclamation of irritation. "Good night,
Mother. Mrs. McKellar is coming on the morrow for the final fittings
for two of the new gowns, and we will be shopping for accoutrements."

She retreated to her room feeling low, but not sure why. She kept
coming back to the near future, and how exasperating it was going
to be to withstand the public exclamation once it was known that
she and Darkefell were to wed. It would be seen as a triumph for her
family, certainly, and there would be much congratulation. Visitors
would swarm the Paragon townhome. Invitations would come thick
and fast. She sighed gloomily. Her pride would be wounded by the
continual marveling over how miraculous it was that she snagged
him. The tabbies in the Assembly Rooms would have a glorious
gossip and her mother would revel in it.

Mary was in Anne's bedchamber sewing by candlelight, while
Robbie, her son, sat at her knee reading aloud from *Gulliver's Travels*.
He had reached a certain exciting part in the land of the
Houyhnhnms and Yahoos, so Anne sat as Mary finished a hem and
Robbie breathlessly recounted an adventurous part of the tale. She
spoke with him briefly about the tale, then said goodnight to the
boy, who, accompanied by his mother, slipped off to his cot in the
bedchamber he shared with her. When Mary returned to help her
mistress prepare for bed, Anne recounted her day, ending with her
conversation with her mother.

"I had to disabuse her of the notion that Tony will be the toast of
Bath and everywhere beloved," she said with a smile, catching
Mary's eye in the mirror. "He will be courted, yes, and feted and
deferred to, but I fear that few will like him or understand him." Her
smile died, and she continued: "Also, she did not want to invite my
father to celebrate. How could she think that I would agree, when
Papa will so dearly love to see Tony and Osei again? I can honestly
say that my father is the parent of whom I am most proud, and most
confident."

"Aye, milady, but you're far too hard upon your puir mother. She hasnae to do but visit and gossip. Your wedding will be her crowning happiness."

"I won't be certain of that until I see her and Tony together. He's likely to offend her and dash all her dreams of showing him off in Bath."

Chapter Eleven

Anne awoke to a dull and dreary day, wind pelting rain against her window, and little change in the light in her room even as the maid opened her drapes. Anne and Mrs. McKellar did their final fittings, and then she took the carriage and they shopped for fripperies. Gloves, hats, shoes, buttons, ribbon, fans, and lace. Fabric for wedding clothes for Mary and Robbie, which Anne decided to commission Mrs. McKellar to sew, though Mary would usually do that for her own dresses and her son's clothes.

After taking an early dinner with her grandmother, Anne retreated to her rooms and readied for another musical night at the Birkenheads'. They adored music and this time had secured a piano player of great ability, Alethea had told Anne in the note of invitation she sent around. Since Lord Westmacott was a supporter of the young pianist composer, he offered to escort Anne to the event, and she gladly agreed. Unlike many an older gentleman reputed to be a roué or rogue in his younger days—Lord West-macott, patched and bewigged, figured in her grandmother's more scandalous tales of the earlier part of their century—she felt completely comfortable in his presence, and wondered if those stories had been amplified by time and gossip, or if he had simply aged past such behavior. He never once made her feel alarmed by too warm a hand press or a suggestive quip.

Dressed in one of her favorite gowns, a lovely indigo watered silk, with a string of pearls and pearl earrings her only adornment, she descended and moments later her escort arrived. She donned her new hooded cloak for warmth, but left the hood off her intricate hairstyle. As always he complimented her look, and how the blue of the gown brought out her eyes. In the dark of the carriage they spoke quietly about the evening ahead.

"How do you know this pianist?" Anne asked.

"One hears of talented young men, you know, and one does wish to support artists, if one has the ability. It isn't all opera dancers, you know," he said with a smile she could hear in the dark.

"I know that, my Lord Westmacott," she said with a laugh. It was impossible to picture the courtly and handsome elderly gentleman as a young hot-blooded rogue, wooing a fair fallen maiden. But she was not one who felt that people of the past weren't just as capable as modern-day ladies and gentlemen of sinning. She had heard too many of her grandmother's tales to imagine that. "You know Quin and Bertie well, don't you?"

"I do. Their grandmother was a great heiress, quite the catch in my youth. Beautiful, with skin like cream, eyes like sapphires. *Heartbreakingly* lovely," he said, his voice quietly contemplative in the dark of the carriage. "Our families were friends. She was my constant companion and I would have married her, but alas, she was wed to another gentleman whose charms were more obvious to her parents."

"She broke your heart?"

"In those days I'm not sure I had a heart for breaking. I was very young, a mere stripling. But . . . perhaps. T'was not her fault, of course, for young ladies had little say in their betrothals in those days. You're fortunate, young lady, that you live now, and within a family that will allow you to choose your husband." He sighed. "I never saw her equal again. I can't say I blame her father. I fear I was not quite the thing in my day, even in my teen years."

"Don't ever tell me that you had a bad reputation," she said with a teasing tone, trying to erase the sadness she heard in his voice.

"I did. And earned, I must say," he said with a sly chuckle that echoed in the carriage. "You would not recognize me as I was."

"You must be happy Alethea and Bertie found each other; I have seldom met a couple so perfectly suited to each other."

"In more ways than you know," Westmacott said, and Anne could again hear the smile in his voice. "More ways than you will *ever* know."

They arrived at Pierrepont Place and were greeted with many of the same guests as last time. The Birkenheads had an exclusive group of friends, and everything was of the highest elegance. Anne smiled to see the same people speaking of much the same topics . . . gossip about absent friends and foes alike.

Finding herself beside Alethea, who was beautifully gowned in green velvet, Anne complimented her, then said, "Where is Mrs. Venables this evening?"

With an arch look, she answered, "Bella has not been here all day. At dawn's light her beau picked her up in his carriage and they took a trot to the countryside to see a property he is considering purchasing to make their home."

"*Outside* of Bath? But I thought he lives in town."

"Oh, he does, but he has a dream of tending goats, or chickens, or bees, or some such madness."

"So speaks the city dweller, my friend Alethea!" Anne chuckled, nodding to some acquaintances. She turned back to her friend, fondly touching her arm. "Do you remember when we were young you told me to call you Thea! For a while you were determined to run away and fight the rebels in the colonies. Then you said you were going to become a pirate and sail the seven seas. You had maps, and spent hours charting your course."

"That was one year," she said with a grin, looking, for a moment, very much as she had at fifteen. "The next, I believe I wanted to become a poet and starve to death in a London garret."

"A poet? I thought you were to become a painter. Remember that shocking painting teacher we had at the academy, the one who was rumored to paint from nude models in his ratty room?"

Alethea sent her a sly look, her eyes alight. "I have a secret, Anne," she whispered. "He did! I *saw* one. I crept away one day and found his hovel outside the village and tapped on his door. He was in the middle of a painting of the most radiant titian goddess . . . a beautiful woman who was completely, absolutely naked, sprawled on a velvet cover on his divan."

Anne, eyes wide, felt a burble of laughter and she giggled uncontrollably, holding her painted fan over her face to hide the outburst. "Oh, my! *Shocking!* Did he invite you in?"

"After much persuasion on my part. I believe I blackmailed him, threatening to expose his dastardly secret to our headmistress if he didn't let me observe."

"So that's where you kept going, am I correct? Did you creep out to visit the painter often?"

"I did."

"You talked of nothing but becoming a painter, like him. You were *madly* in love with him."

Alethea sent her a startled look. "I didn't think you knew of my passion."

"But I did, for all I couldn't understand the attraction of a fellow who could not keep his cravat on straight."

Alethea laughed, her cheeks pink. "I did not think you had plumbed the depths of my soul quite so thoroughly. I was in love, it is true." With a sweet expression, she reached out and touched Anne's cheek. "It is so good to see you, my friend, and to have you here in Bath once more."

Anne covered her hand and smiled. "When I am not here, I think of you often. And I *am* a good correspondent, am I not?"

"You are," Alethea said, patting her cheek. "But it's not the same."

Anne linked her arm with Alethea's and hugged it to her. "You don't know how *good* it is to speak with a friend who has more to talk about than gossip and clothes. To know there is a woman out there who thinks of more than her hair . . . it's wonderful!"

"Though I do still think about my hair," she said, touching her intricate hairstyle, woven with pearls and dyed feathers. "And so do you, don't deny it!"

With a happy sigh, Anne admitted it. "But it's not *all* I think about, and that is my point, my dear friend. It is good to have an ally with whom I can share memories, and speak of real things."

The evening was cheery and comfortable. Anne took a seat near the instrument and listened as the pianist played a few lively Haydn sonatas, the light tripping of his fingers over the keyboard an enchantment. Lord Westmacott sat beside Anne, his fingers counting out the time on his satin-breeched knee as he nodded approvingly.

"He's very good," Anne whispered.

"Isn't he, though? I am determined to help him find his way. He is a retiring young man with no idea how exceptional he is."

After his performance, the young man immediately sought out his mentor and was taken around the room for introduction, his pale face flushed with satisfaction and wine as he was plied by their receptive audience. Bertie seemed particularly taken and invited the young man to come back and play for them again. Westmacott frowned and put his arm over the young man's shoulders, guiding him away to speak quietly to him. Chastened, the musician stayed by the side of the elder gentleman for the remainder of his time among the company. Anne smiled into her fan; Westmacott fancied himself somewhat of an impresario, not just of opera singers but composers and other performers too, and zealously guarded his protégés, wishing to keep all accolades for his discoveries to himself.

After a light supper, which not every person attended, Anne followed the ladies to the drawing room again, where they were joined immediately by the gentlemen. Bertie admitted with a laugh that he saw no point in keeping to the company of gentlemen when there were so many enchanting ladies with whom to speak.

Alethea sent him a look of admonishment across the room, but burst into laughter. "What a flirt my husband is!"

Lady Sharples cornered Anne by the second fireplace and said, with an arch look, "Since our last conversation I have heard much gossip of your spring and summer travels to the north and to Cornwall." She leaned close, her breath smelling of wine and her person of perfume and powder. "You have been having adventures, my friend," she said, tapping Anne's arm with her closed fan. "Having them in the company of a certain elusive marquess, one Lord Darkefell. It is the talk of Bath."

Anne sighed. She had hoped to avoid the topic for one evening at least, but it was not to be. "He is the brother-in-law of a dear friend, Lady Lydia Bestwick. They—Lydia and Lord John Bestwick— are currently in Bath, so—"

"Oh, come, don't play coy with me." Lady Sharples had a gimlet gaze through the lorgnette she employed to good use, and she stared, unblinking, into Anne's eyes.

But Anne would not be broken and would not reveal before she was ready her intentions. She stayed quiet, keeping her countenance placid, and watched their friends chat and laugh. It was a test of wills, and she would not give in.

Finally the woman was forced back into speech by Anne's determined silence. "All right; you are better at this game than my usual victim, but I am not afraid to confront gossip and wrestle it to the ground. I'll tell you plain, rumor has it that you have captured the heart of the dark and mysterious marquess. I have seen the man once, years ago, and I admit, I find it hard to imagine you and he would suit." She eyed Anne up and down critically.

It was insulting that she should be examined and found wanting, but Anne was aware of what charms she possessed and those she didn't so she was determined not to be offended, though the woman's insult was one that she knew would be repeated once the truth came out. "Most would agree with you on that point," she said, with a forced placidity she considered a rehearsal for the next month or more, especially once her engagement had been announced.

"He is terribly intense, with those *eyes* . . . seems like he stares right through you." She shivered, but it was with a smile that tugged the corners of her mouth. "I'll admit though, he is a *very* well-looking man . . . nicely set up, if you know what I mean without saying." She eyed Anne in a calculating fashion. "I fear, though, he is much more the type to choose some fluff-brained girl in her first Season, one he can breed and then ignore. Do you not think? You have no hopes in that direction, I assume?"

Anne took in a sharp breath to retort at such a crude insult to the marquess and more oblique implied insult to her, but then saw on the other woman's face the avid, breathless anticipation. Lady Sharples was goading her, hoping to force some intemperate admission. She let the breath out slowly, then said with a smile, "How *wise* you are, my lady. It is *exactly* what I think of the gentleman. He is imperious to a fault and annoyingly arrogant. Handsome as the devil, as they say, but addicted to having his own way. He should indeed choose a fluff-brained girl." Though he hadn't. "What woman of spirit would ever have him, I ask you?"

After that, smiling to herself, Anne drifted from group to group, evading questions about her rumored romance with the mysterious Lord Darkefell—because of Lady Sharples the rumors were spreading like an untended fire—until she found Quin and Alfred Lonsdale sitting by the fire. She took the low chair by Quin's knee, awkwardly batting down the fullness of her skirts, and viewed Lonsdale with alarm. He appeared ill, his face pale, perspiring, one trembling hand pressed over his stomach. Quin was speaking urgently to him, leaning forward in his chair.

"Anne, help me," Quin said, reaching for her hand. "I am trying to convince Alf to seek medical advice. I offered my own physician, Dr. Fothergill—he is an esteemed and intelligent member of the Religious Society of Friends, a most estimable man and doctor—but he will have none of it."

Anne squeezed Quin's hand in a reassuring manner as she frowned and examined the young man. "Mr. Lonsdale, I would not say this in the normal course of events, but since I have been appealed to by my dear friend, I must agree; you do *not* look well."

"I appreciate the concern. I am perfectly fine, Lady Anne. A touch of indigestion, a corner of cheese, a bit of undigested pudding, that is all."

"I did not see you at the dinner table," she recalled.

"I didn't feel like supping with you all, and didn't wish it to be obvious that I wasn't eating."

Anne was taken aback; this was odd. Quin seemed equally troubled by his friend's words. "Are you *sure* it is indigestion?" Anne asked. "Are you typically plagued by such illness?" There was many a gentleman — and lady — who ate food too rich and drank far too much wine for their stomach. "What have you eaten today that could have led to it, if you didn't eat supper with the company?"

"I lunched with a friend and had a little something at the Pump Room, where I was importuned by Mrs. Noakes and Mr. Doyne to join them in taking the waters, which he does for his health . . . apparently precarious and getting worse. Tedious conversation and even more tedious mineral water. That's what it is, I'm sure. Who of our age suffers the sulphuric water besides you, dearest Quin?"

"I saw you earlier with a glass of wine that Lord Westmacott handed you, my dear fellow," Quin said. "Has it taken to your stomach badly?"

"Surely a little wine could be good for this particular malady. He's a dear old fellow, is he not? I've known Westmacott forever."

"He is an especial friend of my grandmother's and my escort this evening. I know he has known you and your brother for many years too," she said to Quin. "Quite one of the old school, don't you agree, Mr. Lonsdale?"

"I suppose," that gentleman said with a lift to one corner of his mouth. That half smile disappeared as another spasm had him holding his stomach again. Still, he kept his tone light as he said, "In some ways he is the very *essence* of the modern fellow." He pressed on his gut.

Something passed between him and Quin, but Anne could not imagine what it was. "Mr. Lonsdale, are you, perhaps, still upset as you were on Sunday?" she murmured, leaning toward him. "You spoke then of . . . of a dilemma. A moral quandary you were in. Is that what is making you ill? I know when I am upset I sometimes suffer physical ailments, indigestion among them."

He shook his head. "No, I have made my decision, and I plan to follow the moral path. I will do what is right, and hope those who love me understand my choices."

Quin frowned and opened his mouth to speak, but then closed it again, looking concerned.

"I'm sure you'll do what is best," Anne said gently.

"Perhaps you should go have a rest, dear fellow," Quin said. He motioned for a maid, who approached and curtseyed. "Could you show Mr. Lonsdale to the guest bedchamber, the one made up for him? He requires respite."

"Quin, dear boy, you fuss too much," Lonsdale said, but he looked relieved. There was a heartbeat thrumming in his temple, one vein standing out and pulsing irregularly.

"Nonsense. If Bertie were not attending to his company he would insist himself."

"I don't know about that. I am in his black book right now," Lonsdale said.

Anne was about to open her mouth to ask him about that, for she wondered if it had to do with Mr. Thomas Graeme and the scene at the last musical evening, but Lonsdale rose, swaying and clutching onto the back of the chair.

"*Please* let me send for Fothergill!" Quin said, alarm in his voice. "He is right round the corner, a most obliging fellow and a wonderful physician."

"Don't *fuss*, Quin. Tell Bertie to come see me when he has a moment, will you?" He followed the maid out of the room and was gone.

Miss Susanna Hadley gratefully sank down in his vacated chair and sent a pathetic look to Anne, who still perched on the stool by Quin's chair. "My aunt is a wonderful woman, and I do appreciate her letting me stay with her in Bath, but she is so determinedly needy of information and it is fatiguing when she has someone pinned and expects me to help her elicit news."

Anne, who had suffered Lady Sharples's inquisition, sympathized. "My mother is like that. When we are in company I am expected to help her in her quest. They should go out in company together and work as one."

Susanna laughed. "It sounds as if they might make the ideal conspirators."

"Unless their methods are too much alike, then they would cancel each other out."

The pianist was begged for another tune, and he moved to the piano. His elegant playing was a delight. As the music echoed and danced, the small group well entertained, Anne made her way to her hosts, who stood together, arm in arm.

Anne made some slight comment on the pianist, then said, "Bertie, when you have a moment Lonsdale would like to speak with you. He has gone upstairs to rest."

He grimaced. "He has not chosen the best time to want to see me," he said. "I will go soon enough."

Anne drifted away, wondering what was wrong with her usually equable friend. It seemed that the tension between Bertie and Mr. Lonsdale had not abated. Time would solve it, she thought. She had never known Bertie to hold onto a grudge for long.

Alethea was then asked to sing. Bertie replaced the young musician at the instrument, and he and his wife sang a duet.

"I confess, I love to hear them," Anne said, sitting down by Quin. "I've said it before, I know, but it never fails to amaze me; they have what I would call the perfect marriage. It is charming. A true marriage of minds and hearts."

Susanna sighed. "'Tis true," she said, then looked at Quin and blushed. "Would that every lady was so fortunate."

Quin watched her admiringly as applause for the duet erupted. The listeners again broke into groups, gossiping, laughing, flirting and exchanging glances. There was a convivial lightness in the crowd, but Anne was weary and did not take part. Even with her friends she was beginning to feel *de trop*, as Quin and Susanna leaned toward each other and whispered confidences.

Fortunately Lord Westmacott, appearing worn out, approached and bowed. "Anne, dearest child, I hesitate to take you away from your friends, but I'm not as young as I wish I was. It is time for this elderly gentleman to return to his own warm fireplace. I would take you home, my dear, and then deliver this young fellow to his lodgings." At his side was the pianist, his rosy cheeks burnished to red as he bowed to Anne.

"I would not keep you out late for the world, sir. I will get my cloak and we can leave."

She said her goodbyes to Quin and Susanna, begged them to give her farewells to the rest of the company — particularly her hosts, who were still seated at the piano playing requested pieces and laughing with some of their guests — and asked Quin to have Alethea send her a note when she was free for tea. She then exited to the stairwell with Lord Westmacott and summoned the maid. The girl curtseyed prettily and then trotted up the stairs to get Anne's cloak.

A moment later there was a piercing shriek from above. Anne gasped and stared up the stairs as the hubbub in the next room stopped and the piano playing ended with a crash of chords. A few of the male guests raced out to the stairwell, asking what was happening.

"What in heaven's name is going on?" Lord Westmacott asked, his voice trembling with irritation and weariness. The young pianist clutched his arm and, wide-eyed, stared up the staircase.

"I don't know," Anne said. "But I mean to find out." She had gathered her skirts in one hand and had a foot on the bottom step when, white-faced, the maid hurled herself halfway down the staircase and paused, clutching the banister.

"Help, help!" she shrieked, tearing at the lace cap that confined her hair. "Oh, please *help*! Mr. Lonsdale . . . the gentleman is . . ." She paused, blenched, then slumped down onto the steps in a faint.

Chapter Twelve

Bertie, who had erupted into the hall with a couple of his guests, bolted up the stairs, the skirt of his coat flapping. Anne hesitated for one moment but then followed, hastening as quickly as possible, squeezing her full skirts past the young maid, leaving her to be cared for by others.

Alethea had followed her husband to the stairs and cried out, her voice following them upward, "What is going on? Anne, what is it?"

"Take care of that maid; she collapsed on the stairs!" Anne said over her shoulder. "I'm following Bertie. The poor girl said something about Mr. Lonsdale. He was ill earlier." Out of breath, she paused on the landing, turned, and gazed down at Alethea's face in the midst of the upturned faces of others of the company, all with similar expressions of puzzlement mingled with irritation. "Summon Quin's physician friend, Dr. Fothergill, will you?"

"Why? What is . . ."

The rest of Alethea's cry was lost as Anne followed the sound of Bertie's stomping footsteps up the stair and down a hallway. An inhuman wail echoed, followed by guttural sobbing, the sound a wrenching, keening howl of desolation. She picked up her skirts and ran down the hall to an open door through which she bolted, gasping for breath.

Bertie was prostrate across the slight body on the bed, the prone and still figure of Alfred Lonsdale. Anne raced across the room. "Bertie, is he —"

"He's dead! He's . . . *gone*," Bertie wailed.

"He *can't* be," Anne cried as the stench of vomit insinuated itself up her nose, the earthy aroma of defecation competing in her nostrils. She moved to Bertie's side and bent over the bed.

The young man was indeed dead, his skin chilling in the cold room, his eyes open and staring, and his face and body soiled by the vomit and effluence of his last minutes. While below they had laughed and talked and drank, listening to tinkling music and lilting voices, Alfred Lonsdale had been alone, dying in agony.

"I'm so sorry, Bertie," Anne sobbed, taking her friend's arm and trying to tug him away from the body. But he stubbornly clung to the young man's hand and pressed it to his cheek, howling over it, hardly able to catch his breath, his urbane and elegant face a mask of pain and sorrow. "Come away . . . come leave him alone," Anne said. "There's nothing you can do for him now."

"I won't leave him alone. He *died* alone!" He looked around wildly, into the corners of the room, pressing the young man's hand to his lips. "My dear friend; how cruel a fate. Anne, do you think his spirit is here? Oh, Alf, how could you leave us!" His tortured cry finished on a groan of pain.

Alethea entered and saw the scene. "Oh, *no!*" she cried, and sagged against the doorframe. "What happened? How did he . . . ?"

"He was ill," Anne said sadly, turning from her friend, though her hand was on Bertie's shoulder. She could feel how the sobs wracked his whole body. "I spoke with him as he sat with Quin an hour or more ago. He was *very* ill. Quin wished to summon his physician, but Mr. Lonsdale would not have it, so Quin told him to go up and rest. Remember, I told you he was upstairs and wished to see you. Did you, Bertie? Did you come up at any time?"

He started and looked up at her. "I . . . no, I never came up. I wish I had. I so *desperately* wish I had."

Of course, Anne recalled; he had moved to the piano very soon after she gave him the message and had been there until this discovery. "My dear friend, don't blame yourself," Anne said gently. "We didn't know it was illness unto *death*. He seemed frightfully in pain, a digestive upset, but not . . . not *dying!*"

Bertie sagged again over his friend and wept. Voices below rose up the stairwell, and they could hear Quin's above them all. Then, a few minutes later, a plainly dressed gentleman entered the room.

"Doctor, thank goodness!" Alethea cried.

The gentleman was of medium height and middle age, brown-haired, with no peruke over his head. Extreme haste was evident in his unshaven face and mussed hair, his cravat absent, his clothes in disarray. "Where is the patient?" he said abruptly. "I could not get a bit of sense out of anyone below, not even your maid, usually a most sensible girl, nor your footman, Crabbe, who said he knew nothing. Quin didn't appear to know what was happening either. Where is the patient?"

"No patient here, I'm sorry to say," Anne said. "Dr. Fothergill, I assume? Quin's physician?"

The man nodded soberly.

"This young gentleman, Mr. Alfred Lonsdale, has expired," she said, raising her voice to be heard over Alethea's weeping and Bertie's moan of sorrow. "He was ill and we sent him upstairs to rest, but the maid found him dead."

The doctor crossed the room and tried to see Lonsdale.

"Bertie, you must let the doctor have a look," Anne said, trying to take her friend's arm. "Perhaps he can tell us . . . Doctor, how did the poor young fellow die?"

Reluctantly, Bertie allowed Anne to pull him from Lonsdale's side; his satin coat was stained with his dead friend's vomit, but he was too distraught to notice or care. The doctor leaned over and sniffed, then frowned. He touched Lonsdale's cheek, then peered into his eyes, and frowned some more and shook his head. He straightened and looked over his shoulder at the three of them, now standing together, for Alethea had taken her husband's arm and supported him. She looked as ghastly as Bertie, her skin ashen, her eyes still streaming with tears and her lips pressed together but trembling, choking back sobs of horror. Anne supported Bertie on the other side and felt his whole body tremble.

"I cannot say," he said finally.

"That's all? You charlatan, no wonder Quin does not recover!" Bertie bellowed, pulling away from his wife and Anne's clutches. His hands fisted, he stood alone in the dim center of the room. "Not *know*? He has suffered and died. What killed him?"

"Bertie, *please*, you're doing no good raging at poor Dr. Fothergill," Alethea sobbed, folding her arms over her stomach.

"Mrs. Birkenhead, it's perfectly all right," the doctor said, one hand held out to stay her protests. "I am accustomed to the emotions of a deathbed." He turned his gaze back to Bertie, his expression one of profound sympathy. "If you please, who are this young man's closest relations?"

"I happen to know them," Anne said, drawing the doctor's attention. "Mrs. Clary Basenstoke is his aunt, and her home is where this young man lives . . . lived. He has a cousin, Mr. Roger Basenstoke." She told him the Basenstoke address. "That is all the family he has, I think."

Alethea nodded. "He has stayed here on occasion; I . . . I made him up this room in case he could not stand it at the Basenstokes' any longer!" She burst into tears.

The doctor put his head to one side. "Pardon me, Mrs. Birkenhead, but what do you mean by that, Mr. Lonsdale not being able to stand it at the Basenstokes'?"

She shook her head, pressing her lips together.

"She means that Roger Basenstoke is a bully and Alfred is . . . *was* gentle and easily distressed." Bertie swiped one large hand over his face. "The poor boy knew he had a home with us if ever he felt . . . threatened."

A twinge of alarm twisted Anne's stomach. She watched the doctor's shadowed face, how his gaze seemed to turn inward.

"You ask how this young man died, and I cannot answer. I would like to, but I'm no magician. I require more information. Do you think Mr. Basenstoke would allow me to do some investigation?"

"What kind of investigation?" Anne asked before Bertie could say anything.

The doctor frowned as he gazed at her, as if trying to assess her place in the discussion. "I am a physician and a scientist. I have questions, perhaps more than Mr. Birkenhead. Given a few hours with his body, it is possible I may have answers." He paused and looked back at the body. "I'd at least like to try."

Answers; what an innocuous word for what he was implying. "You think he was poisoned," Anne said, even as she thought it.

Alethea gasped. "No!" she cried.

Bertie yelped, "What?"

Fothergill was silent, but his expression spoke volumes. He had not expected anyone to realize his meaning, nor was he prepared to confirm or defend his surmise. "I'll need Mr. Basenstoke's permission."

"Roger? Whatever for?" Bertie roared, his face glowing red as if he had quaffed an entire bottle of port, something he had been known to do at a party in past. "We were closer to Alfred than his closest relatives. Cared for him a damn lot more."

"Mr. Basenstoke is the closest male relation to Mr. Lonsdale, and so legally the one to ask," Anne said. "Is that your meaning, Dr.

Fothergill?"

"It is, Lady Anne."

"But why do you need *his* permission? Surely, as a physician attending the scene, you have a right?" Anne said. "And surely, as the young man died *here*, the Birkenheads have a right to know how he died?"

Fothergill watched her for a moment, then nodded, approval in his expression. "You have a point, my lady. A *good* point. I don't know if it would hold water legally, or is a cracked vessel, but we need to make a decision swiftly. I am willing to risk the family's displeasure in the search for answers." He turned to Bertie. "This is your home, and this poor young gentleman has died in it. Do you so request it, sir? Do you ask me to take possession of the body, and give permission for me to try to find out what killed him?"

"I do," Bertie said, his voice gruff and thick with emotion. "And damn the consequences."

"Then so be it. I'll make the arrangements."

• • •

In the drawing room a wan and trembling Bertie, who had discarded his stained coat and donned another, gathered the company together. He stood in front of the fireplace, with Lord Westmacott standing close by. Alethea was sitting on the edge of the chair where Quin was ensconced, holding her brother-in-law's hand. Quin had been told of the terrible occurrence, and tears rolled down his pale cheeks.

Bertie cleared his throat and looked around at the company. *"Media vita in morte sumus,"* he said solemnly. "In the midst of life, we are in death. Poor Alf . . . Mr. Alfred Lonsdale . . . has passed. We don't know why. I would like to say here and now that he was a lovely young man. A flower of youth, and as sweet-tempered and angelic a boy as I have ever met."

Alethea reached out and took her husband's hand. He nodded and squeezed it, then released.

Lord Westmacott put his arm over Bertie's shoulders and patted. "I'm sorry, dear boy. He seemed a charming fellow." He turned to Anne. "My dear, I am sad and tired. Would you indulge an old man and let me see you home? I feel the need for my fireside and a glass of port before bed."

"Unless you need me, Alethea? Bertie?"

Alethea said, her voice clogged with tears, "You go on home, Anne. Thank you for . . . for helping."

"Helping?"

"Helping decide . . . the doctor . . . you know," Alethea said wearily, waving her hand to indicate the rooms above. "Your resolve has helped immeasurably."

Anne nodded, wordless. Bertie, Alethea and Quin would support each other in this, an hour of sorrow. The rest of the subdued party had either left or was now in the process of leaving. Anne, the musician and Lord Westmacott followed Susanna and Lady Sharples out. It was a silent carriage ride, conversation circumscribed by the presence of the weepy young pianist. He was, it appeared, of the temperament that was sensitive to poetry and death, able to weep equally over a poem or a pyre. Westmacott said he would take the young man back to his lodgings after seeing Anne to her door. Anne felt out of sorts and oddly jealous of the pity shown the young man. Who was he to weep? *He* didn't know Alfred Lonsdale, as she did.

It was, Westmacott explained in a murmur when she remonstrated, because as an artist and an Italian he was a fragile fellow, his sensibility charming, if hard to bear at times. Anne, an Englishwoman, was made of stronger stuff and must make allowances for such a gentle soul, easily bruised by witnessing brutal death.

"He didn't witness *anything,*" Anne whispered to her friend. "I'm the one who saw the dead body, for heaven's sake."

"Don't be petty, Anne dearest," Westmacott said.

Chapter Thirteen

After a restless night with little sleep, as her mirror told her the next morning, reflecting dark circles under her eyes, Anne sent a message to Osei at his lodgings. She wanted to know if Mr. Basenstoke had helped him find something for Tony to rent. Instead of replying, he attended her personally. She was at the breakfast table alone when the butler brought his card in.

"Tell Mr. Boatin to join me. And can you have cook send up some more coffee?" It was, she knew, the secretary's preferred beverage.

Osei was ushered into the breakfast room and bowed.

"Help yourself to coffee and whatever is on the sideboard, Osei," she said. "And sit. I wish to speak of many things, and you are probably my best choice for someone in whom to confide. I'm happy you chose to attend me this morning."

He smiled and adjusted his spectacles. "I have much information and news to impart — I have found his lordship a townhome — and it seemed easier to speak with you than to write it all in a note."

"But food first," Anne said. "I am ravenous this morning. Perhaps death and sadness are for me an appetite stimulant."

"Death?" he said. "What do you mean?"

She related the events of her previous evening; he was suitably shocked. As she spoke, an idea occurred, but she let it simmer in her mind. Once she was done explaining, and they had finished eating and were drinking a cup of coffee, brewed most excellently by the cook, she tentatively made her proposal.

"I'll admit to being most upset by last evening's tragedy, and to some relief that Dr. Fothergill is investigating the cause of young Alfred Lonsdale's death. It seemed to me that the doctor was troubled, too. I understand that the doctor's residence and work rooms are on Henry Street around the corner from my friends' Pierrepont Place townhome. I would like to call on him, for I have a couple of questions. Would you accompany me, Osei?"

He thought about it for a moment, sipping his coffee with satisfaction. He then met her gaze, the sunlight streaming in the window glinting in his spectacles. "I'm sure his lordship would not be pleased with my answer. The last thing he said to me before I left him was to keep you out of trouble."

"So if you think Tony won't be pleased, that means you will do as I wish?"

"I am inclined to obey your request, my lady."

"Good. I don't see how keeping me from this task would keep me out of trouble anyway, do you?"

"I am of the opinion that my aid in satisfying your curiosity and anxiety is a better indemnity against the likelihood of you getting in trouble than would denying you my company. At least this way I can lend you aid if you become mired in a . . . situation."

"A *situation*," Anne repeated. "I suppose I have been in a few *situations*, in Yorkshire, Cornwall, and at home." She was silent for a moment, then said, "But this is different. Surely there can be no harm in trying to find out what killed poor Lonsdale? And regardless, if there are troubles to navigate, I remain undaunted. My friends are in pain, and answers will help, I hope, soothe them."

"Are you certain of that?"

Anne sighed deeply. "No. Sometimes answers simply lead to more questions, or to trouble. But I must try." She smiled at Osei. "You're not worried, are you?"

"About you? No, my lady. You are as intrepid as any warrior I have known."

"I appreciate that, Osei." She paused, but then said, "This won't get you in trouble, will it, you helping me? Tony knows me enough by now to know there is nothing you could do to stop me if I have made a decision to follow a course of action. He was never able to control my actions, so how could you? He cannot say I have tricked him with a meek and placid exterior."

He smiled. "No, you certainly have not deluded him as to your true nature and there is nothing typical about you. I do not fear his displeasure. His anger flashes bright but is quick to burn out. If you'll pardon a moment of impertinence on my part, I would say that what the marquess most values is your inability to behave as any other young lady would."

"Hah. Perhaps, but I think he cares for me in spite of it. Let us go, then; I'm ready, I only require my gloves and cloak. On the way to Dr. Fothergill's you can tell me of the townhouse you have found for Tony."

After a bright and promising start the day had closed in, with dark clouds gathering. The dowager viscountess's carriage, creaky and ancient though it was, had the benefit of being closed to curious Bathonians, and warmer than a lighter, more modern vehicle. Mary was present to lend her respectability, but the maid would stay with the carriage and pick up some weighty packages for her mistress as Anne and Osei did their business. The driver had an intimate knowledge of Bath from a lifetime of driving its narrow streets and squares, so they made their way through the foggy gloom toward the doctor's home on Henry Street.

"So . . . you have found a residence for the marquess, Mr. Boatin?" Anne asked. The secretary was Osei in private, but she tried to remember to call him by his proper name in public.

"Mr. Basenstoke made inquiries and procured for me the addresses of townhomes that were available. As a result, I have found the marquess a most suitable place on Upper Church Street, large enough that he will not feel cramped, but not so large as to be wasteful."

"Close to the Crescent."

"Yes, between the Crescent and the Circus."

"And not directly by Milsom," Anne said with a sly look. Mary smothered a chuckle. "And so not within reach of Lydia's every complaint."

"As you say."

"I'm relieved," Anne said. "I was worried you would secure a place on the Paragon. That would be too close for *my* comfort."

It was his turn to glance her way. "Indeed, there was a place on the Paragon on the list, and though I looked at it, I thought perhaps a little further away from your mother and grandmother would suit you better."

"Your judgment is, as always, impeccable, Mr. Boatin."

The carriage pulled to a halt. Osei jumped down, scanned the street and saw a brass plate with the doctor's name etched on it. He limped to the door and knocked; a maid opened the door, curtseying, eyes wide, as Osei handed her Anne's card. She retreated, but came back to the door a moment later and curtseyed again, then stood aside in the open doorway.

Osei helped Anne down from the carriage and she went directly through the door past the maid as the secretary stayed behind and told the driver to return directly after helping Mistress Mary with her parcels. The Fothergill maid showed them into a tidy front parlor, where they sat in comfortable stuffed chairs by a cheery blaze. The home was neat and well ordered, the furnishing simple but sturdy, with little to clutter the space except for bookcases, which lined most walls and were full to overflowing. Either the doctor was a married man or he had an excellent housekeeper, or possibly both.

A tidy woman entered; she was garbed in a plain blue gown with the faintest hint of woven pattern, and wore a white cap with long lappets over light brown hair dressed severely. She smiled, and her appearance was transformed from severity to amiability. "Lady Anne Addison?" she said, her voice sweet and musical. "I am Mrs. Fothergill. And you are Mr. Boatin?" she said, turning to the secretary. She offered her hand and both shook, a departure from polite greeting that surprised Anne greatly. "Please, have a seat. My husband is coming down directly. I offered to greet you; I hope that's all right."

Anne said, "Of course, Mrs. Fothergill. I'm afraid I'm being a nuisance coming so early."

"I understand completely. You were a witness to that terrible tragedy at the Birkenheads' home last night. How awful!" she said, her voice warm with compassion. "Poor young Mr. Lonsdale."

Surprised that the doctor had shared his work, *and* also amazed by the woman's openhearted warmth, Anne asked, "Did you know him?"

"We were acquainted," she said. "He involved himself in our mission group to the Caribbean working to end slavery there."

"Is your husband related to the Dr. Fothergill from Yorkshire?" Osei asked. "He who was a botanist as well as a physician?"

She smiled and nodded. "He *is* related in some degree."

Anne stared at Osei; was there *any* connection he could not recall? She refocused on the lady. "Again, pardon our intrusion, but I am most anxious to speak with Dr. Fothergill concerning what happened last night."

She nodded, her expression solemn. "A tragedy. A good-natured young man, Mr. Lonsdale was, and very kind. I am disconsolate at his death. Poor Arthur was up all night with his work. He just now had a cup of tea, but he will make time for you, I'm sure." She paused, listening. "There he is now, coming down." She rose. "I'll leave you to speak with him."

"You could stay, if you wish, madam," Anne said.

"I never interfere in Arthur's work, as he never interferes with mine."

She exited to the entry hall, and their voices together, murmuring, whispered into the room. Anne exchanged a look with Osei; what was passing between the spouses? She was his confidante, and perhaps shared with him her opinions of the people they met.

Dr. Fothergill entered and bowed, much more tidy and presentable than the night before in sober dark blue breeches and coat, his cravat tied neatly. "Sit, sit," he said to Osei—who had stood as he entered—after introductions. His dark brown eyes alight with interest—his obvious kindness and intelligence transformed his plain face to one of benevolent good looks—he examined Osei's visage for a moment. "My wife says she hears a trace of Africa in your voice, sir. Is she right?"

"She is! I had fooled myself that I had developed the accent of a proper Englishman," he said with a rueful smile.

"There *is* no inflection of a *proper* Englishman. We are a muddle of accents on this island, not one better than the other. But one thing is true: my wife is exceptionally good at tracing origins through voice, a talent of hers. She has worked with many Africans in London and Bath as well as former slaves from the Caribbean colonies, a part of her mission with our people."

"*Our people?*" Anne interjected.

"The Quakers," Dr. Fothergill replied.

"Oh, yes, I had heard that you were of the Society of Friends," Anne said.

The doctor turned back to Osei. "Where are you from, then? If you don't mind me asking."

"I don't mind at all, sir." Osei explained his origin in the coastal region of Africa, an area south of the great Saharan desert. Though he didn't say it, Anne knew from their past conversations that Osei was named after a great emperor to whom he was related. He, of the

Fante people, had been sold into slavery by a warring tribe to his people, the Ashanti. Once on the slave ship transporting him toward the sugar plantations of the West Indies the conditions were poor and many of his people fell ill, so the slavers, intent on killing them all to claim the insurance, began to throw the alive overboard with the dead. When he had briefly recounted the awful tale, Osei said, "That is how my employer, the Marquess of Darkefell, became my employer. It was he and his brother, Lord Julian, who jumped in the water and saved several of us, including me. He brought me to his estate. I was ill and I still have a limp from an injury sustained in the fall, but he helped me get better. I learned the language from him and his household staff." His recitation, repeated many times over the years, was swift and precise.

"Not just our language," Anne said. "Osei learned Latin, Greek, German and . . ." She eyed the secretary. "I know there are others, but I can't think what they are."

"It is no matter," Osei said, his face burnishing with a coppery hue. He cleared his throat and adjusted his spectacles. "I am very interested in your wife's work, sir. She mentioned a mission to eliminate slavery in the Caribbean. I lost all trace of my sister in the horrible events, as she was on a different ship than I. I have been looking for her ever since, approaching every society I can find to see if she has survived. Perhaps—"

"Of course Elizabeth would be pleased to help you," Dr. Fothergill said. "She, especially, has made every attempt to record the true names of those who were given new names when enslaved, and those who adopted English names to become part of our society. Come back another day and she will show you her list; it's somewhere to start. But . . . you didn't come here for that. How can I help you?"

"I have been deeply troubled all night over that poor fellow's death, Doctor," Anne said. "Have you discovered anything? Was it death by misadventure, a deliberate poisoning, accidental? He was unhappy, I know, because we chatted at length after church on Sunday and he spoke of . . ." She hesitated, but continued, feeling sure her assertion would be kept secret. Softly she said, "He spoke of sins that would finish his calling as a vicar, sins that would be unforgiveable if people knew. He was *deeply* depressed. I dislike saying it, but . . . could his death be attributed to deliberate self-harm?"

He tapped his fingers on his knee and twisted his mouth. It was a serious matter, the thought of suicide, a sin and a crime with grave repercussions for the family of the deceased. "I make no claims, and will not speculate. But I found a most curious thing when I examined the poor lad."

Anne waited, breath bated, watching the physician. Finally, when he hesitated, she said, "Please, sir, do not spare me the details. I am a woman, but no fainting flower."

He smiled at that. "I did not assume so, my lady. Any married man does—or should—know the strength of the female of our species, and a married physician knows even more. I have helped my wife bear children, though the help consisted of sitting by her side while another woman did all of the labor of helping her birth them—no man midwife for her!—and also deliver the few we lost. I have been by the side of other women who strained and suffered to bear children who would see light of day only to die, and I know they would abide the physical pain a *hundred* times to save the life of their child. I have seen women stitch wounds, clean every kind of effluent the body produces, and all without a murmur. I *know* the strength of women."

She was silent in the face of his good-humored acknowledgment of feminine strength.

"I hesitate for the sake of the young man and his family. What I have to say has grave consequences, and I have learned never to rush into pronouncing what cannot be taken back."

"I understand, Dr. Fothergill," Anne said. "But let me assure you; as I rely on *your* discretion in what I have told you, so no matter what you tell me, no one shall know it but us three unless you wish it shared."

Osei nodded. "Lady Anne speaks the truth."

"We are both exceptionally accomplished at keeping secrets."

The doctor nodded, accepting their assurances. "I will take you at your word, though I have learned in my life that secrets are impossible to keep secret. However, I will tell you. In my opinion the young man died from ingesting *taxus baccata* in sufficient amount to poison him."

"*Taxus baccata* . . . what is that?"

"The yew," Osei said.

"The yew . . . as in the yew tree?" Anne exclaimed.

"Does that mean anything to you?" the doctor said, watching her closely, his observant gaze on her face.

"I do know it is poisonous. In fact, Mr. Lonsdale and I walked together in the churchyard of St. Swithin and he pointed out an ancient example of the tree; he . . . he said it was known as the Tree of Death."

They were all silent. Had that been the moment a distraught young man recalled the yew's toxic properties and decided to make use of it? Self-destruction was not, though, the only possibility here. Lonsdale had spoken to her in serious tones of a moral dilemma, of making a choice that would potentially hurt someone he loved—though it would be the right thing to do—or do nothing, and others he cared nothing for would suffer. And he had indicated last night that his soul was calm, for he had decided to do the right thing. At what cost? She pondered, in that moment, the potent enmity between him and Mr. Roger Basenstoke; what if Lonsdale knew something about the fellow, something that would expose him to the law? How much would that hurt Mrs. Clary Basenstoke, whom he loved like a mother, if Lonsdale exposed Basenstoke to justice?

"Dr. Fothergill, I . . . ." She stopped, unsure what to say, how to reveal her deepest fears. It was hideous to speculate on the inevitable direction her thoughts were taking; was she really pondering the possibility that someone had deliberately poisoned Mr. Lonsdale to keep him from doing what he had decided to do? The moral thing, he had said, the one that would hurt someone he loved. She didn't know enough about him to know if there were others who fit that description. "Dr. Fothergill, I am *deeply* concerned, I will not conceal that. It seems to me there is no natural way he could have ingested such a poison, so what you are suggesting leaves us with two possibilities."

He nodded. "I'm afraid I concur, my lady. This was either self-destruction, and I would not like his family to know it was that, or it was murder."

There was little else they could glean from the doctor, for he would not speculate on how Lonsdale ingested the yew. A note came for him by hand as Osei and Anne rose to leave. The doctor appeared angered by the note.

"What is it, Doctor?" Osei asked.

"I sent a note to the Basenstoke household last night, to tell them I had that poor fellow's body, and it appears Mr. Roger Basenstoke is furious. He is threatening legal action."

"On what grounds?" Anne asked.

"Theft of a body." The doctor was shaking, and appeared to be attempting to calm his fury. "He says if I do not return Mr. Lonsdale's body immediately he will have no choice but to accuse me of being a cadaver thief, set on unnatural means to further my despicable research."

"That is outrageous!" Anne exclaimed.

Dr. Fothergill took a deep breath and let it out slowly. In a calmer tone, he said, "For some the body made flesh is sacred. It is a subject concerning which I must be delicate. We don't know; his mother could be the one who is upset with me. I will do my best to smooth it over."

"We must be going, sir; I apologize for any trouble you may have with Roger Basenstoke."

"My lady, worry not. I know what I did was right, and gave us answers we would not have had otherwise."

"What will you do with that knowledge, sir?"

He frowned. "I'm not sure yet. I will ponder that as I prepare young Lonsdale's body for his family."

Chapter Fourteen

The carriage, with Mary inside, awaited them at the doctor's door. "Would you come with me to John and Lydia's, Osei?" Anne asked as he helped her up the two steps.

"I would be happy to, my lady."

Once ensconced and on their way to Milsom Street, she discovered that Mary's business was satisfactorily concluded. She bore with her a trunk containing two of Anne's new gowns, as well as two bonnets, gloves, and a fan suitable for the theater. "Remarkable! To sew the two gowns in such good time Mrs. McKellar must have stayed up all night, and then she had the foresight and kindness to obtain the other items for me as well."

"I'd wager she employed help, milady," Mary said. "She's a canny businesswoman and ambitious; she knows the value of such trade as yours. She'd no' want to disappoint you."

Anne turned to Osei. "It was lovely of you to come with us to church Sunday. Lydia was overjoyed to see you."

"Bath seems to have made me a desirable companion to her," he rejoined dryly.

"She has come to appreciate your perfect good humor. I wonder if Lolly is still ensconced on Milsom? I haven't heard from her." Their stop at Milsom was in vain. No one was home, Anne was informed at the door by the maid. *No* one. "Neither Lady Lydia nor Lord John?"

Nor Miss Broomhall, who had gone out with Lady Lydia, the maid said with a curtsey.

Anne returned to the carriage. "Unusual," she said, settling her gown about her. "Lydia has complained about her inability to go anywhere."

"Mayhap having Miss Lolly there has enabled her to go out and about," Mary suggested.

"But *I* am available; she knows that. I would do *anything* for her."

Mary glanced at her but remained silent.

"What is it? Speak your mind, Mary!"

"Milady, Miss Broomhall is the sort that Lady John would find a comfort, especially in her state, and it may be easier to feel that she is not imposing with Miss Broomhall."

"You're likely right. Let us return to Pierrepont Place, for I wish to call on Mr. and Mrs. Birkenhead, to make sure my friends are recovering from the shock and horror of last night." She had another motive. Who but his closest friends might know if Mr. Lonsdale was likely to kill himself? Two stops would hopefully tell her much, this to his friends and one to the Basenstoke home, to see how Clary was doing after the death of her nephew, upon whom it appeared she doted. Perhaps she could ascertain if Roger's note to the doctor had been prompted by Clary or was his own broadside.

Knowing what it was that likely killed Lonsdale worried her. If it wasn't by his own hand, who could do such a thing? Who had the knowledge necessary to concoct the poison and the opportunity to give it to Lonsdale? Perhaps reconstructing Lonsdale's day would give her some insight and questioning those closest to him would reveal his frame of mind.

The Pierrepont house was transformed by mourning, the knocker off the door and straw quieting the cobbles. A maid was keeping watch, recognized Anne, and let her in. She asked Osei to accompany her and sent Mary home with her burdens to organize Anne's winter wardrobe.

She and Osei were shown into the sitting room that overlooked the narrow street outside. Alethea, solemn and gowned in dark gray, entered. Anne, her composure broken by her friend's evident suffering, advanced across the room and embraced her. Alethea sobbed on her shoulder for a moment, then Anne held her at arm's length, examining her face. Lines and dark circles under her lovely eyes were a haunting visual reminder of the pain of losing a close friend. "How are you, my dear one? Did you sleep at all? How is Bertie?"

Alethea didn't answer, she just shook her head. There was a dragging sound in the hall, and Quin, carrying a book, hobbled into the sitting room, looking wan and weary, his thin frame trembling with the exertion of joining them. Always attentive to her brother-in-law, Alethea bid them all sit, as Anne introduced Osei to them both. They sat close to the fire, the blaze warding off the foggy miasma that enveloped Bath as the day progressed.

"How *is* Bertie?" Anne repeated, after assuring herself that her friends were doing as well as could be expected after the trauma of the previous night.

"He is devastated," Alethea said. "There is no other word for it."

"He seemed particularly attached to Lonsdale, as to a son or nephew," Anne commented. "I knew him but little, however he was an exceedingly polite gentleman, good company. We strolled in St. Swithin's churchyard for a time on Sunday and I came to know him somewhat. Tell me, did he seem unduly distressed to you lately?"

Alethea and Quin exchanged glances.

"He was troubled over his future," Quin said. He passed one hand over his forehead and squinted. "He was unsure he would be able to find a position as a vicar. No livings had been offered so far."

It was more than that, Anne knew from their conversation. Perhaps he had not confided in them, not wishing to worry them unduly. But it was too late to be sensitive to that; the young man was dead, and she wanted to know why. These people who loved him would surely feel the same. "Perhaps that explains something he said to me," she said, watching them both. "He seemed set on disavowing his profession. I know I can speak frankly in this company, or I would not repeat his words, but he spoke of . . . of sins he had committed that made him ineligible for the post. He seemed to think he would be stripped of his theological standing in the Church of England. What could he have meant by that?"

Alethea shook her head and Quin frowned. And yet . . . Anne could see there was something they were not telling her, something they both knew but would not share. Youthful indiscretions? Gambling debts? A secret family of illegitimate children? Not one of those possibilities fit with what she knew of the fellow. She was frustrated by their silence, but how could she blame them for keeping the secrets of a friend now unable to defend himself?

"It's too bad. I felt he was on the point of sharing his burden with me, but we were interrupted," she mused, still watching their faces. Perhaps if they thought Lonsdale was about to confide in her it would reassure them, and it was naught but the truth. But it was no good. She hesitated about revealing what else he had said, about his moral dilemma, and later the decision he had made regarding it. She'd have to think about that.

They spoke of other things for a moment, and Anne raised the topic of Thomas Graeme. "He will certainly be wounded by Mr. Lonsdale's death; they seemed close friends. Bertie appears to dislike Mr. Graeme, though I can't imagine why." She stole a glance at her friends. "He was *most* put out the other night when Lonsdale invited him to the musical evening with the Italian singer. There was an argument; I think Bertie demanded that Graeme leave."

"Anne, what is this?" Alethea asked, her expression hardening into something perilously close to anger. "Why the questions? What are you saying?"

Anne cocked her head and examined her friend. The sudden spurt of annoyance could be completely innocent, brought on by sadness and emotional fragility, or it could be something else, borne of some awareness that there were secrets among friends that could invite grim interpretations. Anne wasn't sure why she felt it was the latter, but it was there, in Alethea's irrational anger. It didn't mean there was any actual guilt or knowledge of guilt, but secrets led to more secrets in her experience. "I'm not *saying* anything, my friend. I'm trying to decipher things I have noticed that seem odd, or unexplainable. Among them Bertie's reaction to Mr. Graeme; as much as your husband says the young fellow is 'not quite the thing,' he did not appear to merit resolute banishment and an argument between two friends as close as Bertie and Lonsdale. I am merely . . . curious."

"I think your curiosity is vulgar," Alethea said, her tone harsh.

"Alethea, please," Quin pleaded. "Lady Anne is our friend; she means nothing bad, I'm sure."

"Quin doesn't know you as I do, does he?" the woman said, glaring at Anne.

Alethea could be hotheaded and impulsive, attributes that had made the two girls close if troublesome companions at a young age. As with many girls, they could be passionately attached friends, then quarrel and become mortal enemies for a time, enlisting other girls into their war; that's the way it was at a boarding school for young ladies, warring factions using rumor and scandalous gossip in the place of swords or bullets. Then a sudden shift; something would bring them together and they would be friends again. Alethea was tempestuous with a brittle temper, but it would not last.

"I don't mean to intrude," Anne said, her tone gentle.

But Alethea's anger had been roused and for the moment the fire could not be smothered. "I know you fancy yourself more intelligent than the rest of us, but you have brought your suspicious prying into my home, and I don't like it."

Her words, razor sharp, stung. "I do *not* think, Alethea, that I'm more clever than others. You should know better. Don't be so . . . so . . . ." She stopped and shook her head. She had been drawn into patterns from their school days, and those were long gone. With sympathy she watched Alethea's expression; her friend was only holding herself together with a great effort. "I'll not quarrel with you, my dear friend," she said gently. "I'm so deeply sorry for your loss."

Osei said, his tone mild and placating, "I cannot help but fear that my presence here is contributing to some misunderstanding, that you cannot speak as freely as you would if I, a stranger, were gone." He glanced back and forth between the two women. "I will leave soon enough and then two such close and dear friends as you ladies clearly are can set your differences aside and make peace." He glanced over at Quin. "As rude as it may be for me to thrust myself forward, I would beg a boon, Mr. Birkenhead. I have recently secured a townhome for my employer in Bath and wish to understand the city before he arrives in a few days. Would it be too much to ask for your assistance? I sense in you a like-minded individual, judging by your reading matter."

The tension in the room wavered and shimmered, but began to dissipate.

Quin smiled faintly. "Mr. Boatin, you find me out." He held up what he was reading, his finger inserted where he had stopped and a pair of spectacles dangling from his other hand. "It is a book given to me by my doctor's wife, a published collection of letters by the late Ignatius Sancho, who passed a few years ago."

"I have read it," Osei said, without mentioning that they had met the doctor's wife that very morning. "He was an accomplished writer and had much to offer to Britons on the subject of those of us born in Africa who now dwell in your country."

Quin frowned. "But how can *I* help you discover the city? You see in me a wreck of a man, barely able to tolerate a carriage ride."

"My employer has allowed me funds to hire a carriage at any time, and I have found a livery that has superior well-sprung vehicles. An hour of your time would give me a better knowledge of the city for my employer's benefit."

"Why not let Lady Anne guide you?" Alethea said, her frostiness a little thawed. "She certainly knows the city."

"Not as well as Quin," Anne said. "I have spent relatively little time here over the most recent years."

Quin put his hand on his sister-in-law's to stay her. "I would be delighted, Mr. Boatin. Alethea, dear, it may help me get my mind off poor Lonsdale. I feel certain I will be safe with this gentleman."

"Perhaps tomorrow then?" Osei said, rising. "I will be guided by you. I understand you must be available to your brother in a time such as this, when he has lost a close and dear friend."

"Tomorrow is perfectly fine."

Anne rose too. There was no point in staying. She turned and to her friend said, "Alethea, I mean no harm. I trust your love of me to know that, in your heart." Her voice broke there, and she cleared her throat. "I will leave now too, and pray I have not offended in a deep sense. I'm going to see Mrs. Clary Basenstoke this afternoon. May I carry any message, or word from you and Bertie? Or has your husband visited there today, perhaps?"

"I think Bertie went there this morning to pay his condolences. But . . . thank you for the kind offer," Alethea said. Her lip trembled and tears welled. She sniffed. "I didn't mean to snap. I feel . . . last night was so dreadful . . ." She trailed off and caught back a sob.

"I understand, my friend," Anne said, hugging her close. "We'll take our leave."

The carriage was awaiting them by the door. They mounted, heading back to Anne's grandmother's house. "Thank you, Osei, for your brilliant intervention," Anne said. She waved to her friend, who stood in the window, then closed the curtain and turned back to the secretary. "Alethea was very angry with me, I'm afraid, and I'm not sure I understand why. What did I say or do to make her so full of ire?"

"I don't think it was anything in particular you said, but . . . may I be frank, Lady Anne?"

"Please do, Osei."

"When you are on the trail—pardon me and understand I truly mean no disrespect—you get a sharp look in your eyes and in your tone. It can seem intrusive, though you don't intend it so. You almost *quiver* with excitement and curiosity and your eyes shine."

"Add that my nose gets wet and you will make me sound like a hunting dog, Mr. Boatin!" she said with a laugh.

"You are offended! I'm sorry, my lady."

"Not at all, Osei, not at all. Dogs and cats are better than most humans I know. But you *have* given me food for thought. I understand how that would feel from Alethea's aspect, when I consider that Lonsdale was a dear friend. My eagerness in the hunt for a solution may have seemed . . . indelicate. I was tactless and forward. I will try to restrain the quivering and sharp look in future."

She returned home to have an afternoon meal and allow Mary to fit some of her new gowns. As she dined with her mother in the woman's room, the countess, looking decidedly weary, did not engage in her usual tittle-tattle.

"Mother, is everything all right?"

The woman looked across the small table. "I suppose I'm saddened by the news of that poor young man. Clary must be devastated. Alfred was like a son to her."

"He seemed such a lovely young man."

"He was. I knew him, of course. Since he arrived in Bath he had often accompanied Clary on her visits here. He was special in so many ways, ways few in society would appreciate."

"What does that mean?"

Her mother simply shook her head, her expression pensive. "I can't explain. He and Clary were close, especially with Roger being as he is."

"As he is?"

"Cold as a codfish. Roger is a good son, but he lacks any depth of feeling."

"I'm surprised to hear you say that, Mother. I did not think that you would have counted that against him." Her mother was not the soul of warmth herself.

"I know what you think of me, Anne," she said, raising her head and glaring at her daughter. "But I have had troubles in my life, things you will never understand."

"I know Jamey is a trial to you, but—"

"*Don't!*" The countess, trembling, stared down at the tablecloth as she raised one hand, palm toward Anne. "Not now. I wish not to speak of this today, please. If you are done . . . ?"

Anne nodded. "Mother, I . . ." She wasn't sure what to say so instead she simply stood, circled the table, and put one hand on her mother's shoulder. It quivered under her touch. "I'll give Clary your sympathies, shall I?"

"Yes, and tell her she can come to me if she needs to talk."

"I will do that."

After a word with her grandmother, Anne engaged the carriage once again. The Basenstokes lived in a newer elegant townhome on Walcot Parade, not a long distance and walkable, but she had other destinations in mind. The fog had burned off. A weak stream of sunlight broke through the clouds, but the day still felt gloomy and damp. The knocker was off the townhome, and an air of desolation clung to the residence.

Anne was known to Mrs. Basenstoke's staff, though, and as the daughter of the mistress's oldest friend she was allowed in. She sent her card in and was summoned to the sitting room on the ground floor.

"Anne, oh, Anne, how good of you to come," Clary cried, standing and holding out her arms.

They hugged and then sat, Clary in a gilt wood armchair upholstered in the delicious figured silk she preferred, Anne opposite her in a morocco leather chair. They were by the window, mellow October light now streaming in through sheer draperies. "Mother sends her warmest regards. You are to go to her when you are able. She hopes she will find you comforted by your family's support through this?" Anne let her tone rise, obliquely asking about Roger's treatment of his mother through a wretched ordeal.

Clary reached over and grabbed Anne's gloved hands, squeezing and staring at her steadily. Mrs. Basenstoke had prominent eyes, dark and lustrous, damp at the moment with unshed tears. "Do you speak of Roger?"

"I hope he has been a comfort to you?"

She dropped Anne's hands and sighed, staring out the window. "I wish . . ." She shook her head.

"You can talk to me, Mrs. Basenstoke."

"Clary, my dear; call me Clary. I know others retreat behind our society's veil of correct behavior, but that is a chilly and lonely place to live."

"Clary, then," Anne said with a smile.

"Do you know, I saw you when you were just days old," the woman reminisced. "By then Barbara already knew Jamey was . . . was going to have problems. You were her saving grace, her beautiful girl."

Anne tried not to show how startled she was. That she should be anyone's saving grace, much less her mother's, was staggering.

"I know you don't realize it, but Barbara loves you dearly . . . in her own way." Clary paused and frowned. "She loves Jamey too, as much as she is able." Clary had neatly avoided speaking of Roger.

"Mother says you were close to your nephew, and that Mr. Lonsdale was a wonderful young man. Are you . . . have you heard how he died?"

Trembling, she nodded. "Mr. Birkenhead was here an hour ago." She clutched her hands together in her lap and sobbed. "He t-told me how poor Alfred died. It's appalling!"

Anne thought of her conversation with Dr. Fothergill. "What did Bertie . . . Mr. Birkenhead say?"

"That poor Alfred died of a digestive ailment, sudden and violent."

Anne nodded. "Truly terrible. I was there and saw him. He suffered only briefly, as far as I can tell, apart from the digestive upset that had plagued him all day."

"But what could have done it?"

"Something he ingested, or some undiscovered ailment exacerbated by something else, perhaps," Anne said, keeping her word to the doctor not to discuss the yew poisoning. "Did he eat with you that morning?"

She smiled weakly, tears glittering in her eyes as she folded her hands together on her lap. "We eat . . . we *ate* together nearly every morning, toast and tea. He was a good boy for a comfortable coze."

"And you did so that morning?"

Clary gazed at Anne with a furrowed brow and nodded. "Roger joined us, though . . . so unusual. He is most mornings gone by the time Alfred and I take . . . took . . . our morning tea and toast. He says he cannot bear our gossip and tittle-tattle."

"But that morning he ate with you?"

"He was most kind," she said. "He even poured. Made a little joke out of it."

A joke . . . Roger Basenstoke joking and pouring tea. Anne's heart thumped as she recalled Lonsdale saying he had a moral dilemma that would, if he spoke out, hurt someone he loved. He loved Mrs. Basenstoke like a mother, and what would hurt her could be something concerning her son. "What was the joke?"

"Something about being the lady of the house."

"Mr. Basenstoke said that?" Clary nodded. "What were Alfred's plans for the day?" Anne asked.

"The usual, I suppose. Go to his club, the Pump Room, see friends."

"But he didn't say anything specific?" As Clary shook her head, Anne said, "Did you see him again that day?"

She again shook her head, one tear coursing down her cheek. "Breakfast was the last I saw him. Roger said he had something to speak to Alfred about and asked where he'd be."

"Did he reply?"

"They walked out together. I don't know if he replied; Alfred seemed . . . dismayed."

"How has he been recently . . . Mr. Lonsdale, I mean? Was he his usual self? Was he upset over anything?"

Pensive, Clary stared out the window. "Something was troubling the dear boy. Something grave. I'll never know what it was now. I let him fret, thinking he'd come to me when he wished to speak of it. Now it's over, and I cannot go back and ask." She sighed and shook her head. "I suppose it doesn't matter. When we leave this world, our troubles leave with our spirit." She turned and frowned, staring at Anne. "Mr. Birkenhead asked the same thing when he visited. Why are you both asking the same things, about Alfred's humor lately? Is there something I don't know about how he died?"

"I'm sure I couldn't say, Clary. Truly. I *cannot* speculate," she added, which was the exact truth; she could not speculate or speak of it because of her promise to the doctor. She twitched her lips. What she would give to look into Lonsdale's room, but to ask would be too peculiar. Maybe she could find a way, but it wouldn't be today. "Bertie is distressed, I think, that Mr. Lonsdale died in his home. They were close."

"Yes, closer than I was aware."

"We're all looking for meaning in his death . . . so young, and gone so tragically."

"He *has* been . . . sad lately. Out of sorts. I know Roger was hard on him—"

"How so?"

"My son is . . . *was* jealous, I think, of my regard for my nephew. But that may be a fond mother's interpretation. I have no real foundation upon which to lay such a charge. Roger was unfair to dear Alfred, *terribly* unfair. He called him weak. He said the boy was manipulating me, that he needed to stiffen his spine and behave in a manner to make his family proud, rather than one that would bring distress and humiliation on us all."

Distress? Humiliation? That seemed excessive, Anne thought. It made her pause; as far as the little she had known of Lonsdale he had seemed mild, intelligent, friendly. Maybe she had too easily translated that to imply every noble attribute possible, but if so the Birkenheads had been similarly fooled, for her friends loved him. "What did he mean by that?"

Clary shrugged helplessly. "I don't know. He would never say when I asked. But that is why I was so pleased that morning when Roger took an interest in Alfred. It was what I had been hoping for."

"I don't like to pry, Clary, but were you offended that Dr. Fothergill took charge of Mr. Lonsdale's body? Did it upset you?"

"Not at all. It was kind of him to take charge, and so I said to him in the note I sent."

"You sent a note?"

"Roger said I should. *He* was upset that Dr. Fothergill had taken poor Alfred's body with him. He thought I should object. That is what he wanted me to say, but how could I? The doctor was doing his duty."

"So you didn't object?"

"Of course not."

"I'm surprised that if your son objected, he didn't write to the doctor himself. Isn't it his place to do so?"

Clary knew what she meant, of course; as her son and closest male relative, Roger Basenstoke had say over much in her life. She frowned. "He . . . he seemed unwilling, for some reason. I don't know why. As my son, and Alfred's cousin, it truly is his place."

Anne considered that. It was unlike the man to shrink from giving his opinion. Was there a reason he didn't want to be the one to protest the doctor's presumption in taking charge of Lonsdale's body? He ultimately did, so why the hesitation? "What did you say in your note?"

"That I was relieved a man of medicine had been there, though it had been too late, and I hoped he would visit me at some point."

That explained Roger's note castigating the doctor, then. It had been written because he could not bully his mother into doing so. It was interesting that Clary's note did not arrive by the same messenger. Try as she might, Anne could not erase her suspicion of Mr. Basenstoke's behavior the very morning of Lonsdale's death. Why would a man who loathed another suddenly pour him tea and desire a private chat?

Chapter Fifteen

Anne took her leave and headed to Lydia and John's home. Lydia and Lolly were home, answering her question about whether Lolly was staying on with the Bestwicks. She was shown to the comfortable sitting room and took a chair by the window overlooking Milsom. It was a busy street, with shoppers strolling, servants bustling, the occasional carriage trundling past, but many more in sedan chairs hefted by broad-shouldered chairmen. With a lively mix of townhomes and shops, it was an ideal home for Lydia, who loved nothing more than to meet and socialize with new people and old friends alike.

Anne thought back to John's request that she intercede for him with Tony to allow them to take over management of their Cornwall property. She would try, she decided, knowing that Yorkshire was grim for a society-loving young lady like Lydia. She wasn't sure yet how much persuasive power she had with her fiancé, but she could test it and see.

Lydia, followed by Lolly, entered after twenty minutes or so. Lydia wore a capacious *robe volante*, or "flying robe," a style from France that was perfectly accommodating for her delicate state. It was of lovely figured green silk, and she looked so beautiful, with her chestnut curls in a tumble and her lovely eyes lowered under fluttering thick lashes.

"You are so lovely, my dear," Anne exclaimed. "You look well."

They exchanged embraces, and Lolly made Lydia comfortable in a sturdy chair near the fireplace, which had a cheery blaze. It suited her friend to have someone fuss over her, Anne decided, and Lolly was the perfect candidate for that position. Perhaps this would be a solution for Lolly's lengthy descent into genteel poverty. If John would allow Lolly to become Lydia's permanent companion, both would be happy.

After exchanging news since the day before—she did not mention Lonsdale's tragic death, as Lydia disliked tragedy in any form, in or out of the theater—Anne sat back and regarded her friend. "I dropped in this morning and found you both out. I was surprised. You are not in general an early riser, Lydia." The two ladies exchanged furtive looks, like naughty schoolgirls found pillaging the box of sugarplums. It was most disconcerting.

"I had some shopping to do, and Lolly was kind enough to accompany me," she said in her most innocent voice.

"Shopping. In your condition."

A mulish expression muddied Lydia's sweet countenance. She rested one hand on her protuberant belly and glared at Anne. "Yes, *shopping*. I have a baby coming. I wish to be sure the nursery is fitted. I . . . I wanted to buy some things for after the baby is born, for m-me, for . . . why must you question me, Anne?"

"I'm sorry, my dear, I did not mean to pry."

Lydia's expression became sunny. "Let us talk of other things. Osei has been by; he says that he found a townhome for the marquess."

"Yes, that is true."

"And Darkefell is to come to Bath?"

"I believe so."

"And will you announce your engagement soon?"

Anne stared at her friend. "*Now* who is being the questioner?" she said with a teasing tone.

Lydia fidgeted, her cheeks blushing. "Anne, do you ever think of Reginald?" she asked. Lydia's brother, Anne's former fiancé, was lost around the time of the Battle of Yorktown. He was not lost in any heroic action, as his family would have it, but for her friend's sake Anne kept up the fiction of a dashing army officer tragically dying for his country. A child at the time of the engagement, Lydia had been looking forward to having Anne as a big sister, but their deeper friendship began a few years after Reginald's death, when Lydia came out in society. The young woman's dainty prettiness won her much interest, but of them all Lord John Bestwick was not only the best in every practical sense, it was a true love match.

Wishing to not wound her friend's sensitive soul, Anne said, "Certainly, I think of Reggie often. He was dear to me. Why do you ask?"

Lydia's eyes widened and her breathing became more rapid. How odd, Anne thought, watching her young friend. What was wrong with the girl?

"No reason. How he would laugh to see me thus," she said, indicating her distended belly.

If he did, it would be the height of rudeness, Anne thought, but bit her tongue. She watched her friend, and then her cousin. Something was up between these two, and it had to do with their spurious shopping trip that morning. She would discover the answer one way or another.

They had tea, and Lolly fussed happily over Lydia. Her cousin's place in the Bestwick household seemed to be secure at least until the child was born, when a special nurse would be engaged. Whenever Anne tried to return to the topic of their mysterious shopping trip that morning, the subject was changed or ignored. Lolly was more skilled at obfuscation and circumlocution than Lydia and could talk about nothing for half an hour, exhausting even the most determined questioner. At length, Anne gave up on discovering the truth from either of them and rose to leave. John arrived home from his club and greeted her warmly. She made her farewells to the ladies, as her future brother-in-law invited her to come into his library for a moment. He had something to ask of her.

His library was a dark chilly chamber of wood and leather, smelling of tobacco, but with few books. John was as different from Darkefell as ever a brother could be. Tending toward portliness, pale of visage and mild of manner, he adored Lydia, and expected nothing more than that she should comport herself as a lady ought, meaning with delicacy and submission.

In Anne he knew that he had met a woman who surpassed him in intelligence, but to his credit he had never countered her strong will with ire, and often consulted her on the best way to take care of his wife when she was dejected, as happened relatively often. There was something on his mind, and as there was something on Anne's mind, too, they were well matched. She sat across the broad wood table behind which he sat, and stared at him.

"Tony will be in Bath soon, Osei says," John started with.

"Yes, in a few days. He has a house now, at least. Will your mother accompany him, do you think?"

He shook his head. "Autumn is a difficult time for her always. She begins to withdraw."

Anne simply nodded. She and the dowager marchioness had spoken of the woman's troubled mind, and Anne now understood her better than she once had. She was surprised that Lady Sophia would not be in Bath to welcome her first grandchild, but she had ever been hard on Lydia, and her presence would agitate the younger woman, so maybe her restraint was best. John looked troubled. "Is everything all right, John? You're not worrying about Lydia, are you? If it helps any, I think Lolly is good for her . . . an excellent companion."

He nodded. "I'm happy that she has Miss Broomhall. And yes, I'm worried. She won't tell me where she was this morning. At first I thought maybe there were things I didn't know . . . things of a delicate nature. But she has never been shy of telling me anything before."

"Did you ask your coachman?"

"Of course. He said he dropped her and your cousin off in front of Miss Broomhall's home. Why would she not tell me that herself? Perhaps it was to pick up some things from Miss Broomhall's home to make her stay here more comfortable?"

Another explanation occurred to Anne, but she didn't want to divulge it to John until she was sure. "If I find out, I'll let you know, as long as it is not compromising Lydia's privacy." He bridled and she hastened to add, "Please don't take that amiss! I merely mean . . . perhaps she is, oh . . . ordering a gift for you for your birthday, or, as you said, doing something of a private nature before she is confined to her bed."

Mollified, he nodded.

"The most likely explanation is that she wished for an outing, a breath of fresh air before her confinement." She rose and watched him for a moment. "Is anything else troubling you, John? Is it just Lydia?"

He sighed. "I feel I can be frank with you, Lady Anne; the thought of Tony living in Bath at the same time as my wife and I is . . . daunting. He is a strong character, as you know, and though I feel I have become known in Bath and appreciated on my own merits, when he comes I will be back to being an insignificant person in the eyes of society."

"John, you have little to fear. I have been in Bath enough to know that Tony will not find many friends here. At first all will dance attendance on him in honor of his title and position, but after, the whispers will begin. He is not suited to Bath. In fact he is more likely to mortally offend all the old gossips of this town than to make conquests. And I promise you, your amiable charm is more winning and likely to please true Bathonians, who value good humor and good manners, neither of which Darkefell has in abundance."

"How well you know my brother," he said and smiled, seeming relieved. "And yet still, you will marry him. I suppose you know what you are doing?" He peered at her anxiously.

She smiled. "Yes, I'm perfectly aware of what I am doing. We shall suit."

"Perhaps it is that I have so rarely been away from home for any length of time, but I have enjoyed staying here. The people of Bath have been uncommonly welcoming."

"John, my advice to you is, you will win a host of friends by being your friendly, uncomplicated self. Don't change, and you will continue to be admired and accepted."

Anne said her goodbyes, but before leaving she had the maid send for Lolly. She was going to get to the bottom of this, now that she had a good idea of where the two had been, and what they had been doing.

Chapter Sixteen

She awaited her cousin in the carriage outside. Lolly climbed in and faced Anne. "What is it, cousin? I must get back to Lydia. I dislike leaving the poor girl alone."

"Lolly, I know where you and Lydia went this morning."

Flustered, the older woman stayed silent, her gaze darting from side to side and finally fixing on the knot fastening her fluffy shawl at her waist. She tugged and worried at it.

She was not going to volunteer the information. "You and Lydia went to the mystic again. Why?" Anne asked. "What did you ask? Or what did she tell you?"

"Oh, you know, the usual thing," Lolly said, fidgeting and not meeting Anne's gaze. "To be sure that Lydia will be safely delivered of a healthy baby, which is all any young woman cares for, you know, not whether it is a boy or girl, or if it has dark eyes or light, or if it has hair or is bald, as so many babies are. You know it never ceases to amaze me that so many children who later grow great thatches of hair are born with none. Why you yourself, Anne, with that lovely thick —"

"Lolly!"

The woman stopped, flustered, but stayed silent.

"That is what the mystic told her last time. What would be the point to go again, just to be told the same thing?"

Still Lolly stayed silent.

"There is more, I know it."

She sighed and fidgeted again, then finally met Anne's gaze. She was going to tell the truth, . . . finally. Anne waited.

"I don't *know* what the mystic said to her."

"What?"

"I left the room. The mystic said she had a private message for Lady Lydia and that it was for her ears only. I was made to go out and wait in the anteroom, like last time."

"You didn't listen at the door?"

"I would *never*," Lolly exclaimed, pressing one hand to her bosom, offense writ in her astonished expression.

"I wonder if it had to do with Reginald? She hasn't spoken of him to me in ages and then suddenly today she did. Perhaps there is something there."

"Perhaps. I'm sure you have other things on your mind, my dear, what with your young friend dying."

"You know about that, do you?"

"Yes, we heard. Lord John said something."

"And it didn't upset Lydia?"

"Why would it? She did not know the young man."

It was true that with tragedies, it was knowledge of those affected that made one experience it more vividly. "He was a recent friend to me, but my dear friends the Birkenheads are in *great* distress. I am deeply saddened and mystified." She paused and looked out the carriage window. One of the horses whinnied and shifted; the carriage rocked. Anne looked back to Lolly. "Do you think Lydia can spare you for an hour? John is home now, and she has the household staff."

"I could ask her. What do you need, my dear girl?"

"I wish to go to the Pump Room. I have not done so since I arrived, and I wish to plumb the depths of the local gossip, you could say, concerning Mr. Lonsdale. There is something wrong there, some oddity. I wonder if there are people I could speak with who might have answers?" Anne had a certain person in mind in particular, but she was not about to share that unless necessary.

Lolly retreated inside and returned donning a warm cloak. Lydia was resting, she told Anne, and a maid was sitting with her for the moment. The two set out across town to the older section, once inhabited by upper-crust Romans living in Bath, and entered the ancient baths through the new portico, built earlier that year, strolling arm in arm to the Pump Room, where at any hour of the day all of the town's society was to be found. It was a good clear day and midafternoon, the perfect time to find the ailing and those who simply wished to be seen, to sample the mineral waters or to exchange news.

There was, of course, music, ubiquitous and adding to the roar of conversation, the din of laughter, the underlying whine of complaint, and ever-present hum of gossip. The sulphurous smell of the mineral water, the odor of bodies, and the overpowering scent of wig powder and perfume assailed her nose. But despite the noise and smell, appearing in the Pump Room was a necessity; it announced one's arrival in Bath. It was where you could be sure of seeing everyone you knew, at some point, if you were persistent enough to spend the morning.

Everyone knew Lolly and liked her, which is what Anne had counted on in taking her cousin along. They were stopped constantly as they strolled, Anne's gaze darting until she saw some she knew and wished to speak with. Subtly, she guided her cousin across the floor, past a septuagenarian in a Bath chair, his attendant bending over him to listen to his complaints, and a group of elderly ladies chattering like magpies, toward a couple who stood together arm in arm speaking in low tones.

"Mrs. Venables, Lord Kattenby, how nice to see you!" Anne cried. "Lord Kattenby, may I introduce my cousin, Miss Louisa Broomhall? Mrs. Venables, Miss Broomhall." She turned to her cousin. "Lolly, Mrs. Venables is cousin to my friend Mr. Birkenhead, of whom you've heard me speak." She turned back to the couple, who appeared slightly disconcerted at her determined hailing of them.

"Oh, you were at St. Swithin on Sunday. Your banns were posted! How *exciting*," Lolly chirped, clapping her hands together. "I do so love a wedding," she went on, clasping them before her in a prayerful attitude. "It gives one such *hope*, don't you think? Especially when the couple is . . ." She drifted off, perhaps about to say "older," then recalling that it was not, perhaps, the most complimentary or politic observation. The baron was closer to her age, but Mrs. Venables considerably younger.

The baron looked a little the worse for wear, Anne considered, examining him. He looked weary. Perhaps being engaged was too taxing for a man who had come to Bath for his health. She turned to Mrs. Venables. "You were not at Bertie and Alethea's last night, when the tragedy occurred," she said, concerning Lonsdale's death.

"No, we traveled out of Bath to see a house dear Kattenby is considering purchasing," Mrs. Venables said, clinging to her older beau.

"That took all day?"

Baron Kattenby cleared his throat and looked off across the room. Anne eyed him with surprise; his wan cheeks were pinkening.

"Er, we did not leave until late morning, and then . . ." He stuttered to a halt.

Mrs. Venables rescued him, patting his arm. "Indeed, we *were* gone most of the day," she said, looking up at the baron. "We stopped at an inn and . . . and had luncheon."

He cleared his throat again and looked down at her fondly. "It was lovely," he said, his tone warm with affection.

Anne examined them through narrowed eyes. An inn; perhaps they had partaken of more than luncheon. "But you wouldn't have been out after dark. It would be a dangerous carriage ride in that case. And cold!" Anne shivered dramatically.

"Oh, no, my lady," Kattenby said. "The house is a mere four miles from the edge of Bath, a quaint villa with a little land."

"And did you buy it?"

"I will think on it. I have not told anyone yet of my plans to settle —"

"We are talking it over," Mrs. Venables said, squeezing the baron's arm to her.

"And when *is* the joyous day?" Lolly asked.

"As a matter of fact, I was telling dear Kattenby that there is absolutely no reason to delay," Mrs. Venables said, placing her free hand on his upper arm. She brushed off a mote of dust and plucked at the fabric. "Neither of us has any impediments to marriage, and if we marry before the holiday season we can establish our home and be comfortable. I *long* to make a home for dear Kattenby, a home where we can be together every day."

That felt rehearsed, Anne reflected, as if it was an argument she had used on him to speed their courtship. She wondered, was the gentleman hesitant? Did his family object? She turned slightly and saw Mr. Thomas Graeme, who had appeared to be heading toward them, veer off to speak with an older gentleman who was at the pump for his cup of medicinal water. A well-dressed voluptuous lady drifted past, pausing by the pump to wait her turn; Graeme bowed to her, then introduced her to the gentleman. Graeme was one of those she had come to the Pump Room to speak with, but she didn't yet want to leave Mrs. Venables.

"Certainly where there are no impediments, there is no reason to delay," Anne replied to Mrs. Venables's statement. "Lord Kattenby, do you have family?"

"I have a son, Tedrick. He remains in London running our business. I wish him to meet dear Bella before we wed."

He was committed to her now though, having had the banns read. To jilt her would be to suffer immeasurably in society. "Would it be too difficult for him to make the journey to meet your bride-to-be? 'Tis not so far from London to Bath."

"He will be coming to spend a few days with me over the Christmas season, and I would like to introduce him to Bella then. He is dedicated to our business, and I should not wish to take him from London before then."

"All the more reason for us to marry *before*," Mrs. Venables argued. "Then I can make your house a *true* home for the holiday season."

Anne watched the baron; he seemed uncertain despite his obvious pleasure in her company. Was he regretting his haste in proposing and having the banns read? It was not too much to ask Mrs. Venables to put off their nuptials a couple of months, but she did not appear willing to wait. Such eagerness did her love great credit, but to Anne it seemed a sham. They were not amorous youths, straining at the leashes of parental authority, after all, but sober reasonable adults.

"How did you meet, if I may ask?" Lolly chirped brightly, looking from one to the other. "I do find such stories so entertaining."

"We met through mutual friends," Mrs. Venables said. She was becoming restive, her gaze darting about.

She wished to be away from them, Anne thought. Mayhap she didn't see any help from Anne or Lolly in hastening the gentleman to the altar.

"Mutual friends . . . how *interesting*," Lolly said. "Here, in the Pump Room, perhaps? Or at the Great Assembly Rooms? So ideal for making acquaintances, I always say. For how else are we to meet suitable gentlemen if we do not meet them through mutual friends?"

Lord Kattenby smiled upon Lolly and her friendly prattle. "Indeed, Miss Broomhall, how true." He turned to Anne. "Mutual friends, correct. I am reminded, my lady, that I do know a friend of yours. How is Mrs. Basenstoke, may I ask?"

"She is grieving over her nephew, Mr. Alfred Lonsdale."

"Yes, a great tragedy. Mrs. Venables told me of it this morning."

Bella cried, "I was devastated last evening when I returned to Bertie and Alethea's and learned the awful events."

"You must have returned very late?"

"We were invited to dinner with friends of Kattenby."

"Perhaps I should make a call on Mrs. Basenstoke," the baron said, blinking and looking down at Bella. "Would you like to join me, my dear?"

The woman didn't answer. Anne said, "It's awful for her, of course, and I'm sure a visit would be a great comfort. Do you know her *well*, sir?"

"At one time we knew each other very well indeed. Our sons are of an age and are friends."

"Roger Basenstoke and your son know each other?"

"Tedrick and he went to school together and attended the Inns at the same time. My son has a law background but takes care of our business currently. I feel deeply for her from the bottom of my heart. I did not know the gentleman well—the late Mr. Lonsdale—but I had heard nothing but good of him. Poor Clary is wounded deeply, no doubt; she has a tender heart."

He had used Mrs. Basenstoke's given name so casually . . . interesting. She glanced at Bella, whose expression was determinedly blank. "She is well enough physically, but mourning the nephew she considered almost like another son."

"I'm not sure a visit from me would be appropriate after all," the baron demurred. "We . . . uh . . . we were once closer than we are now. Please give her my regards when next you see her."

"I will do that, sir. But if you and Mrs. Venables should care to visit I'm *sure*—"

"Kattenby, we *should* be moving along," Bella said. "You know we are promised elsewhere."

"Ah, yes, of course, my dear," he said, patting her hand where it tugged at his jacket. He did not appear to be in any hurry to leave, though. "My lady, you asked about how Bella and I met; it is an interesting story. Most fortuitous, you know, how it occurred—"

"Kattenby!" Mrs. Venables said. "We will be late for our engagement."

"Certainly, my dear. Do you wish to attend the pump?"

"I wish you to take your second cup before we leave."

"So concerned for my health," he said with a fond smile. The baron bowed to Anne and moved a few steps away with his fiancée on his arm. "There is Mr. Thomas Graeme, the very fellow who introduced us to each other; we must say hello to him in passing. Do you know him, my lady?" he said, looking back to Anne. "Such a *delightful* fellow. A tea merchant. Done well to be so successful at such a young age."

Mr. Thomas Graeme interested Anne more and more; he popped up in conversation and in person as the mutual acquaintance of so many. "Perhaps we shall follow you," Anne said, tugging her cousin, as the engaged couple strolled toward the pump. "Lolly, you were saying how you wished to have a cup of the water for your dyspepsia."

"Did I?" Lolly said, startled. She caught Anne's wide-eyed glance. "Of course, my . . . dyspepsia. *So* alarming."

They followed the couple, catching up with them.

"You *must* take the waters, then, Miss Broomhall. It is supposed to aid in digestion greatly," Baron Kattenby said as he strolled at an easy pace. "Though I have not been feeling the good affects promised." He laid one hand over his waistcoat.

"You're not well?" Anne said, frowning.

"It is nothing at all, merely alarm over how his son will feel about our marriage, I am sure," Mrs. Venables said with a slight smile.

Many in Bath, Anne had noticed on past visits, seemed to suffer nothing more than excessive worry over their health brought on by a preoccupation with it. He could be one of them. Others tried to cure with the mineral waters overindulgence in wine or rich food, the curse of wealth. One glance across the Pump Room showed that Mr. Graeme was on the move, strolling toward the door. As he was her next target, there was no time to lose. "Come, Lolly, there is a line at the pump; let us promenade instead."

She took her cousin's arm and moved as quickly as her gown would allow. Lolly was out of breath and protesting by the time they had positioned themselves exactly where Anne wished. She turned and bumped into the young gentleman. "Mr. *Graeme*. I did not see you there. Good day, sir!"

The fellow bowed politely over her hand. "Lady Anne, how charming to meet you here!"

"I was visiting this establishment with my cousin. May I

introduce you to Miss Louisa Broomhall? Lolly, this is Mr. Thomas Graeme, tea merchant, I believe?"

"Yes, though you find me visiting Bath at my leisure."

Lolly peered at him steadily, a frown on her face.

"So successful that you can take time away from your business. How fascinating." Anne took his arm and turned, with him, so that he was rather forced to take Lolly's arm on his other side or appear abominably rude. "Let us perambulate," Anne said.

After a moment or two of chat, she paused by the brilliant light of the window and turned, watching his face. "I'm sure you must have heard by now the terrible news."

"News?"

"About Mr. Alfred Lonsdale. He has tragically died, and so young! I was there when he was found."

"I am devastated, of course. So young to meet his Maker." He sighed deeply, covering his heart with one hand and bowing his head, a theatrical stance of mourning. "I mourn him sincerely."

"You met at Eton, I remember one of you saying . . . or was it at a club?"

He started and opened his mouth, then closed it again.

"Had you seen him yesterday at all?" she asked, intent on reconstructing Lonsdale's day. She wondered if he was the acquaintance with whom he took a midday meal.

"One does, you know."

"One does *what?*"

"See people."

"Did you see him *yesterday?*"

"I believe I did, yes. Bath is a social town; one sees one's friends everywhere: here, the Assembly Rooms, the coffee house."

"Where were you when you met yesterday?"

He gazed steadily at her and cocked his head. "Why the inquisition, my lady?" he asked. He had the sharp look of a fox, with a narrow pointed chin and nose, and squinting eyes.

"Ah, I have been trying to place you, Mr. Graeme," Lolly chirped. "And now I have it. I met you one day on the street where Margaret's Buildings are. I live there, you see, and I know I have seen you strolling, or . . . ." She put her head to one side, peering at the gentleman as he glared at her. "You were speaking with—"

"You are mistaken, Miss Broomhall, for I don't know Margaret's Buildings," he said, his tone gentle. "It is an easy error to make, for I have the kind of face that looks familiar to all. I have never been along there, so you must have seen someone else who looks like me."

Lolly blinked, then nodded. "Of course. I'm sure you're right."

Impatient at the interruption, Anne said, "You were saying, Mr. Graeme, that you saw Mr. Lonsdale yesterday?"

"Was I?" he asked. "I must have seen him, but I cannot say where. One doesn't keep track, does one?"

"So you didn't have lunch with him, or meet him here?"

He waved one hand airily, fluttering his fingertips. "I cannot say, my lady. Now, I must be on my way." He separated himself from them and bowed. "My deepest condolences to the Birkenheads."

"Will you not attend them personally to offer your condolences?"

He nodded and a slight smile tipped his lips in one corner. "If you see them please tell them that I will attend them and we can reminisce together about Lonsdale and their deep and abiding friendship with him." He bowed again then left the Pump Room, his pace rapid.

Anne watched him go. That was a most *odd* exchange. It was as though there was some secret message buried there, something he wished the Birkenheads to know, and he was going to use her to deliver it. Or was she reading too much into a simple expression of sympathy and regard? Not likely, given Bertie's apparent expulsion of Graeme from his home. Anne recalled the look on Graeme's face as he glared up at the Birkenhead home; it was filled with loathing. After such a quarrel he would not likely attend them to offer condolences.

Uncertain about her next step in trying to reconstruct Alfred Lonsdale's last day on earth, she strolled a while longer with Lolly, then sat down to think. As usual, Lolly attracted more than one friend, and it seemed that for many of them the death of Mr. Alfred Lonsdale was cat's meat to a tabby, irresistible fodder for gossip. A plain-countenanced young woman took Lolly aside and spoke for some time, her tone becoming more piercing and cutting as she spoke.

Lonsdale's name was invoked, and the lady commented that

many were saying he had sinned in his life and could no longer bear the weight of it, and so had *destroyed* himself. Lolly, horrified by the suggestion, replied that there was no reason to think that true. If he had been intent on self-destruction, after all, why would he do so in his good friend's home? Would any friend do such a turn to a close companion?

The young lady's gaze bored into Lolly, and her words were perfectly heard even by Anne, several feet away. "It is being whispered," she said, "that Mr. Lonsdale did so *purposely*, to cause as much trouble for Mr. Birkenhead in particular as he could."

The young woman walked away in triumph, having spread a little poison in the place of healing waters. Lolly rejoined her younger cousin.

"I overheard," Anne said, breathless at the cruelty of gossip and how quickly it would spread. But still . . . she had to consider it. As awful as is sounded, was there truth behind it? She reflected back to the conversation she had two short days before, after church. Lonsdale himself had spoken of sinning so deeply he did not think he could uphold the office of vicar. But he also spoke of moral dilemmas in the plural. And he said, as he left, that there was something he had to do that moment while he had the courage. What was all that about? And did it involve the disagreements between himself and Bertie, and himself and his cousin, Roger Basenstoke?

Quin Birkenhead limped into the Pump Room supported on one side by the Birkenhead footman and on the other by Susanna Hadley, now his constant companion. Anne waited as he was greeted by friends and the curious. After fifteen minutes, Quin was clearly tiring and looking about for a place to sit. She beckoned him then, and he gladly hobbled over to her, leaning heavily on Susanna's arm.

He looked terribly sad, his face lined with weariness. Susanna clung to him, but it was clear she did so for his sake, not hers; she was bearing his weight with her own young strength. Anne couldn't tell if their mutual affection was gratitude, love, or friendship. She could not guess at Quin's feelings, but from her knowledge of her friend she suspected on Susanna's side it was love, a swift and complete meeting of the mind and heart. That was something her friend had never found in all the years she had been "out" in London and in Bath. She hoped Alethea didn't get in their way, that she let the two determine their own futures. There were not two more deserving souls in the whole nation.

They all chatted, then Susanna and Lolly stood and moved away to obtain glasses of punch. Anne had only a few minutes. Of anyone she could have told what was worrying her, she instinctively trusted Quin's intelligence and calm reflection the most.

The room was still crowded; she bent her head to his and kept her voice low. "Mr. Birkenhead, I have been sorely distressed today by what I have heard from the gossipmongers who use this place to spread their tales."

"I'm sorry you've been disturbed," he said, the lines of discomfort on his narrow face beginning to ease as he sat at his leisure. "What gossip in particular has upset you?"

"I think you know it must have to do with Mr. Lonsdale and his untimely death," she said, watching his expression.

He nodded, sadness on his pale face. "I'm not surprised. It was bound to be spoken of."

"The worst of it is, some are saying that he could not bear to live any longer, and so effected his own death and chose Bertie and Alethea's home purposely to embarrass them."

Quin still did not appear surprised. "My lady, if that is all that is disturbing you, I would advise you let such malicious gossip die aborning. It is not worth dignifying by denying."

"There is something in what you say, sir." While she acknowledged his methodology, she suspected that in this case it might be better to fight the gossip than let it go. Rumor, like a creeping weed, could send snaking tendrils into each crack and crevice, crumbling in time the sturdiest edifice, even one as strong as the Birkenhead family. "But there is more to my concern; when I walked with Mr. Lonsdale on Sunday, he was clearly in distress. He spoke of sins that would keep him from taking his position as a vicar if he should be offered one." She was silent for a long moment. "I don't understand what he meant."

"You don't think I know what was in his mind or heart?" Quin replied. "Or that, even if I did, I would feel free to spread such information about a fellow I considered a friend? It would be a . . . a desecration of his good name, and for naught, since he is gone. It's not as though we can solve his problems after death. I will stoutly defend his name wherever I hear slander, but I will never reveal anything about his personal life."

She would have expected nothing less from the gentleman. "Your brother is going to miss Mr. Lonsdale."

"Yes," he replied. "They were close." And that was all he would say, though he was clearly pondering what she told him.

She felt a little better for having shared her worries with him. Anne returned Lolly to the Bestwick home. She had not forgotten her concern for Lydia, and her secretiveness over visits to the mystic. The last thing she said to her cousin was, should Lydia go again to the mystic, Anne would like to be there. She must learn of it ahead of time, though.

"A message will find me any time of day, Lolly. Please, for Lydia's sake, don't fail me."

"I don't know if I will be able to, Anne, dear, but I will do my best."

It had been a long, sad day with little concrete information to help her understand how and why Alfred Lonsdale died. It was not her mystery to elucidate, and yet . . . it was a puzzle, and unsolved puzzles were anathema to her. She *must* uncover the explanation.

Chapter Seventeen

The next morning Mrs. McKellar again attended Anne and they fitted more wardrobe items, including the dress she would wear to marry Darkefell. The gown was colorful and alluring, everything she wished to be for her husband. Made from scarlet silk, it was trimmed in gold embroidered vines that lined the stomacher and the neckline of the gown. With it she would wear her ruby parure, the necklace of which would drape perfectly in her décolleté. She shivered, thinking of her husband-to-be. He was unlike any man she had ever met, and despite all they had already been to each other, it was beyond comprehension that soon they would be man and wife.

She gazed at herself in the mirror, her hair still down in nighttime abandon, her eyes heavy-lidded from a night of little sleep. She touched the low bosom of the gown, tracing the neckline, imagining Tony's hand instead of her own, his palm broad and strong, thick fingers surprisingly gentle. Shivering, she turned away from the mirror to the seamstress.

"This is wonderful, Mrs. McKellar. I think you can take in the waist of the bodice somewhat, and the skirt too."

"Yes, milady." She picked up her paper of pins and stuck some in her mouth, getting down to business.

Anne sighed and daydreamed. Tony . . . long winter nights with him alone (but for a large retinue of servants) in a big, drafty, cold Yorkshire castle. There was so much about marriage to him that she anticipated with unadulterated joy and desire and yet . . . and yet . . . she had reservations, fears, and gloomy moments of doubt. It was tiresome, and there was no one in whom she could confide, or at least no one who understood her deep uncertainties. All dismissed her concerns with airy certainty that she would settle in to wifehood with ease.

In her agitation she had moved. Mrs. McKellar begged her to stay still; she did not want to poke Anne. Taking a deep breath, Anne stilled herself. Irusan, who had been napping on a new velvet cushion Mrs. McKellar had sewn for him, stretched and yawned and looked up at her, blinking sleepily. He rose from the cushion, sauntered over and rubbed his whole body against Anne's legs, purring loudly. Somehow, the cat always knew when she needed him. Mrs. McKellar smiled and rubbed Irusan's cheeks as he stretched out his legs and clawed happily at the Turkey rug. The seamstress picked him up and put him in Anne's arms. She nuzzled his fur and shook the gloominess away. It was the happenings of the last few days that had her despondent. She must cheer up and trust she was making the right decisions. She was deeply in love with Darkefell, and believed he returned that love with an equal fervor. All the rest they would work out between them.

Anne put Irusan down and he resumed in place on the beautiful velvet cushion made from gown scraps in a gorgeous array of gold and azure, scarlet and emerald. He purred loudly and stretched, as the new cushion gave him room to luxuriate. Her mother and grandmother were again by the fire, this time going over visitors' cards. Lord Westmacott was due to attend them that afternoon, and the two women exclaimed over his most recent purchase, a high-perch phaeton, made popular by the young and fashionable Prince of Wales but exceptionally lively for a gentleman of his years.

"He's one o' them who goes to see the mystic," the seamstress whispered to Anne, past a mouth bristling with pins. "I wouldn't doubt it was her as put the notion of the carriage in his head."

"Lord Westmacott? How do you know he visited her?" Anne said, looking down at her as she rapidly pinned the waist, then moved up to the last seam on the bodice, tugging it to fit and inserting a line of pins.

Taking the last pin from between her lips, Mrs. McKellar inserted it and then gave it a pat. Her green eyes sparkling in the window's light, she said, "I hear much that goes on. The mystic's maid, Bridie—poor girl—is friends with my sister's char, Tompkins."

"And Lord Westmacott goes? Who else whose name I would recognize?" Anne asked.

"Baron Kattenby," she said. "Do you know that gentleman?"

"As a matter of fact, you have heard me speak of Alethea and Bertie Birkenhead. His new fiancée is Bertie's cousin, Mrs. Bella Venables."

"It is said that he chose her because she was so strongly marked for him by the spirits. The mystic herself foresaw it!"

"Was he seeking a wife?"

"As much as many men do, someone to be a comfort to him in

his later years, yes. The gossips say he had already begun to court another before taking up with Mrs. Venables."

"How was she brought to his attention?"

"The mystic foretold in coffee grounds that a certain lady was about to come into his life, and affect it powerfully. He was to make her his bride to ensure a long life of good health and wealth. She named the lady's height, hair color, and even her initials, BV!"

She frowned. "How very . . . specific."

"So when he met her, he knew."

"Interesting. I was told yesterday that it was a Mr. Graeme who introduced them to each other."

"The hand of providence, perhaps," Mrs. McKellar said lightly.

"Maybe," Anne said doubtfully. She had some thoughts on that, and was beginning to get a glimmer of an idea that was, as yet, amorphous. "So you know the mystic's maid? I recall her, a small girl with a nervous manner."

"Nervous, perhaps," the seamstress said with a grim tone. "But mayhap it's not her disposition but her position, if you understand. I've heard that the mystic has a foul temper and lashes out at the child."

"Is that so? What a pity. I've always thought it is a dangerous thing to mistreat your serving staff. Loyalty cannot be bought with money; it must be earned with kindness."

"You're wise for a young woman, milady." As Mrs. McKellar helped her out of the pinned bodice and gown, then turned to fold the pieces into the trunk she would use to take it back to her rooms to do the final sewing, Anne had an idea, which led to a plan. She would need help to effect it, though. "You say your sister's charwoman is friends with Bridie?"

"Aye. As much as the poor girl has time to be friends with anyone," Mrs. McKellar said, standing and turning to watch Anne with curiosity in her bright, quick eyes. "We have rooms not too far away from the mystic's. Why do you ask, milady?"

How well did Anne know the seamstress? Not enough to confess everything, but enough to reveal some of her thoughts, she decided. "Please, sit for a moment."

The seamstress did, at the table by the window, and Anne sat opposite her. Thin light streamed in through the window, burnishing the dusty pink of a vase of late roses with warm golden light. "I have concerns that the mystic is leading people astray," she said carefully, folding her hands together in front of her. "I worry that she's using her skills to instill fear, or inspire her clients to do things they wouldn't normally do."

"Such as what, milady?"

Anne shook her head. That was more than she had intended to say. "I don't know what I mean, exactly, but I am suspicious. Perhaps her advice leads simply to making a ridiculous acquisition, as Lord Westmacott's high-perch phaeton. I'm a rational creature, and as such I have no patience with anyone who believes that old fraud can see the future, or speak to the dead. It's got to be a trick, but I can't explain it."

"You'll not be believing, then, that she foretells the future?" There was a glint of knowing humor in the seamstress's eyes as she said it.

"I do not," Anne said with an answering smile. "There must be some method, a way she learns things. I want to know how."

The seamstress looked down at her work-worn hands and frowned, pensive. "I believe there are things we don't know, milady, things beyond the veil. I don't believe we see and know everything there is to know, for the very air about me is filled with mysteries, the wind I cannot see though it tosses the treetops, fairy circles in the woods, the spirit of my mother, who comes to me in my sleep." Then she looked up and with a smile said, "For all that, I'll agree that yon Mystic of Bath is likely not a reader of things beyond that veil. But begging your pardon, milady, why do you care?"

"My young and impressionable friend, Lady John Bestwick, is, I fear, in the woman's clutches. She's with child, and vulnerable. She's going there and . . ." Anne stopped and leaned forward. "*Please* don't say this to anyone else," she murmured.

Mrs. McKellar acknowledged the plea with a nod.

"Lydia is lying about it, to me and to her husband, who she knows doesn't approve. It worries me. I am the one who took her to see the mystic in the first place and I wish I hadn't. What is the woman saying to her that has Lydia so afraid?"

"How do you think that poor Bridie can help?"

Anne gazed at her steadily. "Mrs. McKellar, though many of my acquaintance refuse to acknowledge it, servants know more about a household than anyone else. There are no secrets where there are servants. Bridie *must* know how the mystic goes about telling her clients about their lives and their future. Where does she get information from? How much is inspired guesswork? How much does she glean from the conversations she has with other clients?" For the moment she decided not to go into what she really wanted to know, how the woman knew who was looking for a spouse, and what would attract them. "I'd like to meet her . . . the little maid. Can your sister's char arrange it?"

The woman looked pained but hesitant. "Milady, you're not wrong in one respect; servants know a lot about what goes on in the household. But . . ." She shook her head and fidgeted.

"I hope you know you can be honest with me."

"I wouldn't want to offend you, milady." She leaned forward across the table and said softly, "You do see that Bridie's continuing to work requires discretion? You cannot think I'd bring her to you and you'd winkle out all the mystic's secrets?" The seamstress shook her head. "That's hardly fair to the girl. It's a risk I'd not ask her to take. It's nothing to you, but *everything* to her."

Anne felt a moment of shame; in her eagerness to solve a mystery, she had disregarded the real consequences for someone vulnerable to the moods and annoyance of a bad-tempered employer. "I understand." She drummed her fingers on the tabletop. "She doesn't enjoy her position, didn't you say?"

"The mystic is a harsh mistress."

"What if I could arrange for a better job? One in a happier household?"

"Why would you do that, milady?"

"Let's say, if I am right, she may not have a job for long anyway." If she was right and could prove it, the mystic might be chased out of Bath. "I'd rather the girl have somewhere safe to go."

The seamstress examined her face for a moment, one intelligent woman to another, and nodded. "I'll see what I can do, milady."

After the seamstress departed, Anne excused herself from her mother's company and repaired to her own tiny sitting room, a dim little closet off her dressing room, to write some notes, still wearing a type of banyan gown she liked for morning. She *must* get organized. She wrote down all the puzzles and mysteries perturbing her sleep. The chat with the seamstress had been illuminating. She wanted to discover more about the matchmaking the mystic seemed to be doing and, if she was correct, Mr. Graeme's part in it.

Young Mr. Graeme was the common factor linking the other enigma confounding her, the more pressing puzzle of Mr. Lonsdale's death. There was a mystery there, one that worried her, nagging at her brain no matter how much she tried to distract herself with her curiosity about the Mystic of Bath and her influence over people, including her puzzling meetings with Lydia. Her deepest question about the strange death was, how had Mr. Lonsdale died of yew poisoning? Surely it was impossible to ingest yew accidentally?

Truffle entered her sitting room, holding a silver salver. "The post, milady," he said, bowing.

She took the stack of letters. There were notes from Osei, Alethea, Lolly and Mrs. Basenstoke. From Clary, for *her*? Curious, she opened that one first. It *was* to her. The lady wrote as to a friend, brief and to the point:

Lady Anne Addison
Everingham House, The Paragon
Anne, I need your help. Something is wrong, and I don't understand it, and I cannot speak to Roger about it. Can you come? This morning? Please?
Mrs. Clary Basenstoke
Gordon House, River Street

Her breath caught. Clary was worried about Alfred's peculiar death; that was the *only* interpretation she could put on such a note. She set the letter aside. Clary Basenstoke would be her first visit of the day.

Three more notes were in the stack. Osei's was brief and to the point: the marquess would arrive on Monday, the sixteenth day of October. The secretary had informed him by return post of the townhome rental, and that all would be ready; his employer could send staff ahead to prepare his temporary home. Anne felt a pleasurable trill down her backbone, one of anticipation and nervousness combined. They had been apart for weeks. What would a first meeting be like?

She shrugged off those thoughts to open the next note, addressed to her in a sloping, scrawling hand. It was from Lolly, and betrayed an anxiety about Lydia that reanimated Anne's own worries. Lolly would not hide it from her dear cousin; Lydia was going to visit the mystic again that very morning. Lydia had seemed relieved after their private meeting, but late yesterday had lapsed again into abstracted anxiety. Something preyed on her mind, something she would not divulge to Lolly. Lolly thought that Lydia was not normally a secretive lady, but she was hiding something. Would Anne come, in the afternoon, and talk to the young woman? Please?

Of course she would. She had wanted to attend the mystic with Lydia, but perhaps that was not practical, not right now, anyway. She opened the last, from Alethea. Her friend was deeply worried about Lonsdale's death, true, but also what it was doing to their social standing. Folks who would normally visit were ignoring their invitations and shunning them in public. Did Anne know what was wrong? Did she have any information? Could she visit? *Would* she visit?

Given the scandalous rumor she had overheard in the Pump Room, it was no wonder Bath residents were avoiding the Birkenheads. Gossip was spreading that Lonsdale had deliberately killed himself at the Birkenhead home as a way to harm his friends. People were superstitious, and suicide was a shockingly reckless deed, one that inspired a deep sense of dread.

She would visit and do her best to allay her friend's worries. She hastily scrawled replies to all, gave them to Truffle for immediate post, and retired to her bedchamber. As Mary dressed her hair for a day of visits, Anne pulled on her stockings, tied them above the knee, then gazed at her trusted confidante's reflection in the mirror. "Mary, I have need of you and Robbie today. Do you mind him performing a few tasks for me?"

The maid grimaced, her mouth full of hairpins. She concentrated on tidying the elaborate style, smoothing the curls and pinning some loose waves, then forming the ringlet that would drape artfully over Anne's left shoulder. She met her mistress's gaze in the mirror. "If t'were just boxes to carry, you'd no' ask me, milady. May I know what Robbie is to do?"

"Of course. I would never ask him to do anything without consulting you first." Anne slid her feet into nankeen half boots — sturdy enough for a day of visits in uncertain weather — and Mary laced them. Anne stood, and there was silence for a few minutes as Mary tied her stays, helped her into her petticoat, tied her pockets and bum roll, then dropped, over her head, the skirt of her gown. The silent maid tied the waist. "You'll be there too, Mary, with Robbie," Anne said, picking up their conversation as she tied a pretty lace tucker over her shoulders, carefully draping her coiled ringlet over her shoulder again.

She turned and faced her maid, putting her hands on Mary's shoulders and gazing directly into her eyes. "Nothing amiss will go on. I merely wish him to pester the kitchen staff and gossip with the lowest of the servants. It's about Lydia and John's household. I want to know of any irregular mail, any notes she has been getting. Something is worrying her, and John is concerned. Lolly is beside herself. No one is confessing to delivering notes to her, but I wonder if one of the underlings is being employed to take them to her in secret. Lydia can be devious. She is both sly and determined to get her own way even if to do so she must act in a furtive manner." And though those traits had irritated Anne in past, she was beginning to see that for some women, it was the only way to both keep peace and live with some measure of independence. She would not blame her friend in future.

"You're sayin' she's a mite crafty, milady?" Mary said, handing Anne what she habitually carried in her pockets: money, a handkerchief, smelling salts, her gold watch, and a magnifying glass.

Anne sighed. "She is. Lolly doesn't know her like I do, and thinks she is just a pretty, sweet, mild-mannered young lady. But I don't blame Lydia. Has any woman alive gotten through life without employing some deception to get what she wants or needs? It is, unfortunately, how we are raised, for to men goes the lion's share of power in the world."

She paused, frowning and staring off into the shadowed corner of the room. "I must confront her concerning her secretive meetings with the mystic, but she may put me off with some claim about doing it for entertainment. I no longer believe that. She is too upset, according to those closest to her. There is something more going on. I wish to be sure of my standing *before* confronting her, though, for I think that what is upsetting her is coming to her by way of messages delivered by hand. A potboy or scullery maid may say to Robbie what they would not dare divulge to anyone else."

"You wish him to be your spy." Mary, as always, cut through her babble.

Taking a deep breath, Anne nodded. "Yes." She put her arms through the bodice of the gown then turned, so Mary could lace it and pin it in place. "He's a clever boy, and more than once he has noticed something I haven't seen, or brought me information that has helped. I'm worried about Lydia, and so is John. Even Lolly is concerned."

Mary nodded. "Aye, milady. But mind . . . if he gets in a problem wi' the Bestwicks' housekeeper, it's your task to get him outta trouble."

"Yes, Mary, of course." She took a deep breath and gazed at herself in the mirror, pulling on her gloves. "There are more stops today, but I don't imagine I'll have Robbie do the same tasks at the Basenstokes' and certainly not at the Birkenheads', so you will be home long before me. Mrs. McKellar may, at some point, send a note," she said, and explained about Bridie, the mystic's maid.

"What is all o' this in aid of, milady?"

"There are assorted mysteries in Bath, odd goings-on with the mystic, and now this death at the Birkenheads'. Too many puzzles. My friends are suffering. I will sort out Lydia and find out what is troubling her, and try to help Alethea. My poor dear friend is in terrible distress over the rumors, so I am determined to find out who killed Alfred Lonsdale."

"Who killed him? You think it murder?"

Anne stared in the mirror, her mouth pinched in a frown. "Unfortunately, I do. I want to know who, and why."

"On the trail again of a murderer," Mary said, tsk-tsking between her teeth. "What would the marquess say?"

"If he's wise, nothing. Could you fetch my shawl? This weather is unpredictable, the sun shining one moment and gloom gathering the next."

"Sounds like life, milady," Mary said, draping the shawl around her mistress's shoulders."

Chapter Eighteen

John was not in at the Bestwick house on Milsom, and Lydia was resting, or so the maid who answered the door said. She did not wish to see Anne, for she was unwell. Or was she avoiding Anne, afraid her friend would see through her? Mary and Robbie went around to the back door, of course, to descend to the kitchen to visit with the cook and Lydia's lady's maid, who Mary knew from their time at the Darkefell estate.

Lolly, white-faced and worried, met Anne in the main-floor reception room.

"Why won't Lydia see me?" Anne asked, turning from the window overlooking Milsom. "I'll not believe that she is unwell. That is when she wants company the most."

Twisting her hands over and over, Lolly paced, and then perched on an embroidered corner chair, staring at Anne, her pouched eyes clouded with worry. "We got back from our visit to the mystic and Lydia retired to bed, exhausted. It was the same as before; I went in with her, but then was sent out to sit in the antechamber while the two had a private session. Last time at least she was happy after, but this time she was not. She seems afraid. The girl is not getting enough sleep. I'm *so* concerned. She is keeping something from me, and I *can't* share my worries with Lord John. It would be . . ." She shook her head.

"Presumptuous. You haven't known her long enough to tell her husband she's troubled by something."

Lolly nodded.

"He already suspects, Lolly; he said as much to me. But you're right not to betray her trust. Let me handle this for now." Anne confessed that she had Mary and Robbie downstairs, hoping that the boy, with his quick intelligence and likability, would be able to discover if there were any secrets belowstairs that would explain the mistress's low mood. "I'm worried about this mystic, Mother Macree, and what she's up to." She explained that she was hoping the mystic's maid might be tempted by a new job to give her employer up, but it was a risky task. "Lolly, you've lived in Bath many years; do you think I can find the girl another job? A better one than as maid of all works for that woman? She treats the child shabbily, I've been told."

"Bath is insular, my dear. It may not be as easy as it would be in London. But I *will* prick up my ears, I vow it. I have many friends. One of them may know of a situation. Even my landlady—"

"Not her! I'll not have that child leave the mystic to work for a slattern like that."

Lolly nodded. "I'll see what I can do for the child."

"If Lydia wishes to confide in you—"

"I will listen."

"But will you tell me what she says, even if she swears you to secrecy?"

Lolly clutched her hands together. "God forgive me, yes, I will. I wish what is best, and must be guided by your better knowledge and love of her, and your wisdom."

"Thank you, dear Lolly," Anne said. Judging she had given Robbie enough time, she rose and departed to the carriage outside. When Robbie and Mary joined her, she could see the signs of success in the clever lad's broad grin. "Did you find something out?"

"Aye, milady," he said. "The potboy, Willie Wag, he tolt me in secret, he sed as how there is a fellow as gives 'im a note many a day to hand Lady John in secret. Pays 'im tuppence each time. *Tuppence!*" he said, his bright eyes wide at the bounty. "Willie nicks up the back stairs—he don't dare get caught; if he was caught upstairs he'd be beat black n' blue by the housekeeper—an' leaves it for her ladyship under her pillow."

"Under her *pillow*?" Anne was astounded. *Beyond* risky, it was unthinkable that the boy had been put up to such a thing. Tuppence was a staggering sum for the boy, she supposed, but if he was found out, he would be cast out onto the street. "Tell me, did you think to find out what this fellow looks like, the one who leaves messages for Willie to put under her ladyship's pillow? And perhaps where he gives it to the boy?"

"Aye, he sed as how the toff is goldy-haired, all shiny like a half guinea he seen once."

Golden hair; it was not an unheard-of color, but her first thought was of Mr. Graeme. "A toff . . . that means a well-dressed gentleman, correct?"

The boy nodded. "An' milady . . . Willie sez as 'ow her ladyship twice in th' last few days give 'im a velvet sac with somethin' heavy in it, to give to the same feller."

Mary, wide-eyed, said, "Oh, milady, I know what must be in the sac. Lydia's maid is in a fair takin'. Seems there are things missing from her ladyship's jewel case. Not first-rate jewels, but little trinkets. She's in quite a tizzy for fear her ladyship'll accuse her, but I said Lady John would no' do that."

Anne nodded, thinking. There was one inescapable conclusion: the items in the velvet sac were some kind of gift or payment from Lydia to the fellow who brought the notes. But for what? "Mary, can you ask at the door if Lolly will come out to the carriage? I have something more to ask her."

Lolly, wrapped hastily in a woolly shawl of her own knitting, climbed up into the carriage and squeezed breathlessly in next to Mary. "What is it, Anne, dear? What have you forgot?"

Anne told her what Robbie had discovered from the potboy, knowing that of all people Lolly could be counted on to not get the lad in trouble. "He is receiving those secret notes from the hand of a well-dressed gentleman with golden hair. The description puts me in mind of one Mr. Graeme; you remember. We met him at the Pump Room. In fact . . ." Anne paused a moment. Of *course*! She reached across and took her cousin's hand to focus her attention. "Lolly, when we met, you said to him—though he denied it vehemently— that you saw him on the pavement outside of Margaret's Buildings," she said urgently, squeezing her hand. "You were about to say who with when he denied it, interrupting you. Who was it you saw him with?"

"Oh, yes! T'was the mystic's little maid. Very sly, he was . . . very sly *indeed*, with that side-to-side gaze, as when you are hoping no one you know sees you. He tugged her into a doorway and gave her something."

"How interesting," Anne said. It was the connection she was looking for between the mystic and Mr. Graeme. And perhaps illuminated part of the mystery, those "introductions," though it didn't *explain* them. Was it some harmless matchmaking or something more underhanded? And this information didn't help at all with learning why Lydia was so upset by the notes—if what

Anne surmised was true and it was the notes that unsettled her — or what connection any of it had with Mr. Lonsdale's tragic death. And there was the other matter . . . Anne told Lolly about the items from her jewel box that Lydia was probably giving to Graeme, or sending by way of him to someone else. "I need to find out what is in those notes. Would Lydia have kept them? I'm sure she would. Lolly, could you look through Lydia's things to try to find them?"

Lolly appeared horrified, pulling her hand free and rearing back as if she had seen something terrible. "I could *never* do such a thing to Lady Lydia. Telling you what she confides to me is bad enough, but . . . oh, that poor child! Paw through her possessions? How could you ask such a thing, Anne?"

Anne glanced around and saw the same horrified look on Mary's face. It was too far. If she applied it to her own life, she realized how angry she'd be if someone searched her private possessions. "All right, don't pry. But if she is inclined to confide in you — to confess what is worrying her — you *will* tell me?"

"I already promised I would. As . . . as long as she doesn't *swear* me to secrecy," Lolly said, mollified. She bid adieu, and climbed down out of the carriage and went in.

Anne told the driver to take her to the Basenstokes', and from there to return Mary and Robbie to the Paragon, before coming back to await her.

Inside Gordon House Clary was anxious and pacing. "Anne, thank heavens you have come!" She strode forward and took Anne's gloved hands, her own quivering with emotion.

Looking over her shoulder and waiting until the door to the sitting room was closed, Anne then led her older friend to the settee and sat, pulling her down to sit beside her. "Tell me what it is that is upsetting you, Clary."

The woman took in a deep shuddering breath and let it out slowly. Anne's presence seemed to be calming her, though the dark circles under her eyes spoke of a sleepless night or two. And yet she had not been so agitated when last Anne spoke to her. Sad about her nephew's death, yes, but not agitated. Something had happened.

But Clary would say nothing until tea was brought, with an array of sandwiches and cakes on a platter. Anne, looking at her mother's friend intently, saw enough that she, too, was willing to wait until they had drunk and eaten. She encouraged Clary to do so, urging her to a sandwich and a cup of tea. They ate, and finally the tray was cleared away, another cup of restorative brew poured and waiting.

"Now, what is upsetting you?"

"I found letters, in Alfred's room, and I don't know what to think of them." She pressed a black-edged handkerchief to her mouth and choked off a sob. "I thought them love letters. Maybe they are. Maybe not."

"I don't think I understand you, Clary," Anne said, baffled. "Love letters? Surely that's obvious if they are or are not?"

"No, no, you don't understand. They're from . . . they are from another *man*."

Chapter Nineteen

"Another *man*?" Anne felt her heart thump. She had heard of such things as those who loved others of the same sex. She had no idea that Mr. Lonsdale was of that persuasion. There was no mark, or sign, no stigma that pointed him out, so, how could she know? She shook off her inward gaze and instead listened to her friend.

"Another *man*! I feel such a fool," Clary sobbed. "I kept throwing young ladies at him. I even asked, when I visited that woman, that mystic, Mother Macree, would my beloved nephew Alfred find a good wife to love him? Would he find happiness with a suitable young lady? I had your mother trying to find a good match for him, a nice girl who . . ." She stopped and shook her head.

"What did the mystic say?" Anne asked.

"That the future was unclear," Clary said. "No wonder."

"Who is he, the writer of the letters?"

"There is no name, just endearments. Alfred is Dearly Beloved and the other man is Tulip."

"How do you know it's a man, then?"

"He writes of . . . of things they have done."

"Oh." For all that it was scandalous, it shed some light on Mr. Lonsdale's concerns about "sins" the church would defrock him for. "I'm sorry it shocks you, Clary."

"Doesn't it shock you?"

Anne examined her heart. It did *surprise* her. And yet, it was deeply personal to him and didn't affect her memory of the young man who had seemed lonely, sad at times, but sweet-natured and good. "I suppose, but Clary, he was your nephew. He loved you and you loved him. Nothing you have learned changes that."

Tears streamed down her face and she dabbed at her swollen eyes. "What breaks my heart is, how could I not have known? How could he have kept such a secret, an affair with another man!" she whispered. "I was his aunt, but he was like the son I never . . . . I mean, Roger is a good son, but Alfred was *exceptional*." She paused, mouth open, and her eyes grew wide. "You don't think . . . could Roger have known about . . . about Alfred's affair?"

Anne frowned down at her gloved hands and pulled at a loose thread. "I suppose he may have." It would explain Roger's aversion for him. If so, Roger may have worried that others would discover Lonsdale's secret and it would all come out, shaming their family. She couldn't ask Clary this, but she did wonder . . . what would Roger do to prevent that? Given his position in Bath society, how his business relied on connections, what would he *not* do to keep the secret? She looked up and examined her friend's teary face. "What do *you* think? Could your son have known?"

"Men gossip as much as women, though they don't call it gossip of course. And gentlemen have so many connections in society that we don't, associations we ladies have no knowledge of."

Her way of saying *in all probability.* "What have you done with Mr. Lonsdale's letters?"

"I have them here," Clary said, pulling a stack tied with a slim blue ribbon from her pocket. "I didn't read them all. I only read the first couple, enough to know . . ." She shook her head and compressed her lips.

"Do you want to know who the other gentleman is? Would you like to return the letters?"

Clary nodded and sniffed back the last of her tears. "You've helped me think of this a different way. He was such a lovely boy, and this changes nothing. I wish he could have told me."

"How would you have reacted if he did?"

Clary shook her head. "I don't know. I'd like to think I would have been gentle but . . . I don't know. I wonder, now, if perhaps there is someone else out there mourning poor Alfred as I am, but unable to show it. He should have his letters back, if it is at all possible. But how can I return the letters when I don't know who it is?"

"Would you like me to try and figure it out?"

"Would you?"

Anne nodded and took the letters. "I'll do the best I can."

"Thank you."

"Has anyone else read these letters? Did you show them to your son?"

"No. I would never tell Roger, or anyone else."

"Has anyone else been in his room?"

"The maids have been in to dust, of course, and clean the fireplace, but he had no valet, and these were in a locked case. I found the key in his pocket when I was getting a suit of clothes for the undertaker. I'm the only one who has been through his things."

Anne took a deep breath. "I have a favor to ask, my dear Clary. I'm deeply concerned about your nephew's death." She hesitated, but there was no way around this. "I have reason to believe that it was not natural."

"Not natural? What do you mean?"

"I cannot tell you more. Please just know this: I don't believe it was natural, but neither do I believe it was by his own hand."

"But that means . . ." Clary paled, the faintest hint of color ebbing from her cheeks.

Anne let her come to the natural conclusion. "May I look through his room?"

She choked back a sob. "If you think it would help, please do," she said, her voice thick. "I'll take you up now, if you like, to look around."

"I would appreciate that. Can we be discreet, though? I don't wish Roger—or anyone else, for that matter—to know I've been looking through his things."

Clary observed her closely for a minute, then nodded. "Roger is not home at the moment and won't be for a few hours, and the maids are busy with preparations for visitors this afternoon. Some of my friends will be dropping around this afternoon, I'm sure, to express their sympathy. Now is a good time."

• • •

In Alfred Lonsdale's room, Anne threw back the heavy draperies, letting in the light. It was a large, airy chamber, with a full testered bed draped in blue damask, a mirrored wardrobe, and a dressing table. There was a chest of drawers with various toiletries upon it: brush, comb, clothing brush, a valet case, hair pomade, and scent.

And a Bible. She opened it and sat on the end of the bed. He had marked, with torn slips of paper, certain sections of the Old Testament, especially Leviticus, and in the New Testament, Jude. She understood why the sections were marked, and it saddened her. She had never thought of it one way or the other, she supposed—she had never *had* to think of it beyond her Bible readings—but to believe that who you were made you an outcast in the eyes of God . . . it could not have been an easy life, especially for a man pursuing the church as a career. Was that why he went to the church for a vocation? Had he been looking for hope, or peace or . . . salvation? There was nothing else in the Bible, no notes or letters to give her the answers she sought, so she set it back where she had found it.

She wished more than anything to read the letters; that was her most likely source to figure out who the other man was. However, she had access to this room for a short time, and she had best make haste. She thought of Dr. Fothergill; what would he want to know, if he had this opportunity?

Immediately she began to go through the wardrobe looking for any medicine or bottles. When she found one, a tonic, she examined it closely, pouring some into the washbasin. No green residue, no yew needles. Still . . . she made sure the stopper was firmly in and slipped the slim bottle into her pocket. There was a part bottle of brandy. No residue, no greenish tint, and no yew needles as far as she could tell from the little she poured into the water pitcher after shaking the bottle. She could not possibly take it, though she *would* tell the doctor about it. His portable writing desk contained financial papers and other items, but nothing of deep interest. Relentless, she searched every last inch of the room, and in a deep dark corner of the wardrobe she discovered, wrapped in oilcloth and tied with a ribbon, a small leather book, handwritten.

She untied the ribbon and opened the book, sitting down at the dressing table and reading the frontleaf. It was a journal, and had his name, Alfred Gabriel Lonsdale, then, in script, the words *Not for the world would I expose my secret heart to the scorn of men.* She closed the book and held it to her chest. It was a plea for privacy, and it rent her heart. "I wish I could abide by your wishes, Alfred," she whispered. "But we *must* discover who killed you. I promise, nothing revealed within shall be exposed to the ridicule or contempt of others."

She descended and told Clary about the journal, asking to take it with her—that wish was granted—then bid her farewell, promising to do her best to discover both who to return the letters to and who may have had any responsibility for his death. She left her with another warning not to tell another living soul, including her son and Anne's mother, what they had discussed and what she had taken away.

Her soul was weary. Her sadness over Alfred Lonsdale's death was growing, not receding, perhaps as a result of her visit to Clary. But still, she must go on. She would visit Alethea, as she promised, and see how the Birkenheads were doing after the wrenching few days they had suffered. If they were being shunned, as Alethea feared, she *would* suffer. Alethea lived for company and gaiety far more than Bertie, who was not afraid of solitude. She arrived at their door at the same moment as Osei returned Quin, after their jaunt. Quin, pale with weariness, asked them both to come in and take tea — or something stronger — with him. Anne agreed, but Osei said he must return the rented curricle to the livery.

"I will wait upon you this evening, my lady," he said to Anne. "If you don't mind."

"I'd like that, Mr. Boatin. I have some things to discuss with you."

Quin was helped in to the ground-floor sitting room on the shoulder of a footman — Quin called him Crabbe when he thanked him — followed by Anne.

Alethea, hearing them enter, descended. "Darling boy, how pale you are!" she said to her brother-in-law, rushing to help him. "I *knew* that was a bad idea, Mr. Boatin and you going out," she scolded.

"Enough, Alethea, it was my choice. I do still *have* a choice, do I not?"

"Of course."

Anne had never heard Quin so impatient, but it must become wearying, she thought, to have everyone fussing over you all the time. He was ill, but not lacking in mental facilities, and he knew his own limits better than anyone else. If he wished to test them, it was his right.

"Miss Hadley is visiting this afternoon," he said, casting his sister-in-law an impatient look. "I hope you'll be polite to her."

"Of course I will." Alethea's chin went up. "You needn't be rude, Quin." She glanced over at Anne. "Are you here to visit me, or him?"

"Either. Both," Anne said, taken aback. Grief was something that cut through every human emotion, leaving devastation in its wake. "I got your note. I'd be happy to visit with you together, or separately; I'm yours to command."

"Come upstairs when you and Quin have had your chat." She turned and swept from the room.

"There is tension between you," Anne said, sitting down by the fire, opposite Quin. She stripped off her gloves and held her hands out to warm them. "I've never seen that before. You've always been so close."

"I suppose I was a little cutting toward her." He passed one bony hand over his face and squinted wearily. "She thinks I'm being foolish," he said, glancing at her, then staring fiercely into the fire. "I have asked Susanna to marry me."

Anne leaped from her chair and hugged him in an excess of joy. After the last few dreadful days the Birkenheads deserved happiness. "Oh, Quin, I'm overjoyed for you both! Susanna is a dear girl. I think you two suit most admirably." Tears prickled her eyes. "And I know it is shocking for me to say, but I think she is already deeply in love with you. I'll presume she said yes?"

He nodded and slumped back in the chair. "I'm grateful to hear you say that, Anne, that you're happy for us. Bertie and Alethea had almost convinced me I was being unbearably selfish, sentencing her to a life of looking after an invalid."

She gasped and stared. "They didn't *say* that, did they?"

"Not in so many words, but if I hear one more time about a woman's *appetites* . . ." He shook his head.

"I suppose it is because of their own relationship in the . . . their *physical* relationship, I mean. They think everyone as lusty as themselves." She smiled, making her little joke.

Quin shook his head and didn't respond.

"I'm sorry if my jest fell flat, dear boy. I didn't mean anything by it."

"Do you know them as well as you think?" he finally said, staring at her. His tone was exasperated.

"Know them? Of course I know them. What do you mean?"

"No marriage is without . . . without some difficult times. Some tension and distance." He sighed. "It's nothing, don't listen to me.

I'm tired. I think I'll have a rest before Susanna comes. We are planning our wedding. I would enlist Alethea's help, but you see how I am left to my own devices, though I'm sure Lady Sharples will assist once she learns Susanna is as determined as I, my income is more than sufficient and I'm prepared to be generous in the settlements." He rang a bell beside him. "Alethea will be in her sitting room upstairs."

The footman came.

"Crabbe, I am going to have a rest in the small salon," Quin said. "I'm too weary to ascend." The footman helped Quin to his feet and the two shuffled off, down the hall toward the back of the townhome.

The entire household felt fractured, like the death of Alfred Lonsdale had broken something wide open, leaving a raw wound. She fingered the stack of letters in her pockets, and the journal, too. What would it reveal? Taking in a deep breath she ascended. The drawing rooms on the first floor were sectioned off by folding screens. "Alethea?" she called out.

"Here," came her friend's ghostly voice from beyond the screens.

Anne followed the voice to the dim withdrawing room to find Alethea sitting, staring into the ashy cold fireplace. Her hands were folded in front of her, and her attitude was listless.

"My dear, let me ring for a servant to stir the fire." Anne ordered the Birkenhead staff around as if it were her own. It seemed shockingly poorly managed to her, with no housekeeper to direct the staff. Within minutes of her brisk commands there was a fire blazing in the hearth and a steaming pot of tea on the table in front of the settee where Alethea still sat, an island of stillness in the household whirlwind. "When did you last eat?" Anne asked.

Alethea lifted one hand and let it fall without answering.

"Sandwiches for your mistress," she said to the maid, who was departing the room. She'd have a second luncheon herself; food was the magic elixir to brighten the spirit, she hoped. At the very least, it would sustain life.

"Nothing seems to matter right now," Alethea said, her tone dead of inflection.

"It's been a shock," Anne said gently. "Someone dying in your home, a dear friend, at that. I didn't know you were so close until recently. How is Bertie?"

"Beside himself."

"You said in your note that your acquaintances are shunning you. Surely that can't be true?"

"Bertie says I'm imagining it, and maybe I am. I thought you had deserted me, too."

"Oh, Alethea! I never would, you know. I never will."

The other woman's eyes teared, but she shook her head. "I have no certainty right now. I feel as though a rug has been pulled out from underneath us all, and that the world is now neither so sure nor so steady as I once thought it." She brushed away the tears and impatiently shook her head.

They drank tea, and again Anne forced food on a grieving woman, her role for the last few hours, it seemed. Anne delicately hinted at Lonsdale's secret life, but her friend was deaf to subtlety and didn't appear to know of anything amiss. Finally Anne said, putting down her teacup, "Alethea, I am looking into Alfred's death. I know how deeply you are concerned, not only for that but because of the gossip you feel is swirling around you, and how you suspect you are being ostracized because of how his death occurred. Will you come with me to the Assembly Rooms for the next ball? You must not let people send you and Bertie to Coventry. It's not fair, and I'll not have it."

"I know I asked you to come to me, I know I said I was upset about it, but even if it is true, do you think we care right now?" She looked mulish, her face set in a hard expression of disdain. "I won't go. Let society banish us; we have each other and Quin."

"Has your friend Mrs. Hughes been to visit?"

Alethea merely shook her head.

"I'm sorry, my dear."

"I don't *care!*" she cried, a wail of misery. "I don't care about *anything* right now. It is all wrong and false and people are horrible!"

In times of trouble one did not exhort a friend to cheer up, one provided love and comfort. However, it was her place to help her friend look forward. "You may not care now, but in time you will, and it will be too late. Society is fickle, and once they've taken against you . . ." She shook her head. "Please, Alethea, say you'll come. *Please.*"

"No. I am done with them all."

Anne sighed, but Alethea had always been dramatic when overwrought. "If you change your mind, you know how to find me. Now . . . I have some questions about Alfred Lonsdale. I know he was a friend, but how close?"

Alethea looked up and met Anne's eyes. "I don't know what to say. He was more Bertie's friend than mine." She shifted in her seat, and when she spoke again her voice had changed. It was higher, lighter, and she looked away from Anne into the fire. "*You* know how good Bertie is. Alfred was almost like another little brother."

Cautiously, Anne probed deeper. "Did you know of his other friends? Alethea, I am asking in particular about Mr. Graeme. I know Bertie didn't like him and ejected him from your home. Why?"

"You know my husband; once he takes against someone, he can be rigid and unforgiving. And . . . the gentlemen do get about more than we do. I assume he knew something unsavory about Graeme."

"But what?"

"I don't know, Anne, *truly!*"

Alethea was weary and irritable, and Bertie still was not home. "Will you tell your husband I wish to see him?" Anne asked, standing. "And do me a great favor; be kind to Quin about Susanna. You may have concerns, but I've known her for years. If your apprehension is for her, please, don't worry. I have never seen her happier than when she and Quin are together."

"You mistake me, Anne. My concern is not for her, but for him. I worry that she will expect from him what he cannot give."

"Isn't that for the two of them to work out? Weren't there things you and Bertie had to work out when you first married?"

Alethea looked startled for a moment, and stared at her friend, her gaze searching, questioning. She shook her head and looked away, her voice indistinct when she replied, "Of course, yes, you're right, Anne."

• • •

When she arrived back at the Paragon townhome, her grandmother and mother were in the sitting room entertaining two of their friends, a powdered and wigged widow of gossipy repute

165

and Lord Westmacott. Though she couldn't bear to drink another cup of tea without a moment alone with a bordelou, Anne did visit.

As the three ladies chatted, Westmacott, sitting beside Anne, put one hand over hers. "How are you, my dear? Have you recovered from the awful scene at the Birkenheads'?"

"I'm all right, but Alethea is still devastated and Bertie . . . he's taking this dreadfully hard. As disbelief wears off, melancholy takes its place."

"Truer words were ne'er spoken."

"Did you know Lonsdale well?"

"Not well, I wouldn't say. He was often at the Birkenheads' of late, since he came to stay with Mrs. Basenstoke in August."

"Mr. Roger Basenstoke didn't care for his cousin. Why, I wonder?"

"They are very different gentlemen, Anne. Not everyone gets along."

"Mr. Basenstoke has always seemed somewhat disagreeable to me, though he's been helpful of late, with advice for the marquess's secretary, Mr. Boatin, on where to find him a townhome to lease for the winter season."

"Ah, yes, Mr. Boatin. What a dignified-looking young man he is. I find him most intriguing."

"He is a wonderful person. He found a new secretary for my father, one who can ably assist his research. Papa is thrilled." She paused, and ensured that her mother and grandmother were still taken up with gossip. She leaned into Lord Westmacott and murmured, "I was with Clary today. She is more upset than before, and I'm becoming deeply concerned. When I spoke with Mr. Lonsdale last he spoke at length about his concerns for his future, and his uncertainty of his chosen profession, the church, whether he was fit for it or not. He was melancholy, but many are saying he was self-destructive. I don't think that. I'd appreciate any help I can get socially to counter that horrible rumor. It is hurting the Birkenheads and their social standing."

"That is so sad!" He seemed torn and uncertain. Finally he said, "I beg your pardon, Anne; I will do what I can but do you truly think the other alternative, that he was murdered there, is to be preferred? Does that not put them in a worse light?"

She gasped and stared at him, meeting his pale protuberant eyes, lined with wrinkles he tried to hide with powder. "Has it come so far? Do people not still think it was natural causes?"

"There has been gossip. It is unusual for a young man of such obvious good health and in the flower of youth to die suddenly."

"I see." It was urgent that she hasten her investigation, and to do so she must approach it in a more organized fashion, rather than rambling about listening to gossip. Someone murdered Alfred Lonsdale. The first step to finding out who could have poisoned him was to establish his day, where he had been, who he had seen. She knew its beginning, with tea and toast at home, the tea served by Roger Basenstoke, suspicious enough in its unusualness. But for the rest . . . "Do you know Mr. Thomas Graeme?"

The gentleman eyed her with a frown. "That supposed tea merchant? I *have* seen him about. Young fellow seems to know everybody. Why do you ask?"

She hesitated. She didn't wish to speak of her suspicions of Graeme's involvement in some marriage scheme . . . not yet anyway. Nor could she reveal what she knew, that Lonsdale had been poisoned. She had promised to keep that to herself. What a tangled web information was, for how could she foresee what would lead to what? It came back to her that moment that her old acquaintance had been one who gave Lonsdale something to imbibe that night. For all she knew the yew could have been in the wine he handed Lonsdale, though she had no reason to think it possible. It was ludicrous to suppose it on purpose, but the older gentleman *could* have been used as an innocent carrier of the glass. How could she frame that question? It was impossible. For all his affectations the gentleman was astute and would see through any pretense.

She needed to know more, first. Perhaps she could use Lord Westmacott's vast social network to improve her knowledge.

"My dear, I can see you are struggling with something. Surely you can trust me, your grandmother's oldest friend?"

Of *course* she could trust him. She was being unnecessarily labyrinthine in her thoughts. "If Alfred Lonsdale's death was not suicide, what do you think it was? You hinted at . . . you hinted at murder. What did you mean by that?"

He shrugged, a helpless look on his face. "I don't know, my dear;

truly, I don't. Who would want to kill such a harmless, delightful young fellow? How well did you know him?"

"I came to know Mr. Lonsdale first by word, through Mrs. Clary Basenstoke. But then I found he was a friend of the Birkenheads', who are friends of yours as well, of course. We were just speaking of Mr. Thomas Graeme; he approached us all quite boldly as we were out walking, which is when I first learned of him as a friend of Mr. Lonsdale's. I saw the fellow again at the Pump Room, and Lolly saw him outside of the Mystic of Bath's rooms. How weblike Bath society is, a spider's trap of links!"

"Yes, I suppose that is true," he said, watching her, his pale intelligent gaze fixed on her face. "An astute observation, Lady Anne."

"There is something not quite right about Graeme. I cannot find out for sure how they met each other, him and Lonsdale. I have varying accounts . . . Eton, a club—"

"A club? What kind of club?"

How odd, Anne thought, staring at him. That was exactly Alethea's reaction when she said something about a club. "Why do you ask?"

"No particular reason. But Bath is not London, you know, with a hundred gentlemen's clubs. It is, as you yourself have noted, a narrow society. What kind of club do you mean, Anne?"

"I don't know. Graeme said they knew each other from a club. A gentlemen's club, I assumed. What other kinds are there?"

"Oh, so many," he said airily. "You know these young gentlemen, with their varied interests. Astronomy, science, four-in-hand driving . . . it could be anything."

"But you said Bath was not like London and there were not so many clubs."

He took out his pocket watch. "Oh, dear!" he exclaimed with a start. "I had no idea it was so late. I believe I must go," he said, rising. "Good day, Lady Anne. If I discover anything, I will share the knowledge with you." Pausing, he eyed her with a look somewhere between curiosity and suspicion. "Though, it gives me pause . . . why *are* you inquiring? We spoke of murder; I cannot fathom it, myself. Do you *truly* think there is something about Lonsdale's death that is suspicious?"

"What could I possibly know about it one way or the other?" she said, dismissing his query with an evasion. "You have known me, my lord, for many years; I'm perpetually meddlesome and think I know better than anyone else." She smiled, to show her humorous intent, and to pass it off as lightly as she could, but the fiction was impossible to maintain. "It would be best for everyone if we knew how the fellow died," she said, her tone somber. "I know Bertie and Alethea would feel better if they understood it. Perhaps it will come out that it was some shocking and sudden illness."

He nodded with a thoughtful look, bowed, and said his goodbyes to the ladies. Anne excused herself soon after to retreat upstairs, and the relief of the bordelou. She must soon change for dinner and the evening's concert at the Upper Assembly Rooms, which she had decided to attend. Concert director Venanzio Rauzzini mounted an ambitious and entertaining musical program for the Bath Season, and it invariably drew everyone who cared about music, along with everyone else who cared about others *thinking* they cared about music. She sent a note to Lolly asking if she'd like to go, and considered inviting Osei. As subscribers her family was entitled to seats, and the marquess's secretary enjoyed music as much as anyone, she supposed. If he attended her, as she hoped he would, she would ask him.

But first . . . the letters and the journal. She was nervous but eager, and hopeful that one or the other would provide clues as to who would wish Alfred Lonsdale dead.

Chapter Twenty

She retreated to the privacy of her bedchamber, sat on her low chair by the dressing table and picked up the first letter on the stack. It was a poem dedicated to Lonsdale, badly written verse, accusations of his "cold manner" in public, and how much the writer longed for "one sign, one touch, one lovely gesture of true affection." Irusan demanded her attention, and she patted her lap; he jumped up and sprawled. She pet him as she read it all the way through, with the paragraphs after the poem. It seemed that perhaps the two had not formed any relationship yet at that point. But the writer was persistent, there were a couple more along the same line, but then from the tone of the next letter, it was clear that he was at long last rewarded with the love he so desperately sought.

"My Dark-haired Darling," the writer called Alfred — a name he must have used before settling on the "Dearly Beloved" nickname — then went on with the extensive praise that proved beyond doubt that Clary was right; both lovers were male. Anne's cheeks burned as she read the lines, which effusively described male anatomy. "How shocked would Mother be to know what I am reading?" she said aloud. Irusan purred and lolled; she ruffled his fur. "She'd be even more shocked at how well I understand these descriptions of male physique."

But then it went on to softer fulsome praise:

My dear one, how different we are, you with your dusky gazes and visage, and me with my sunny locks and light eyes, each of us convinced the other is the handsomest man he has ever seen!

She shifted uneasily. Sunny locks. Light eyes. Could it be . . . ? She set that letter aside and read another:

Dearly Beloved . . .
How I long to be with you! My day is dreary, as I go from Pump Room to club, and delight in all company pales in contrast to your dear voice in my ear, your sweet breath on my cheek, your endearing eyes watching me, only to seek what you insist are my perfections, and I see as my faults.
Please . . . do not worry about me. You say I have been too busy lately,

with my many schemes, to spend my time with you at the Sacred Theban Club.

The Sacred Theban Club . . . was it at that club that they met? Probably. Why did the word *Theban* ring some distant dusty bell at the back of her mind? She stared into the fire and sorted through her muddled thoughts. Theban . . . was her memory of that word from something in her father's studies? Thebes she knew of as an important place in Greek myth. How the gentlemen did like their classical references! But *Theban* . . . there was something else. She shook her head. She'd think of it later.

She read on:

Trust me, my dearest, you know I think only of you. Do not be jealous, but one must be social. You know that well; have you not introduced me to many gentlemen who have proved to be of value to me? You don't approve; you say I am wicked. But a fellow must make a living, yes?

Anyway, I have other services to render, you know, beyond my schemes. There are many engagements at the Pump Room, and I must dance attendance on the ladies at the Assembly Rooms, or our little secret will be revealed. And so many introductions . . . where would the sickly old gents of Bath be without me to find them a nursemaid to marry? I wink as I write this, and blow you a kiss . . .

I am, as always, your precious Tulip

Anne sat up straighter at this, and stared at the page as Irusan grumbled his displeasure. It was beginning to seem like her guess as to the identity of the lover/letter writer was correct. She set that on the stack of those she had read and picked up the next note. It was much less loving and had a more serious tone.

Do not think to threaten me, Dearly Beloved, nor to say I should not do what I do. I know so much about you. More than you know, for like a faithful terrier I have done some digging. I know of your past . . . shall we call them friendships? Your past close friendships. You would not want those revealed, would you? Those with whom you have shared your body before me? And you would not like all your exquisite writings, your pretty praise of my male beauty, to be revealed? I kept them, you know, though you thought them committed to memory and burned. I have them still in your own dear hand, one that could be compared to your other letters and noted.

Eyes wide, Anne stared down at the stack; he had kept Alfred's letters, had he? And yet told Lonsdale he was destroying them. Alfred had kept his, as well, so there was that. She unfolded the next.

Dearly Beloved . . . I begin to think you false, since you have yet to bring me into your inner circle, your web of close friends. I don't wish to think you a trickster, but what else am I to imagine? What would I do then, hurt and abandoned?

Destroy this letter, as you have done my past, and I vow I shall do the same this time. I promise, on everything we have shared . . . do not disappoint me, dear fellow.

Anne frowned down at the spidery writing slanting across the page, racing to an end. There were phrases and hints that were nothing but threats. The author of the letters was seeking something, an introduction to Alfred's inner circle. Lonsdale was resisting. Was he afraid others would discover his secret life?

And both men assured the other that they had destroyed the letters, while both kept them. If Lonsdale had kept the other man's letters as protection against blackmail, Anne doubted it would work. As a man of the cloth and a member in good standing of society, Lonsdale had much to lose while the other man . . . if it was who she suspected, he had little to lose, since his whole identity seemed cloudlike, vaporous and ethereal, with little substance.

The last note in the stack, dated Sunday, October 8, was a chilly little missive, written after a spat, and confirmed for Anne what she had been thinking.

How can you allow B____ to speak to me that way? I could cry a thousand tears, but I begin to fancy you unworthy. Have I wasted my love? Perhaps. Know, anyway, that I have far less to lose than you, my Dearly Beloved (how the words seem a hollow mockery now that you have allowed me to be so cruelly turned away from your company!), should our affair be revealed. I could live on without the Sacred Theban Club, or your cruel friend, or any other Bath-ing gents. I could disappear, invent myself elsewhere. I've done it before; I can do it again. There are other men than you, you know. Ones who would reward me for my gifts.

The writer thought Lonsdale too concerned with the opinions of others, too taken up with friends the writer was not close with, perhaps the very ones who formed his "inner circle." He thought that Lonsdale did not care enough, or he'd defy those friends. "Tulip" *then* asked for money, something that had been paid in past, he said. Should Lonsdale choose *not* to send the money, perhaps, Tulip said, there would be a bishop who might care to learn what naughty business Dearly Beloved was up to in Bath.

Blackmail. She knew it.

She took a moment to let it all sink in. Was "Tulip" Mr. Thomas Graeme, as she now suspected? On the surface there were enough clues pointing to the conclusion that she felt she must be right. And if she *was* right . . . had his threats led him to violence? She reread the letter. Why kill Alfred, when he was a source of money? Or had Alfred threatened something worse than the withholding of money, like turning him in to the law? Anne shook her head; as Tulip intimated, Lonsdale would have been risking much more than the other man with such an action, for he was the one with family, friends and social standing. Graeme could, he had made clear, assume a new name and start over somewhere else.

For Alfred the stakes were much higher. If he was arrested for sodomy his whole family would be shamed beyond thinking, even beyond the physical punishment of incarceration or worse for the gentleman himself. And there was worse than imprisonment; the law on the books stated that one punishment for such a crime was death.

Was the answer to the mystery of his death so simple, ultimately? Had he taken his own life after all, to prevent his secret from destroying his family?

"No!" she said, slapping her hand on her dressing table. Irusan started and growled. "Sorry, dear one," she said, making him settle back down. Reason demanded one conclusion: if Alfred had been about to kill himself to conceal his failings, surely he would have destroyed the letters and the journal! She shuffled the letters together and slipped the ribbon on the bundle. He was struggling with a moral decision, and had decided to do the right thing, he told her himself. Was Lonsdale about to turn Graeme in to the magistrate, no matter the personal consequences? What a risk that would be. She contemplated it, trying to imagine how much courage it would take to expose Tulip—Graeme—knowing that to do so might result in exposure of an illicit love so dangerous to reveal that it could lead to prison.

Their society had many paths to ruin, each more perilous than the last. Gambling debt was shameful. Drink or drugs in excess also. But neither would result in a scandal so devastating it could not be recovered from. Sex was another matter altogether. For a lady the road to ruin was clear; sexual activity before marriage was perfectly scandalous. As an example, if someone were to tell the world about the sexual experimentation she had engaged in with Tony, she would be fallen, her name so sullied that she would be considered a disgrace to her family. They would have no alternative but to banish her to the country, and even there she would have to live in a cottage away from Harecross Hall. No morally upstanding family would visit her home.

In theory this was all true, though in practice her reputation would be rescued by marriage to Tony and her moral failings would be forgotten except for being dredged up as spicy gossip.

But for a gentleman like Lonsdale there could be no rescue from ruin. Once accused of the crime of sodomy he would be shunned at the very least, imprisoned, more likely. It was dreadful to contemplate and she no longer wondered at his depression as he contemplated his fate should he choose to expose Graeme's blackmail. *If* that was what had him in the doldrums. She still didn't know if that was what had him so downhearted.

Anne slipped the ribbon off the journal and opened again to the flyleaf, then turned past it. Irusan batted at the ribbon, but she kept it away from him and set him down. What would his own words reveal? The journal started the year before, then there was a break when he did not write, perhaps while he was ill. He resumed when he came to stay with the Basenstokes. He was so grateful for his aunt, and wrote of it with fulsome praise for her love, dedication and support. Anne would share some of what he said, if she wished to hear it. He had found in her a true friend, he wrote, when he felt friendless.

Mr. Roger Basenstoke was a different story. He could not understand his cousin, Lonsdale wrote. Roger was antipathetic toward him. They never argued, but his cousin was subtly cruel and derided him at every opportunity. He made cutting remarks, insulted him. He cautioned his mother against Alfred, and tried to break their affectionate bond. It had become so Alfred avoided Roger whenever possible.

Anne felt a cold shudder pass through her. Who had access to Alfred better than someone who lived in the same home as he did? The open hostility Alfred wrote of could not be ignored. But it appeared that Alfred was puzzled by Roger's animosity toward him, which indicated that his cousin was not in on the secret of his life. That he knew of, anyway. How often in life did one think he or she had concealed some aspect of their life only to find that the truth was clear to many?

She read on. Over the months Lonsdale made friends in Bath. He spoke of a club he belonged to where he found joy and friendship. Westmacott had asked what she meant when she said something about a club, and it had put her in mind of Alethea, and her reaction. Did they know about Lonsdale, and this Sacred Theban Club he and Graeme apparently belonged to? Men gossiped, though they preferred to call it conversation, and knew more of some aspects of life than they would ever speak of in front of a lady.

Alfred wrote most days. He used coded language, never completely open, afraid, perhaps, that his deepest secrets would be plumbed. Toward the end it was clear how troubled he had become. He wrote of someone he loved but who did not love him in return, or at least not in the same way. Could that have been reflective of his disappointment in young Graeme? Did he at last conclude that the fellow was using him for an introduction to society, or as a bank from which to withdraw funds?

Or was there someone else? She read on. One passage in particular was revelatory. *I have betrayed the one I love most,* Lonsdale wrote. *I've been weak, and lost myself in the sensual attractions of novelty. In doing so I've disappointed someone who is, to me, as important as a god of old. I can cry a thousand tears, but I will never be able to make up for a loathsome error of deep disgrace. I'll never forgive myself.*

But there was more beyond his troubled love life. There were hints that seemed to indicate that he, too, had visited the mystic. He wrote of his mistrust, and his worry about others being led astray from the true path to one of a dangerous belief in magic and reliance on potions and talismans. He evasively referred to something or someone he was intent on exposing, but it was not clear if he spoke of the mystic.

And yet . . . potions, magic! She shook her head, confused and irritated by Lonsdale's writing style. He had coached himself to write in such an indirect manner that even when speaking of something straightforward, that wouldn't be harmful if someone came upon his journal, he could not be frank.

A maid entered and curtseyed. "A visitor, milady; Mr. Boatin to see you, in the sitting room."

She gathered the letters with the journal and locked them in her writing desk, pocketed the key, and then descended—followed by Irusan, who thump-thump-thumped his way down the stairs—to find the gentleman perusing, from the shelf, a book of poetry. His spectacles glinted in the lamplight, and she paused in the doorway to watch and smile. How many times had she seen him thus in her father's library, book in hand, spectacles glinting? "Good evening, Mr. Boatin," she finally said, and he started, jumping to his feet.

Irusan gave a meow of pleasure—Osei had rescued him once from Anne's rowdy unpleasant cousins, and so was one of the cat's favorite people—and ran to the gentleman, leaping into his arms. He struggled to right himself and keep from dropping the book. "Good day, my lady," he said with a gasp of laughter. "You catch me in perusal of Pope. I find him entertaining."

"Do you read *The Rape of the Lock*?"

"I prefer the *Essay on Man*."

"The proper study of Mankind is Man?" she said with a smile.

He smiled in return and bowed. "Indeed. It is a sentiment with which I concur."

She took a seat and with a wave of her hand invited him to sit. He did so, settling Irusan on the chair beside him. "And so . . . what have you learned in your study of man?" Anne asked. "Any further information on how Lonsdale died? Does the doctor have a guess as to how long the poisoning would have taken?"

He shook his head, setting the book aside on the table, clasping his hands and leaning forward into the pool of lamplight, his brow wrinkled in thought. His clasped hands dangled between his knees and he twined his fingers. Irusan jumped down and sat on the rug before him, nudging his hands. Osei obeyed the command and petted him. "Dr. Fothergill says there is not enough information. That is, there has not been enough study on the ingestion of poisonous substances, and how much or how long it takes for death to follow to know for sure."

"May I ask, if it is not indelicate . . . how *does* he know it was *yew* poisoning that killed poor Lonsdale?"

"That is interesting. Dr. Fothergill tells me that he removed the fellow's stomach contents, and there found one single bit of a yew needle. From that, because there is no other reason for it to be in his stomach, and the substance produces symptoms readily recognized, the doctor extrapolated the deadly poison. He cannot be certain, of course, but he is as certain as one could expect."

Anne found it fascinating and considered a whole branch of science research that was, perhaps, the future of investigation into causes of death, when so much currently was guesswork. "One *single* tiny portion of a yew needle?" she mused. "And from that he extrapolates yew poisoning?"

"The symptoms of taxine poisoning have long been known. Julius Caesar recounted how Cativolcus, king of Eburones, committed suicide using, as he said it, the 'juice of the yew.' So Mr. Lonsdale's symptoms of poisoning, united with the bit of yew needle . . ." Osei shrugged. "It is beyond the stretch of imagination to believe he would willingly eat such a thing, so he thinks Lonsdale must have been given it in something he ate or drank that day. One tiny bit of the needle was left in the brew or food accidentally."

"How would the so-called juice be isolated? I don't understand."

"The poisoner must have distilled the toxin by infusion, as one brews tea leaves, the doctor said, then strained it."

"Like Socrates, and the infusion of the hemlock plant," she mused. "How positively diabolical." A chill raced over Anne. She pictured some shadowy figure in a kitchen, distilling yew needles, perhaps smiling as they made the distillation, knowing the end result. It was sickening that such resolute evil existed. "I have been trying to piece together Lonsdale's day, to see who could have given him the infusion. So far I know he had breakfast with Roger and Mrs. Basenstoke, lunch with a friend, and imbibed something at the Pump Room." She glanced at the secretary and said, "Roger handed the tea around to Alfred and Mrs. Basenstoke, which was so unusual that my friend commented on her son's action. He was not in the habit of taking breakfast with them. If he was of a murdering state of mind he could easily have introduced the yew infusion to the poor young gentleman's cup, I suppose." She shook her head. "I cannot believe he would do that to a kinsman."

"Though history is threaded with many accounts of those who murder a relation out of anger, or greed, or some kind of gain."

"But for what purpose? I fail to see how he gains by Lonsdale's death."

"Perhaps Mrs. Basenstoke was going to leave young Mr. Lonsdale money if she had the disposition of a private fortune, and Mr. Roger Basenstoke objected?"

"Clary does have her own money, I know, so that is possible," Anne said, frowning down at her hands. She stretched out her fingers, imagining the moment . . . handing a cup of tea to someone, knowing you were killing them. She shuddered and closed her fist. "It's inconceivable."

"There could be other reasons we cannot know."

"Like jealousy over his mother's regard of Alfred, who she told me was more a son to her than Roger."

"Jealousy is a powerful sentiment."

"Roger is a cold fish. I cannot think that he would be so jealous of his mother's regard that he would kill his cousin, who, after all, was not living with them permanently, but merely for the autumn. Basenstoke is so calm, so unruffled . . . cold even."

Osei shrugged. "I do not know the gentleman well enough, but it is said that *Smooth runs the water where the brook is deep* . . ."

"Henry VI Part 2, correct?"

Osei smiled. "The phrase is older than that, I understand, but I do quote Mr. Shakespeare, who writes it most elegantly. An old fable puts it that *There's More Danger in a Reserv'd and Silent, than in a*

Noisy, Babbling Enemy. Mr. Basenstoke may have resentments, even old ones, that he conceals beneath a calm and undemonstrative appearance, while beneath he could seethe and roil with anger."

"How vivid a picture you paint," Anne murmured.

"I find your language most useful at times."

"But there are numerous other possible sources for the poison," Anne mused. "The gentleman may have taken the waters at the Pump Room, and he did imbibe wine at the evening party at the Birkenheads'; the glass was handed to him by Lord Westmacott."

"He was already ill at the evening party, was he not?"

Anne sighed with relief. "You're right, Osei. Perhaps I can strike him from the list."

"Perhaps. Though you cannot say for sure that Lord Westmacott did not provide refreshment to the gentleman earlier?"

She acknowledged it with a nod. "There may be other possibilities. In fact, I was able to look in his room and brought away with me a bottle of some medicine he was taking. Would you be able to take it to the doctor for his analysis?"

Osei said, "Gladly, my lady.

"There was brandy also in his room, but I could not bring that away without arousing suspicion. I would not wish Clary to know the direction of my thoughts. Not yet, anyway."

"I will take the medicine bottle to the doctor. He has, by the way, reported to the magistrate his suspicions concerning the young man's death," Osei said, watching her face. "He felt it was his duty."

"Otherwise his death would have been reported as the result of illness."

"Yes, my lady. And a murder would go undetected. It is fortunate that you were so perspicacious as to command Dr. Fothergill to take the body."

"Anyone would have done the same," she said, heat rising in her cheeks.

"No, my lady. Not one in a hundred would have done so."

"I may have caused more problems for my friends than if I had kept my nose out of it, which is one reason I feel an obligation to help solve it. The poisoner was counting on it looking like natural death. I wonder how many have died, thus, as a result of poisoning, made to look natural?" She considered the problem and glanced up at Osei. Of all the people in the world—or in Bath at the moment, anyway—she trusted him most: his intelligence, his discretion, his unique outlook. "I have something to share with you, something with which I was entrusted on my vow not to tell a soul."

"You had better not share it with me then, my lady," he said promptly. "I would not have you break a vow."

"Neither would I, but I consider this possibly a vital link in the chain of events that led to Lonsdale's death. You see my dilemma; I believe Alfred Lonsdale was murdered. There are secret aspects of his life that may provide the clues to lead to who killed him, and I am not free, as a woman, to move in circles where I can discover what I need to know. On the other hand, I do travel in the right circles to get other pieces of the puzzle. I have already made a start in solving the problem, but I would confide in you, and enlist your aid."

He nodded solemnly. "You know I am at your service, my lady. And I will protest no further; my curiosity has been piqued."

"First, though, I have a favor to ask: are you free to go to the Upper Assembly Rooms this evening to attend the concert?"

"I am at your command."

"Good. I'm inviting Lolly too. I have consulted with her on a separate matter—"

"Concerning Lady Lydia's moods?"

"Yes, as you say . . . and I wish to speak with her. But first . . . have you ever . . ." Distressed, she paused and sighed, examining the pattern on the Turkish rug beneath their feet. Irusan turned to her and pushed his cold nose into her hands. She ruffled his mane of fur and sighed. Finally she looked up and met Osei's gaze. "I feel ridiculous saying this. I have no idea if I am about to be offensive, or if I am making too great a thing about something you will consider of no importance."

"My lady, say what you will. I will neither think it ridiculous nor offensive. I know you well enough to believe you incapable of either."

"Thank you, Mr. Boatin. Have you ever heard of men who are attracted to other men? Is it . . . in your culture, or . . ."

As she stammered, he came to her rescue with a smile, saying, "Yes, I understand the concept. In my people there were men who were known to be . . ." He frowned. "I am now the one struggling, but it is to translate a word from my language. I suppose . . . 'boy wife' would be the closest. Or 'man wife,' men who choose to be with other men, and commit their fidelity, as to a spouse."

She sighed, relieved, and nodded. "Thank you."

"Am I to assume that Mr. Lonsdale was one who preferred the company of men?"

"Mrs. Basenstoke discovered a cache of love letters when she was looking for a suit of clothes for his burial. It was a shock to her when she found that the love letters were from a man."

"Who is the other gentleman?"

"He signed the letters with a pet name, Tulip."

"Do Mr. Lonsdale's friends know this about him?"

"I'm not sure. But I'm wondering if Roger knows. His behavior toward Mr. Lonsdale was . . . troubling. He was rude and cutting. Lonsdale remarked on it in his journal."

"And you think it was because of his preference for men? I would not make that assumption. As we have already discussed, there could have been some other conflict between them, since they were family and lived in the same house. Perhaps it was something else of which Mr. Lonsdale was unaware, or, as we postulated, jealousy over Mrs. Basenstoke's love of her nephew."

"You're right, of course, Osei. I have a tendency to race ahead in my thoughts and make assumptions. Anyway, I wish to enlist your help to do a few things." She told him of the concern Alethea and Westmacott had both expressed over the word *club* in association with Lonsdale and Mr. Graeme. "I wonder what that means, if . . . if Mr. Lonsdale belonged to some kind of club consisting of men who felt as he did, and if it is a matter of gossip among the gentlemen of Bath. I don't know if you can learn anything about it, but you may. Tell me . . . you have a self-taught classical education. What do you think of when you hear the word *Theban*?"

"Thebes is a Greek city mentioned often in classical literature."

"Yes, of course, but there is something in my mind to do with the word *Theban* in particular. I feel I have heard the word before, but the reference escapes me."

Osei pondered, and his eyes widened behind his gold-rimmed spectacles.

"What is it? You've thought of something," she exclaimed,

eagerly sitting forward.

"I can think of one thing, my lady. It may connect to what you were saying. In history it is known that there was a group of soldiers, a unit, formed of men and their younger lovers."

"Male lovers? How odd to make up an army unit in that way."

"It was thought that they would fight more earnestly to protect their loved ones."

"And . . . ?"

"It was called the Sacred Band of Thebes."

Chapter Twenty-one

"That's it! I knew I had heard of it in some connection, though I think the part about male lovers was expurgated from my education. I was told they were friends."

He smiled. "It would have been difficult to explain to a young girl, perhaps."

"I suppose. I think I can safely assume that in Bath there is a club called the Sacred Theban Club—that was in the journal—of men of Lonsdale's persuasion. He met Graeme there."

"And yet both were young men. There must be older men involved, hence the club name?"

"I suppose. I don't know who those gentlemen would be, though. But Osei, this explains some of what I read! How valuable a weapon it would be if one had a blackmailing bent to know the gentlemen of such a club."

"True. If there were men there with reputations to protect it would be a rich hunting ground for a blackmailer."

"I'll have to sort it out in my brain. However, there are a couple of other things: as I said, I am attempting to reconstruct his day, where Mr. Lonsdale went, with whom, and what he did. Also, I wish to prove my suspicions correct. Alfred's lover was Mr. Thomas Graeme, who was in the end blackmailing him with the threat of exposure; of that I'm virtually certain. Graeme was threatening to reveal all, I think, perhaps to Lonsdale's friends and relatives, and even to the church. And yet there is more. Lonsdale spoke to me of a moral dilemma, of a need to right some wrong, but I believe it was something more than his love affair."

"What do you mean, my lady?"

"I have a sense that there is more to young Mr. Graeme than his preference for men and willingness to blackmail his lovers. I fear that he is behind some matchmaking scheme of sorts. But how could he profit from such a thing, and how is he allied with this Mystic of Bath? There is a connection there, I'd wager."

Mr. Boatin smothered a grin. "Is that all you investigate, my lady? A trifling. A matter of hours."

She smiled. "You've caught me, Mr. Boatin. It is, indeed, a complicated puzzle, with many mysterious pieces to it." Sobering, she said, "I wish to solve Mr. Lonsdale's murder because I see how deeply hurt my friends are, and how it is affecting their lives. There is gossip going around about the fellow dying in the Birkenheads' home, and I don't like it. I must, therefore, be where people gossip, and nowhere do they gossip more than the Assembly Rooms and the Pump Room. So we shall attend the concert tonight, and tomorrow I will go to the Pump Room and try to speak with Mr. Graeme. Let me get that medicine bottle for you to take to Dr. Fothergill."

• • •

Anne sent a note to Mr. Tyson, the Upper Assembly Rooms' master of ceremonies, about the Marquess of Darkefell's impending arrival in Bath, and added a note introducing his secretary, Mr. Boatin. She mentioned that gentleman's desire to attend the concert. It was enough, as she had surmised, to ensure he would be welcome. And so, gowned elegantly, she entered the Upper Assembly Rooms on Mr. Boatin's arm. As she'd hoped, their entrance made a stir, conversation swelling and swirling across the room in ripples of hisses, whispers, sighs and muttered exclamations.

Lolly, on the secretary's other arm, avidly glanced around, waving with her fan to her various friends. She was giddy with excitement, for the concerts were in general out of her limited budget. It was a treat, an auditory sweet.

The concert would be in the tearoom, but it was not yet open to patrons. Anne did not often like arriving early, but tonight she wished to make Mr. Boatin known to her acquaintances. Quin, who adored music, was sitting in the Octagon Room with Susanna Hadley, waiting to be seated. Anne, Lolly and Mr. Boatin made their way through the crowd toward them, nodding and bowing to all who greeted them. Quin was happy to see Osei again, and introduced him to Susanna. Swirling around them were many others who Anne introduced, including Baron Kattenby and Mrs. Venables, and Lady Sharples, who examined the African gentleman with undisguised interest.

Drifting past her she saw Mrs. Noakes and Mr. Doyne. She managed to attract their attention and introduce them to Osei, who bowed and engaged them in small talk. Anne had filled the secretary in on as many of her suspicions as she could remember, on their way over, so he was well-equipped with Bath gossip. Fortunately Mr. Doyne, who, it turned out, had been to Tunisia on the African continent, lingered. As Mrs. Noakes attempted unsuccessfully to appear interested, they spoke of a recent outbreak of plague in that area. Plague of different sorts was a recurring problem in Europe, Africa and Asia, with no solution, no cure that anyone could come up with beyond avoiding the plague-ridden.

Skillfully, with a natural polish and finesse of which Anne wished herself possessed, Osei brought the conversation around to the subject they agreed would be interesting to pursue. When Mr. Doyne had asked him a little about his life in Africa before his enslavement, he spoke briefly, then said, "I wish I could disabuse the English of the notion that all of the African continent is plagued by witch doctors and magic men. There is, unfortunately, great fear of me for that reason; people see me and once they learn of my origin, immediately think of shamans, and even cannibals."

"Outrageous!" Mr. Doyne said with horror. "I apologize for my fellow Englishmen."

Anne smothered a smile at Osei's skillful manipulation. He had both interested and engaged the gentleman.

"No apology necessary, sir; I could amaze you with the tales *my* people heard of the European travelers they encountered. The Spanish were considered especially barbaric. But I was therefore surprised, when I got to know your country better, that the same people who say my people are superstitious go to mystics and seers here in England. In fact, I have heard there is one in Bath that I should visit, a woman by the name of Mother Macree. I'll admit, I am tempted simply out of interest. Have you heard of her?"

"Indeed I have, Mr. Boatin," Mr. Doyne said eagerly, his plain face alight, his jaundice-yellowed eyes wide. "My dear fellow, please do *not* dismiss what you have not experienced! She is most interesting, a real character, and I believe she does have some power of sight through the veil between this world and the next. In fact, I have her to thank for this lovely lady entering my life!" he said, patting the gloved hand of Mrs. Noakes, resting on his satin-clad arm.

"Is that so? How is that possible?"

"I visited the mystic," Mr. Doyne said, his tone now serious and sober. "I had heard marvelous things about her accuracy from many sources but I was, I'll admit, skeptical. Her reading was uncanny! She told me things she could *not* have known without being a visionary. I went back again, and then, on my third visit, she told me I would meet a woman with blue eyes and reddish hair, a lady who would hale from Sussex and would be a child of October—all the best spiritualists make a study of the stars and know the ancient secrets of the zodiac—and then I was introduced to Mrs. Noakes! It was simply *astounding* how much we have in common," he cried, his volume rising in conjunction with his enthusiasm. "I discovered we share a passion for King Charles spaniels, and the reintroduction of the white stork to England; the species died out after the civil war, you know . . . great shame. Anyway, it is *uncanny* how perfectly suited we are to one another." He cast her an affectionate look and squeezed her arm to his side. She returned the smile with a coquettish simper.

It was as if Mrs. Noakes had been made to order for him, Anne thought, listening in. How many ladies did she know who adored dogs and were avid bird fanciers concerned with reintroducing the white stork to England? Mrs. Noakes would be the first, if it was in any way true, which she doubted.

"Who introduced you, sir, if I may be so bold to ask?" Osei said.

"Oh, a young fellow . . . very congenial sort. Mr. Thomas Graeme."

Of course; it *would* be Mr. Graeme, but it was not news to her, as Anne had already surmised it. She asked, "Pardon me, Mr. Doyne; how well do you know Mr. Graeme?"

"Met him as one does in the Pump Room, you know, a casual acquaintance."

"I have heard various tales of his past," she said. "And a friend said he had met him at some club," she said, regarding the gentleman closely. But he did not flinch at the word *club*, as Alethea and Lord Westmacott had. Perhaps the salacious gossip had not reached the prosaic and provincial Mr. Doyne. He was not a longtime denizen of Bath, as her two friends were.

"Club? Can't say. Don't belong to any. I came here for my health, you know, not to carouse."

"And how *is* your health, sir?"

"Middling."

Her attention was claimed by friends who desired to introduce her to another lady. That was merely a pretext to gossip, she feared, as one pulled her aside, and, with an avid look, said, "You were at the Birkenheads' musical evening the night Mr. Lonsdale died, were you not?"

"Yes, I was."

The two ladies exchanged glances and one said, "I heard he killed himself over a love affair gone wrong."

"Is that so?" Anne replied, stiffening. "Where did you hear it from?"

The lady recoiled from Anne's brusque tone. "One does hear things, you know, here, there—"

"But where did you hear this *particular* piece of gossip?" she said, her annoyance quickening and her cheeks flushing hot. She did not need a mirror to know they would now be a most unbecoming shade of livid red. She slapped her fan against her skirt. "You *must* remember."

"I know the Birkenheads are your particular friends and I fear that I have offended," the acquaintance said, curtseying and then turning away to her companion.

Curses on her intemperance. Anne shook her head. She must take lessons from Mr. Boatin on retaining a sense of decorum even when outraged.

A chime indicated the concert hall was ready, and as the doors were opened the sounds of the orchestra tuning up drifted to them. The two women swept away, heads together, no doubt gossiping now about Lady Anne Addison's highly inappropriate reaction. Susanna and an Assembly Rooms footman helped Quin to his chair, as Osei took Anne and Lolly on his arms and—despite his slight limp—guided them skillfully through the crowd to sit with their friends.

Anne adjusted her skirt while Osei politely chatted with Lolly. The conductor bowed, then turned and the music flowed. In moments the soothing effects of it lifted Anne, improving her temper, the program inspired, as usual. Mr. Venanzio Rauzzini, the famous castrato who had retired as a soloist singer to become the music master of the Upper Assembly Rooms, led the orchestra in a series of Telemann overtures. The lovely acoustics of the tearoom ensured that the music soared into the heights, reaching even to the back of the seventy-foot room effortlessly.

Anne glanced to her left; Osei was enjoying it greatly. She would be sure to let Darkefell know that if he didn't wish to go to a concert — he was no great lover of music, he had confessed, while she deeply appreciated great musical performances — that his secretary would be more than an adequate replacement. Lolly, on the other hand, was looking about at the crowd with interest and paying little heed, it appeared, to the music surrounding them. She was, as always, interested in everything, but there was not the air of gaiety in her mien that Anne was accustomed to.

Finally, there was a break. "Let us amble, Lolly, while Mr. Boatin accompanies Quin and Susanna to the card room for tea." They strolled to the fireside in the Octagon Room, where there were fewer people, though the babble of chatter humming was still ever-present, cocooning them in muffled conversation. Anne leaned into her cousin. "Did you discover anything about poor Lydia?"

"What I have discovered is most distressing," she said, grabbing Anne's hand. "Lydia's maid is beside herself, and finally confided in me. I don't know what to do."

"What is it?" Anne asked. "Tell me now, or I'll fear the worst."

Lolly stared up at her, tears welling in her bloodshot eyes. "You won't let darling Lydia know what I've told you and how I found out? The maid is desperately afraid, both for herself and her mistress. Please, Anne . . ."

She watched her darling cousin's pouchy lined face, drawn down with an unusually sober expression of worry. One tear swam over the red rim of her eye and took a wayward zigzag path down her soft, wrinkled cheek. "I promise," Anne said. "But I may have to do something about it, you know. If I must speak to her, I will conceal the source of my knowledge. She won't question it; she knows I am relentless where my curiosity is aroused."

The tears became a flood, dripping down her cheeks and spraying as she vigorously nodded and sniffed. Anne offered her a handkerchief, and she dabbed at her eyes. "You're so clever, I'm sure you can figure this puzzle out. I want the darling girl to be relieved of her worry."

"Then *tell* me, so I can help, what is going on," Anne cried softly, becoming impatient. "Did it start the day we went to the mystic?"

"Oh, no, Anne, it was *before* that," Lolly said, hastily dabbing at her tearstained cheeks with a handkerchief. "It was the reason she wished to go to the mystic in the first place." She blew her nose, and a couple glanced over at her in horror. "Poor dear Lydia is *deathly* afraid that her baby and her family are under a curse."

"A *curse*?"

"Yes."

"Of all the featherbrained—"

"Anne, do not be cruel!" Lolly said, glaring up at her with a rare stern tone. She took Anne's gloved hands in her own. "*Listen* to me!"

"Yes, Lolly," Anne said.

"Not long ago, Lydia found a note on her dressing table addressed to her. She opened it. It contained a message; she had been enchanted by the evil eye. Her baby, it said, was doomed to be born a monster."

"How *hideous*!" Fury rose in Anne's heart and a sick taste flooded her mouth. Those around them turned and gazed at her with interest. She lowered her voice and hissed, "To trick a gullible girl like Lydia, to prey upon her fears—"

"Shush, Anne," Lolly said, squeezing her hands. "Poor child. She is desperately seeking a hunchback—"

"A hunchback? Whatever does that mean? She spoke of it to me several days ago."

"A hunchback can ward off the evil eye."

Anne sighed and opened her mouth, but then closed it. She had nothing to say. Railing against Lydia's folly would not help. She needed to focus on solutions.

Lolly released her cousin's hands and fidgeted with her fan, flicking it open. She glanced around as those closest returned to their own gossipy chatter, drifting away. Bending closer to Anne again, Lolly said, "Listen: her maid tells me that the note said the only way to counter it was to not speak of it to anyone, but to find a magic practitioner, someone who understood how that kind of evil spell worked. The maid knows because she was curious; Lydia threw the note in the cold hearth, but the girl took it and read it before destroying it. Lydia's only hope, the note said, was a talisman to ward off the evil eye and a potion of protection for the babe."

Fear clutched her stomach. Potion? Her breath caught as she considered that if Dr. Fothergill was right, Lonsdale had died as the result of drinking a potion, of sorts. "*That* is why Lydia was so intent on going to see the mystic."

"Yes. I don't understand why that woman wanted to see Lydia in private, though. How did she know the child is suffering such an enchantment? She truly must be a mystic."

Anne regarded her with an incredulous gaze. "Lolly, listen to yourself! Think! From whence did the curse note come if not the mystic herself?"

"Oh. *Oh!*" Lolly stared, her eyes bulging. "It's like those sellers of quack medicines who diagnose an illness and sell you the exact cure. You never had the illness, but feel the good effects of the cure completely."

"Exactly."

"Because you believe," Lolly mused, frowning. "I had not thought of it that way around. It never occurred to me that the original note was from the mystic, or someone in her employ. I *trusted* her! I was *kind* to Mother Macree," she exclaimed. "Giving her an ointment for her poor cramped hands, even. How *could* she trick poor Lydia in such a cruel manner?"

The bell was rung for the second half of the concert, and arm in arm they strolled back. "It wasn't just her, Lolly. She had the aid of a confederate who wrote and carried that execrable note. I have a feeling I know *exactly* who is responsible. If I am correct I can uncurse Lydia swiftly."

"But can you convince *her* it is all a sham?"

That gave Anne pause. Lydia had a stubborn streak that usually became evident when it was least convenient. How did one eradicate the effects of irrational dread on one who was deeply superstitious?

The second half of the program was a lilting set of Vivaldi *concerti con molti strumenti,* the sound of the strings singing and dipping among them: mandolins, violins and cellos, and even the theorbo, a lute with bass strings. Then the sweet woodwinds— flutes, oboes, the resonant bassoon, and the chalumeau, with its lovely folk music lilt—and the happy harpsichord to round it out.

But all Anne could think of was her plan; the so-called Mystic of Bath and one Mr. Thomas Graeme had overreached themselves when they frightened Lydia. She was determined. She would stop them from persecuting the gullible, but there was more. She must uncover the matchmaking enterprise, and how they benefited from the matches they made. To that end she must employ her mother's genius at recalling a piece of alarming gossip Anne vaguely remembered from one of her first days in Bath.

Lives could hang in the balance.

Chapter Twenty-two

Morning dawned with a cold rattle of wind at her window. After her morning tea, she set her plan into action. First, to gather every scrap of information she could. "Mother, may we talk?" Anne stood in the open door of her mother's bedchamber, a large dim room papered in a cheerful floral William Kilburn print, as her maid, Eloise, pinned in a length of false hair and swept it up into the coiffure that was the Countess of Harecross's unique style.

The woman turned and regarded Anne with surprise. Unpowdered, her face was surprisingly youthful, the faint lines in her forehead and beside her blue eyes less noticeable. "Of course, Anne. I have been wanting to speak with you these last few days, but you are always rushing in and rushing out, visiting and gallivanting. What would you like?"

Anne hesitated.

"Come, sit," her mother said, indicating the end of the elegant testered bed. Her maid selected more pieces of false hair, combed and pinned them, then adorned the resultant style with silk flowers, feathers and pearls. "I will start. When is the marquess arriving?"

"Monday, Osei says." A flush of heat crept up Anne's body from her toes to her cheeks.

"You look like you have a fever. You aren't sickening, are you?" Lady Harecross met her daughter's gaze in the mirror and stared, narrowing her eyes.

"I'm in perfect health, Mother. Mr. Boatin has engaged a house for the marquess—"

"Why he's not staying with the Bestwicks is beyond me. Frivolous waste of money."

"—and is making sure it is fitted up as Tony . . . uh, Darkefell prefers. He is not particular about much, but he is about a few things."

"I wish, of course, to hold a party to celebrate your engagement. When is best?"

"Never," Anne said bluntly. "He'll hate it. He'll insult half the people there without meaning to and your friends will take against him."

"You make him sound an ogre, as though he is the rudest man on the face of the earth."

"I'm trying to keep you from false hope, Mother. He does not suffer fools gladly."

"Are you saying my friends are fools?"

Anne bit her lip and stayed silent.

She harrumphed loudly. Her maid waited a moment for her mistress to calm, then resumed her task. "I will not believe someone as well raised as he is, with such an illustrious title and so much a gentleman, would misbehave," Lady Harecross said, sliding her gaze sideways to her daughter." He was perfectly charming to your grandmother and me."

"I think we can fairly assume I know him better than you, Mother."

Lady Harecross caught her smile and said, "You enjoy his bad temper, don't you?"

Anne smiled more widely, surprised by her mother's perceptiveness. "I suppose I do, for I never need to apologize when I lose my own temper, or say something in haste. He more than matches me for irritability, and yet he doesn't frighten me in the least. When he is angry at me I let him rage. Once he gets over it, which he does quickly almost always, we carry on and do what I wish."

"I'll never understand you, Anne."

"That coming from a lady who also likes to get her own way? We are identical in that, Mother, though we diverge in our methods."

"You are a most contrary young lady."

"I have captured a marquess," she said with a sigh. "He is securely in my leg-hold trap. Doesn't that please you?"

"Don't be vulgar. Of course it pleases me, but I'd be happier if I could speak of it to my friends."

"Soon enough, Mother. I've already told you . . . once he is here and settled we will announce our engagement. He can share that horror with me, though I'll bear the brunt of it, no doubt, from disappointed females trying to understand how I snagged a marquess with my limited charms." She sighed heavily. "But that is talk for another day. I have something I wish to ask you. The first day Mrs. McKellar was here for a fitting, you and Clary were speaking of a Mr. Court-something-or-other, who died soon after marrying."

"You rarely listen to gossip. Why do you care?"

"How much do you know about him? How did he come to meet his bride? Who is she?"

Lady Harecross stared as her maid pinned in one last spray of silk flowers. "You never do or say anything without purpose, Anne." She examined herself in the mirror, then nodded and flapped her hand at her maid to dismiss her. "Tell me why you want to know and I may indulge you."

"You know how I am; I can't help but poke around in things. I have recently come across a couple of odd matches between ailing men of means and younger ladies who appear to have come out of nowhere. They were introduced by a young gentleman I have met. I'm curious."

"What does that have to do with Courtland, who died?" Lady Harecross said.

Curses, Anne thought, her mouth twitching in irritation. She hadn't wanted to explain, just to learn more. "I don't know," she said honestly. "Probably nothing."

The maid stowed the other pieces of false hair in their boxes along with various feathers, lengths of ribbon and hair combs, then assembled the countess's clothes for the day, laying the various pieces on the bed behind Anne.

"All right, I will tell you what I know." Lady Harecross turned to face Anne. She wore her daytime hair, but still had on her night-gown, an oddly disparate look to which Anne was unaccustomed. "Mr. Cleveland Courtland was a widower with two children, both of whom are married and settled in London. He came here two years ago for the waters, taking a home on Upper Church."

"Was he wealthy?"

"Anne, that's vulgar to ask!" She shrugged, then said, "Of *course* he was. Moderately. Perhaps more than moderately. He had a woolen factory that has contracts with the military. And his children were independent, one in government, and the eldest manages the manufactory . . . owns it now, I suppose, since Courtland's death. I knew him because Clary had some hopes in that direction. You don't realize it but she's lonely, and Roger is not a good companion in many ways. What son is? Besides, he'll marry at some point and no doubt expect her to find her own house.

"I held a soiree and a literary afternoon—so tedious!—because she asked me to. Mr. Courtland fancied himself a poet. Poor Clary." She sighed but then shook herself and straightened. "At least she now has some hopes of this Mr. Smythe, though I am doing my best to run to ground any information about him; it is vaguely said he is *also* a woolen manufacturer with deep pockets. However, no one seems to know him, or his background or his people. I prefer someone with anchors in society. I prefer *proof* that someone is who they say they are."

"Indeed you do," Anne murmured.

"Don't be snide, Anne."

"Mother, I actually agree with you. A proven history is the safest bet, in marriage and otherwise."

Lady Harecross eyed her daughter with suspicion, but then continued. "Anyway, about Courtland . . . ten months ago or so he met a widow, Mrs. Breckenridge, and within weeks they were engaged to be wed, and in two months they were married. He then proceeded to buy her an extravagant number of gowns, and jewels, a horse and carriage, even a townhouse in London, in *her name!* No woman was as showered with gifts as she. It was the talk of Bath for a time."

"Really? Generous man."

"He was besotted. She was, he claimed, perfect for him. She enjoyed poetry, especially the poetry of Goldsmith; she quoted 'When Lovely Woman Stoops to Folly' — you know, from *The Vicar of Wakefield* — when first they met, if you can believe it."

"What an odd choice to quote to a gentleman."

"Easy to memorize and hinting at a tendency to, shall we say, *stoop to folly?*" Lady Harecross raised her eyebrows with a significant look. "For gentlemen of a certain age who have been without female companionship for a time but are too fastidious to stoop to conquer," she said, quoting another Goldsmith work, "that would be enough to heat his blood and hasten his footsteps down the aisle."

"*Mother!* You are being unusually outrageous." Anne bit back a smile, which she easily defeated when she thought that the gentleman was now dead after hastening down that aisle. "It sounds as though you do not believe the random nature of their meeting. Who introduced them? Do you know?"

"I do. They met through a lovely young fellow . . . ingratiating. I know him but slightly. He was especially kind to your grandmother in the Pump Room when her Bath chair would not go over the door sill. Rushed to our aid when those lazy attendants could not bother to stir themselves."

"A young man? Unusual one would be bothered with two . . ." She was about to say two elderly ladies, but she stopped herself. Her mother was on the wrong side of fifty, but she was still attractive and spirited.

"He was absolutely charming and stayed by our side, fetching water for your grandmother. She was quite taken, I must say. He sat beside her and gossiped the afternoon away. It gave me some time to myself to spend with friends. When I came back, she *still* was in no hurry to depart."

"*Grandmother?*" What a little male attention could do, Anne mused.

"She was flattered by his interest. Such a nice-looking fellow: beautiful golden hair, nicely dressed, enjoyed all the tittle-tattle and gossip most men do not."

"And his name is . . . ?" Anne asked, already knowing the answer.

"Mr. Thomas Graeme."

• • •

It was enough, Anne thought as she evaded her mother's further questions and returned to her room, to go on. Graeme's name was everywhere, entwined in Bath society like a parasitic vine to such a degree that she could imagine where he got enough information, if what she suspected was true, to fuel his marriage brokerage, arranging introductions guaranteed to lead to the altar. There was a sick feeling at the pit of her stomach. What she feared was too fantastical though, and surely could not be true.

As Mary dressed Anne's hair for the day, she said, "Mrs. McKellar sent some of the new gowns this morning, milady. And along with them, she sent a note, addressed to you and sealed."

Anne held out her hand, Mary gave it to her, and she broke the seal. It was short and to the point: she had met with Bridie. The girl was frightened but willing to tell what she knew if it would gain her a better position. Should Mrs. McKellar arrange a meeting of some sort? She thought the girl would be able to give Anne much information that would interest her.

Once her hair was dressed, Anne sat down at her desk and wrote a note to Mrs. McKellar, who had rooms with her sister on Catherine Place, around the corner from Margaret's Buildings. Anne would arrange to be at Lolly's Margaret's Buildings rooms at noon, if Mrs. McKellar could get word to Bridie. It was a great risk the child was taking, and one for which Anne must be ready to compensate her.

She sat for a moment, tapping her teeth with the pencil, then recorded what she knew of Alfred Lonsdale's day and the possible places he could have ingested poison. Breakfast with Roger and Clary Basenstoke, with Roger pouring his tea, then speaking to him privately. Lunch—perhaps with Thomas Graeme, if that young gent was indeed Tulip, for another bout of blackmail?—or perhaps with someone else. Water, possibly, in the Pump Room. Wine at the Birkenheads'. She had to fill in the rest.

Other than that she jotted down a list:

Club? Who belonged to the Sacred Theban club?
Why did Roger dislike Alfred?
Is Graeme Tulip?
Did Alethea and Bertie know about Alfred's secret life?
How does Mother Macree know what she knows?

Given what she had learned of her grandmother's gossipy chat with Mr. Graeme, she had a feeling she knew the young gentleman's best source of information: every elderly lady or gent who spent time at the Pump Room and who spoke to him. But there had to be more to it, because the mystic appeared to know about Quin's dead sister, about whom none of them ever spoke. It would not be a topic of conversation. Was it a case of an extraordinary guess, or was she adept at reading people? Also, she jotted down:

How are Graeme and Mother Macree connected? (Maybe find out from Bridie?)
What benefit in helping men find wives?
Is Lonsdale's death connected to his secret life, or was he poking into the same thing I am, the matchmaking?

She folded the list, telling her maid the contents of it as Mary helped her into her gown. Whether it was all interwoven—Graeme seemed, to her, to have his thumbs in so many pies that he was the center of all that was going wrong in Bath—or whether there were pieces of the puzzle that had other sources, was yet to be established. Alfred Lonsdale's murder was by far the most serious event, however . . . was his the latest in a line of suspicious deaths? Mr. Courtland's untimely demise, which had enriched his tailor-made bride, troubled her. There were, it seemed to her, far too many perfect spouses, all coincidentally foreseen by the mystic, but unless there was some manufactory somewhere turning them out, she could not imagine where they came from. Mr. Lonsdale's murder was out of keeping with the others, in any case, and there were suspects in his suspicious death that had nothing to do with the mystic, suspects like the victim's own cousin.

But her first priority had become Lydia, and the poor girl's belief that she and her baby were cursed. What had the mystic told her about how to defeat it? What had Lydia already done, what potions had she taken, what talisman had she bought? Anne decided a visit to the mystic was in her immediate future. Maybe the woman already knew she was coming, she thought, with a grim smile.

As Mary tied the last bow and pinned the last pin, Anne picked up her pencil and list and said to her, "If you would, please be ready to go with me if I need you. I am going to get to the bottom of all of this nonsense or know the reason why."

"Aye, milady," Mary said with a smirk.

"Why are you smiling?"

"I'd no' like to be the culprit who thinks himself—or herself—safe from discovery when you're on the job, milady. I'd bet on you every time."

"I am the nag most likely to win," Anne said with a grim smile and a tug at her waist. "I will not rest until this is satisfactorily concluded."

She sent a note to Osei to meet her at the Pump Room, for she valued his astute regard of people, and was interested to know if the doctor had found anything more out. The day was brilliant and brisk, with a limitless sky across which clouds scudded, like horses across a blue meadow. Above all things she would have enjoyed a good long ramble in the park of her home in Kent, or the wilder environs of Darkefell's moody, sullen castle, which she had come to adore. Living there with her husband for most of the year was going to be a challenge, though, despite her love of it. She was a social creature, and the castle was lonely.

She would have to write to her father; the marriage settlements *must* include language that allowed her the freedom to spend some time at her father's estate, visiting him and her brother and even, as much as she had dreaded it, time in Bath to visit her mother and grandmother. Freedom was an illusion, especially for women. That which she had so far experienced had come about because of a lack of entanglement. In future her life was about to become very entangled indeed, and as much as the idea of that kind of bondage frightened her, being Tony's wife would inevitably have rewards that would have to make up for it.

Enough gloomy wonderings; she must go to the Pump Room for an early meeting with Osei, assuming he had received her note. He had, and awaited her outside. He bowed, then took her arm, guiding her in as she explained her various tasks that day. She had attended in the morning, knowing that several of those who came to partake of the waters would be there to begin their mineral regimen for the day.

"There, my first quarry," she murmured to Osei, nodding toward Baron Kattenby, who stood alone. "My lord," she said, sweeping toward him. "I saw you last night at the concert, but you were otherwise engaged. How do I find you today? Taking the waters, I see," she said as he was handed a glass of the warm murky liquid.

"My lady," he said, bowing. He held the glass up and peered at it nearsightedly. "Yes, you find me taking the first of the three my doctor has advised for the day."

"May I introduce to you Mr. Osei Boatin, secretary to the Marquess of Darkefell? Mr. Boatin is in Bath engaging a house for his lordship and arranging his subscriptions."

"Good day, sir," the baron said, bowing. If he was startled to be introduced to a secretary, he did not show it. "You must be sure to write your name in the book here, in the Pump Room, Mr. Boatin."

"Thank you, sir; I will."

"I am so happy for you and Mrs. Venables. Have you decided on a wedding date yet?"

"No, I would not say that," he answered, his tone full of caution.

"We have some time." They had three months after the reading of the banns in which to marry. "I am still anxious to wait until Christmas. It seems to be happening so swiftly, but I see no reason to jump into it."

Anne wondered how Mrs. Venables felt about that. The woman was anxious for an establishment away from the Birkenheads, and who could blame her? Marriage, for her, would mean more freedom than what she now had as a poor relation of sorts. "Sir, I have noticed you are friendly with the people of Bath. You appear to have established yourself here. Tell me, did you know a gentleman by the name of Mr. Courtland?"

"I certainly did; we were ardent foes across the whist table. Poor fellow! Recently deceased."

"Was it unexpected?"

"Unexpected?" He frowned. "I suppose so. He had been unwell, but nothing that any of us thought would take him."

"What were his symptoms?"

An expression of uncertainty became bewilderment. "I . . . surely that is . . . he was unwell. I think that is enough to know."

"I understand from my mother, Lady Harecross, that Mr. Courtland was recently wed."

"Recently? Well, early in the year. A lovely lady, Mrs. Breckenridge she was, before their marriage."

"Is she still in Bath?"

He shook his head. "No. Poor lady. They were so deeply in love." He sighed sentimentally. "Never saw Courtland so happy in those first days, though he was not feeling quite the thing, you know. His experience with his lady wife was what made me think I should try marriage again."

"But she is not still in Bath," Anne said, persistent.

He frowned. "She moved to London after his death."

"But he died just a couple of weeks ago?"

"That is so but his son came to Bath and took possession of his townhouse. There was some disagreement between him and the widow, so rather than quarrel she departed. So sad."

"But not unavoidable. She had a right to stay in the house while in mourning, surely, do you not think?"

"Perhaps she did not wish to face the opprobrium the young man threatened. We may think the son was being most unreasonable, but grown sons and daughters do not always understand that a parent still wishes for companionship." He frowned still and stared at her. "See here, my lady, why are you asking about Courtland's death?"

She had pushed too hard too fast. "Conversation, sir; I was passing the time of day." She made some light comment about another topic, and they spoke for a minute about the weather, if rain was expected, and what assemblies both would attend. But Anne still had questions. "Tell me . . . do you know if Mr. Thomas Graeme introduced Mr. Courtland to Mrs. Breckenridge? And had Mr. Courtland been to the Mystic of Bath?"

"I couldn't say."

"Was anyone a closer friend to the late Mr. Courtland? Perhaps his son is still in Bath settling his estate?"

"I'm sure I do not know, my lady, and I am most concerned at this line of . . . this gossip! You must excuse me, madam, if I halt our conversation here."

Chapter Twenty-three

She had offended him with her clumsy questioning. There was nothing to do but be gracious. "Sir, I wish you and Mrs. Venables *both* well."

He bowed. "Thank you, my lady."

As she walked away with Osei she could not resist saying to him, "I wonder if the new Mrs. Courtland escaped Bath just ahead of the magistrate?"

"What do you suspect, my lady? You appear to be on the trail of some mystery, and yet surely there can be nothing wrong between the baron and your friend Mrs. Venables?"

"I don't suppose so," she mused. "It's not the same at all as these other marriages and engagements." She explained her suspicions regarding the Courtland marriage and the Doyne/Noakes engagement, both examples of aging gentlemen and genteel widows who appeared to be eerily perfect, as if made for their tastes. "The baron and Bella's engagement is different, of course. Bella is Bertie's cousin, deeply loved by him; marriage, for her, will be a welcome relief to her penury, but that's no rare thing in this world where women have no ability to work in a profession, and so no alternative but to marry for financial security. It's no wonder if she perhaps pretends a little more love than she feels."

"You think that's the case? That she doesn't love the baron as much as she seems?"

Anne frowned. "I don't know. She is an interesting woman. She has traveled and seen life; I suppose I assume the prosy baron would bore her."

"Perhaps her idea of a good life has changed from the excitement a younger person would welcome to one with security and comfort."

"You are likely correct, Osei. She said as much the first day I met her, that she only wished for a quiet life. The baron's lineage is impeccable and his income comfortable. She is a handsome woman and he a lonely man; it's an ideal match in many ways." She sighed. "Sorting my suspicions from reality is a difficult task. My curiosity has been aroused because of the several 'perfect' matches foretold by the mystic. I am likely suspicious without cause in most cases."

"It is said that once one has encountered a snake in a tree, every vine becomes a snake."

She smiled up at him. "How perfect a proverb that is! Tell me, Osei, what more have you learned from the doctor? Does he still doubt that Lonsdale would have committed suicide?"

"His conclusion is that death by ingesting yew poison would be an unlikely way to kill oneself."

"I agree. And so, we are still left with murder." She glanced around the room, then turned to walk with him.

The Pump Room was beginning to fill with the usual gentlemen and ladies there for their daily mineral water and exercise, walking about chatting and ogling the others. She had been hoping to get her astute friend's opinion of Graeme, but he was unfortunately absent. Anne had a busy day ahead, so she and Osei parted ways. He had a plethora of duties to see to, to ensure that the townhome was fitted up for Lord Darkefell.

Her carriage awaited; Osei handed her up into it, bowed and strode off to see to his duties. Inside the carriage Irusan awaited in fluffy splendor. Many a lady carried with her a small dog as companion. Anne had decided that if her cat chose to accompany her—unlike a dog, a cat must choose for himself—she would welcome it, as eccentric as it would undoubtedly appear. Today was one of the days he had followed her out to the carriage.

They traveled a short distance, and then Anne told the driver to wait; she entered the Milsom Street residence of the Bestwicks. Lady John was not receiving visitors, the maid informed her, but Anne tartly told her to summon Lolly. Her real aim was to enlist her cousin's aid to interview the mystic's maidservant, so she was perfectly content not to see Lydia that day. Lolly was, as always, willing to help in any way possible.

Shortly thereafter they were let down at Margaret's Buildings. Anne stiffened her back. "Lolly, if you will wait for me in your rooms, I have some business with the mystic."

"Is it about poor Lydia?"

"It is indeed."

"May I go up with you, Anne?"

"I think this is something I had best do on my own."

Lolly did not argue. Anne, with Irusan prancing at her side, strode down the street, ignoring the amazed expressions of passersby. She entered, greeted young Bridie with a nod and a wink, and said she would see the mystic, if the woman was free. The child, with a frightened look, told her there were no patrons present and bade her ascend and sit in the anteroom. The girl hastened to her employer. Anne could hear the murmur of voices, a shout and a slap. She started up from her chair, but Bridie, her cheek red and tears in her eyes, came out to the anteroom, curtseyed and bid her enter. Anne sailed in, followed by Irusan, who proceeded to investigate each corner of the room, his tail swishing, his whiskers twitching, and his nose wiggling. His entire attitude, watchful and alert, indicated that there were mousies afoot.

The mystic was seated in her spot and sent a baleful look at the cat but did not object. "What do you want, lady?" she asked. "You're here to make trouble for me."

Anne sat. "Perhaps."

A quivering Bridie offered Anne tea, but she shook her head. "No, I'm not here to have my leaves read, or my palm, or my fortune or future."

The mystic stared at her. "Why are ye here?"

"I'm here to set you straight. As long as you are just taking people's money to feed them a line about their supposed future, I was not your enemy. But you are harming someone I love."

"I harm no one," the woman said. "I tell them their . . . their future."

Anne paused; there was something in the old woman's voice, a quavering tone. Her eyes darted, and she appeared to shrink in her seat. This did not fit with Anne's view of her as a bold teller of lies for profit. Was she a cat's-paw, in someone else's control . . . perhaps a certain gold-haired gentleman? It was an interesting thought, and one she would have to ponder, but not now. "You are going to deny what I have to say, but I know the truth. My name is Lady Anne Addison."

"I know who you are." The woman was sullen, uneasy, slumping humpbacked in her chair.

"Do you? Do you know which of us—you or me—a magistrate is most likely to listen to?"

The woman's beady eyes dilated and protruded; it was the

reaction of someone frightened. *Good,* Anne thought. Perhaps she should not bully an old woman, but a message must be sent, a lesson imparted.

"I came here with a young woman who was heavy with child. I did not know it at the time, but you and your henchman, Mr. Thomas Graeme, had a wicked, vile plot to wrest from her money and jewels using fakery and intimidation. You heard of her somehow, likely from some other of your clients." The Bestwicks had been in Bath two months and had made some acquaintances in that time, many of whom no doubt visited the mystic. It was the only way the woman could have learned of Lydia, and how soft a victim of the swindle she would be.

The mystic made no move nor protestation.

"You sent her a note, saying she and her baby were cursed, and that she needed a purveyor of magic so she could uncurse herself. You were the obvious choice; what other seer, or prophetess, would she have heard of but the woman all of Bath is exclaiming over? And like a *fool* I delivered her to you, the perfect sweet *stupid* victim." Her voice shook. She took a moment to contain it, to submerge her rage with reason. She took a long deep breath and sat ramrod straight. "Since then she has given you money — or jewelry, more likely, for she has little money of her own — and in return you gave her talismans and potions to uncurse her unborn child."

The woman was as still as a statue, but behind her, Anne heard the maid squeak like a mouse. Irusan growled, and there was a thud. When she turned, she saw that he had pounced and dispatched a rather large gray rat. He hunched beside it, one paw holding it down though it was clearly dead, licking it all over. He then sat up straight and began cleaning himself meticulously. He would not eat the rodent, for he was far too well fed to dine on such grubby fare. It was enough that he had killed it.

Anne turned back to the mystic, who watched her with squinted eyes set in wrinkled pockets. The fear had dissipated, replaced by a cunning furtive wiliness. "Madam, don't deny what I have said, for I know it's true. I don't know why you targeted poor Lydia, but you will stop immediately and never communicate with her again. Tell your courier to leave her alone. If she comes here, or if she writes to you, you will tell her the curse is gone, and that she and her baby are safe." Anne rose, pushing the chair back with an impatient movement. "If you do *not* abide by my rules, beware; I have powerful friends. I will make sure that you and your . . . *confederate* will receive a visit from the magistrate in your future, whether you foresee it or not."

The woman's mouth worked but no words came out. But finally she said, her voice hoarse, "Ye should not threaten an old woman, lady."

"Or what? You will curse *me*?"

The woman stared at her in surly silence.

Anne put two hands on the table and leaned over it, staring directly in the mystic's beady pale eyes. "I don't believe in your curses, and I don't believe in your visions. You are a trickster, a *fraud*. You make your living off the fear and gullibility of sad and needy people."

"All who can afford to give *me* a shilling or two!" she cried.

Anne straightened and acknowledged it with a nod. "If you had stayed with that, with a pittance in exchange for a dream and a hope, I would have left you alone. But you abused your place, and I suspect . . ." She stopped and shook her head, watching the woman, who appeared once again to be in the throes of some unnamed terror. Out of pity she softened her tone. "Do what I ask. I bid you good day. If I were you, I would pack up and leave Bath. You have wrested enough money from Bath idiots; your time here is growing short."

The woman glared at her.

Anne had been about to leave, but given what she suspected, she had to issue a warning. It was her first hope to stop any future deaths. "Remember, madam, while I thought it harmless diversion I was content to be silent, but I suspect there is more, beyond your poor fortune-telling, something deadly, if I am right." She watched the mystic for some sign she was close to the truth, but there was nothing, just a baleful glare and a chin quivering, her mouth working to withhold some emotion. "I pray, for your sake, I am not correct." What she suspected seemed infamous, unthinkable, *impossible* and yet . . . she turned and headed for the door. "Come, Irusan."

She descended the stairs, her cat prancing before her, and went to Lolly's rented rooms down the street. Irusan followed her in the door, which frightened the landlady. The woman shrieked in dismay and slammed the door on her section of the townhome. Anne ascended.

"I heard my landlady scream," Lolly said, opening her door to Anne. "Was it the sight of Irusan?"

"She looked terrified. I don't know why, when she saw him last time."

"You carried him in that time. She's nearsighted; I'd warrant she thought him a dog. She is one of those who are superstitious about cats. I'm so sorry, Sir Irusan," Lolly said in a sweetly facetious apology to the large cat.

Ears and whiskers twitching, he set about examining Lolly's rooms, following her as she dusted and opened windows to air out the stale smell after several days away. There was a vase of dead flowers to dispose of and several pieces of mail the landlady had slipped under the door. As she fussed, Irusan sneezed at the dust she disturbed. Anne told her what she had said to the mystic.

"I hope you haven't stirred up trouble," Lolly fretted, turning, cloth paused in her tidy work.

"I'll not have Lydia's trusting nature abused in that way." She wasn't about to reveal her darker suspicions to her cousin, not yet. Anne checked her pocket watch. "It is past noon. Mayhap after what she heard Bridie will not dare to come."

Lolly, by the window, glanced out. "Oh, there she is now!"

Anne raced down the steps, huffing from the exertion, and threw open the door. "Bridie, come in, come in! Swiftly, girl!"

The girl shrank back and cast her gaze sideways in alarm. "I d-don't know—"

"Come inside, at least," Anne said, tugging her sleeve and glancing up and down the street. There were some strolling, but no one she recognized. "Come upstairs. I hope my visit to Mother Macree did not frighten you."

The girl climbed the steps, trembling with apprehension. The familiar sight of Lolly calmed her greatly, but it was seeing Irusan that completely chased away her nerves. "Oh, he is such a *beautiful* puss!" she cried, sitting down abruptly on the floor and watching him, wide-eyed. "I so wanted to pet him when he was examining the room, but I didn't dare, not in front of Mother Macree."

He stepped toward her, sniffed delicately, nudging her chin and rubbing softly against her cheek, and then climbing into her apron-clad lap with the assured step of a monarch. The girl hummed in delight and put her slender arms around the huge cat, hugging him and nuzzling her face deep into his ruff of neck fur. She sighed happily. "What is his name?" she mumbled, her voice muffled.

"He is Irusan, King of the Cats." Anne exchanged a look with Lolly. This was a fortunate turn of events, the girl's infatuation with Irusan, and she would take advantage of it. "He seems to like you," Anne said, sitting in a chair near the maid and folding her gloved hands in her lap. "He does not do this often. In fact, he dislikes most people. You must be exceptional."

The child looked up and blinked, her face pinkening and her eyes wide. "Oh, no, milady, I'm just an orphan girl, not special at all."

"Irusan thinks differently, and I know him to be an extraordinarily good judge of character." Anne let a moment pass. The child stroked the cat, and Irusan began his throaty murmuring purr as he curled himself into her lap and closed his eyes, stretching out at his leisure. "Would you like to brush him?" she said, and took the cat's brush out of her pocket.

"May I?" The girl accepted the brush and began stroking the cat's fur, and his purr became louder, more throaty, a hum of pleasure.

"You must be a very special girl, *anyway*, Bridie, for you work for the mystic. How wonderful to be in the seer's company at all times. What insight she must give you!" She paused, then said, "What sight into your own future!"

The girl kept her gaze down on Irusan as she murmured, "My mother woulda said t'was all a hum."

"Is it?"

The maid sighed gustily. "Milady, the mystic sees no further into the future than a few coins will take her."

Anne hesitated, uncertain how to elicit more information. "Is she not a true seer, then?"

"You know she isn't. You said so yourself, milady," Bridie said with a shrewd glance at Anne.

"I know I said so, but still, I acknowledge that she has made the most startling pronouncements. I accused her of deception, but I cannot explain the things she knows of her clients unless she has the key to the mind."

"It's all a trick, milady, *all* of it." Words tumbled from the girl in rhythm with her brushing strokes. "If you could only see . . . the walls have ears."

"What do you mean?" Anne asked, exchanging a puzzled look with Lolly.

Bridie then explained how the rooms were constructed, with listening tubes in the walls. Anne, eyes wide, recalled sitting in the anteroom, chatting with Lolly, Lydia and Quin. What had she said while there? Lydia had spoken of her fears for her child, and Quin had spoken of Bertie and Alethea. The listening tubes would have conveyed information to the mystic, who used it to her benefit, making it seem like otherworldly intelligence.

"But there are things she cannot have overheard," Anne said, thinking of Quin's confession that he had a sister who had died in early childhood. They had most certainly not discussed that in the anteroom. However . . . there was a possible connection, and she must learn about it. "Tell me, Bridie," she said softly, "does she have a gentleman who brings her gossip? A blond gentleman?"

"Her grandson, you mean?"

Grandson? Anne blinked rapidly. "Are you saying that Mr. Thomas Graeme is the mystic's grandson?"

"She calls him Tommy." She threaded her fingers through Irusan's fur and pulled out a tangle. He growled and swatted at her, but she soothed him with a murmured apology whispered into his ear, and he settled once more. Bridie looked up, her pale face alight with mischief. "Mother Macree doesn't know I know, but I overheard him calling her Grandmam and cursing her out for being slow. He brings her tidbits of gossip and news. He tells her all he has heard in the Pump Room, and from whispered confidences in some club he belongs to. He makes friends everywhere, and carries gossip when he returns. Madam has the most amazing memory. Many a time when someone comes to her, and she learns their name, she has already much information about them."

And that likely provided the source of the information about the late Birkenhead daughter. Lonsdale, being an intimate of the family, would know about the daughter from conversation with his friends, and perhaps in passing revealed it to Thomas Graeme, who then relayed it to his grandmother, among all the tidbits of gossip. She was inspired to bring it out at the exact right moment with Quin to astonish and inspire belief.

Oh, how tangled was Thomas Graeme in all of this, all that had lately happened. For it was he who took the curse notes to Lydia. "Bridie, does the gentleman—the mystic's grandson—does he bring things back for her? Did he perhaps give you something in a little sac one day?"

"Aye, milady. Not just that time, but others. Gifts, me mistress calls them . . . offerings."

If she had known all of this, about Graeme's familial connection to the mystic, before she upbraided the woman about the curse she could have more readily made the woman quiver in fear of the magistrates, knowing that Graeme was not just a confederate but her grandchild. Such a threat would have carried more weight, certainly. Her anger burned again, flaring at the information; criminality ran in the family, it seemed, and the connection made sense out of much that had seemed absurd. She took a deep breath. "Do you recall some of the gentlemen who have come to the mystic, especially those who are looking for romance or companionship?"

Irusan turned over and stretched, lying over her lap like a large furry blanket, giving her the ability to brush his other side. Bridie continued on, almost in a trance as she spoke. "Oh, yes, there have been many."

"A Mr. Courtland?"

She nodded.

"And a Baron Kattenby?"

"Yes, milady. And Mr. Doyne, and many others. But ladies, too."

Ladies, looking for love . . . Anne's stomach lurched. "Tell me, has a Mrs. Basenstoke come to the mystic?"

"Yes, milady. Certainly."

She must find out more about Mrs. Basenstoke's suitor, Mr. Smythe. "And what does the mystic tell them, when these gentlemen and ladies come looking for love?"

"Why, first she learns all there is to know of them, what kind of lady they like, tall or short, stout or slender, and hair color. And what they prefer: poetry, or music, books or science . . . that sort of thing. That is at the first meeting."

"And then?"

"And then she tells all to Mr. Graeme, you see. The next time or the time after that she tells them they will meet such and such a type of lady, and to look about them."

The conclusion was clear. Mr. Graeme somehow found or created the perfect lady for the gentleman. Chilled, Anne considered the unnatural finish of it all; in some cases it appeared to end with the death of the well-to-do husband. An unnatural death? If she was right about this, it was a horrible murdering scheme, an appalling conspiracy, but she had not a scintilla of proof. She must *find* the proof, before it was too late for some other gentleman or lady. Perhaps the warning she had issued to the mystic was enough to halt their wicked plans for now, but she must make haste. "Bridie, do you happen to recall a gentleman by the name of Mr. Alfred Lonsdale?" The girl nodded. "Did *he* visit the mystic?"

"Aye, milady, more than once. The first time he came alone."

"Alone? Did he speak with the mystic?"

"Yes, milady. They whispered. He was unhappy, I could tell."

"Did you overhear what was said?"

"No. Or . . . not exactly. I did hear the gentleman say something like *if you won't stop him I must*, or something like that. When he came the next time it was to meet Mr. Graeme."

"To meet Mr. Graeme? What day was that? Do you recall?"

"A few days ago, milady. Oh . . . Tuesday, it t'were."

Tuesday . . . the very day Lonsdale died he was there, at the mystic's abode. "Morning or afternoon?"

"T'was . . . around this time of day, milady."

"Was there anyone else there?"

The child looked a little frightened at her questions. "My mistress sent me out, milady, to get her some boiled sweets and some broth for her dinner."

"How long were you gone?"

"Some time, milady. Mr. Lonsdale was gone when I got back."

The mystic had wanted Bridie out of the way. "Before you left did you happen to overhear aught that was said that day?"

The child stopped brushing and met Anne's gaze, but Irusan nudged her hand and she set to her task once more. "I did," she said meekly, working out a knot in the cat's fur. "You'll no' think me a terrible sort, milady? It is a small place, those rooms, and you can't help but overhear sometimes."

There was something in the girl's tone . . . "And has it been your job to overhear sometimes, Bridie?" Anne asked gently. "And then to tell the mystic what you have heard?"

The girl nodded, blinking back a tear that nonetheless spilled down her cheek.

"I've heard tell you're treated badly by the mystic. Is that so?"

Bridie, tears welling in her eyes, gazed up at her and nodded again. "She's hasty, milady, and she slaps me. But other girls elsewhere get worse, I know, beaten and . . ." She shrugged, unable to explain further, but Anne understood what she could not say.

"But *some* other girls are treated much better, safe and unharmed, a warm bed and nice clothes, left to work in peace." Anne watched the child. "I'll see that you're never mistreated again, Bridie, I *promise*. You need not even go back there, if you don't like. I have friends, and know many places you could go instead."

The girl dropped her eyes to Irusan again with a sigh of satisfaction. She nuzzled the cat and fluffed his mane.

"Will you tell me what you overheard that day between Mr. Lonsdale and Mr. Graeme, before you were told to leave?"

"It was a terrible argument. First, though, Mr. Lonsdale was a-waiting for Mr. Graeme, and Mother Macree said why didn't he sit down and she'd read his tea leaves? So he had a cup of tea—"

"Wait . . . did you see him drink it?"

"Aye, milady."

"And who made it for him?" Anne asked.

"Why, *I* did, milady."

"Oh." Deflated, Anne slumped. "Go on, what happened next?"

"Mother Macree read his leaves; she told him he must keep his own counsel or he'd be sure to bring down a heap of trouble on his own head, and that of people he loved."

That was as bold a threat as could be, Anne thought. "What else did she say?"

"Naught, for then Mr. Graeme arrived."

"You said there was a quarrel?"

"Mr. Graeme has a terrible temper. Mild as mild can be sometimes but when he is crossed . . . his eyes go dead, like Friday's cod, you know." She shuddered. "Mr. Lonsdale looked upset. He said he couldn't let Mr. Graeme go on with his schemes, that no matter what it cost him in his personal life, he would expose Mr. Graeme to the magistrates."

Anne felt her stomach lurch; she had said the same to the mystic. "And then . . . ?"

"I were sent away, milady. When I came back I saw him leavin', down the street."

"Alone?"

"Aye. Alone."

"And there was no one with the mystic when you got upstairs?"

"Just Mr. Graeme. Him an' my mistress muttered together for a minute, and Mr. Graeme said loudly that he'd stop Miss Molly in his tracks, or know the reason why."

Anne, confused by the new name, said, "Miss Molly?"

Lolly, close by, muttered, "A gentleman who prefers the company of other gentlemen, Anne."

"Oh. *Oh!* I see." Lonsdale had threatened that he would turn him in for his dastardly scheme, and Graeme was set to stop him. It was Bridie who prepared the tea, but there may have been an easy opportunity to introduce the poison yew infusion. Mother Macree could have done so herself, if Anne assumed she was in on the scheme. Now that she knew Graeme was the mystic's grandson, it made it all the more likely. Still, Anne could not rely on that conclusion when there were others who harbored ill will toward the gentleman. "Thank you, Bridie. My offer of help stands; if you don't wish to, you don't have to go back to Mother Macree's ever."

The child looked up, then gently set Irusan on his feet on the floor and scrambled to stand. She straightened her gown and apron, a look of determination on her pretty face. "Milady, an' it please you . . . I'll go back to Mother Macree for now. I've heard tell of the poor gentleman Mr. Lonsdale's death. Was he murdered?"

"We think so."

"Is it the mystic or Mr. Graeme you suspect?"

"Among others. But I am in no way certain, not at all."

She took a deep breath. "I'll go back for the moment, then."

"Are you sure?"

"If I didn't, wouldn't they suspect I was telling tales to the magistrate?"

"They might think that if you deserted her service suddenly." In retrospect, threatening the woman was an unwise action to have taken. She had intended to force them to stop whatever plots they had in action, but was there not a possibility that it would simply accelerate their plans?

Plucking gray cat fur from her apron, she said, "I'll go back and keep my ears open, milady, as little as I like Mr. Graeme, especially. But I'd be obliged if you found me another place."

"I will find you a new position, I swear it." Anne put one hand on the girl's shoulder and looked her in the eyes. "I will be guided by your wishes. But be *careful*, child. You can get a message to me whenever you need to through Mrs. McKellar's household maid. Leave immediately if you are in danger, and come here." She wrote down her mother's address on the Paragon.

Chapter Twenty-four

After the girl left, Anne considered her next move. "I think, Lolly, I shall go and visit my friend Mrs. Basenstoke. May I set you down at Milsom?"

They descended to the waiting carriage and wound through the narrow streets, stopping on Milsom in front of the Bestwick residence. Irusan, in a huff over the child's abrupt cessation of combing—he preferred to nap once he had been cosseted into drowsiness—appeared to blame Anne for his ruffled feelings, so when Lolly got out of the carriage on Milsom, head held high, he followed.

"I think Irusan would enjoy a visit to Lydia. Do you think she'd mind?" Anne asked, leaning out the carriage window, smiling at her haughty cat's irritation.

"It would be a distraction for the poor young lady," Lolly said, picking him up and cradling him in her arms.

Anne considered for a moment, then said, "I can't let Lydia worry needlessly. I need to tell her that there is no curse, that she has been deluded."

Lolly reached out one staying hand to Anne. "My dear cousin, may I make a suggestion?"

"Certainly," Anne said.

"Let *me* set the child's mind to rest. You will charge in, tell her she's a fool, make her cry, and she will not believe you. I would never set myself over you, dear Anne—"

"But you have a much better chance of soothing her fears than I. I don't mean to be hasty with her, you know."

"You're very good to her, my dear cousin," Lolly said gently.

"But in this instance you are the best person to give her truth and reassurance at the same time," she said. "I know it because when I was young, you were so with me, the very best at soothing my fears and worries with a kind word. Thank you, my dearest Lolly. I will come back and fetch Irusan in an hour."

Anne headed to the Basenstoke residence. As she was let down by the coachman, Mr. Roger Basenstoke was striding up to the door. "My lady," he said with a deep bow. "Are you here to visit my mother?"

"I've come to pay a visit of condolence," Anne said. "I know how deeply she mourns Alfred Lonsdale's passing," she added, watching his face as he opened the door for her.

"Yes, rather more than she should," he said dryly. "I'll never understand what she saw in my cousin, a droopy mopey young fellow, all sentiment and no action."

Anne bit back her retort, which would have been that some gentlemen were more welcome for their conversation and gentility, which many men lacked. "It is clear that you didn't like him yourself, sir, and yet the morning he died you served him tea. Poured it yourself, and then asked to speak to him after. I wonder why that was?"

He stopped in the shadowy hallway and stiffened. "That is surely none of your business, my lady, but as an old friend, I will confide in you. Yes, I stopped for breakfast and served tea, trying to unbend with a little joke, trying to get Alfred to warm to me. As much good as it did me," he said, disdain in his voice. "I wished to discover something."

"What did you wish to discover?"

"From whence came the man who has been paying court to my mother. Lonsdale knew; he's the one who introduced them. Him or that wheedling friend of his, Graeme. I'll not have my mother cheated by a card sharp or swindler."

"What did he tell you?"

"I . . . never got to speak with him, as it turns out. He was in a hurry. I told him I'd see him the next day."

Was he in a hurry, or did he merely wish to avoid Roger? Or . . . was Basenstoke lying? "But he died that night. Why were you so angry the doctor took his body?"

His face reddened. "It's disgusting the lengths doctors will go to to get a corpse!" He stopped. "I'm sorry to be indelicate, my lady, but you don't know the ways of the world as I do. What those resurrectionists will do, it would curdle the blood." He narrowed his eyes. "Now see here, my lady, what are you getting at?"

"Nothing . . . nothing at all." She passed by him as a footman approached. "Should I send in my card?"

"No need, my lady," he said, giving the footman his hat and gloves. "My mother will be in the drawing room. You know where it is, I'm sure. Go ahead."

Anne stiffened at the casual arrogance, but then realized that this *was* his house to command, in truth, and not his mother's. "I'm so sorry you did not see the value in Mr. Lonsdale. I found him to be a lovely young man."

"Yes, all the ladies did, as little hope as any lady could ever have of bringing him to the point of a marriage proposal."

She paused and turned back to him as she was about to enter the drawing room. "What do you mean by that?"

"He had little time for the ladies unless it was to coddle him," Roger said with a sardonic lift to his dark brow. "If you don't understand me beyond that, I do not care to elaborate. If you'll excuse me." He bowed, slightly, then headed for the stairs as the footman opened the sitting room door for her, then retreated to dispose of the master's hat and gloves.

His dislike for Alfred Lonsdale survived the young man's death, it appeared. It was disturbing, since it was evident that he knew of his cousin's preference for male company. It made her suspect him despite his ready explanation of why he had stayed for breakfast on the day of Lonsdale's death, of all days. She didn't *wish* to suspect him of Lonsdale's murder, knowing how it would devastate his mother.

And yet he had the perfect opportunity that morning during a breakfast that was said to be unusual, at least.

She entered the sitting room and spied a flash of quick movement, Mrs. Basenstoke hurriedly escaping the embrace of a gentleman who sat beside her on the settee. Anne cleared her throat and strolled across the dimly lit room toward her friend, whose cheeks were flushing a dull red.

"Anne, how good of you to visit," Clary said, standing and shrugging her shawl up over her shoulders.

"Clary, it's good to see you. I only entered so because Roger was at the door and told me I would find you here, and to come right in."

The lady gestured for Anne to join her and her caller. "Lady Anne Addison, may I introduce to you Mr. Herbert Smythe?"

Anne curtseyed, and the nice-looking gentleman of about forty bowed over her hand. With all that she had so recently learned she regarded him with suspicion, struggling to keep her expression neutral. She sat, forcing the gentleman to take the morocco leather chair, as Clary sat back down beside Anne on the settee.

There was silence for a moment, but Anne could not be quiescent, not when someone as dear to her as Clary was concerned. "Mr. Smythe, I have heard that you are in woolens manufacture. Where is your business located?"

He flipped back the skirt of his frock coat and pushed one shapely leg forward. "I have recently begun the process of selling my business," he said.

"Oh? Why?"

With a glance at Clary he said, "Dreadfully complicated business, you know, woolens and all that. Tedious. Manufactories, machinery, thread . . . I would not bore you ladies with such matters. Not when there are so many other delightful things of which to speak: music, books, the theater! Have you read the latest novel, called *The Errors of Innocence*, by a Miss Lee? Five volumes!"

"I do so enjoy a good book, Herbert," Clary said, a beaming look on her face. She held out her hand, oddly, and declaimed, "Whosoever should love me must love books and music and art, I say!"

Anne saw the flash of gold on her finger. She hesitated as the gentleman smiled and Clary beamed. "Is that a new ring?"

She smiled, the lines of her face pulling into brackets for her thinning lips. "It is," she said, her voice clogged with emotion. "Herbert—Mr. Smythe—has asked me the sweetest of all questions." She grasped his hand and stared into his eyes. "And I have said yes." She held out her hand for the ring to be admired.

Anne, stunned into speechlessness, took her friend's hand and stared at the ring, a poesy ring circled by vines and flowers.

"It says on the inside, *As gold is pure, so love is sure.*" She took back her hand and held the ring to her heart. "We are to be married! Within the week, if we can secure a special license."

Chapter Twenty-five

"You are to *marry*? And so . . . so *soon*?" Anne exclaimed, her heart thudding. She had thought she'd bought enough time to investigate, but marriage . . . it was a permanent state. She could not bear for Clary to be put in such danger as she suspected.

"For what do we have to wait?" She beamed and smiled at Mr. Smythe.

"What does your son have to say?"

Clary's smile died, and she shifted uneasily. "I . . . have not yet told Roger—"

"Not yet told me what?" Roger asked, emerging from the shadows. He had entered so quietly they had not noticed him.

"That she and Mr. Smythe are to wed," Anne blurted, still shocked and alarmed by the news. As little as she liked male oversight of a woman's business, in this case it could save a life.

Clary paled to an ashen shade, and Mr. Smythe stiffened, two dots of high color blooming on his cheeks.

"Wed?" Roger bellowed, striding closer, hands fisted at his sides. *"Wed?* What madness is this? Mother, you will *not* wed this upstart, this jumped-up parvenu."

"Roger, I am not your child, you are *mine*," Clary said, her voice tight with tension and high with anxiety. "Remember that!"

"I'm responsible for you. You can't marry this . . . this nothing," he said, flailing one hand toward the trembling Mr. Smythe. "This zero, this nothing, this false gentleman."

His voice tremulous, Mr. Smythe said, "Mr. Basenstoke, remember there are ladies present. I will not allow you to badger your mother, my love, the light of my life, for—"

"Shut up!" Roger screamed, choleric tone rising, his face red. Anne, alarmed by the fear she saw on the gentleman's face, turned to watch Roger Basenstoke.

"You're a fortune hunter," he exclaimed. "You're nothing but a cheat, a swindler, out to honey an old woman with a smooth tongue."

"Roger!" Clary cried in anguish as Anne gasped at his crude allusion to his mother.

"Mother, I'm sorry!" Roger took a deep breath and in a quieter tone said, "My lady, Mother, I beg your pardon. I will ask, Lady

Anne, that you leave us, as we must have a family discussion."

"Anne, you need not go," Clary said, her voice trembling.

Anne watched Roger; he was calm once more, the choleric red in his cheeks ebbing. However, the view into his quick and mercurial fury was frightening. What might he do, given the impetus? She turned to Mrs. Basenstoke, who was calmer, too, seeing her son settle down. Mr. Smythe still trembled and was wide-eyed with alarm. "I will stay if you need me."

Clary took a deep breath and let it out, the sound a hiss in the sudden quiet. "No, it's all right." She was unhappy, but calmer, and tilted her chin up, glaring at her son. "Please go. We'll work it out," Clary said, though her fiancé appeared unconvinced.

"Mr. Basenstoke, would you walk me to the front door?" Anne said, rising. She bid the others adieu, and followed Basenstoke. At the door, she requested her carriage be summoned, and the footman was dispatched. She turned to Clary's son. "What do you intend to do about your mother's marriage?"

"Prevent it," he said, his mouth turned down in bitterness. "She is not in her right mind since Alfred's death, and so shall I argue."

Anne felt a cold fist clutch her stomach. "What do you mean, *and so shall you argue*?"

"If she insists on going forward I will have no choice but to see her committed to an asylum until she regains her sanity."

"You cannot do that!" Anne gasped. "Mr. Basenstoke, think what you are *saying*! It's shocking. *Unnatural* for a son to say such a thing. She is a woman of intelligence and sensibility."

"I know, I *know*! I would never truly do that. It would look very bad in society."

"Is that your only concern?"

"No, of course not, but . . ." Expressions flickered over his dour face: anger, fear, anxiety, bitterness. "How else am I to think? She loses Alfred, and instantly she is transformed into a desperate widow, looking for solace in the arms of who knows what he is?" His emotions were again rising, the color flooding back into his pale face. "*Mr. Herbert Smythe* . . . no one has heard of him before he arrived in Bath! I have inquired the length and breadth of England. He is a *nothing*. I thought it a harmless flirtation, a mere pleasant acquaintance. She *never* would have met him but for my cousin and his sly friend. If he weren't already dead, I'd strangle Alfred with my bare hands."

Anne trembled at his fury. Trying for a tone of calm, she said, "I understand your concern, but Clary is no—"

"How do you know what my mother is? You and your friends . . . the Birkenheads," he said, spitting their name out of his mouth like it was bile. "In truth, more than Alfred, I blame *them* for all for this."

"What? How . . . ?" Anne, puzzled, stared at him alarmed and perplexed. "I do not understand."

"Do you not know of Alfred's loathsome, disgraceful . . . *habits*?" That word too was spat out as if it were some much more disagreeable term.

As she had suspected, he knew of Lonsdale's predilection for the male over the female. "I will not pretend to misunderstand you, Mr. Basenstoke," she said, with a haughty rise of her chin. "But I certainly do not see what that has to do with Bertie and Alethea, unless it is because they offered Mr. Lonsdale a place of refuge, which I now understand, given your cruelty, may have been a necessary haven away from your vile disgust." Or perhaps a protection from actual physical danger; the image of Mr. Basenstoke offering a cup of poisoned tea to Mr. Lonsdale vividly rose in Anne's mind. She could envision him doing it. Or . . . could she? Poison? That was sly and sneaking. He would be far more likely to strangle Alfred in a passion than poison him.

His expression had chilled to ice. "You know *nothing*. Go, ask your friends . . . ask your *Bertie* about his friendship with Alfred. *Ask* him."

"What are you saying?"

"I am saying you should ask your dear friend, Mr. Bertram Birkenhead, about his *friendship* with Alfred, his close *close* friendship! Ask your friend about the Sacred Theban Club. Men share vital information, you know; we have noticed this foul stain on the face of our city. It disgusts us all, my friends and business acquaintances! If they don't disband I will personally call on the magistrate to root out such a morally bankrupt institution."

The carriage arrived. Roger had already turned and was striding away into the shadowy interior, going back to berate and badger his mother, no doubt.

"Mr. Basenstoke!" she called out. He turned and regarded her, his gaunt face a mask of impatience and anger. As much as she wished to rail against him, she *must* attempt a conciliatory tone if she was to keep him from precipitous action. "I would ask, as concerns Mr. Smythe and your mother . . . I have reason to believe it may not be a problem soon. I agree that she should not marry without knowing more about her fiancé, but . . . give me a day or two. I don't think she'll marry in that time."

"Why do you ask such a favor, my lady?" He strolled back toward her, appearing calmer.

"You know me, Roger; we may not have been close, but you know me to care deeply about your mother, my mother's closest and beloved friend. Give it a day or two. Be kind to her. *Please.*" She could not think of another thing to say, because his words about Mr. Lonsdale and Bertie had inspired, in her heart, a sudden trepidation, a violent, lurching doubt. What did she know? What did she *not* know?

He stared at her through narrowed eyes, but finally took a deep breath and said, "I will not turn Mr. Smythe in . . . yet, and I will never — *would* never, despite my hasty words — send my mother to an asylum."

"And you will take no action against this club you spoke of?"

"Why?"

"If we wish to smooth things over with the least amount of nasty gossip concerning Alfred, his purported membership in this club, and if you truly care about your family's good name, you will help me in this matter. Alfred is dead. Any past he had with the supposed club cannot harm you now, and to stir up trouble will only revive gossip. Please say you will do nothing for the time being."

Appealing to his familial concerns over gossip had done the task. He nodded, shortly.

"And do not belittle, berate or punish your mother again," she said, her tone suddenly steely. "She deserves your care and concern, not your anger."

"You forget yourself, my lady. I have promised not to send her to an asylum. I would never lay a hand on her, but neither will I allow her to make such a grave misstep as to marry so far beneath her."

• • •

The short trip to the Birkenheads' townhome was taken up with whirling speculation, fearsome thoughts, worries, frightened wondering. Her friends were home to her, she discovered, as she sent her card in. Trembling, close to collapse, she could go no further than the ground-floor reception room, where, to her surprise, Mrs. Venables was sitting in Quin's usual chair. The lady was warming herself by the fire, book in one hand, glass of sherry in her other. Anne staggered in and collapsed in the other chair, staring at the fire and seeing not flame but question marks.

"My lady," Mrs. Venables said, starting up in alarm as she shut the book and set it aside. "Are you ill? How may I help?"

Anne could not respond, she could only stare with unseeing eyes.

"Lady Anne, you're frightening me," the lady exclaimed. She pressed her glass of sherry into Anne's hand and helped her raise it to her mouth. "Take a draught; you look as white as my best notepaper."

Anne gulped some, sputtered, and sat back.

"Alethea is upstairs; may I summon her for you?" She picked up the bell to ring for the maid.

"No, Mrs. Venables, no, let me sit and think," Anne said, reaching out and staying her hand, the bell tinkling faintly as the other woman set it down. For the moment, she could not bear to see Bertie or Alethea. She took a deep breath and drank the rest of the sherry, the warming liquid igniting a trail down her throat to her stomach, where it burned. Mrs. Venables refilled the glass and she drank that, too. She sat back in her chair. The whirling had stopped for the moment.

Mrs. Venables watched Anne with a troubled gaze, her clear intelligent eyes clouded by alarm. "My lady, have you heard something that has distressed you?"

She nodded.

"Concerning . . . someone in this household?"

"I was at the Basenstokes' residence. Mr. Roger Basenstoke is a *loathsome* man . . . hateful. He disliked Mr. Lonsdale deeply, but more than dislike, he . . . he reviled him, for . . . for his . . . his . . ." She shrugged and shook her head, not knowing how to go on.

"He is one of those who disdain and condemn men who love

other men, is that it?"Mrs. Venables said delicately. "And it appears that you know . . . ?"

"That Mr. Lonsdale was one of those men, yes. I have been sorely troubled by his death in this house, among our friends. Mrs. Basenstoke is a *dear* friend of my mother's . . . *and* of me, and she, too, was troubled by his sudden death. She didn't like the suggestion that Lonsdale's death was anything but the result of a brief, terrible illness."

"There has been gossip that what occurred was self-destruction," Mrs. Venables murmured. She leaned toward Anne. "I have heard it, though I loathe tittle-tattle. It has distressed me, too, for the sake of my cousins, who surely do not deserve how they have been shunned by some in society on the merest speculation. But how did you come to . . . I mean, how did you learn of Mr. Lonsdale's sad situation?"

"Mrs. Basenstoke learned of his predilection from letters in his room. She summoned me, brokenhearted and fearful of what she might learn. She asked me to help."

"To help? How?"

"She was desperate for the truth of how he died. I think she, too, feared that he had done away with himself," Anne said. It was all tumbling out of her. Mrs. Venables was as close to Bertie and Alethea as Anne . . . much closer, in fact, by virtue of old family ties. Perhaps she could help Anne understand where Roger Basenstoke's nasty insinuations came from. She met the other woman's sympathetic gaze. Mrs. Venables was calm—serene, even—but there was something there, something she was not saying to Anne.

"I started to ask questions, to try to figure out how it came about . . . his death, I mean. I searched his room, looking for a clue into his fate; I read his journals, and letters from . . . from a gentleman." She took in a long, deep breath and met Bella Venables's frank gaze, in which she saw calm acceptance. "I know of his relationship with Mr. Thomas Graeme." The lady's eyebrows rose and a faint smile curved her lips. "But Roger Basenstoke said . . . he *implied*, rather, that Bertie and Alfred . . ." She shook her head, not knowing how to go on.

Gently, Bella Venables said, "Would you be greatly dismayed if it were true?"

Anne froze and her head spun, dizziness overcoming her again. She put out one hand to steady herself and took a deep breath. "I would be shocked. I have known him for years and never *ever* suspected. You're not saying it's *true*, are you, that Bertie . . . ?"

"I'm saying nothing," the woman said. "It is not my place."

But with that prim refusal to comment she was *clearly* confirming what Basenstoke had implied, that Bertie and Alfred were more than friends, that there was a relationship between them. "It's not possible. I won't believe it."

"Won't believe it, or don't *wish* to believe it?"

Anne moaned in her throat, trying to grasp what Mrs. Venables was all but saying. "My poor dear Alethea. How *shocked* she will be when she discovers—"

"Oh, come, my lady, do you think a woman could be married as long as Alethea and not know the truth about her husband?"

Mrs. Venables was right about that; the intimacy of the marriage bed, of the shared secrets, the closeness she envisioned in her own future . . . surely, Alethea *must* know. "But how can she live with her husband having . . ." She shook her head.

"You're naïve, Lady Anne," Mrs. Venables said with a soft smile. "Has it not occurred to you that Alethea not only knows but knew before she wed? That perhaps that is why Bertie and Alethea are the perfect couple?"

Perfect couple; she had called them that herself. Perfectly amicable, perfectly aligned in every way, perfectly in each other's confidence. Could it be? She was beginning to suspect something she never would have imagined, and as puzzling as it was, it answered many questions.

Mrs. Venables appeared troubled and worried. "I have been so alone in my thoughts, my concerns. It is a relief to speak with someone other than Bertie and Alethea." She leaped up from the chair and paced to the window, then back, to stand by the fire and warm her hands. She stole a glance at Anne, then back to the fire. "I should have said nothing, but I had no one in whom to confide, not willing to break Bertie and Alethea's confidence, and now I have babbled. But I trust you, my lady, I know your love of them both. I confess, I feel a certain weight lifted."

"Weight?"

"The weight of worry, of speculation; when young Lonsdale died right here in Bertie's home, I worried for my cousin, for what people would say if they found out . . . if their relationship was discovered."

"What are you saying, madam?"

"Nothing, nothing at all, of course. *Nothing.*" She paced away from the fire again and covered her face, sobbing into her hands, her breath catching in gasps. She turned back to Anne, her form lost in the shadows of the room beyond the firelight. "I'm profoundly worried for Bertie." She strode back and collapsed in the chair, burying her face in her hands once again. "He and Lonsdale fought so dreadfully over Alfred's f-friendships outside of Bertie," she said, her words muffled. She took them away from her face and clasped them in front of her, wringing them together in agitation. "My cousin was wounded, *deeply,* by Alfred's defection. He loved young Lonsdale so intensely. You would not think it, but . . . it's true."

"They were . . . lovers?"

"For a time. But Lonsdale fell into an affair with Graeme and then discovered too late that the other man was unworthy. Poor Bertie . . . he was bitterly disappointed in Lonsdale."

"They fought . . . Bertie and Alfred Lonsdale?" Anne said, caught by the revelation.

Mrs. Venables shook her head. "No, not . . . not fought. I should *never* have said that. It was arguments, nothing more."

Still trying to comprehend all she had heard and the possible implications behind Mrs. Venables's words, Anne frowned and examined her gloves, peeling them off and laying them aside on the table. Her hands were cold. She was icy all over, though her cheeks flamed with heat. What she had learned was difficult to fathom, but it did make sense of some of Alfred's journal entries, about deep love for someone. "I should go," she said, her voice sounding hollow and brittle to her own ears.

There was a sound in the hall. "Bella, are you here?" Alethea entered the room. "Oh, Anne, I didn't hear you come in. Why did you not come up to me? I could use a friend today." Alethea looked at her, then at Bella Venables, then back to Anne. "What has happened? Why are . . . what . . . ?" She examined Anne's face. Whatever she saw there was enough. "Who told you?" she said, her tone hollow, her expression dull.

"Roger Basenstoke said something, and then . . ." She glanced at Mrs. Venables.

"Bella! How *could* you? We trusted you," Alethea cried.

Anne jumped up. "Alethea, I am your bosom friend from childhood. How could you not . . . I don't know what to think." What *did* she think? Bella had implied much more than Anne would ever have imagined otherwise, and now she was deeply confused.

"Lady Anne came here knowing some of it, anyway, about Bertie and Alfred." Bella shrugged. "It was out before I knew it."

"I don't need this now," Alethea said. She fled the room, racing upstairs.

"Alethea, *Alethea*!" Anne cried.

"Let her go," Mrs. Venables said. "Poor child . . . she has much to worry about."

"What do you mean?"

"She worries about Bertie, of course."

"Why?" Anne asked, even as she thought of reasons to worry. She remembered how angry Bertie appeared at Alfred as they argued about Thomas Graeme, and Bertie evicted the young man from his home. She had always thought of her friend as a calm thoughtful soul, but she had never seen him thwarted in a love affair. Being rejected for another could twist a man's heart and cause him to behave violently.

But she would assume nothing. "What do you *mean*, Mrs. Venables?"

"Nothing. I just . . . nothing at all."

"I'll go to Alethea." Perplexed and worried, Anne passed a maid in the hall and headed up the stairs. She found her friend, who was in her sitting room on the third floor, perched on the edge of a chair staring into an empty cold fireplace. She looked up when a floorboard creaked, and stared, her eyes empty of emotion, at Anne. "What do you want?"

"The truth, I suppose."

"The truth? About what? My most intimate life? I owe no one an explanation about that."

"Alethea, I am your friend, not an enemy."

"*Are* you my friend? Then come in. Come, and I'll tell you all."

Anne entered and sat down in a chair opposite Alethea. The air between them crackled with tension. Alethea's lovely face was hard with anger, a look Anne had never seen in all the years they had been friends. "I don't understand any of this," Anne said. "Bertie is . . . he's . . ." She didn't know how to describe her thoughts.

"A sodomite? Say it, if that's what you mean."

"Alethea, stop it! Don't assume you know what I am about to say. I *want* to understand. I'm *trying* to understand. This has all come as a shock to me, and I don't know what to say." She paused, but Alethea stared stonily ahead. "Did you always know? Was Bertie like this when you married?"

Her friend met her eyes, her own widening with dawning comprehension. "You don't understand at all, do you?"

"No, so tell me!"

"It's *both* of us. We're both . . . different. He loves men." Alethea stared at Anne steadily and said, "I love women."

Anne restrained a gasp, knowing her friend's intent was to shock.

Still staring steadily, Alethea went on: "We married knowing who we were, *what* we were. We married the only other person who would understand, so the world would not stare and condemn us. My whole life I have hidden who I am, as has Bertie, and now it is all coming out. We will be destroyed, shunned, driven away," she cried, her voice guttural with a mingling of anger and fear. "And all because Alfred Lonsdale could not keep from visiting that club—"

"The Sacred Theban Club," Anne said, her tone hollow.

"Lonsdale let that little rat Thomas Graeme seduce him, and wrote him love letters," she said, her voice hissing with anger. "Alfred is gone, but *we* are the ones who will inherit his legacy of shame, becoming social outcasts, and after we have devoted so much effort, so much care, to secrecy." She caught her breath and let out a long sigh. "We will have to leave England, perhaps go to Italy."

"No, Alethea, you *cannot* go!"

"What have we to hold us here?"

"Quin, your friends, your family—"

"And censure and gossip and danger. I'll not let Bertie suffer, Anne. There are benefits to being a woman; I will escape legal trouble. But Bertie . . . he's too good for this country, and these hideous laws, that force a man to be what he is not." She shook her head. "Go home, Anne. I wish to be alone."

Chapter Twenty-six

Anne didn't sleep, *couldn't* sleep. Late into the night she sat by her fire reading Alfred's journal, rereading the letters, thinking of her friends and trying to decide what to do. How had she been so blind to the truth about Alethea? What had her friend been going through, alone in her own thoughts and feelings, when they were at school together?

She had no answers. Everything seemed bleak and gray and without joy, and she was left questioning everything about life and love and friendship. Even Irusan was out of sorts and pacing, as if he knew something was deeply amiss.

She tried to sleep but tossed and turned. By dawn she was shivering and wretched, with a fever. Perhaps it was because she had eaten little the day before, nor had she rested. Saturday passed in restless aching, confined to bed by Mary, her only comfort Irusan, who would not leave her side. Finally, in the evening she drank some broth and ate toast, entertained by Wee Robbie, who read her more of *Gulliver's Travels*, and Irusan, who played with a twist of paper tied to a length of wool, something he normally would not deign to do.

She slept fitfully, but awoke the next morning knowing that she was better. The weather had turned; a miserable, sleety day dawned gray and brooding over Bath. Even the Bath stone buildings, usually a warm mellow butter color, appeared dull and dismal, cold gray in the morning light. Determined to return to the problems at hand, Anne bathed and dressed carefully in the pale blue striped *robe à la polonaise*, hoping she would be lifted by fresh finery.

Attendance at St. Swithin was thin. Osei met Anne and her mother in their family box. He asked after Lady Everingham.

"I was ill yesterday, and my grandmother is feeling poorly today. I'm pleased she stayed home; the weather is increasingly cold and damp, and her fire is warm. The chill wind affects her awfully now. Irusan has deigned to visit her, and she has surprisingly taken to him after calling him a filthy creature the first time she saw him."

Osei smiled. "King Irusan has a way of overcoming objections." His spectacles glinted in the light from the lanterns, lit on such a gloomy day, and he shivered. "On days such as this I close my eyes and remember home."

"Your home lands are close to the equator, I recall," she murmured, watching the congregation gather in the pews below their box. "You must miss the warmth."

"But in England there is much to make up for what I lost."

"You're good at finding consolation, Osei, but I know your life is not all it could be." She glanced over at him. "Have you spoken to Mrs. Fothergill further about her work with Africans in England?"

"I spent the day with her and the doctor yesterday; I dined there, too. We have started to go through her lists. She is a remarkable woman, one who gives me hope for the future. Wherever possible she has provided both the English name an African is known by and the name they were given at birth, so we are starting there. I have been looking for Akosua among them, with no luck so far. But one day later this month she and Dr. Fothergill are going to London, and I shall accompany them. There are more lists there, with their society." He hesitated and pushed up his glasses, meeting her eyes briefly, then looking away. "Mrs. Fothergill has asked if I would like to join the Society of Friends."

"Will you?"

"I haven't yet decided. I'm not sure I believe wholly as they believe."

"I'm not sure I believe wholly as *anyone* believes," Anne muttered and Osei smiled. "What is it about their tenets you do not go along with?"

"They are determinedly peaceable. As much as I admire that aim, I was raised a warrior. I believe that violence, as abhorrent as it is, becomes necessary when one's loved ones or national survival is at stake. If we had won the battle that ended with our people being slaughtered, neither I nor my sister would have been taken as a slave. My parents and grandparents would be alive. I would go back and fight even harder and be victorious if I could."

"Blessed are the peacemakers, for they will be called the children of God," Anne said.

"*There is a time to love and a time to hate, a time of war and a time of peace.*" He looked down at his hands, clutching a Bible. "I'm not sure my beliefs are compatible with the Friends."

She had been thinking deeply about love and friendship, home and family, over the last two days. Softly she said, "Osei, I hope you someday get a chance to see your home again, and I pray you find your sister, Akosua." She regarded the gathering congregation. Though scattered, Anne could pick out one couple she knew: "There is Baron Kattenby and Mrs. Venables," she murmured. "In attendance for the second publishing of the banns."

"Why do they not marry by special license? I'm astonished they will wait for the banns," he replied.

"I know he could afford a special license. It could be he is thrifty, or . . . perhaps he's delaying marriage."

"Why would he do that?"

"Maybe he's not as eager to be wed as she is. Perhaps he is having second thoughts. I have heard an argument between them. He would prefer to wait until Christmas, after his son has had a chance to meet and approve of her, while she is anxious to be married. I know she feels her dependency upon Alethea and Bertie weigh on her." And perhaps, she thought, the Birkenhead home was not as congenial as Bella Venables would have everyone think.

"It is a matter of two months, correct?"

"Yes."

"I should not think it a burden for the lady to wait so little time."

"True," Anne said, pondering Osei's statement. Why *was* Mrs. Venables in such a hurry? It seemed possible that Bella had simply worn out her welcome in their home. The gossip about Bertie and Alfred . . . had it come from Bella Venables? With her intimate knowledge, how easy it would be to accidentally let something spill.

The service was much as the last one. One week, Anne thought; just one week ago she had wandered in the garden with Alfred Lonsdale. He had poured out his troubles to her—all his doubts and fears about how his life conflicted with his profession—in veiled language that she could now see through. His preference for the intimate companionship of men was weighing heavily on his heart. He had been contemplating different choices, it seemed, and wondering how those choices would affect his future.

At the same time she now knew he was dealing with an estrangement from Bertie over his affair with young Thomas Graeme. Two days and the reading she had done had taught her so much. Graeme was threatening Lonsdale with exposure, judging from the letters, not only of himself, but also . . . of his nearest and dearest. Tulip had said something to that effect in one of the letters, and now that she knew the truth about her friend she wondered . . . was Graeme threatening to expose Bertie? What would Bertie do if he found out? Graeme loomed like a sinister shadow over the events that culminated in Lonsdale's death.

The banns were again read for the baron and Mrs. Venables. As her mother chatted with friends, Anne descended from the family box on Osei's arm and they made their way through the group of well-wishers to the couple. The baron appeared sickly; Mrs. Venables seemed anxious, clinging to his arm and watching his face as he courteously thanked their friends and fellow congregants.

"Sir, are you feeling all right?" Anne asked him as his fiancée was distracted by a group of ladies asking her when the wedding was to take place.

He sighed, one hand on his stomach. "Please, my lady, do not concern yourself. I have been a martyr to complaints of the stomach for years."

Anne nodded, relieved to hear it was not a new illness.

"I think there has been too much excitement lately," he fretted, touching his mouth with a lace-trimmed handkerchief. "My son is coming to Bath to meet Bella in a week. While I look forward to it, I'll confess to some trepidation. If he doesn't approve . . ." He sighed and shook his head. "She still would like to marry by special license . . . something about it being the done thing, quite fashionable."

"A wise man sets the fashion instead of following it."

He smiled faintly. "I don't see what is wrong with doing it by the banns, a good old-fashioned notion. I have been tempted to procure the special license and marry just to get it done, but I am determined to hold fast to the old ways, which were good enough for my parents and are good enough for me."

"And so you should, Baron, stand to your decision," Anne said.

He glanced around and dropped a wink. "I am delighted she is so eager. Stodgy old codger like me . . . don't know what she sees in me."

A comfortable home and an income, the best protection from a life of want and poverty, Anne thought. But she said instead, "My good sir, you seem a kind and interesting gentleman to me. Do not underestimate the attraction of benevolence and geniality as traits of choice in a mate."

• • •

The rest of Sunday passed at the Bestwick home, where she and Osei were guests for dinner and whist. Lydia was inattentive and nervous, clearly uncomfortable as her time of confinement fast approached, though Lolly bustled about her, attending to her every need in a fussy manner. Anne, Lydia and Lolly spoke of her approaching confinement privately, when they retired after dinner. Her midwife had visited to consult with the expectant mother, and had engaged a wet nurse who would live in when the joyous event finally took place.

But the gentlemen soon joined them after dinner — John and Osei did not have a lot to speak of since their tastes and manners were very different — and the whist table was laid. While Lolly sat to one side and knitted something tiny for the coming baby, they played a couple of games. John and Osei won, much to Anne's chagrin; she was highly competitive and it took all of her self-control to keep from berating Lydia for her inattentiveness. After, there was tea, sherry, cakes, and desultory conversation. Anne sighed in exasperation. She had not been able to get a word alone with her friend, and she did wish to discover if the lifting of the "curse" had been of any benefit to her at all.

Finally, as Lydia yawned and was helped to her feet by her husband, Anne said, "Let me see you upstairs, Lydia. I have something to ask you."

John looked to his wife for acquiescence, and she nodded. Anne and Lolly helped her up to her bedchamber, but Lydia insisted on stopping at another room, a small dark chamber with a narrow bed draped in dark bedclothes, as Lolly went ahead to make the room comfortable for her young friend.

"This is the confinement chamber. Is it not dreadful? I don't wish to have my baby here, but the midwife insists, and I cannot make John listen to me. Will you talk to him for me, Anne? I'm sure he will listen to you over me, because he is always saying how sensible and intelligent you are." She pouted, her puffy face shadowed and full of discontent. "He thinks me silly and uninformed. He regrets marrying me, I know it. I'm sure he would rather be married to you."

Anne smiled into the dark at the notion of her and John married. "My darling girl, you know that John adores you above anyone," she replied, putting her arm around the young woman's shoulders. "He is happy here in Bath with you, and wishes to make a home with you somewhere you can be together and away from Darkefell Castle. He adores you and wants your little family to be alone. Is that what you would want, my dear friend?"

"Oh, yes, above all things," she whispered. "To be away from the dowager marchioness would be lovely. She frightens me sometimes."

Cosseted and comforted, Lydia let Anne guide her to her warm bedchamber, where she sat down in a chair by her dressing table as her maid entered. Anne reacquainted herself with the girl, who she knew from Ivy Lodge. But when the maid and Lolly left the room to fetch hot water, she took advantage of being alone for a moment.

As best as she could in her heavy gown she crouched down by her friend's chair and gazed up at her, taking her hand and squeezing. "Lydia, my dear, have you heard word about . . . about your worries? I know what was upsetting you, the curse. Is it all sorted out now?"

Tears welled in Lydia's eyes and she nodded, the wet trails on her cheeks glowing in the candlelight. "You're not going to tell John, are you? About the jewelry I lost to that horrible old fraud? Lolly told me it was all a hum, that you made her admit it."

Anne hadn't been able to do that, but she thanked Lolly in her mind for thinking of that one piece of fiction that would reassure her friend.

"I thought . . . oh, Anne!" Tears dripped down her cheeks and onto their clasped hands. "I believed what the first note said. How could they know, I wondered, whoever sent it. I felt pains and . . . and oh, this *awful* squeezing feeling in my belly!" She freed one hand and touched her curved belly. "They said my child would be a monster!"

"Are you all right now?" Anne asked with alarm.

"Oh, yes, the midwife told me to drink, and gave me a tisane. And she told me how to lie to help with the squeezing feelings. She says it happens to many ladies. But I was so frightened in case I lost the baby. I can't help but feel there is a curse lingering. Are you *sure* it was all a hum?"

"As sure as sure can be. And you trust me, don't you?"

Lydia nodded. "That woman sent me a note, you know. It was hard to read — the handwriting was awful — but I think it said she was mistaken, that she had been wrong and there was no curse."

Deeply grateful that her younger friend was now confiding in her, Anne was careful not to belittle Lydia. "There was no curse, dearest," Anne said gently. "It was not that she was mistaken; it was a sham to swindle you out of money. There are people in this world who live by tricking others, though generous good people like you would never know it. You and your baby are safe."

Perhaps Anne's threats had worked, and the mystic was now in fear of being turned in to the magistrate. That might still happen; if what Anne feared was true, and the plot was deeper and more devious than she had at first thought, there would be awful consequences. Tenderly, she said goodnight to her friend, kissing her cheek. Lolly waited and walked out with Anne, reassuring her that she would stay with the girl until she was asleep.

Tomorrow, Anne thought; tomorrow was Monday. *Tomorrow* Tony — so longed for, so desired — would arrive in Bath. She touched her flaming cheek; how she missed him . . . he was like a fever in her blood. But . . . she resolutely turned her mind toward the puzzle at hand, the one irritant that kept her from fully enjoying the anticipation of reuniting with her love. *Tomorrow* she would get to the bottom of all the nonsense that had been going on. *Tomorrow* she would find out, once and for all, if her darkest fears were more than just fears.

Chapter Twenty-seven

Monday dawned bleak, the awful weather having settled in for a prolonged stay. Cold, rainy, windy: it was the antithesis of the golden warmth of a week ago. It had rained all night but slowed to a drizzle for a time in the morning, though the leaden skies looked ready to let loose a torrent at any moment. Anne took advantage of the break, donning her new hooded woolen cloak and taking a sedan chair to the Pump Room. It was thin of society, though even with the inclement weather the sturdiest of husband hunters were there in force. As Lydia had informed her there were far more women eager to wed than men willing to be caught. It took dedicated effort to find a husband in such surroundings.

Mr. Thomas Graeme was there. His swift and noticing gaze swept over her, and he quickly turned his back, engaging himself with an older gentleman in a Bath chair, whose attendant was waiting behind a group of ladies for the glass of Bath water that he would inevitably quaff, one of many, perhaps, mandated by his doctor. Graeme bent over the fellow — a widower Anne would bet — and spoke nonstop, taking breaks to straighten and glance about the room, his gaze hurried and anxious.

Anne turned and caught sight of a beautiful middle-aged lady who traded a look with Graeme, glanced at *her*, then drifted away, claiming a group of acquaintances before disappearing out the door. Interesting. Had Graeme been about to bring the beautiful lady to the elderly man's attention?

She noted, among those awaiting a glass of Bath mineral water, the footman from Bertie and Alethea's home who attended Quin when he went out. She approached. "Crabbe, correct? You are Mr. and Mrs. Birkenhead's footman."

"Yes, milady," he said with a perfect bow. He was good-looking, as most footmen were, but did not have the air of haughtiness and conceit that tainted the attitude of some of his tribe. His eyes were kind, his mien humble.

"Is Mr. Quin here, then?" she said, glancing around the room.

"No, milady. He is having his treatment with Dr. Fothergill at the Cross Bath. He finds the water here more palatable to drink, though, so I am fetching him this glass for his first of the day. He will come here after for his next."

"Thank you, Crabbe. I may see him if I am still here. How long does his treatment last?"

"About an hour, milady."

Anne swept away to stand in a gloomy shadow near a window and stared at the few faithful who had ventured to the Pump Room for their daily dose. More would come later to gossip and pretend to listen to the music that had not yet started at this early hour.

It was in her quiet refuge that she first saw Mrs. Bella Venables speaking with an unlikely lady, Mrs. Honoria Noakes. She had thought a lot about Mrs. Venables since two days before, the revealing conversation that had shocked Anne so much, at first, and now left her sad and worried for her friends. In the past Bertie's cousin had shunned Mrs. Noakes, condemning the lady as someone with no wit and less grace.

Anne stirred uneasily; the conversation she was having with Mrs. Noakes seemed intense. Two hard red spots of color were on Mrs. Venables's high cheeks, and the other lady appeared cowed, shrinking back and putting up one gloved hand in a gesture of negation or self-protection. But when Mr. Doyne entered the Pump Room and scanned it, looking for his lady, their attitude changed in a twinkling.

Mrs. Venables said something to the other woman, then straightened, taking one step back. When Mr. Doyne joined them there were smiles and nods all around. As Mr. Doyne took Mrs. Noakes on his arm and strolled with her toward the pump, though, the look on Mrs. Venables's face changed again in an instant. The expression was one of baffled fury.

As a child, Anne had loved traditional pantomimes of the "dumb show" style. In those harlequinades all the action was silent, with exaggerated gestures and expressions accompanying the action. As entertaining as the dumb show she had just witnessed was, and as expressive of the various characters' parts, it left her with one question: why had Mrs. Venables until now concealed how well she knew Mrs. Noakes? For it was evident by their body language, as seen from a distance, that they may be friends or adversaries, but in either instance it was a relationship much closer than what she had been led to believe.

Mrs. Venables turned and her gaze met Anne's. She approached, both women nodding, the bare minimum of acknowledgment. "How lovely to see you on such a grim day, my lady! Attendance is so thin I was forced into conversation with Mrs. Noakes, who I know only slightly."

"An acrimonious conversation, if it is to be judged from afar," Anne said, lessening the boldness of the accusation with a smile.

"Acrimonious? How so?"

"You seemed at odds."

"Oh, I suppose from a distance . . ." She nodded and then, with a hardening expression, said, "I'll admit it; I reacted badly to something she said, something she likely did not mean as I took it."

"What was that?"

"She . . ." Mrs. Venables compressed her lips and looked away. "I heard that she was . . . was spreading a rumor around about my cousin. *You* know the rumor of which I speak. Bertie is dear to me, and I will *not* hear him maligned, not by anyone, certainly not by the likes of her, who is not fit to touch his hem."

Anne felt a twinge of remorse for suspicions she had been entertaining. Any defender of Bertie was a friend of hers. "I have heard no rumors other than from Mr. Roger Basenstoke, as I told you the other day," she said.

"Maybe no one else will either, now."

"What did she say that was upsetting?"

"I won't be one to gossip; it's not important." She took the sting out of her words with a smile. "Now when I think about it," Mrs. Venables said, "I probably overreacted and mistook something she said to someone, something about that poor fellow Mr. Lonsdale and his demise in my cousin's home. You know how concerned we all are that his passing is seen as what it was, a brief sudden illness that hastened death."

"I hope it *was* a mistake, if Mrs. Noakes is gossiping about that. I would not for the world see Bertie or Alethea injured. If it helps, I had thought Mrs. Noakes rather stupid, but not vicious."

She nodded swiftly. "Good, good. That was my own thought. I hope I *didn't* overreact," she fretted. "I would injure no one's feelings. Do you think I should apologize?" She looked across the Pump Room to where Mrs. Noakes was clinging to Mr. Doyne's arm.

"I wouldn't," Anne advised. "You'll make it worse by giving the possible rumor more weight than it should have."

"Perhaps you're right." Baron Kattenby entered and slowly made his way to the pump attendant. "I had better join him," she said. "Excuse me, Lady Anne."

Mrs. Venables met her fiancé, he took his glass of mineral water, drank it down, and they slowly headed to the door, though they were stopped occasionally by people, likely for congratulations and questions. Nothing like an impending marriage to make one popular, Anne thought, reminded that she would soon be the one fending off invitations to dine and attend parties when she and Darkefell announced their engagement.

Mr. Thomas Graeme sauntered back in but appeared tense, his eyes underlined with the purple shadows of someone who hadn't been sleeping. He glanced at the older couple, but then swiftly looked away. Anne wished to speak with him. His blackmailing letters troubled her deeply. That he could treat Lonsdale so, when they had been so intimate . . . it was dastardly. She had questions, too, about his matchmaking and his familial connection to the mystic. What would he say if she asked him why recent grooms had passed swiftly and unexpectedly after their marriages? She fretted, uncertain about whether to approach him alone. She had sent Osei an early request to join her and hoped he would be there before she confronted the young man, but if Graeme departed, her questions would stay unanswered.

She couldn't wait. He spoke to a Pump Room attendant and slipped him a coin; the fellow nodded and slipped away. "Wretched weather we're having. How do I find you today, sir, well, I hope?" she said brightly.

He started and slowly turned, an arid blankness in his expression. He traded it quickly for his public face, the cheery veneer of a friendly fellow. "Good day, my lady!" he cried, his face wreathed in a broad artificial smile. "How surprising to find you here on such a raw and unfortunate day. Bath is generally blessed with good weather, but as you say, it is not the case today, is it?"

"The weather today *is* unfortunate," she said, examining him, interested in the public mask he donned so easily. It appeared his natural expression was one of detachment, and perhaps reflected an inner cruelty that had been revealed in his letters. "I was just speaking with Mrs. Bella Venables. Do you know her well?"

He shrugged. "Does anyone really know *anyone*, my lady?"

"Of course we do, Mr. Graeme. I have met her but a few times, and yet I feel I know her moderately well: her history; her sufferings; her feelings for her cousin."

"Perhaps." He glanced around and moved restlessly. Attendance in the Pump Room had thinned even more. "I'll warrant you don't know the lady as well as you think," he said, still glancing around with a restless air. "I doubt even Mr. Birkenhead knows her as well as he thinks."

"Whatever do you mean by that? She is his cousin, the intimate of his youthful years!"

"Who knows the *real* Mrs. Venables?" he muttered.

She stared at him, perplexed.

"For that matter, who knows the real Lady Anne?" He met her gaze and smiled, sweeping his golden hair from his high forehead. "Please do me the very great kindness of ignoring my ill temper, my lady," he went on, his voice once again unctuous. "You find me out of sorts, and I would not have you think ill of me for the world. I fear I am affected by the weather today, beset with gloom."

"Perhaps you are affected more deeply than you expected by the unfortunate death of Mr. Lonsdale. It was a grave tragedy, and you knew him well. *Very* well, I believe."

He was silent, but watchful, his eyes narrowing.

"Mrs. Venables said she has had to speak out against rumors that his death was unnatural. What say you to that?"

He appeared agitated. "What is it to me?"

"You were his particular friend. Come, admit it; you do care that his manner of death is discovered, do you not? He deserves that much, doesn't he? I knew him only slightly, and yet I am concerned. It would defang the gossipmongers if the truth could be found. Gossip thrives on uncertainty. As Mr. Birkenhead's cousin, Mrs. Venables is alarmed that he will suffer by the rumors surrounding Mr. Lonsdale's death."

"It is not my affair. It is an unfortunate event, but nothing to do with me."

This was getting her nowhere. Time to be more blunt. She took a deep breath, stiffened her backbone and said, "Mr. Graeme, I have found you an interesting subject to study."

"Have you indeed, my lady?" he said. "I am flattered, indeed, to be the object of such fascination to you."

Her anger rose, and with it her recklessness. "*Don't* be flattered, sir; I have decided you are a likely candidate to have *murdered* Mr. Alfred Lonsdale."

She had expected him to threaten her or bluster. She did *not* expect him to flinch, a bead of sweat popping out on his forehead.

"What say you, sir?" she prodded when he stayed silent, glancing back and forth hastily, as if looking for an avenue of escape.

"I say you are out of your mind," he said, finally finding his bluster.

"I know he saw you that day, and I know where. You had the best opportunity to kill him, and you did it. I imagine he discovered your scheme," she said.

"Scheme?" His wide smile had died, replaced by a look of uneasy vigilance.

"Your matchmaking and swift dispatching scheme, cooked up with the aid of your grandmother, that so-called Mystic of Bath!"

He stared, blinking and blanching. She noticed his sweat-slicked brow, the rapid increase of his breath, a vein popping on his forehead, and his eyes bulging slightly.

"You go t-too far, my lady, too far indeed. Your imagination has taken flight." He wiped his brow with one shaking hand.

Had she flushed the partridge, and would he now fly away? It was too late to go back. "What a tidy plot: discover wealthy widows and widowers looking for a last chance at marriage, tailor-make a spouse, using your grandmama's mystical maunderings, set them up to meet, get them wed, and poison them. I can only imagine you are somehow finding a way to profit." Putting it into words sped her mind. "Ah, of course," she cried. "You charge the made-to-order spouses to set them up. Or do you take a portion of their inheritance, perhaps, after all is done?"

He backed away from her, then surged forward, thrusting his face close to hers, his face transformed by fear and anger. "You don't know what you're saying," he hissed, tears trembling in his blond lashes. "How *dare* you?"

She could feel his spittle on her face. "I say only what I see."

"I didn't . . . I *introduce* people, that's *all* I do and you can't prove a thing otherwise."

"But Alfred Lonsdale, your close confidant, suspected," she continued, staring into his eyes as she wiped the dampness from her cheek. She recalled the letters in which Graeme complained about Lonsdale considering him wicked, though she doubted the vicar knew the whole story. Graeme quivered but he didn't reply. His gaze darted right and left. Anne said, pressing her advantage, "You had something on Mr. Lonsdale—I know what it was, sir—and were blackmailing him, all the while ensuring that he would say nothing, even after he had figured out part of your scheme."

"You're mad! No one will believe you . . . *no* one!"

"I would bet a garden of *tulips* that I am right."

He gasped and staggered back, then whirled and stomped away without another word. She sighed in frustration. She had hoped to bait him into revealing all, to panic him into saying something incriminating, but she had overplayed her hand. Time to go; where, she had not decided. Perhaps to the Birkenheads', to test her theory on Alethea, or hopefully Bertie. With all the benefits of being a man, Bertie could summon the magistrates and raise the alarm in time to prevent Graeme from having someone else poisoned, or keep him from fleeing Bath to reinvent himself elsewhere, as he had threatened to Lonsdale.

The weather, as seen out the big windows of the Pump Room, appeared to be getting worse, rain sheeting against the glass intermittently. She headed to the passage toward the door, hoping to find an attendant to get her a chair. There was a sudden uproar behind her in the Pump Room, calls of *She's fainted!* reaching her. In the normal course of events she would go back and see who had swooned, as were others heading to where the commotion was. But it was likely just Mrs. Noakes, who had feigned ill health at the party to evade an unpleasant situation. A faint was one way to avoid unpleasantness. Anne had things to work out in her head, so she slowly walked toward the doors as others hurried in the other direction to view the tumult. Someone was loudly asking if there was a doctor present, for Mrs. Noakes had collapsed. She smiled grimly to herself; her guess had been correct. There would be a doctor there in a trice. One could not throw a stone in Bath without hitting a physician who catered to the wealthy infirm.

Near the doors she saw Mr. Graeme. He was beckoning to Mrs. Venables behind the baron's back, as the gentleman stood just inside the doors. Anne shrank back, brows knit in puzzlement; it was terribly familiar of him to beckon to the lady. It implied a close connection, one she had not suspected before this moment.

Anne peeked back out. Mrs. Venables said something to the baron, who was tapping his cane impatiently as he strode toward the doors to the street. He nodded and continued out, looking, probably, for a Pump Room attendant, who would order a carriage for them. Mrs. Venables followed Graeme to a pillar, slipping around it out of sight of the doors.

Anne's curiosity enlivened, she slipped along the wall to the other side of the pillar, hoping to listen in. She could not understand what they were saying at first. He mumbled, his tone urgent but incoherent. She hissed something back, and then Anne heard loud and clear what he said next.

"But Mother, what if she knows even more than she is saying? What if she has proof?"

Mother? Anne put her gloved hand over her mouth to keep herself from exclaiming out loud. What did he mean, what—In her astonishment she had lost some of the conversation that followed. She took a deep, quiet breath and settled herself.

"Go back in and *find* her," Mrs. Venables muttered urgently. "Discover what she knows and don't talk to me until you do."

"She kept talking about you. She knows enough," he whined. "I was never so frightened, Mother—"

"Stop calling me that! I'll whip you until you bleed, you little blighter."

Anne blinked, eyes wide, at the suddenly harsh tone in the genteel Bella Venables's voice.

"Mama, *please* . . . Granny an' me can go off to Brighton or Lyme Regis or Tunbridge Wells and you can follow when you can. I've made money before, I can do it again."

"From what, *smuggling*? This is as good as it gets, Tommy, and you'll stick with it. If I have to make up to those sodomites and sapphists I'll do it, and if you have to find a way to shut up high-an'-mighty Lady Anne then you will."

"Can't you do 'er like ya did the other?"

"I stepped in to protect you, idiot. You chose the wrong feller to blackmail, didn't you? Who knew Lonsdale would have iron bollocks and fancy himself some savior? You wouldn't do 'im in, so I had to."

Anne swallowed back a cry. Bella Venables had been the fatal instrument in Lonsdale's death? How could it be?

"But Mama, Alf woulda come round. I had 'im, I did," Graeme whined, his careful accent degrading with emotion. "He cared fer me!"

"He was about to turn you in to the magistrate even if he 'ad to swing on Tyburn's gibbet for sodomy." Her accent coarsened, her precise diction faltering too.

"There ain't no Tyburn gibbet no more," he muttered mulishly.

"You listen to me, you puling idiot; you start pullin' your weight or I'll make sure the hangman's noose is round *your* neck. I don't care how you do it, just shut her mouth. We aren't ready to be done yet. Your granny is too old to be shunted round the countryside. She's got a soft billet, cooing into idiots' ears about love and health and money."

"But Mama—"

"Just do it. I promise it'll be all right," she said more softly. "Come, Tommy . . . do what I say, take care of that woman and we'll leave off for a while, sit pretty until after I get myself settled. I have my own task, to make sure the baron stays on the hook."

"But why'd you 'ave to kill Alf? He was kind to me," Thomas said, his tone sullen.

"Shut it and be off! Lonsdale was a threat. I'll *not* go back to jail, Tommy, lad. I'll see you dead first, my son, and don't you forget it," she said, her tone venomous with a hard edge. "That Spanish jail was enough to do me for a lifetime. Now go! Before my old fool waddles back and sees us talking."

Heart pounding, Anne slid around the column as Graeme trotted past. She waited a moment, but there was no way she could go past Bella Venables and the baron. If she was faced with Bella now she would betray her knowledge, she was certain. Instead she retraced her steps, hastening back into the Pump Room, her stomach roiling and her mouth flooding with the bitter taste of bile. Her mind was whirling with all she had heard. It was *far* too much to take in all at once. How was it possible that Bella Venables had a son? Bertie had never said anything about his cousin and her husband having a child, and especially not Thomas Graeme. And jail, in Spain? It was incomprehensible.

She reached the Pump Room and tried to compose herself. Thomas Graeme approached her immediately, though, before she got herself under control.

"My lady, do you need an attendant?" he said, his tone back to a soft respectability. "You don't look at all well, if it is ever permissible to say that to a lady. Shall I fetch you a glass of the mineral wa—"

"No!" she yelped, putting out one hand, unable to stop the exclamation. She was not going to drink *anything* this fellow brought her. Huffing with exertion and anxiety, she backed away from him. She needed to get away and think. All of this was too much. She had settled her mind that Graeme was the killer, but Bella Venables had confessed, in so many words.

Graeme examined her face, noting how out of breath she was and that she was shivering. His expression went dark, the light fading from his eyes, and his gaze chilled. "You follered me, didn't you? You follered me out and—"

"Overheard you, yes. You . . . *and* your mother!" She put one hand over her stomach. "Leave me alone or I will scream."

"As you wish, my lady," he said with a mocking bow.

Chapter Twenty-eight

Anne stumbled from the Pump Room into a narrow passage, one of the hallways to the hot baths, where there was little traffic on a day of such wretched weather. She had to *think*. She leaned up against the stone wall, heated to warmth by the hot springs that bubbled beneath them, as her mind whirled. All of her ideas of guilt and innocence were upset.

Mrs. Venables had appeared the picture of an upright and virtuous woman. But she had lied about so much. How could she have a son? How could Bertie have a young cousin in Thomas Graeme he didn't even know about? She'd think of that later. Right now she had other worries. Given what she had overheard she was alarmed at the baron's increasing illness, and what it could mean. Mrs. Venables had been pressuring him to wed before his son could arrive. Perhaps she feared the baron's son would sniff a fraud? Did she dread that the assurance of love would not be so easy to counterfeit in the seeking gaze of a younger man whose inheritance depended on his father not spending it frivolously on an unworthy woman?

If there was one family she had to warn about Bella Venables, it was the Birkenheads. She had to find Quin: sensible, intelligent, calm Quin. From Crabbe she knew he was at the Cross Bath with his doctor. She must seek out Quin and Dr. Fothergill and return, with them, to the Birkenhead home.

Bella would have departed with the baron by now, and she suspected Graeme would follow, needing to speak with his mother about what Anne knew. She pulled her shawl more closely about her shoulders and left the Pump Room, walking swiftly down Stall Street, then onto Bath Street. The day darkened and the rain returned, a thin, cold drizzle that quickly soaked her cloak. She pulled the hood up carefully over her hair and tried to shield her face. She should have ordered a sedan chair. What was she thinking?

The answer to that was, she *wasn't* thinking, she was reacting. Her brain was buzzing with thoughts and mysteries and half-baked theories. Where was poor Alfred Lonsdale poisoned that day? Probably as she had suspected, right there at the mystic's table. Why kill him at all? Bella Venables had told her son that Lonsdale knew too much, and she could not let him ruin her one hope of financial security, marriage to the baron.

She stopped and put out one hand, leaning against the wall of a shop that was closed for the morning, trying to catch her breath. She must be a sight, her soggy cloak heavy, her hair matting with the intermittent drenching rain despite the hood. Her recurring problem with shortness of breath had come back with the damp air and too much exertion.

She swept a lank lock of wet hair out of her eyes, tucking it into the hood, and glanced around. The street was deserted, residents and visitors alike preferring the warmth of hearth and home. Only one carriage passed her, and no sedan chairs. Her mind kept mulling over what she knew, looking desperately for one piece of information that would exonerate Mrs. Venables. But her own ears could not have deceived her. Bella had killed Lonsdale.

The betrayal of the Birkenheads was breathtaking! Bertie had given Bella a home, safety, and the opportunity to find comfort and a path out of the penury in which she had been left by illness and the death of her husband. To believe the woman a poisoner she had to believe that she was in league with that awful woman, the Mystic of Bath. And to believe that, she had to believe that everything she knew was wrong, that a well-bred, well-connected woman of Bella Venables's gentility would align herself with a common . . . *common* . . . Anne stopped dead, and the sound of her own footsteps seemed to echo back to her.

How had she missed the one unavoidable logical truth? If she had been in her right mind she would have grasped the truth immediately. Bella was Thomas Graeme's mother; he had said so and she had not protested, and in fact had acknowledged her son. And Anne knew now that the mystic was Thomas Graeme's grandmother, which meant she was Bella Venables's mother.

How could that be? Anne wiped rain out of her eyes and walked on, toward the Cross Bath, shivering from the damp that had soaked down to her skin. What had Thomas Graeme said in their earlier conversation? He told her that she didn't *know* Bella Venables. That her own cousin, Bertie Birkenhead, didn't *know* Bella Venables.

Graeme meant that quite literally. She had to acknowledge the truth as she now understood it: they did not know her. Bella was not really Mrs. Bella Venables, long-lost cousin to Bertie. She was some schemer, a cheat who imposed herself on Bertie and Alethea as his long-lost cousin Bella, a swindler who, with her mother and son, was bringing in money from any number of schemes. Her mind raced and dashed back and forth, through theories, around impossible hurdles, her confusion becoming deeper with every stumbling, weary step.

But this was no time for bewilderment. Resolve coursed through her, stiffening her spine and hastening her pace. Bath Street turned, and Hot Bath Street merged with it. There ahead was the Cross Bath. When she stopped again she heard footsteps behind her, but when she turned, she saw no one. She shivered and huddled under her cloak, wiping ineffectually at the rain blowing in under her hood, misting her eyesight, then hurried onward.

Was Quin even at the bath? If her mind hadn't been so clouded, if she hadn't been so confused by the conversations she had just had, it would have occurred to her that Quin may have left his appointment early, for she knew that the Cross Bath, once you were past the door and changing room, was open to the sky. What invalid would brave the raw cold rain for a hot bath?

She looked up from her halting, stumbling walk. She was here now, she thought, and may as well find out if Quin was inside waiting out the rain. A misty miasma drifted, swirling, around her. It emanated from the hot springs encountering the cold air. The Cross Bath was a newer structure, rounded in front and squared off at the rear, with three doors on three sides. She wiped rain from her eyes again, wondering which of the doors was unlocked, and if anyone would be about in such foul weather.

Cursing her impatience and impulsivity, she tried one door but it was locked. On the other side, though, was the pillared semicircular roof over the main entry; the words *The Cross Bath* were engraved and picked out in gold. That door was open and she slipped in, looking about for an attendant. There was a pump room, but it was deserted.

The foggy spa mist pervaded the interior of the bath. Overhead thunder rumbled, trembling through the structure, and the sky loosed a torrent of rain, the drumming of which drowned out all other sound. *Enough* of indecisiveness; she must find *someone*, and if she startled an almost naked invalid it was too bad. She was about to enter a narrow passage to her left when the door behind her opened and she whirled, hoping it was an attendant returned from some errand.

Bella Venables, as drenched as Anne, entered and shut the door behind her. "Lady Anne, I fear there has been a misunderstanding between us," she cried, her lovely face twisted with emotion.

Her heart pounding from being startled, Anne put one hand over her chest. She drew herself up and glared at the woman. "I don't think there is any misunderstanding," she said, her voice guttural with fear and echoing in the stone structure. Another clap of thunder rumbled. Staring at the other woman in the sheltered gloom of the entry, she steadied herself, summoning all her courage, and said, "In fact, I think I know the true story behind your actions. When I thought you were Mrs. Bella Venables and believed you guilty of killing poor Mr. Lonsdale, I thought what a betrayal it was, knowing how much your cousin loved him. But now . . . *now* I know that Bertie is not your cousin at all. You are *not* Mrs. Bella Venables."

The woman blinked and stiffened. "You're out of your mind," she said, taking one step forward, her tone guttural and tense. "You've completely misunderstood, as I feared. I knew you were dangerous, but *now* you sound like a veritable raving lunatic. No one will believe a word you say."

"I think the authorities will believe me," Anne replied, taking a step backward. "All they have to do is trace your actions before you arrived on Alethea and Bertie's doorstep. You used the money you stole from the real Bella Venables and funds provided by Bertie to travel here from Spain, perhaps with your *son*, and your *mother*! The Mystic of Bath. What a joke!" Anne said, pouring all the disdain she felt into her words. "You set your mother up to swindle the gulls of Bath. And then you thought of further ways to use her 'sight'; to find lonely hearts the ideal mates, someone to leave wealthier when they died."

"You're mad, and so I shall tell everyone with whom I speak." Her tone was haughty but her expression was calculating and her eyes hard, like dark glistening marble.

"You will find that people are more than willing to listen to me, the daughter of the Earl of Harecross—"

"With a lunatic brother, and showing signs of lunacy herself!" she cried, advancing toward Anne.

"Don't you *dare* speak so of my brother!" It was time to find Quin and Dr. Fothergill, and if they were not present, someone who could summon a chair for her to get to the Birkenheads'. Anne swept toward a passage, hoping to find an attendant. In the eerie silence of the passage her heels clattered on the stone floor, echoing; the structure had the air of being vacant. But surely it would have been locked if no one was there? "Hello?" she called, her voice echoing. "Is anyone here?"

The attack took her by surprise, for who would expect an elegantly gowned lady of forty to briskly seize another woman and wrestle her through a door? But that is what the woman who was *not* Mrs. Venables did.

Breath taken by the surprise, off-kilter and slack with amazement, Anne was no match for the ardor and strength of a desperate woman, and soon she was wrestled, stumbling, beyond the open arches to the hot bath, steam arising even as rain steadily roiled and rippled the surface. She rasped, her old asthmatic injury reasserting itself in such close, humid confines. Coughing and wheezing, she found her footing and her voice in the same moment, and shouted for help as she struggled with the surprisingly strong lady. The rain intensified, and the wail of the wind carried away Anne's voice. But she would not be beaten.

She staggered close to the pool, her cloak and skirts tangling in her legs causing her to lurch, though the iron hold of the older woman kept her upright for the moment. She stared up at her and trembled at the red, enraged face looming over her. Bella bent her backward. The pavement was wet. Anne slid and hovered precariously at the edge of the pool until the other woman shoved her hard, the bruising force of her hands on Anne's chest taking her breath away in its suddenness. Desperately she reached out, but as hard as she tried to clutch at her assailant's dress, it slipped from her grasp as her opponent cried out in victory.

Her sudden backward entry to the water was shocking. She descended down, down into the depths, the water closing over her face as she was gasping; she choked on water and desperately tried to spit it out and not inhale it, but all she could do was close her mouth, even as she did not have enough air in her lungs to sustain her. The water's buoyancy lifted her and she rose up — or what felt like up — floating, trying to kick but unable to from the tangling torment of her feminine garb, layers and layers of cloth that weighted her, wet and clinging and all-encompassing.

She broke the surface, choking and gasping; she could not draw in a deep breath and felt as though she was suffocating. But then the heavy wool of her cloak dragged her back down. She was unable to kick or even paddle. The water again closed over her head, the warmth saturating her until she wanted to let go, to breathe in and stop fighting, stop trying to find a way to the surface again. All remaining air bubbled out of her, and she struggled to keep from breathing in water, smothered and swamped by the heat and cloth, a shroud swaddling her limbs.

She got one arm free of the cloak, finally, and flapped, pushing against the water and triumphantly breaking the surface, sputtering and coughing. She looked up through the rain, water and hair streaming in her eyes, trying to find purchase on the edge of the bath pool with her gloved hands.

The fraudulent Mrs. Venables leaned over the edge and hissed, "Oh, no, you don't!" She put one hand on Anne's head and tried to shove her under the water. Anne twisted away, desperately trying to find footing, but the woman grabbed a handful of hair and pushed. "You *will* drown," she shrieked against the wail of the wind. "And no one will *ever* know why you were here!"

"Except *me!*" rang out a voice. Anne, thrashing and flailing at her assailant's hand, could see through water-misted eyes as Quin limped toward them. He gave his doctor a shove away from him, shouting, "Dr. Fothergill, restrain Mrs. Venables!" His doctor grabbed the woman by the arm, clutching her harder as she fought him; he successfully pulled Bella back from the water's edge and she tumbled to the stone pavement, screeching in protest, her wild wails torn from her by the battering wind. Quin limped closer, battered by the sudden gale but indomitable for all that, and knelt by the pool's edge. He put out his hand to Anne, who flailed and wallowed. "Come, my lady; let me help you," he hollered above another rumble of thunder.

He grabbed her hand, but her glove came loose and he fell

backward, just the glove in his grip. He clambered to his feet and again knelt at the edge, this time grasping her bare hand, slippery from the mineral water. But his bony hand clutched hold of her. He wasn't strong enough to pull her out, of course, but the sight of his dear, determined face and his hand holding her fast gave her the courage to find her footing—she discovered that though deep, the bath was not truly over her head—and take it, clinging there until two burly attendants, drawn by the noise, arrived. One helped her climb awkwardly out of the water, assisted by Dr. Fothergill, who had tersely explained to the other attendant that Mrs. Venables must he held until a magistrate was summoned.

Quin stoutly stated loudly that whatever else had gone on, he had *seen* Mrs. Bella Venables try to shove Lady Anne Addison's head under the water, so to drown her. He would happily charge her with attempted murder.

All of them retreated inside the shelter of the Cross Bath enclosure, a constant stream of abuse Bella Venables's only addition to the conversation. Dr. Fothergill, shocked and appalled, ensured that the bath attendants kept hold of her, for she was a danger to Lady Anne and possibly to herself, judging by her threats, accusations, and statements that she would drown herself. Quin repeatedly pleaded with her to calm herself and explain; why was his cousin trying to hurt their friend?

"She's not your cousin, my dear Quin; this is *not* Mrs. Bella Venables."

He lapsed into confused silence and stared, shaking his head in puzzlement.

• • •

A local magistrate, roused from his warm and comfortable fireside, arrived within minutes at the Cross Bath and spoke to the accused as a bath attendant pinioned her arms behind her. A courtly gentleman of advanced years, he was taken aback by her stream of insults and epithets, her tone and words becoming coarser as time went on. Given the victim's identity as the daughter of an earl, he was willing enough to accept Quin's assertion that he wished to lay charges of assault and attempted murder against the woman for her attack on Lady Anne Addison.

He pronounced himself satisfied that the events warranted the charges, then advised them all to go to their firesides as he was going to his until he had sorted it all out. Anne clutched his arm and the old gentleman, taken aback, patted her gloveless hand and kindly asked what he could do for her.

"There is another, her accomplice and her son; you *must* arrest Mr. Thomas Graeme. He is known by many in the Pump Room, and was an accomplice to murder by either her or her . . . her mother. He must be seized before he leaves town in the company of his grandmother."

"Who is his grandmother, young lady?" the magistrate asked.

"She is none other than the infamous Mystic of Bath, sir, and can be found most likely at Margaret's Buildings. Anyone along there can direct you to her rooms," she replied as Dr. Fothergill and Quin looked on, twin expressions of amazement on their faces.

"It shall be done, my lady," the magistrate said.

Chapter Twenty-nine

An hour later Quin, Dr. Fothergill and Anne were ensconced at the Birkenhead townhome. Anne would not countenance being taken home in her bedraggled state, knowing it would distress her mother to see her, and send her grandmother to her sickbed at the scandal of it. Anne had explained in brief what she now knew, but there would be further explanations required. Alethea, horrified by Anne's ordeal, loaned her one of Bertie's banyans and had her maid help Anne untangle and dry her long, luxurious hair. They sat in Alethea's bedroom, by the fireside, Anne luxuriating in the warmth and protection it offered.

"I cannot believe that Bella—or whoever she is—did such a thing!" Alethea exclaimed, sitting opposite her friend as the maid finished and put aside the brush. "She always seemed so . . . so—"

"So *ladylike*? You would not have thought so if you saw her expression as she tried to drown me." Anne's throat was sore from yelling and screaming. She took a long draught of sweetened tea, soothing and warm. "And if you had heard the names she called me, Quin and the magistrate! I didn't even *know* some of the words. I cannot think of it without shuddering. Let us speak of something else."

"Like what?"

Anne studied her old friend, thinking of all she now knew. She waited until the maid had left the room and took Alethea's hand, chafing it between hers. "My friend, I will say now what I did not say, in my shock, the other day; you could have told me long ago, you know, of your . . . your secret. You could have . . ." She sighed and shook her head, wishing she had more eloquent words of reassurance. "I wouldn't have cared."

"You think that now." Alethea's eyes swam with tears. "Secrecy has become a habit, a trick of survival in an unfriendly world, and I do not trust easily. I've been betrayed before. Both Bertie and I learned early what it was to place our trust in unworthy people and have those people turn on us and use our truth against us as a razor, cutting deep in many directions."

"I'm sorry," Anne said simply.

Alethea squeezed her hand. "You may have been the one person I could trust with my secret, but I could not know that."

"But you know now?"

"I do."

Anne thought of something and started. She looked at her friend, who gazed back with a question in her eyes. "The other day you told me of sneaking off to the artist's cottage, the tutor who taught us art. You said you had a passion for him. So that was a lie?"

"*You* implied I had a passion for him, but all I said was I was madly in love."

Anne's eyes widened. "Oh. *Oh!* With the model?"

Alethea sighed and her eyes held a dreamy expression. "Ah, yes, the *beautiful* model. She was his lover." She cast a glance at her friend. "And mine, too. I was so young . . . what were we, fifteen? She taught me much. She was divine, a Titian goddess who loved equally men and women, though in truth I don't think she loved anyone but herself. She broke my heart, but at least she taught me that I was not the only woman like myself, that there were others who shared my attraction for the same sex."

They were silent for a moment, but thoughts could not long be kept from the dramatic events of the day. "Poor Baron Kattenby!" Anne said with a sigh. "What will he do when he learns the truth about his delightful Mrs. Venables?"

"Perhaps he will see the true value in a woman like Mrs. Basenstoke. She is kind and good, and she would make him happy."

"You're right about that; she knows the truth about Alfred now and doesn't care one bit."

"Kattenby and Mrs. Basenstoke were once close to an understanding until Bella set her sights on him."

"Clary has a new beau, though, a Mr. Smythe, who . . ." Anne stopped, mouth open, eyes wide. "Oh, dear," she said at last. "I fear that my mother's friend may be in the same plight as the baron, in which case—"

"You think Mr. Smythe is one of the swindlers?"

Anne sighed. "I fear so. Perhaps she and the baron can console each other." It occurred to her in that moment to wonder if the baron's recent bout of ill health had been a sign he was being poisoned with some accumulative toxin that would culminate in his death after marriage; it was safe to assume he was not to be murdered until *after* that event. She shuddered and shared her thoughts with her friend, who agreed that she should tell the doctor and the baron at the earliest possible moment—the doctor would need to examine him to be sure no harm had been done—but that he was not likely to be in danger now, not with his fortunate escape from his jailed fiancée.

"Mrs. Basenstoke deserves someone as kind as Kattenby. I have learned to value goodness and kindness over an assumed beauty of face and form." Alethea mused. "Seeing Quin happy has taught me much; Susanna loves him sincerely, and between them is a trust I wish to emulate. And a love I seek."

"Don't be too hard on yourself, my dear friend," Anne said. "It cannot be easy, to hide your truth and yet find love."

"I think sometimes I have it, and then it slips away from me."

Anne knew she was referring to Mrs. Meredith Hughes, and the woman's husband's precipitate removal of her from Bath. She didn't know how to answer.

"What are we urged to do?" Alethea continued, a hint of desperation in her tone. "Women are told to hide their innermost light, or they will shine too brightly and surpass the gentlemen. Even I . . . I fear I have absorbed the lesson all too well. But how can we ever find love unless we are our true selves, our honest best, while seeking someone to love?"

"You make finding love sound impossible," Anne said gently.

"Isn't it? Other than our darling Quin, who is the essence of gentle manliness, and sweet Susanna, I have never seen it."

"Speaking of my own experience, I have found that not every man is frightened of a strong woman. I have fought and berated and quarreled with my Tony. I have defied him, run away from him, scolded him, and yet . . . he says he can love no one but me. I have found real love with Darkefell."

Alethea stared into the fire and then met her friend's steadfast gaze. "How do you know it is *safe* to love him, that he won't break your heart?"

"I don't," Anne replied.

"Then how do you have the courage?"

"It's not some magical sense of it being right, Alethea. I've tussled with it in my mind, knowing I give up my independence, as illusory as it is, when I marry Tony. But I have to take the chance. It is a risk; I know it. I have seen miserable unequal marriages. But for every fault he has, I have a virtue, and for every virtue he has, I have a fault. We balance. I hope it's enough. All I know is, I can't imagine life going on, knowing he was in the world, and not be with him."

Alethea smiled and nodded. "Then you are indeed fortunate, my dear friend. I will not say your path has been simpler but . . . I have not been so lucky. Mayhap someday I will, and if so, I hope I have the courage to accept such good fortune. Bertie *could* have had love with poor Alfred. Between the church and society, and appearances, they never had a chance. Bertie was too careful to give himself fully other than at their club."

"On Lonsdale's side, he had been raised to think he was an aberration, I'm afraid," Anne replied. "I have read his journal; he began to loathe himself, I fear, as all around him conspired to tell him he was deviant and wrong to feel as he did. He excoriated himself constantly. It was a war within him."

Alethea sighed. "Bertie became impatient with his uncertainty. He stopped going to their club when he and Alfred fell out."

"What is the club, anyway?"

"It's a place for gentlemen like Bertie to go and be themselves. There is lovemaking, yes, from what I understand, but it is also a place to talk, and play billiards and dance, to be open and playful and laugh."

"Why is it called the Sacred Theban Club, Alethea? Do you know?"

"It began as a little joke among the gentlemen, based on the old Theban story of an army made up of lovers, one young and one mature."

"So Osei was right about the meaning of the name," Anne mused, staring down at Alethea's hand, which she still held.

"You knew about it? What do you mean, Osei . . . that is Mr. Boatin, correct?"

Anne explained what she and Osei had learned and figured out from Alfred's journal and letters. Her friend looked alarmed, but Anne reassured her that Osei was the soul of discretion. "I think Bertie would be comforted by Mr. Lonsdale's journal. In it he tells of the one love who escaped him, of whom he was unworthy. I read it late one night. It is sweet and poetic, how he speaks of Bertie."

Alethea nodded. "Perhaps you can let him read it. It was a dreadful tangle, you know . . . the two of them trying to find a safe place in an unsafe world. And then Thomas Graeme seduced Alfred away, courting him with coquetry and soft words. He offered a thrilling vision of youthful passion, rather than Bertie's rather conservative caution, and it quite bowled poor Alfred over. He was so young and vulnerable. Graeme exploited his insecurity and doubt in his love with my husband. You never knew him at his best, before all his troubles, but Alfred was sweet and honest and humble, and Bertie loved him deeply before Graeme came along." She sighed. "And as for me . . ." She shrugged.

"I'm sorry, my friend."

"At least I have Bertie," she said. "He is the best friend I will ever have, and the only one who fully understands me. If that is not a basis for a good marriage, I don't know what is."

"I think I agree with much of what you say," Anne replied gently.

There was a commotion below, a din that rose up to them along the staircase. Anne stiffened . . . that voice! That shouting, hectoring, angry, beloved *voice*! "It's him! It's Tony!" She rose and dashed through the door, long hair streaming behind her, and went to the top of the staircase, leaning over the railing. "Tony, I'm here!"

"*Anne!* Anne, where is here?"

Laughing, she said, "Come up. You will see me!"

Such a thudding on the stairs, then, as he took them two at a time! It shook the house. He hove into view and stopped, staring up at her. "My darling Anne!"

"I look a fright," she said, pulling back her streaming hair.

"You look *beautiful*," he said, charging up the rest of the steps and grabbing her roughly, pulling her to him, and kissing her.

Swirling into his magnificent grasp, taken by his ferocious love, she relaxed and for the next few blissful minutes thought of nothing but how she had missed this ardor, this resolute passion that flared between them. The proof of his passionate love pressed against her, and she was lost, head swimming, gaze misty, feeling the hunger grow.

"You two should marry by special license and not wait a second more."

Anne pulled away, her lips moist from his kisses, her gaze misty, to see Alethea grinning and watching them from her doorway. "Oh, goodness, I completely forgot where I was. Tony, this is Alethea, one of my dearest friends," she said, stretching out her hand. "Alethea, this is . . ." She shrugged. "My Tony." She put one hand up to cup his cheek as he stared down at her, his dark eyes still hungry.

"I would never have guessed," Alethea said dryly.

Bertie had climbed the steps after the marquess's hasty ascension. "Do you believe me now, my lord? We are not holding Anne captive. I'll admit, her being in my banyan does not look proper at all, but she can assure you of the complete innocence of the occurrence, despite how it appears."

Hand flat on his chest, Anne said, "Tony, you didn't accuse them of holding me captive, did you?"

"If you had heard your mother you would not be surprised. That note you sent her . . . it was most mysterious. What has happened? And more to the point, what did you tell her about what happened?"

"It's a long and complicated story," Anne said. "And I'm famished. Alethea, do you have any food? And where is Quin? Is my hero all right?"

"Who is Quin?" Tony said, his dark brows drawn down over his eyes. "And why is he your hero? An honor I reserve for myself, by the way." He kissed her again, and closed his eyes, breathing heavily. "Must we stay?"

"Yes. Collect yourself, Tony," she said, secretly enjoying every bit of his unrestrained delight at being with her again. "These people are my friends, and when you hear the story, Quin will be your hero too."

"I'd rather go somewhere private with you than hear the story."

"Do you not care how I almost died at the hands of a swindling female?" she asked archly.

He grumbled but agreed that his ardor would have to wait.

• • •

The magistrate arrived to get all of the information needed for the charges, and to update them on what had happened in the hours since the dramatic events. Anne, dressed in a too-tight gown of

Alethea's, descended and with the help of Bertie, Alethea, Quin and Susanna, told what she could of the tale. It was slow, and tedious, for she was mindful that there were parts of the story too damaging to her friends to admit, and she had to find a way around it.

In return the magistrate, an amiable elderly gentleman, told them what they had discovered. The so-called Mystic of Bath had balked at leaving Bath with her grandson, too old and too tired to flee. She confessed much, and it was revealing. Mrs. Bella Venables was not who she said she was; she was, in fact, Mother Macree said, her daughter, Miss Betty Macree, never married to Tommy Graham, whose natural son Thomas Graeme/Graham was. The magistrate told them his conclusion, that Mother Macree was more than a little afraid of her daughter.

"I think that is probably true," Anne said. "That woman had an iron hold over both of them, I think, her mother and her son. I saw fear in their eyes, fear of her."

"She fooled me," Bertie said sadly. "I have sent out letters to two people I know who lived where Bella last lived; I hope they can find out what happened to her. I'm assuming that this woman, Betty Macree, knew Bella in Spain, where my dear cousin lived with her husband. In one of her letters she spoke of a 'Betty' who did her laundry. She was most likely a camp follower. Bella probably fell ill, after her husband died, with the same wasting fever. As awful as it is, I think that she died alone, with just this woman to receive her letters."

Anne had no proof beyond conjecture, and it made no sense to deepen Bertie's pain by giving voice to her suspicions, but she feared that something much more sinister may have occurred. Given her behavior in Bath, Anne thought it possible that Betty Macree killed Bella Venables to assume her identity. If it was so her friend would know soon enough, but Anne thought it possible, especially given her vague allusion to a Spanish prison.

"She had enough information to fool you," Anne said softly.

"I didn't know what had happened to poor Bella. When this woman wrote, I was so overjoyed . . . I don't suppose I questioned closely enough. Her writing was altered, compared to Bella's fine hand, but she had been ill, I reasoned. I sent her money and she came home to England."

"But you recognized her as Mrs. Venables?" the magistrate said, setting aside his glass of sherry.

Bertie shrugged. "It had been so long since I saw her — we were practically children when last we met, over twenty years ago — and I suppose she had enough of a similarity to my poor cousin, and had her family jewelry and my letters to lend her charade credence. I was fooled because I wanted to be fooled. I *wanted* it to be Bella."

There was no question of the perfidy of the Macree-Graham alliance, and their cheating of so many. Those suspected of being confederates of Betty Macree and Thomas Graeme had been apprehended. The supposed Mr. Herbert Smythe had been caught fleeing Bath in the company of the lady who had been presented to society as Mrs. Honoria Noakes. Both had been supported in their charade by Thomas Graeme, and both were out-of-work actors. Smythe had answered an advertisement for genteel gentleman actors, was given a history, clothes, rented rooms, and enough money to splash about, and set a task: to romance into marriage Mrs. Clary Basenstoke, whose sizable estate would become his upon marriage. Mrs. Noakes was a friend, he told the magistrate, meaning, Anne supposed, his lover. He swore he only wanted a soft place to land, and was, he claimed, genuinely fond of Mrs. Basenstoke.

Meanwhile, the widow of Mr. Courtland was being sought in London.

The magistrate asked Anne how she figured out the scheme. Surprised to be asked by a gentleman of his years — she had expected to be ignored — she lied, the only way to protect the existence of the love letters, which had exposed Graeme's blackmailing machinations, and the journal, which had relayed a vague hint of Lonsdale's suspicions. Instead of revealing the written record, she told him a tale, that she and Mr. Lonsdale had chatted a couple of days before his death and he told her that he was suspicious of Mr. Graeme/Graham. He had asked the young man to explain why he was lying about their friendship — they did not have a long-standing friendship, as the fellow had been saying — and had threatened to turn him in if he discovered anything untoward going on. That, Anne said, was likely why the fake Mrs. Venables gave him poison (slipped into his tea by Mother Macree, most likely, though that would probably never be proven) when he visited the mystic's rooms the morning of his death. Bridie was cooperating with the magistrate and had confirmed Mr. Lonsdale's presence there that day, she learned.

The magistrate appeared to accept her fictional account of a conversation with Lonsdale. The rest was gossip and suspicion, she told him. She began to see Graeme's sly insinuation in Bath society, and how many times ailing gentlemen married ladies he had introduced them to, or in some cases, had inveigled Lonsdale to introduce, and a pattern of deaths after marriage. Anne wrote down, for the magistrate, the list of those who had died after marrying one of Graeme's made-to-order ladies: Mr. Courtland was the most recent. Could they prove it was murder? Perhaps not, but the death of Mr. Alfred Lonsdale most certainly was, as Dr. Fothergill would attest, and a distillation found in the mystic's abode was being examined by the doctor even now, to see if it was the same concoction.

"No matter what Miss Betty Macree says now to blacken Mr. Lonsdale's name, or anyone else's name," Anne said to the magistrate, exchanging a look with Bertie, whose shadowed expression held a trace of concern, "you *must* not believe her. She will tell wild lies in an attempt to evade her fate." Anne remembered the mystic's warning to Quin about secrets of those he loved, and how they should pay handsomely to keep those secrets. The woman clearly knew from her grandson all about Alfred Lonsdale and Bertie Birkenhead's relationship, and was issuing a warning that she hoped would be conveyed back to Lonsdale about paying the blackmail Graeme was demanding. Quin didn't know about the extortion and apparently did not pass on the message. His alarm that day had likely been in response to the mystic's mention of 'secrets,' of which Bertie had an abundance. The Macrees never missed an opportunity to press their advantage. Anne was determined to undermine the credibility of any accusation they might make.

With a comfortable chuckle, the magistrate said, "I hope I know a liar when I hear one, after a lifetime of listening to them. The woman has already tried to buy her freedom with what she called scandalous secrets." He shook his head, his peruke slipping sideways. He had been fed a great deal of very good sherry. "I told her I'd see her gagged before I'd let her blacken the names of Bath's best citizens," the magistrate assured her. "I no more countenanced her ridiculous tales than that a man could fly."

Finally, the matter had been thoroughly explained and examined. The magistrate heaved himself to his feet, saying, "I must go. There will be more arrests, but at least we have the worst of them."

He was walked to the door by Bertie. Anne followed and listened in. Bertie thanked the magistrate warmly and said, "One more thing, sir; I would consider it a great favor if you can obtain from that woman the amber cross she wears around her neck. It was given to the real Mrs. Bella Venables by her husband on her wedding day, and she treasured it."

"I will do my best."

As the door closed behind the good magistrate, she watched Bertie, noting his gaunt face and haunted eyes. "How are you, dear friend?" Her voice echoed strangely up the stairs and to the high ceiling.

He turned from the door. "I can't help feeling if I had just not argued with him poor Alf would still be alive," he said, a catch in his voice.

She threaded her arm through his. "Don't blame yourself. You had a right to be upset; Lonsdale wronged you, and then flaunted his lover in front of you."

"That's not true!" he cried.

"No, but that's what it seemed like to *you*. How were you to know Graeme was threatening Lonsdale—and you—with exposure?" She was silent for a moment, then squeezed his arm and said softly, "You loved him, and you lost him. I am truly sorry."

Bertie nodded. "He was such a lovely boy, sweet and intelligent and . . . he went to his grave trying to rectify his mistakes."

"You agree with me, that Lonsdale had decided he must turn in Graeme's family no matter the cost?"

He nodded. "He had decided to do the right thing and, knowing Alfred, was going to tell Graeme the honest truth, that he would be turning them all in. It cost him his life. But at least I know. And I have *you* to thank for knowing that in his last day he was trying to weigh the balance of harm and do the right thing." He shook his head and gave her a rueful look, smiling down at her. "This must all seem so odd to you, who only learned of . . . who only learned about Alethea and me so recently."

She pondered it a moment, turning her thoughts inward. "I was surprised at first, but I am not shocked. My father taught me to keep my eyes and my heart and my mind open."

"Thank you for discovering his killer," Bertie whispered, tears clogging his throat. He took her free hand and brought it to his lips. "Thank you. I'm only sorry I sheltered her for so long, held her to my bosom, called her my beloved cousin. You never knew Bella, but she was the sweetest friend I had in my youth, the one who made me feel I was not lost. This woman . . . she felt like a hollow sham the whole time, but I needed to believe her. My dear Bella was the real thing. She knew what I am, and she didn't care."

"Neither do I, my friend, neither do I." They returned, arm in arm, to the sitting room.

• • •

Finally, it was all drawing to a close. Anne looked around at her friends. Quin, wrapped warmly in a blanket, sat by the fire with Susanna on a low stool at his side, her cheek laid on his knee. Alethea and Bertie stood nearby, arms twined about each other, looking as loving as any couple could. It was good that they had each other.

Darkefell stood by Anne's chair. He cleared his throat. "I would like to say, to you all . . . thank you for looking after Anne." He raised his glass and bowed, saluting them all. "And to Mr. Quin Birkenhead I offer my most sincere congratulations; you are indeed, as Anne said, the hero of the hour."

"And to my wonderful Dr. Fothergill," Quin said softly, loath as always to take credit to himself. "It was he who ensured that Betty Macree did not escape justice."

Chapter Thirty

Much later she and Darkefell sat in the Everingham townhome with Lady Harecross, Lady Everingham (who was napping, truth be told) and Osei. Anne's mother knew only the vaguest hint of what her daughter had suffered that day. She was beaming and gloriously happy. Darkefell and Anne had agreed to an engagement supper in three weeks, followed by a wedding in Bath at St. Swithin, rather than in London, in two months or so, close to Christmas.

Anne had insisted that her father be invited, and Darkefell said he would invite his mother but wasn't sure she would travel so far, especially since Anne and Tony would be going north almost immediately after the wedding. The butler entered with a note on a silver tray. Though Lady Harecross held out her hand, the butler crossed to Lord Darkefell instead and bowed.

Tony took the note up, read it swiftly, and started up in surprise.

"What is it?" Anne asked. "What's going on?"

"It is Lydia; she is about to give birth."

"Oh! I must go to her, poor girl."

"Are you sure?" Darkefell said with an ironic lift of his brow. "Even in the best of times Lydia has a tendency to dramatize herself. Can you imagine what she will be like having a child?"

"Don't be rude, Tony. Of *course* I must go to her. The poor girl has suffered intolerably—"

"Through her own stupidity," he said.

Anne stiffened and glared at him. "Don't be cruel; Lydia is frightened. If you cannot be sympathetic about something you will never suffer, then you should keep your criticisms to yourself." Anne stood, noting her mother's look of horror at her manner of speaking to her fiancé. "Do you not agree, Mother, that with no fear of ever suffering the life-threatening condition of pregnancy, perhaps men should take the old adage to heart, that silence is wisdom . . . at least in this instance?"

Lady Harecross hesitated, but with a lift of her chin she said, "My lord, as seldom as it happens, I think I must agree with my daughter. Having gone through the condition many times, though only twice successfully, my sympathies lie with Lady John."

The marquess, outnumbered and out-reasoned, bowed. "Ladies,

I will bow to your superior knowledge and agree; in this case I will never know the truth of it. I retreat in the face of your inexorable reason."

"Thank you, Tony."

"Don't thank me for admitting I am wrong."

"Why not?"

"Would you expect thanks from me if you were ever to admit being wrong?"

She smiled as he took her hand. Looking up at him and winking, she said, "Since it is unlikely to happen, I may never know what I would—or would not—expect. Nonetheless . . . I thank you for doing what so few men are capable of."

Osei politely declined going with them; he had work to do at the marquess's rented townhome, now filled with staff arranging for their master's comfort. Anne took Mary with her, and they repaired to the Bestwick home on Milsom. It was late. Lydia had been suffering through contractions, laboring with the friendly coaching of the midwife. But at long last, late in the night, the birth had been accomplished. Mary and the midwife, along with a young maid of the house, helped Lydia with the necessary labors after birth to expel the afterbirth and clean herself and the baby.

Anne, exhausted and feeling faint after viewing the birth, was considerably buoyed by how Lydia, who most considered silly and fragile, was stoic through the process, putting all of her effort into the delivery and immediate aftermath. It was miraculous, in a way, how Lydia seemed to mature through the process, and how the midwife, an experienced woman of advanced years and sturdy health, patiently coached the young woman, supporting her and giving her courage with homely good sense and composure.

John, who had been frantically pacing outside the birth chamber for hours, poking his head in the door many times, only to be expelled time and again, was finally invited in to view his new baby. He broke down in tears when given his little daughter to hold, and Lydia, wearily beaming, chuckled at the sight.

Anne left them alone and crept out to find Darkefell. He was in John's library, restlessly pacing.

"Is Lydia all right?" he asked, his face much more drawn with anxiety than she would have expected.

"She's wonderful. Oh, Tony, it was remarkable, and frightening and . . . overwhelming."

He took her in his arms and held her against his chest. She felt the steady reassuring rhythm against her cheek. "After *such* a day and *such* a night I'm *so* tired," she sighed. "I don't know how she did it, how she stayed so strong. I have a new respect for Lydia."

"Despite her getting bamboozled by that mistaken mystic?"

"Fear will turn anyone foolish. I won't judge her for it, Tony. The poor girl has been through enough. We've always known she was superstitious, but she's not alone in that. My own mother will never allow a white tablecloth to stay on the table overnight."

"What will happen if she does?"

She looked up at him and grinned. "We would, apparently, need a shroud soon after. It defies examination, I know, to explain how one thing follows the other, but she always says *better safe* when reproached." Anne examined his face in the dim light of one branch of candles. "Do you wish to see the baby?"

"I'd much rather stay right here with you in my arms." He tightened his grasp on her, squeezing until she was breathless and murmured a complaint. He loosened his hold a fraction. "I feel like I will never get enough of this. I'm more than a little frustrated, my lady, if you must know." His hands traced the curve of her waist and roamed up to touch her neck and thread into her hair. "The thought of having to wait, now, until we are wed, to be alone with you . . ." He sighed.

Anne smiled in the dark. "Then let's not wait long," she said, shuddering in delight at his caresses. "Get a special license and let us marry within the week." She felt him tremble against her.

He held her away from him and stared into her eyes. "Are you being serious, Anne? Don't you wish all the fuss leading up to it? Don't you want your mother's engagement party, and the congratulations of friends, and the—"

"All I want is you, Tony, truly."

He sighed. "Just hearing you say that . . . I can wait. Let us do this right, for the sake of your family, especially. I would bear a hundred engagement parties, knowing you will be mine at the end of it. Two months, Anne . . . let us wait the two months. I will stay in Bath, Lydia will recover her strength, your mother can glory in having a daughter well wed, and your father can complicate the marriage settlements to his heart's content to protect you. Julius and mother can attend, if they wish, and your friends can give us party after party. I want every single bit of it."

She sighed and he folded her back into his sturdy embrace. "Two months, then, Tony; two months and we'll be married here, in Bath."

"I love you, my lady. Now . . . shall I go and make faces at a new baby?"

"Let's stay here a moment longer," she replied. "I've missed you so, Tony. Let's not be apart ever again."

About the Book

A writer must research many odd things while writing. When I was looking for a poison to use in *Lady Anne and the Menacing Mystic* I *considered* many and *discarded* many for various reasons. I finally settled on the yew; I already knew it was poisonous, discovered how lethal while researching, and coincidentally discovered a reference to St. Swithin's churchyard having a hedge of yews. Perfect. I let Osei, the most learned person in the novel, have his say when he speaks of a historical reference to poisoning from the "juice of the yew," but Anne does chime in, as she remembers from her own education how Socrates died from an infusion of hemlock.

Lady Anne and the Menacing Mystic takes place in 1786, a year in the late middle of the Georgian era in England. Sometimes I wonder, do readers know how lewd and slyly suggestive books and songs were in this era? I think we too often believe that folks of the past had a more restrictive outlook on sex, but nothing could be further from the truth, as anyone who understands Shakespeare will acknowledge.

For example . . . "My Thing Is My Own," a song mentioned, is a real English folk song with an *extremely* naughty meaning; the "Thing" of the title (remember, the song is sung by a lady!) is a lady's most intimate parts and she states quite tartly that the "thing" is her own and she will not let anyone have it, no matter how cunning or handsome or witty they are, without marriage. The song first appeared in print in a large six-volume collection of songs published by Thomas d'Urfey (*Wit and Mirth – or – Pills to Purge Melancholy*) between 1698 and 1720.

Read below the entire lyrics, and imagine the meanings, which are all frankly bawdy and sexual. To hear a delightful rendition, look on YouTube and find the incomparable Wilson sisters—yes, *those* Wilson sisters, of the rock group Heart fame—singing their version.

Lolly singing it may seem out of character, but she has lived a long life, and though she is a lady, she knows a thing or two about life, men and sex. Her past is mysterious; she doesn't speak of it much. I like to imagine a slightly scandalous and perhaps tragic love story for her. As sentimental and silly as she sometimes seems, there are depths to the woman that make her a favorite relation of Anne's.

In short, her singing the song is a suitable saucy moment for her character!

And speaking of sex (*we were, weren't we?*) research often leads one down fascinating paths. When Lady Anne needs to rope in the marquess's estimable secretary to help her investigate the rumors of homosexuality (not a word in use until a century later, by the way) and the Sacred Theban Club, she must first find out what he understands about same-sex attraction. I'll say it again; surprises are in store for the naïve researcher who may think of "olden days" as more strict and constrained when it comes to sex and sexual expression. Though it is true that same-sex activity was criminalized in the UK and some other countries, that does not tell the whole story.

I discovered that shame of, and criminalization of, same-sex attraction and conduct is a relatively modern reaction to an ancient and widely accepted behavior. Mr. Osei Boatin's invocation of the phrase *boy wife* from his language comes from my research into homosexuality among the African nations. There are, in many of the continent's cultures (and many *many* ancient cultures!) a frank acknowledgment of same-sex attraction dating back to artistic depictions on cave walls from millennia ago. In fact, the Sacred Band of Thebes referenced in *Lady Anne and the Menacing Mystic* was, as far as can be ascertained, true, an army regiment made up of older men and their younger male lovers.

In England in the late eighteenth century, though homosexual activity was a criminal offense—the language of which lingers in our vernacular (words such as *bugger*, etc.)—it was common enough, according to reports of the time. In some cases reports of its occurrence in society were weaponized to whip up a religious fervor for moral reformation. Reforming preachers made it their mission to convict homosexuals, even if they had to entrap and trick them, or *invent* accusations.

There did not seem to be the same fervor to accuse and convict women who loved other women, a sociological phenomenon that I find bewildering but fascinating. Historical research is an absorbing rabbit hole for the historical fiction author to disappear down.

I'll leave you with this thought: understanding the past can lead to a calmer present. There have always been times of great suffering.

Moral panics, crime waves, pandemics, heartbreaking wars, *all* are tragic. We are in this together, my friends and beloved readers, this world, this life. But through it all and beyond, the human spirit of love endures.

Wishing you love and light,
Victoria Hamilton

*Read below the delightful "My Thing Is My Own"!

My Thing Is My Own
(English Folk Song)

I a tender young Maid have been courted by many,
Of all sorts and Trades as ever was any:
A spruce Haberdasher first spake me fair,
But I would have nothing to do with Small ware.
My thing is my own, and I'll keep it so still,
Yet other young Lasses may do what they will.

A sweet scented Courtier did give me a Kiss,
And promis'd me Mountains if I would be his,
But I'll not believe him, for it is too true,
Some Courtiers do promise much more than they do.

(Chorus Repeated) My thing is my own . . .

A Master of Musick came with an intent,
To give me a Lesson on my Instrument,
I thank'd him for nothing, but bid him be gone,
For my little Fiddle should not be plaid on.

(Chorus Repeated) My thing is my own . . .

An Usurer came with abundance of Cash,
But I had no mind to come under his Lash,
He profer'd me Jewels, and a great store of Gold,
But I would not Mortgage my little Free-hold.

(Chorus Repeated) My thing is my own . . .

A blunt Lieutenant surpriz'd my Placket[1]
And fiercely began to rifle and sack it,
I mustered my Spirits up and became bold,
And forc'd my Lieutenant to quit his strong hold.

(Chorus Repeated) My thing is my own . . .

A fine dapper Taylor, with a Yard[2] in his Hand,
Did profer his Service to be at Command,
He talk'd of a slit[3] I had above Knee,
But I'll have no Taylors to stitch it for me.

(Chorus Repeated) My thing is my own . . .

Now here I could reckon a hundred and more,
Besides all the Gamesters recited before,
That made their addresses in hopes of a snap
But as young as I was I understood Trap,
My thing is my own, and I'll keep it so still,
Until I be Marryed, say Men what they will.

Notes:
1. A *placket* is an opening or slit in fabric; I think you can guess what it implies.
2. *Yard*, in this instance, refers to a yardstick; again, I think you can guess the euphemism!
3. Again with the naughtiness!

About the Author

Victoria Hamilton is the pseudonym of nationally bestselling romance author Donna Lea Simpson. She is the bestselling author of the Lady Anne Addison Mysteries, the Vintage Kitchen Mysteries, and the Merry Muffin Mysteries. Her latest adventure in writing is a Regency-set historical mystery series, starting with *A Gentlewoman's Guide to Murder*.

Victoria loves to read, especially mystery novels, and enjoys good tea and cheap wine, the company of friends, and has a newfound appreciation for opera. She enjoys crocheting and beading, but a good book can tempt her away from almost anything . . . except writing!

Visit Victoria at www.victoriahamiltonmysteries.com.

www.ingramcontent.com/pod-product-compliance
Lightning Source LLC
Chambersburg PA
CBHW050831190726
48286CB00007B/2038